AWAIT YOUR REPLY

Copyright © 2009 by Dan Chaon

Published in the United States by Ballantine Books, an imprint of The Random House Publishing Group, a division of Random House, Inc., New York.

BALLANTINE and colophon are registered trademarks of Random House, Inc.

Grateful acknowledgment is made to Henry Holt and Company, LLC, and The Random House Group Ltd. for permission to reprint an excerpt from "The Road Not Taken" from the book *The Poetry of Robert Frost,* edited by Edward Connery Lathem, published by Jonathan Cape. Copyright © 1916, 1969 by Henry Holt and Company, copyright © 1944 by Robert Frost. Reprinted by arrangement with Henry Holt and Company, LLC, and by permission of The Random House Group Ltd. Rights in the United Kingdom are controlled by The Random House Group Ltd.

LIBRARY OF CONGRESS CATALOGING-IN-PUBLICATION DATA
Chaon, Dan.
Await your reply : a novel / Dan Chaon.
p. cm.
ISBN 978-0-345-47602-9 (hardcover : alk. paper)
1. Identity theft—Fiction.   I. Title.
PS3553.H277A95 2009
813'.54—dc22   2009021245

Printed in the United States of America on acid-free paper

www.ballantinebooks.com

2 4 6 8 9 7 5 3 1

FIRST EDITION

Book design by Dana Leigh Blanchette

For Sheila

PART ONE

✦

I myself, from the very beginning,
Seemed to myself like someone's dream or delirium
Or a reflection in someone else's mirror,
Without flesh, without meaning, without a name.
Already I knew the list of crimes
That I was destined to commit.

—ANNA AKHMATOVA,
"Northern Elegies"

1

We are on our way to the hospital, Ryan's father says.
Listen to me, Son:
You are not going to bleed to death.

Ryan is still aware enough that his father's words come in through
the edges, like sunlight on the borders of a window shade. His eyes
are shut tight and his body is shaking and he is trying to hold up his
left arm, to keep it elevated. *We are on our way to the hospital,* his father says, and Ryan's teeth are chattering, he clenches and un-
clenches them, and a series of wavering colored lights—greens,
indigos—plays along the surface of his closed eyelids.

On the seat beside him, in between him and his father, Ryan's severed hand is resting on a bed of ice in an eight-quart Styrofoam
cooler.

The hand weighs less than a pound. The nails are trimmed and there are calluses on the tips of the fingers from guitar playing. The skin is now bluish in color.

This is about three A.M. on a Thursday morning in May in rural Michigan. Ryan doesn't have any idea how far away the hospital might be but he repeats with his father *we are on the way to the hospital we are on the way to the hospital* and he wants to believe so badly that it's true, that it's not just one of those things that you tell people to keep them calm. But he's not sure. Gazing out all he can see is the night trees leaning over the road, the car pursuing its pool of headlight, and darkness, no towns, no buildings ahead, darkness, road, moon.

2

A few days after Lucy graduated from high school, she and George Orson left town in the middle of the night. They were not fugitives—not exactly—but it was true that no one knew that they were leaving, and it was also true that no one would know where they had gone.

They had agreed that a degree of discretion, a degree of secrecy, was necessary. Just until they got things figured out. George Orson was not only her boyfriend, but also her former high school history teacher, which had complicated things back in Pompey, Ohio.

This wasn't actually as bad as it might sound. Lucy was eighteen, almost nineteen—a legal adult—and her parents were dead, and she had no real friends to speak of. She had been living in their parents' house with her older sister, Patricia, but the two of them had never been close. Also, she had various aunts and uncles and cousins she hardly talked to. As for George Orson, he had no connections at all that she knew of.

And so: why not? They would make a clean break. A new life.

———

Still, she might have preferred to run away together to somewhere different.

They arrived in Nebraska after a few days of driving, and she was sleeping, so she didn't notice when they got off the interstate. When she opened her eyes, they were driving along a length of empty highway, and George Orson's hand was resting demurely on her thigh: a sweet habit he had, resting his palm on her leg. She could see herself in the side mirror, her hair rippling, her sunglasses reflecting the motionless stretches of lichen-green prairie grass. She sat up.

"Where are we?" she said, and George Orson looked over at her. His eyes distant and melancholy. It made her think of being a child, a child in that old small-town family car, her father's thick, calloused plumber's hands gripping the wheel and her mother in the passenger seat with a cigarette even though she was a nurse, the window open a crack for the smoke to trail out of, and her sister asleep in the backseat mouth-breathing behind their father, and Lucy also in the backseat, opening her eyes a crack, the shadows of trees running across her face, and thinking: *Where are we?*

She sat up straighter, shaking this memory away.

"Almost there," George Orson murmured, as if he were remembering a sad thing.

And when she opened her eyes again, there was the motel. They had parked in front of it: a tower rising up in silhouette over them.

It had taken Lucy a moment to realize that the place was supposed to be a lighthouse. Or rather—the front of the place, the façade, was in the shape of a lighthouse. It was a large tube-shaped structure made of cement blocks, perhaps sixty feet high, wide at the base and narrowing as it went upward, and painted in red and white barber-pole stripes.

THE LIGHTHOUSE MOTEL, said a large unlit neon sign—fancy nautical lettering, as if made of knotted ropes—and Lucy sat there in the car, in George Orson's Maserati, gaping.

To the right of this lighthouse structure was an L-shaped court-yard of perhaps fifteen motel units; and to the left of it, at the very crest of the hill, was the old house, the house where George Orson's parents once lived. Not exactly a mansion but formidable out here on the open prairie, a big old Victorian two-story home with all the trappings of a haunted house: a turret and wraparound porch, dormers and corbeled chimneys, a gable roof and scalloped shingles. No other houses in sight, barely any other sign of civilization, barely anything but the enormous Nebraska sky bending over them.

For a moment Lucy had the notion that this was a joke, a corny roadside attraction or amusement park. They had pulled up in the summer twilight, and there was the forlorn lighthouse tower of the motel with the old house silhouetted behind it, ridiculously creepy. Lucy thought that there may as well have been a full moon and a hoot owl in a bare tree, and George Orson let out a breath.

"So here we are," George Orson said. He must have known how it would look to her.

"This is it?" Lucy said, and she couldn't keep the incredulous-ness out of her voice. "Wait," she said. "George? This is where we're going to live?"

"For the time being," George Orson said. He glanced at her rue-fully, as if she disappointed him a little. "Only for the time being, honey," he said, and she noticed that there were some tumbleweeds stuck in the dead hedges on one side of the motel courtyard. Tumbleweeds! She had never seen such a thing before, except in movies about ghost towns of the Old West, and it was hard not to be a little freaked out.

"How long has it been closed?" she said. "I hope it's not full of mice or—"

"No, no," George Orson said. "There's a cleaning woman coming out fairly regularly, so I'm sure it's not too bad. It's not abandoned or anything."

She could feel his eyes following her as she got out and walked around the front of the car and up toward the red door of the Lighthouse. Above the door it said: OFFICE. And there was another unlit tube of neon, which said:

NO VACANCY.

It had once been a fairly popular motel. That's what George Orson had told her as they were driving through Indiana or Iowa or one of those states. It wasn't exactly a *resort,* he'd said, but a pretty fancy place—"Back when there was a lake," he'd said, and she hadn't quite understood what he meant.

She'd said: "It sounds romantic." This was before she'd seen it. She'd had an image of one of those seaside sort of places that you read about in novels, where shy British people went and fell in love and had epiphanies.

"No, no," George Orson said. "Not exactly." He had been trying to warn her. "I wouldn't call it romantic. Not at this point," he said. He explained that the lake—it was a reservoir, actually—had started to dry up because of the drought, all the greedy farmers, he said, they just keep watering and watering their government-subsidized crops, and before anyone knew it, the lake was a tenth of what it had once been. "Then all of the tourist stuff began to dry up as well, naturally," George Orson said. "It's hard to do any fishing or water-skiing or swimming on a dry lake bed."

He had explained it well enough, but it wasn't until she looked down from the top of the hill that she understood.

He was serious. There wasn't a lake anymore. There was nothing but a bare valley—a crater that had once held water. A path led down to the "beach," and there was a wooden dock extending out into an expanse of sand and high yellow prairie grass, various scrubby plants that she imagined would eventually turn into tumbleweeds. The remains of an old buoy lay on its side in the wind-blown dirt. She could see what had once been the other side of the lake, the opposite shore rising up about five miles or so away across the empty basin.

Lucy turned back to watch as George Orson opened the trunk of the car and extracted the largest of their suitcases.

"Lucy?" he said, trying to make his voice cheerful and solicitous. "Shall we?"

She watched as he walked past the tower of the Lighthouse office and up the cement stairs that led to the old house.

3

By the time the first rush of recklessness had begun to burn off, Miles was already nearing the arctic circle. He had been driving across Canada for days and days by that point, sleeping for a while in the car and then waking to go on again, heading northward along what highways he could find, a cluster of maps origami-ed on the passenger seat beside him. The names of the places he passed had become more and more fantastical—Destruction Bay, the Great Slave Lake, Ddhaw Ghro, Tombstone Mountain—and when he came at last upon Tsiigehtchic, he sat in his idling car in front of the town's welcome sign, staring at the scramble of letters as if his eyesight might be faulty, some form of sleep-deprivation dyslexia. But no. According to one of the map books he'd bought, "Tsiigeht-chic" was a Gwich'in word that meant "mouth of the river of iron." According to the book, he had now reached the confluence of the Mackenzie and the Arctic Red rivers.

WELCOME TO TSIIGEHTCHIC!

Located on the site of a traditional Gwich'in fishing camp. In 1868 the Oblate Fathers started a mission here. By 1902 a trading post was located here. R.C.M.P. Constable Edgar "Spike" Millen, stationed at Tsiigehtchic was killed by the mad trapper Albert Johnson in the shoot-out of January 30, 1932 in the Rat River area.

The Gwich'in retain close ties to the land today. You can see net fishing year round as well as the traditional method of making dryfish and dry meat. In the winter, trappers are busy in the bush seeking valuable fur animals.

ENJOY YOUR VISIT TO OUR COMMUNITY!

He mouthed the letters, and his chapped lips kept adhering to each other. "*T-s-i-i-g-e-h-t-c-h-i-c,*" he said, under his breath, and just then a cold thought began to unfold in the back of his mind.

What am I doing? he thought. *Why am I doing this?*

The drive had begun to feel more and more like a hallucination by that point. Somewhere on the way, the sun had begun to stop rising and setting; it appeared to move slightly to and fro across the sky, but he couldn't be sure. Along this part of the Dempster Highway, a silvery white powder was scattered on the dirt road. Calcium? The powder seemed to glow—but then again, in this queer sunlight, so did everything: the grass and the sky and even the dirt had a fluorescent quality, as if lit from within.

He was sitting there by the side of the road, his book open in front of him on the steering wheel, a pile of clothes in the backseat, and the boxes of papers and notebooks and journals and letters he had collected over the years. He was wearing sunglasses, shivering a little, his patchy facial hair a worn yellow-brown, the color of a coffee stain. The CD player in his car was broken, and the radio played only a murky blend of static and distant garbled voices. There was no cell phone reception, of course. An air freshener in the shape of a Christmas tree was hanging from the rearview mirror, spinning in the breath of the defroster.

Up ahead, not too far now, was the town of Inuvik, and the wide delta that led to the Arctic Ocean, and also—he hoped—his twin brother, Hayden.

The man said, "Above the wrist? Or below the wrist?"

The man had a sleepy, almost affectless voice, the voice you might hear if you called a hotline for computer technical support. He looked at Ryan's father blandly.

"Ryan, I want you to tell your father to be reasonable," the man said, but Ryan didn't really say anything because he was crying silently. He and his father were bound to chairs at the kitchen table, and Ryan's father was shuddering, and his long dark hair fell in a tent around his face. But when he looked up, he had a troublingly stubborn look in his eyes.

The man sighed. He carefully pushed the sleeve of Ryan's shirt up above his elbow and placed his finger on the small rounded bone at the edge of Ryan's wrist. It was called the "ulnar styloid," Ryan remembered. Some biology class he had taken, once. He didn't know why that term came to him so easily.

Above the wrist . . . the man said to Ryan's father . . . *or below the wrist?*

———

Ryan was trying to reach a disconnected state—a *Zen* state, he thought—though the truth was that the more he tried to lift his mind out of his body, the more aware he was of the corporeal. He could feel himself trembling. He could feel the salt water trickling out of his nose and eyes, drying on his face. He could feel the duct tape that held him to the kitchen chair, the strips across his bare forearms, his chest, his calves and ankles.

He closed his eyes and tried to imagine his spirit lifting toward the ceiling. He would drift out of the kitchen, where he and his father were pinned to the hard-backed chairs, past the cluttered construction of dirty dishes piled on the counter by the sink, the toaster with a bagel still peeping up out of it; he would waft through the archway and into the living room, where a couple of black-T-shirted henchmen were carrying computer parts out of the bedrooms, dragging matted tails of electrical cording and cables along behind them. His spirit would follow them out the front door, past the white van they were tossing stuff into, and on down his father's driveway, traveling the rural Michigan highway, the moonlight flickering through the branches of trees as his spirit gained velocity, the luminous road signs emerging out of the darkness as he swept up like an airplane and the patterns of house lights and roads and streams that speckled and crisscrossed the earth growing smaller. *Woooooooooooooooooooo*—like a balloon with the air let out of it, a siren, a wailing wind. Like a person screaming.

He squeezed his eyes, tightened his teeth against one another as his left hand was grasped and tilted. He was trying to think of something else.

Music? A landscape, a sunset? A beautiful girl's face?

"Dad," he could hear himself saying, through chattering teeth. "Dad, please be reasonable, please, please be—"

———

He would not think about the cutting device the man had shown them. It was just a length of wire, a very thin razor wire, with a rubber handle attached to each end of it.

He wouldn't think about the way his father wouldn't meet his eyes.

He wouldn't think about his hand, the wire looped once around his wrist, his hand garroted, the sharp wire tightening. Slicing smoothly through skin and muscle. There would be a hitch, a snag, when it reached the bone, but it would cut through that, too.

And Lucy awoke and it was all a bad dream.

She was dreaming that she was still trapped in her old life, still in a classroom in high school, and she couldn't open her eyes even though she knew that there was an asshole boy in the desk behind her who was flicking stuff into her hair—boogers, or possibly tiny rolled-up pellets of chewing gum—but she couldn't wake up even though someone was knocking at the door, a secretary was at the door with a note that said, *Lucy Lattimore, please report to the principal's office. Your parents have been in a terrible accident—*

But no. She opened her eyes, and it was merely an early evening in June, still sunny outside, and she was asleep in front of the television in the alcove room in George Orson's parents' house, and an old black-and-white movie was playing, a videotape she had found in a stack next to the ancient cabinet television set—

"Why don't you stay here awhile and rest, and listen to the sea?" said the lady in the movie.

She could hear George Orson chopping on the cutting board in the kitchen—an intent tapping rhythm that had woven its way into her dream.

"It's so soothing," said the woman in the movie. "Listen to it. Listen to the sea. . . ."

It took Lucy awhile to realize that the tapping had stopped, and she lifted her head and there was George Orson standing in the doorway in his red cook's apron, holding the silver vegetable knife loosely at his side.

"Lucy?" George Orson said.

She sat up, trying to recalibrate, as George Orson tilted his head.

He was handsome, she thought, handsome in a collared-shirt-and-sweater intellectual way that you hardly ever saw back in Pompey, Ohio, with close-cropped brown hair and a neatly trimmed beard and an expression that could be both sympathetic and intense. His teeth were perfect, his body trim and even secretly athletic, though in fact he was, he said, "a little over thirty."

His eyes were a stunning sea-green, a color so unusual that at first she'd assumed it was artificial, some fancy colored contacts.

He blinked as if he could feel her thinking about his eyes.

"Lucy? Are you okay?" he said.

Not really. But she sat up, straightened her back, smiled.

"You look like you've been hypnotized," he said.

"I'm fine," she said. She put her palms against her hair, smoothing it down.

She paused; George Orson gazed at her with that mind reader look he had.

"I'm *fine*," she said.

———

She and George Orson were going to be living in the old house behind the motel, just for a short time, just until they got things figured out. Just until "the heat" was off a bit, he told her. She couldn't
tell how much of this was a joke. He often spoke ironically. He
could do imitations and accents and quotations from movies and
books.

We can pretend we are "fugitives on the lam," he said, wryly, as
they sat in a parlor or sitting room, with fancy lamps and wingback
chairs that had been draped with sheets, and he put his hand on
her thigh, petting her leg with a slow, reassuring stroke. She put her
Diet Coke onto a doily on the old coffee table, and a bead of perspiration ran down the side of the can.

She didn't see why they couldn't be fugitives in Monaco or the
Bahamas or even the Riviera Maya area of Mexico.

But— "Be patient," George Orson said, and gave her one of his
looks, somewhere between teasing and tender, bending his head to
look into her eyes when she glanced away. "Trust me," he said in
that confiding voice he had.

And so, okay, she had to admit that things could be worse. She
could still be in Pompey, Ohio.

She had believed—had been led to believe—that they were going
to be rich, and yes of course that was one of the things that she
wanted. "A lot of money," George Orson had told her, lowering his
voice, lowering his eyes sidelong in that shy conspiratorial way.
"Let's just say that I made some . . . *investments*," he said, as if the
word were a code that they both understood.

That was the day that they left. They were traveling down Interstate 80 toward this piece of property that George Orson had
inherited from his mother. "The Lighthouse," he said. The Lighthouse Motel.

They'd been on the road for an hour or so, and George Orson
was in a playful mood. He had once known how to say hello in one

hundred different languages, and he was trying to see if he could remember them all.

"*Zdravstvuite,*" George Orson said. "*Ni hao.*"

"*Bonjour,*" said Lucy, who had loathed her two required years of French, her teacher, the gently unforgiving Mme Fournier, repeating those unpronounceable vowels over and over.

"*Päivää,*" George Orson said. "*Konichiwa. Kehro haal aahei.*"

"*Hola,*" Lucy said, in the deadpan voice that George Orson found so funny.

"You know, Lucy," George Orson said cheerfully. "If we're going to be world travelers, you're going to have to learn new languages. You don't want to be one of those American tourist types who assume that everyone speaks English."

"I don't?"

"Not unless you want everyone to hate you." And he smiled his sad, lopsided grin. He let his hand rest lightly on her knee. "You're going to be so *cosmopolitan,*" he said tenderly.

This had always been one of the big things that she liked about him. He had a great vocabulary, and even from the beginning, he'd treated her as if she knew what he was talking about. As if they had a secret, the two of them.

"You're a remarkable person, Lucy." This was one of the first things that he'd ever said to her.

They were sitting in his classroom after school, she had ostensibly come to talk about the test for the next week, but that had faded away fairly quickly. "I honestly don't think you have anything to worry about," he'd told her, and then he waited. That smile, those green eyes.

"You're different from other people around here," he said.

Which was, she thought, true. But how did *he* know? No one else in her school thought so. Even though she did better than anyone else in the entire school on the SAT, even though she earned A's in nearly all her classes, no one, neither teachers nor students, acted as if she were "remarkable." Most of the teachers resented her, they didn't really like ambitious students, she thought, students who wanted to leave Pompey behind, and the other students thought that she was a freak—possibly crazy. She hadn't been aware that she had the habit of muttering sarcastic things under her breath until she discovered that quite a number of people in her school thought that she had Tourette's syndrome. She didn't have any idea where or when such a rumor had started, though she suspected that it might have originated with her honors English teacher, Mrs. Lovejoy, whose interpretations of literature were so insipid that Lucy could barely contain—or apparently had failed to contain—her scorn.

But George Orson, on the other hand, actually liked to hear what she had to say. He encouraged her ironic view of the great figures of American history, actually chuckled appreciatively at some of her comments while the other students stared at her with stern boredom. "It's clear that you have a brilliant mind," he wrote on one of her papers, and then when she came to see him after class to talk about the upcoming exam he told her that he knew what it was like to be different—misunderstood—

"You know what I'm talking about, Lucy," he said. "I know you feel it."

Perhaps she did. She sat there, and let him turn his intense green eyes on her, an intimate, oddly probing look, both ironic and heartfelt at the same time, and she drew in a small breath. She was well aware that she was not regarded as pretty—not in the conventional world of Pompey High School, at least. Her hair was thick and wavy, and she could not afford to have it cut in a way that made it more manageable, and her mouth was too small and her face was too long. Though maybe in a different context, she'd imagined hopefully, in a different time period, she might have been beautiful. A girl in a Modigliani painting.

Still, she wasn't used to being looked in the eye. She fingered the silk scarf she was wearing, an item she'd found in a thrift store, which she thought might have a slight Modigliani quality, and George Orson regarded her thoughtfully.

"Have you ever heard the term 'sui generis'?" he said.

Her lips parted—as if this were a test, a vocabulary word, a spelling bee. On the wall were various inspirational social studies posters. ELEANOR ROOSEVELT, 1884–1962: "NO ONE CAN MAKE YOU FEEL INFERIOR WITHOUT YOUR CONSENT." She shook her head, slightly uncomfortable.

"I don't know," she said. "Not really."

"That's what you are, I think," George Orson said. "Sui generis. It means 'one of a kind.' But not in the phony, feel-good, self-help way—everyone is an individual, blah, blah, blah, just to boost the self-esteem of the mediocre.

"No, no," he said. "It means that we invent ourselves. It means that you're beyond categories—beyond standardized test scores, beyond the petty sociology of where you're from and what your dad does and what college you get into. You're outside of that. That's what I recognized about you right away. *You invent yourself,*" he said. "Do you know what I mean?"

They looked at each other for a long time. Eleanor Roosevelt waved down at them, smiling, and a hope tightened inside her, like a warm, soft fist. "Yes," she said.

Yes. She liked that idea: *You invent yourself.*

They were making a clean break. A new life. Wasn't that what she'd always wanted? Maybe they could even change their names, George Orson said.

"I get a little tired of being George Orson," he told her conversationally. They were driving through the middle of Illinois in his Maserati with the top down and her unmanageable hair was rippling behind her and she was wearing sunglasses. She was gazing critically at herself in the side mirror. "How about you?" George Orson said.

"How about me, what?" Lucy said. She lifted her head.

"What would you be if you weren't Lucy?" George Orson said.

Which was a good question.

She hadn't answered him, though she found herself thinking about it, imagining—for example—that she would like to be the type of girl who had the name of a famous city. *Vienna,* she thought, that would be pretty. Or *London,* which would be wry and vaguely mysterious, in a tomboyish way. *Alexandria:* proud and regal.

"Lucy," on the other hand, was the name of a mousy girl. A comical name. People thought of the television actress, with her slapstick ineptitude, or the bossy girl in the *Peanuts* comic strip. They thought of the horrible old country song that her father used to sing: "You picked a fine time to leave me, Lucille."

She would be glad to be rid of her name, if she could think of a good replacement.

Anastasia, she thought. *Eleanor?*

But she didn't say anything because a part of her thought that such names might sound a little vulgar and schoolgirl-ish. Names that a low-class girl from Pompey, Ohio, would think were elegant.

One of the nice things about George Orson was that he didn't know much about her past.

They didn't talk, for example, about Lucy's mother and father, the car wreck the summer before her senior year, an old man running a stoplight while the two of them were on their way to the Home Depot to buy some tomato plants that were on sale. Killed, both of them, though her mother had lingered for a day in a coma.

The fact that people at school had known about it had always felt like an invasion of privacy. A secretary had given Lucy condolences, and Lucy had nodded, graciously she thought, though actually she found it kind of repulsive that this stranger should know her business. *How dare you,* Lucy thought later.

But George Orson had never said a word of condolence, though she guessed that probably he knew. He knew the basics, anyway.

He knew, for example, that she lived with her sister, Patricia, though Lucy was relieved that he had never actually seen her sister. Patricia, herself only twenty-two, not very bright, Patricia who worked at the Circle K Convenient Mart most nights and with whom, since the funeral, Lucy had less and less contact.

Patricia was one of those girls that people had been making fun of for almost all the years of her life. She had a thick, spittley lisp, easily imitated and cartoonish, a bungler's speech impediment. She wasn't fat exactly, but lumpy in the wrong places, already middle-aged-looking in junior high, with an unfortunately broad, hen-like figure.

Once, in grade school, they were walking to school together and some boys chased them, throwing pebbles.

> *Patricia, Patrasha,*
> *Has a great big ass-a!*

the boys sang.

And that had been the last time that Lucy had walked with Patricia. After that, they had begun to go their separate ways once they left for school, and Patricia had never said anything; she had just accepted the fact that even her sister wouldn't want to walk with her.

After their parents died, Patricia had become Lucy's guardian—perhaps officially still was? Though now Lucy was almost nineteen. Not that it mattered in any case, because Patricia had no idea where she was.

She did feel a pang about that.

She had the image of Patricia and her pet rats—the rats' cages stacked in the eaves, and her sister coming home late from her job at the Circle K, kneeling there in that red and blue vest with the name tag that said PATARCIA, talking to the rats in that crooning voice, the one rat, Mr. Niffler, with an enormous tumor coming out of its stomach that it was dragging around and her sister had paid to have the veterinarian remove it and then it *grew back*, the tumor, and still Patricia persisted. Showering the dying creature with love, buying it plastic toys, talking baby talk, making another appointment at the vet.

Lucy was glad that she had never told George Orson about Mr. Niffler, just as she was glad that he'd never seen the house she had grown up in, where she and Patricia had continued to live. Her father used to call it "the shack," affectionately. "I'll meet you back here at the shack," he'd say when he left for work in the morning.

It didn't occur to her until later that it *was* basically a shack. Ramshackle, haphazard, a living room and kitchen that bled into each other, the bathroom so cramped that your legs touched the edge of the bathtub when you sat on the toilet. A garage stuffed with car parts, bags of beer cans that her father never took to the recycling center, the hole in the plasterboard wall of the living room through which you could see the bare two-by-fours, the carpet that looked like the fur of a worn-out stuffed animal. Some stairs led up to an attic, where the girls, Lucy and Patricia, had their beds. The ceiling of the bedroom was the roof, which slanted sharply over them while they slept. If George Orson had seen it, she imagined, he would have been embarrassed for her; she would have felt dirty.

Though—she couldn't say that she was particularly happy to be *here*, either.

In the middle of the night, she found herself wide awake. They were in the old bed of George Orson's parents, a king-size expanse, and she was aware of the other rooms in the house—the other empty bedrooms on the second floor, the trickle of a pipe in the bathroom, the toothy rows of bookshelves in the "library," the flutter of birds in the dead trees of the high-fenced backyard. A "Japanese garden," George Orson called it. She could picture the small wooden bridge, the bed of stunted, un-flowering irises choked with weeds. A miniature weeping cherry tree, still barely alive. A granite Kotoji lantern statue. George Orson's mother had had an "artistic bent," he'd told Lucy.

By which he meant, Lucy assumed, that his mother had been a little crazy. Or so Lucy gathered. The place—the motel and the house—seemed as if it had been put together by someone with multiple personality disorder. A lighthouse. A Japanese garden. The living room with its gruesome old sheet-covered upholstery, and the room with the television and the big picture window that looked out onto the backyard. The kitchen with its 1970s colors, the avocado-green stove and refrigerator, the mustard-colored tile floor, drawers and cabinets full of dishes and utensils, an old wooden butcher block and an almost obscenely large collection of knives—George Orson's mother had apparently been obsessed with them, since they could be found in almost every shape and length a person could imagine, from tiny filet blades to enormous cleavers. Very disturbing, thought Lucy. In a pantry, she found three boxes of china dishes and some disturbing canning jars, still full of dark goop.

On the second floor, there was the bathroom and three bedrooms, including this one she was in right now, the very room, the very bed where his parents had slept, where his elderly mother had continued to sleep, Lucy imagined, after the husband had died. Even now, many years later, there was still a vague hint of old-lady powder about it. A few hangers still in the closet, and the empty dresser sitting darkly against the wall, and then the stairs that led up to the third floor—to the turret, a small octagon-shaped room with a single window, which looked out away from the lake, out onto the cone of the faux lighthouse, and the courtyard of motel rooms. And the highway. And the alfalfa fields. And the far distant horizon.

And so—she couldn't help it, she couldn't sleep, and she lay there staring up at the swimmy darkness that her brain couldn't quite process. The door was closed, the window shade was pulled, so there wasn't even moonlight or stars.

Suggestions of shapes floated across the surface of the dark like protozoa seen through a microscope, but there wasn't too much for the optic mechanisms to actually hold on to.

She slid her hand beneath the covers until she came up against the shoreline of George Orson's body. His shoulder, his chest, the ribs rising and falling underneath his skin, his warm belly, which she pressed against—until at last he turned over and put his arm over her, and she felt her way along the length of it until she found his wrist, his hand, his pinkie finger. Which she held.

Okay.

Everything would be fine, she thought.

At the very least, she wasn't in Pompey any longer.

6

Miles's twin brother, Hayden, had been missing for more than ten years, though probably "missing" wasn't exactly the right word.

"At large"? Was that a better term?

When the most recent letter from Hayden arrived, Miles had pretty much decided that it was time to give up. He was thirty-one years old—they were both thirty-one years old—and it was time, Miles thought, to let go. To move on. So much energy and effort, he thought, squandered, pointless. For a while Miles felt a new determination: he was going to live his own life.

He was back again in Cleveland, where he and Hayden had grown up. He had an apartment on Euclid Heights Boulevard, not far from their old house, and a job managing a store called Matalov Novelties, an old storefront mail-order establishment on Prospect Avenue that dealt primarily in magicians' equipment—flash paper and smoke powder, scarves and ropes, trick cards and coins and top hats and so forth, though they also sold joke gifts and gags, useless gadgets, risqué toys, some sex stuff. The catalog was somewhat unfocused, but he liked that. He could organize it, he thought.

Was it what he had hoped to do with his life? Probably not exactly, but he had a good brain for receipts and orders, and he felt a certain affection for the stock on the shelves, the carnival aura of the trashy occult and bright plastic legerdemain. There were times, sitting at the computer in the dim windowless back room, when he thought it wouldn't be a bad career after all. He had grown fond of the old proprietress, Mrs. Matalov, who had been a magician's assistant back in the 1930s, and who now, even at ninety-three, had the stoic dignity of a beautiful woman who was about to be cut in half. He had a good rapport with Mrs. Matalov's granddaughter, Aviva, a sarcastic young woman with dyed black hair and black fingernails and a narrow, sorrowful face, whom Miles had begun to imagine he could probably ask out on a date.

He had been thinking about going back to college, maybe getting a degree in business. Also, possibly, getting some short-term cognitive therapy.

So when Hayden's letter arrived, Miles was surprised at how quickly he had fallen back into his old ways. He shouldn't have even opened the letter, he thought later. And in fact, when he came home to his apartment building that day in June and opened the mail cubbyhole and saw it there among the bills and flyers—he actually decided that he should leave it unopened. *Set it aside,* he thought. *Let it rest for a while before you look at it.*

But no, no. By the time he had gone up the three flights of stairs to his apartment, he had already torn open the seal and unfolded the letter.

My Dear Miles, it said.

Miles! My brother, my best beloved, my only true friend, I'm sorry that I have been out of touch for so long. I hope you don't hate me. I can only pray that you understand the grave situation I have found myself in since we last spoke. I have been in deep hiding, very deep, but every day I thought about how much I missed you. It was only my fear for your own safety that kept me from contact. I am fairly certain that your phone lines and email have been contaminated, and in fact even this letter is a great risk. You should be aware that someone may be watching you, and I hate to say this but I think you may actually be in danger. Oh, Miles, I wanted to leave you alone. I know that you are tired of all of this and you want to live your own life, and you deserve that. I'm so sorry. I wanted to give you the gift of being free of me, but unfortunately they know we are connected. I have just lost someone very dear to me, due to my own carelessness, and now my thoughts turn to you with great concern. Please be wary, Miles! Beware of the police, and any government official, FBI, CIA, even local government. Do not have any contact with H&R Block or with anyone representing J.P. Morgan, Morgan Stanley, Goldman Sachs, Lehman Brothers, Merrill Lynch, Chase, or Citigroup. Avoid anyone associated with Yale University. Also, I know that you have been in contact with the Matalov family in Cleveland, and all I can tell you is DO NOT TRUST THEM! Do not tell anyone about this letter! I hate to put you in an awkward position, but I urge you to get out of Cleveland as soon as possible, as quietly as possible. Miles, I am so sorry to have involved you in all this, I truly am. I wish I could go back and do things differently, that I could have been a better brother to you. But that chance is gone now, I know, and I fear that I won't be in this world much longer. Do you remember the Great Tower of Kallupilluk? That may be my final resting place, Miles. You may never hear from me again.

I am, as always, yours, your one true brother,
and I love you so much.

Hayden

So.

What does a person do with a letter such as this? Miles sat there for a while at the kitchen table, with the letter spread out in front of him, and opened a packet of artificial sweetener into a cup of tea. *What would a normal person do?* he wondered. He imagined the normal person reading the letter and shaking this head sadly. *What could be done?* the normal person would ask himself.

He looked at the postmark on the envelope: *Inuvik, NT, CANADA X0E 0T0.*

"I'm going to have to take some personal time, unfortunately," Miles told Mrs. Matalov the next morning, and he sat there with the phone pressed to his ear, listening to her silence.

"Personal time?" said Mrs. Matalov, in her old-fashioned vampire accent. "I don't understand. What does this mean, personal time?"

"I don't know," he said. "Two weeks?" He looked at the itinerary he had planned out on the computer, the map of Canada with a green highlighter mark running a jagged, rivering way across the country. Four thousand miles, which would take, he calculated, approximately eighty-four hours. If he drove fifteen or sixteen hours a day, he could be in Inuvik by the weekend. It might be difficult, he thought, but then again didn't truck drivers do it all the time? Weren't they always making marathon drives such as this? "Well," he said. "Maybe three weeks."

"Three weeks!" Mrs. Matalov said.

"I'm really super sorry about this," Miles said. "It's just that— something urgent has come up." He cleared his throat. "A private matter," he said. *Do not trust the Matalov family,* Hayden had said, which was crazy, but Miles felt himself pause.

"It's complicated," he said.

Which it was. Even if he were to be completely honest, what would he say? How could he ever explain the ease with which these old longings had come back to him, the lingering ache of love and duty?

Perhaps to a therapist it would seem simply compulsive—after all this time, after all the years that he had already wasted—but here, nevertheless, came that same urgency he'd felt when Hayden had first run away from home all those years ago. That same certainty that he could find him, catch him, help him, or at least get him locked up somewhere safe. How could he explain how badly he wanted this? Who would understand that when Hayden left, it was as if a part of himself had vanished in the middle of the night—his right hand, his eyes, his heart—like the Gingerbread Man in the fairy tale, running away down the road: *Come back! Come back!* If he were to tell this to someone, he would seem as crazy as Hayden himself.

He had thought that he was past such feelings, but, well. Here he was. Packing his things. Taking the milk out of his refrigerator and pouring it down the drain. Sifting through his old notes, printing out long-ago emails that Hayden had sent him—the various hints and clues of his whereabouts dropped into fantastical descriptions of invented landscapes, the angry rants about human overpopulation and the international banking conspiracy, the late-night suicidal regrets. And then Miles sat at his desk examining with a magnifying glass the envelope of the letter that Hayden had just sent him, that postmark, that postmark. Rechecking the directions. He knew where Hayden was going.

And now he was almost there.

Miles sat in his car by the side of the road, casually reading through one of Hayden's journals as he waited for the ferry that would take him across the Mackenzie River. Some rails ran up from the slate-gray muddy bank and into the green wrinkled lobes of tundra, but otherwise there wasn't much sign of human habitation. A toilet house. A diamond-shaped road sign. The river was a calm reflective surface, silver and sapphire blue. Once he was across, it was only about eighty miles to Inuvik.

Inuvik was one of the places Hayden had gotten fixated on.

"Spirit cities," he called them, and he had written extensively about Inuvik, among other places, in the journals and notebooks that Miles now had in his possession. For years now, Hayden had been taken with the idea that Inuvik was the site of a great archaeological ruin, that on the edge of Inuvik was the remnants of the Great Tower of Kallupilluk, which had been a spire of ice and stone, approximately forty stories tall, built around 290 B.C. at the behest of the mighty Inuit emperor, Kallupilluk—a figure whom Hayden believed he had contacted once in a past life.

None of this was true, of course. Very few of the things Hayden was obsessed with had much basis in reality, and in the last few years he had strayed even further into a mostly imaginary world. In actuality, there had never been a tower or a great Inuit emperor named Kallupilluk. In real life, Inuvik was a small town in the Northwest Territories of Canada with a population of around thirty-five hundred people. It was located on the Mackenzie Delta—"nested," according to the town's website, "between the treeless tundra and the northern boreal forest," and it had existed for less than a century. It had been constructed building by building by the Canadian government as an administrative center in the western Arctic, incorporated at last as a village in 1967. It wasn't even, as Hayden seemed to believe, on the shores of the Arctic Ocean.

Nevertheless, Miles couldn't help but think of Hayden's drawings of that great tower, the simple but vivid pencil sketch Hayden had done, reminiscent of the Porcelain Tower of Nanjing, and he felt a small, dizzy quiver of anticipation pass through him as the Mackenzie River ferry appeared on the horizon, approaching. Miles had spent a good portion of his life poring over Hayden's various journals and notebooks, and even longer living with Hayden's various delusions. Despite everything, there remained a tiny core of credulity that glowed a little brighter as he came closer to the town of Hayden's fantasies. He could almost picture the place at the edge of the town where the Great Tower once rose up out of the folds of tundra, stark against the wide, endlessly shining sky.

———

This had always been one of the problems: this was maybe one way to explain it. For years and years and years, Miles had been a willing participant in his twin brother's fantasies. Folie à deux, was that what they called it?

Since their childhood, Hayden had been a great believer in the mysteries of the unknown—psychic phenomenon, past lives, UFOs, ley lines and spirit paths, astrology and numerology, etc., etc. And Miles was his biggest follower and supporter. His listener. He had never personally believed in such stuff—not in the way that Hayden appeared to—but there had been a time when he had been happy to play along, and perhaps for a while this alternate world had been a shared part of their brains. A dream they'd both been having together.

Years later when he came into possession of Hayden's papers and journals, Miles was aware that he was probably the only person in the world capable of translating and understanding what Hayden had written. He was the only one who could make sense of those stacks of composition notebooks—that tiny block-letter handwriting; the text and calculations that ran from edge to edge and top to bottom of each page; the manila envelopes full of drawings and doctored photographs; the maps Hayden had torn out of encyclopedias and covered with his geodetic projections; the lines across North America that converged at places like Winnemucca, Nevada, and Kulm, North Dakota, and Inuvik in the Northwest Territories; the theories, increasingly serpentine and involuted, a hodgepodge of crypto-archaeology and numerology, holomorphy and brane cosmology, past-life regression and conspiracy theory paranoia.

My work, as Hayden had at some point begun to call it.

Miles often tried to remember when Hayden first began to use that term: "My work." At first it had just been a game the two of them were playing—and Miles even remembered the day they had started. It was the summer that they turned twelve, and the two of them had been poring over books by Tolkien and Lovecraft. Miles had been particularly fond of the maps that were included in the novels of *The Lord of the Rings,* while Hayden had been more inclined toward the mythologies and mysterious places in Lovecraft—the alien city beneath the Antarctic Mountains, the prehistoric cyclopean cities, the accursed New England towns.

They had found one of those old gold-leaf hard-bound atlases, 25 x 20, on the shelf in the living room with the *World Book Encyclopedia,* and they had loved the feel of it, the sheer weight, which made it feel like it could be some ancient tome. It had been Miles's idea that they could take some of the maps of North America and turn them into fantasy worlds. Dwarf cities in the mountains. Scorched goblin ruins on the plains. They could invent landmarks and histories and battles and pretend that in the olden days, before the Indians, America had been a realm of great cities and magical elder races. Miles thought it would be fun to make up their own Dungeons and Dragons game with real places and fantasy places intermingled; he had some very specific ideas about how this would develop, but Hayden was already bending over the map with a black ink pen. "Here is where some pyramids are," Hayden said, pointing to North Dakota, and Miles watched as he drew three triangles, right there on the page of the atlas. In ink!

"Hayden!" Miles said. "We can't erase that. We're going to get in trouble."

"No, no," Hayden said coolly. "Don't be a fag. We'll just hide it."

And this was one of those early secrets that they had—the old atlas hidden beneath a stack of board games on a shelf in their bedroom closet.

Miles still had the old atlas, and as he waited there at the edge of the river for the ferry to come, he took it out and paged through it once again. There, on the northern coast of Canada, was the tower that Hayden had drawn, and Miles's own clumsy attempt at calligraphy: THE IMPATRABLE TOWER OF THE DARK KING!

How ridiculous, he thought. How depressing—that he should still be following the lead of his twelve-year-old self—an adult man! Over the years that he had been looking for Hayden, he had often thought about trying to explain his situation. To the authorities, for example, or to psychiatrists. To people he had become friends with, to girls he had liked. But he always found himself hesitating at the last minute. The details seemed so silly, so unreal and artificial. How could anyone actually believe in such stuff?

"My brother is very troubled." That was all he ever managed to tell people. "He's very—ill. Mentally ill." He didn't know what else could be said.

When Hayden first started to exhibit symptoms of schizophrenia, back when they were in middle school, Miles didn't really believe it. It was a put-on, he thought. A prank. It was like the time when that quack guidance counselor decided Hayden was a "genius." Hayden had thought this was hilarious.

"Geeenious," he said, drawing the word out in a dreamy, mocking way. This was at the beginning of seventh grade, and it was late at night, they were in their bunk beds in their room, and Hayden's voice wafted down through the darkness from the top bunk. "Hey, Miles," he said in that flat, amused voice he had. "Miles, how come I'm a genius and you're not?"

"I don't know," Miles said. He was nonplussed, perhaps a bit hurt by the whole thing, but he just turned his face against his pillow. "It doesn't matter that much to me," he said.

"But we're identical," Hayden said. "We have the *exact* same DNA. So how can it even be possible?"

"It's not genetic, I guess," Miles had said, glumly, and Hayden had laughed.

"Maybe I'm just better at fooling people than you are," he said. "The whole idea of IQ is a joke. Did you ever think about that?"

When his mother started bringing in the psychiatrists, Miles thought about that conversation again. *It's a joke,* he thought. Knowing Hayden, Miles couldn't help but think that the therapist their mother consulted seemed awfully gullible. He couldn't help but think that Hayden's so-called symptoms came across as melodramatic and showy, and, Miles thought, easy to fake. Their mother had remarried by that time, and Hayden hated their new stepfather, their revised family. Miles couldn't help but think that Hayden was not above using an elaborate ploy—even to the point of imitating a serious illness—just to stir up trouble, just to hurt their mother, just to amuse himself.

Was he faking it? Miles had never been sure, even as Hayden's behavior became more erratic and abnormal and secretive. There were times, lots of times, when his "illness" felt more like a performance, an amplified version of the games they had been playing all along. The "symptoms" Hayden was supposedly exhibiting, according to the therapist—"elaborate fantasy worlds," "feverish obsessions," "disordered thoughts," and "hallucinatory perceptual changes"—these were not so much different from the way Hayden usually behaved when they were deeply involved in one of their projects. He was, perhaps, a little more exaggerated and theatrical than usual, Miles thought, a little more *extreme* than Miles felt comfortable with, but then again there were reasons. Their father's death, for example. Their mother's remarriage. Their hated stepfather, Mr. Spady.

When Hayden was institutionalized for the first time, he and Miles were still working on their atlas pretty regularly. It was a particularly complicated section—the great pyramids of North Dakota, and the destruction of the Yanktonai civilization—and Hayden couldn't stop talking about it. Miles remembered sitting there at dinner one night, his mother and Mr. Spady watching stonily as Hayden pushed the food around on his plate as if arranging armies on a model battlefield. "Alfred Sully," he was saying, talking in a low, rapid voice as if reciting memorized information before a test. "General Alfred Sully of the United States Army, 1st Minnesota Infantry, 1863. Whitestone Hills, Tah-kah-ha-kuty, and there are the pyramids. Snow is falling on the pyramids and he's amassing his armies at the foot of the hill. 1863," he said, and pointed at his boneless chicken breast with his fork. "Khufu," he said, "the second pyramid. That's where he first attacked. Alfred Spady, 1863—"

"Hayden," their mother said, sharply. "That's enough." She straightened in her chair, lifting her hand slightly as if she'd considered slapping him, the way you might a hysterical person who is raving. "Hayden! Stop it! You're not making any sense."

That wasn't true, exactly. He *was* making some sense—to Miles at least. Hayden was talking about the Battle of Whitestone Hill, near Kulm, North Dakota, where Colonel Alfred Sully had destroyed a settlement of Yanktonai Indians in 1863. There were no pyramids, obviously, yet what Hayden was describing was fairly clear, and even quite interesting to Miles.

But their mother was unnerved. The things Hayden's therapist had been reporting had upset her, and later, after Hayden had gone back upstairs and when she and Miles were washing dishes, she spoke in a low voice. "Miles," she said, "I need to ask you a favor."

She touched him lightly, and a piece of soapsuds transferred to his forearm, the bubbles slowly disintegrating.

"You need to stop enabling him, Miles," she said. "I don't think he would get nearly so stirred up if you didn't encourage it—"

"I'm not!" Miles said, but he withdrew from her reproachful look. He wiped his fingers over his arm, the wet spot where she had touched him. Was Hayden sick? he wondered. Was he pretending? Miles thought uncomfortably about some of the things Hayden had been saying recently.

"I'm thinking that I might have to eventually kill them," Hayden had said, his voice in the darkness of the bedroom late at night. "Maybe I'll just destroy their lives, but they actually might have to die."

"What are you talking about?" Miles had said—though obviously he knew who Hayden was referring to, and he felt a little frightened; he could feel the pulse of a vein in his wrist and could hear the soft tiptoeing sound of it in his ears. "Man," he said, "why do you have to say crap like that? You're making people think you're crazy. It's so *extreme!*"

"Hmmm," Hayden said. His voice curled sideways through the dark. Floating. Musing. "You know what, Miles?" he said at last. "I know about a lot of stuff that you don't know about. I have powers. You realize that, don't you?"

"Shut up," Miles said, and Hayden laughed, low, that wistful, teasing chuckle that Miles found both comforting and galling at the same time.

"You know, Miles," he said. "I really am a genius. I didn't want to hurt your feelings before, but let's face it. I'm a lot smarter than you, so you need to listen to me, okay?"

Okay, Miles thought. He believed and he didn't believe, both at the same time. That was the condition of his life. Hayden was a schizophrenic, and he was faking. He was a genius, and he had delusions of grandeur. He was paranoid, and people were out to get him. All of these things were at least partially true at the same time.

In the years since Hayden had gone missing—slipping out of the psychiatric hospital where he had been confined—he had become more and more elusive, harder and harder to recognize as the brother that Miles had once loved so dearly. Eventually, perhaps, that old Hayden would disappear entirely.

If he was, in fact, a schizophrenic, he was one with an unusually practical streak. He covered his tracks skillfully, moving stealthily from place to place, changing his name and identity, managing, along the way, to hold down various jobs and appear, to the people he met, convincingly normal. Personable, even.

Miles, on the other hand, had been the one to live a life of near-vagrancy. He had been the one who must have come across as "feverish" and "disordered" and "obsessive" as he trailed behind Hayden's various aliases. Too late, he came to Los Angeles, where Hayden had been working as a "residual income stream consultant" named Hayden Nash; too late in Houston, Texas, where he had been employed as a computer services technician for JPMorgan Chase & Co., named Mike Hayden. Too late, Miles arrived in Rolla, Missouri, where Hayden had been masquerading at the university as a graduate student in mathematics named, cruelly, Miles Spady.

Too late, also, at Kulm, North Dakota, not far from the White-stone Hill Battlefield historical site, not far from the place where Hayden had once imagined *the great pyramids of the Dakota . . . the Giza, Khufu, and Khafre . . .* It was February, and fat flakes of snow fell on the windshield, the wipers flapping like big wings as Miles imagined the shape of the pyramids emerging out of the gray blur of snowfall. They weren't really there, of course, and neither was Hayden, but at the Broken Bell Inn in nearby Napoleon, a motel clerk—a sullen pregnant young woman—frowned over the enlarged grainy photo of Hayden.

"Hmmm," she said.

From the photo, it would have been difficult to guess that they were identical twins. The picture had been taken years ago, not long after they had turned eighteen, and Miles had gained quite a bit of weight since then. Who knew, maybe Hayden had as well. But even in childhood they had never been truly indistinguishable. There was an aspect of Hayden's face—brighter, more avid, friendlier—something that people responded to, and an aspect of Miles's that they didn't. He could see it in the motel clerk's expression.

"I think I recognize him," the girl said. Her eyes flicked from the photo to Miles and then back. "It's hard to say."

"Take another look," Miles said. "It's not a very good photo. It's fairly old, so he may have changed over the years. Does it bring to mind anyone you've seen?"

He looked down at the photo with her, trying to see it as she might. It was a Christmas photo. It was that horrible winter break, their senior year in high school, that had ended with Hayden institutionalized once again, but in the picture Hayden looked completely sane—a kind-eyed, smiling teenage boy in front of a tinselly tree, his hair a bit shaggy, but no sign whatsoever in his face of the trouble that he was causing—would continue to cause. The girl's mouth moved slightly as she looked at it, and Miles wondered if perhaps Hayden had kissed her.

"Take your time," Miles said, firmly, remembering episodes of a police procedural he'd seen on television.

"Are you a policeman?" the girl said. "I'm not sure if we're supposed to give out that information."

"I'm a relative," Miles said reassuringly. "He's my brother, and he's been missing. I'm just trying to locate him."

She examined the photo a little longer, then at last came to a decision.

"His name is Miles," she said, and she gave him a brief but hooded look, which made him wonder if she was simply being recalcitrant, choosing not to reveal some important tidbit of information she had decided to hold back for no other reason but that she didn't like him as much as she liked Hayden. "Cheshire was his last name, I think. Miles Cheshire. He seemed like a great guy."

He remembered how his heart had contracted when she'd said this, when she'd repeated his own name back to him. It *was* just a joke, he thought then—a complicated, nasty prank that Hayden was engaged in. *What am I doing?* he thought. *Why am I doing this?*

That had been almost two years ago, that trip to North Dakota. He had packed up his things and driven back home, darkly aware that the whole Kulm adventure had been nothing but an elaborate tease. Hayden had been in one of his mean and jolly manic moods, and when Miles got back to his apartment, there was a book waiting for him: *No Tears for the General: The Life of Alfred Sully,* and an 8 x 12 manila envelope that contained an article torn from the pages of *The Professional Journal of American Schizophrenia,* a passage high-lighted in yellow marker. "If one twin develops schizophrenia, the second twin has a 48% chance of developing it as well, and fre-quently within one year of the first twin." There was also an email waiting for him from generalasully@hotmail.com, just one more cheerful dig. "Oh, Miles," it said. "Do you ever wonder what people think of you going around with your posters and crummy old pho-tos and your sad story about your crazy evil twin brother? Do you ever think that people are going to take one look at your raggedy-looking self and they aren't going to tell you anything? They'll think: *Why, it's actually Miles who is the crazy one.* They'll think: *Maybe he doesn't even have a twin brother! Maybe he's just out of his mind!*"

That was it, Miles had thought then, reading the email and blushing with humiliation. He was so furious that he'd thrown the book about Alfred Sully out the window of his apartment, where it landed with an unsatisfying flutter in the parking lot. That was it! he promised himself. They were finished. No more of my time—no more of my heart!

He would forget about Hayden. He would get on with his own life.

He remembered this resolution. It came back to him vividly, even as he sat there in the car, unshaven, unshowered, sorting through the flyers that he'd printed up on simple, durable card stock. HAVE YOU SEEN ME? at the top. Then the photograph of Hayden. Then: RE-WARD! Though that was probably stretching the truth a little.

He angled the rearview mirror and examined himself critically. His eyes. His expression. Did he look like a crazy person? *Was* he a crazy person?

This was the eleventh of June. 68° 18′ N, 133° 29′ W. The sun wouldn't set again for about five weeks.

7

In the waiting area of Enterprise Auto Rental, Ryan checked through his identification materials again. Social security card. Driver's license. Credit cards.

All the flotsam that proved that you were officially a person.

In this particular case, Ryan was officially Matthew P. Blurton, age twenty-four, of Bethesda, Maryland. Ryan didn't think that he looked like he was twenty-four, but no one had ever questioned him, so he supposed that he must not look suspicious.

He sat there politely, thinking about a song that he was learning on the guitar. He could picture the tablature in his mind, and his fingers moved inconspicuously as he thought of the positions on the frets, the ham of his hand on his thighs, palm up, the fingers posed into various combinations like sign language.

He knew that he ought to be paying more attention; he was going to screw things up if he didn't take better care. That's what Jay—his father—would probably tell him.

———

And so he lifted his head to see what was going on.

At the counter, there was a middle-aged African American woman in a navy-blue coat and a small purple hat, and Ryan observed her surreptitiously as she withdrew a billfold from her purse.

"My grandmother is ninety-eight years old!" the lady was saying. She regarded her billfold as if she were playing a game of pinochle, frowning, then withdrew a bent ancient-looking credit card. "Ninety-eight years old!"

"Mmmm-hmmm," said the young man behind the counter, who was also African American. The young man's eyes were on the computer screen, and he typed out a burst of letters onto the keyboard.

"Ninety-eight years old," he said. "That's a long time to be alive!"

"It certainly is," the woman said, and Ryan could sense that they were on the verge of settling into a comfortable conversation. He glanced down at his watch.

"I wonder how long my lifeline is," the young man at the computer mused, and Ryan watched as the woman nodded.

"Only the Lord knows," the woman said.

She set her credit card and driver's license upon the counter.

"You know," the woman said, "it's not easy at that age. She doesn't talk much at all anymore, but she does sing a lot. And prays. She prays, you know."

"Mmmm-hmmm," the young man said, and typed again. "Does she have amnesia?" he said.

"Oh, no," the woman said. "She remembers things okay. She recognizes the folks that she wants to, at least!"

They both laughed at this, and Ryan found himself smiling with them. And then—at least partly because he was stupidly smiling at an eavesdropped conversation—he felt lonely.

Back home in Iowa, where he'd grown up, there were practically no black people to speak of, and he'd noticed since coming east that it seemed like black people were always nice to one another, that there was a camaraderie. Maybe that was a stereotype, but still he felt an unexpected sense of longing as the man and woman chuckled. He had an idea about ease, warmth, that private sense of connection. Is that what it was really like? He wondered.

Lately, he had been thinking about contacting his parents, and there was a letter he had in his mind. *"Dear Mom & Dad,"* obviously.

"Dear Mom & Dad, I'm sorry that I haven't been in touch in so long, and I thought I should let you know that I'm okay. I'm in Michigan—"

And then, right, they would want to know, or they would figure out. *"I'm in Michigan with Uncle Jay, and I know that he is my biological father, so I guess that is one thing we can stop pretending about—"*

Which started already to sound hostile. *"I'm in Michigan with Uncle Jay. Staying here for a while until I get some things figured out for myself. I'm writing some songs, earning some money. Uncle Jay has a business venture that I've been helping him out with—"*

Bad idea to even mention "business venture." It came off immediately as shady. *Jay?* they would think. What was the nature of this "business"? Immediately they would think drugs or something illegal, and he had already promised Jay that he wasn't going to tell anyone.

"Swear to God, Ryan," Jay had said as they sat on the couch in the cabin in Michigan, playing video games together. "I'm serious. You've got to swear that you're not going to breathe a word of any of this."

"You can trust me," Ryan said. "Who am I going to tell?"

"*Anybody,*" Jay said. "Because this is extremely, extremely serious stuff. Serious people could become involved, if you know what I mean."

"Jay," Ryan said, "I understand. Really."

"I hope you do, buddy," Jay said, and Ryan nodded earnestly, though truthfully he didn't understand much about the project they were engaged in.

He knew that it was illegal, obviously, a scam of some sort, but the actual purpose was elusive. One day he'd be Matthew P. Blurton and he'd rent a car in Cleveland and then drive the car to Milwaukee and return it at the airport, and then he'd board a plane in Milwaukee using an ID card for Kasimir Czernewski, age twenty-two, and fly to Detroit, and then later, online, he'd transfer bank funds in the amount of four hundred dollars from Czernewski's bank account in Milwaukee to the account of Frederick Murrah, fifty, of West Deer Township, Pennsylvania. Was it simply a very complex shell game, one person sliding into the next person and so on down the line? He assumed that there must be financial gain involved somehow, but if so he hadn't seen evidence of it yet. He and Jay lived in basically a hut in the woods, a little hunting lodge, lots of top-notch computer equipment but very little else of value as far as he could tell.

But Jay looked so serious and stern. He had straight shoulder-length hair, surfer hair, Ryan thought, black with a few threads of early gray running through it, and the droopy army surplus clothes of a teenage runaway. It was hard to imagine him projecting an attitude that wasn't mellow, but suddenly he was startlingly fierce.

"Swear to God, Ryan," Jay said. "I'm serious," he said, and Ryan nodded.

"Jay, trust me," Ryan said. "You trust me, don't you?"

And Jay said, "Sure I do. You're my son, right?" And then he gave Ryan that grin that, despite himself, Ryan still found pretty dazzling, even breathtaking, like he'd almost got a crush or something—*You're my son*, and that deliberate eye contact, both unnerving and flattering, and Ryan, all flustered, was like:

"Yeah, I guess I am. I'm your son."

This was one of the things that they were still figuring out—how to talk about this stuff—and it was all still very uncomfortable, they would start to talk about it, and then neither one of them knew what to say, it required a certain language that was either too analytic or too corny or embarrassing.

The basic fact was this: Jay Kozelek was Ryan's biological father, but Ryan had only found out recently. Up until a few months ago, Ryan had thought that Jay was his uncle. His mother's long-estranged younger brother.

Ryan's existence had been due to the usual teenage mistakes; that was the short version. Two sixteen-year-olds getting carried away in the back of a car after a movie. This was back in Iowa, and the girl's, the mother's—Ryan's mother's—family was strict and religious and didn't believe in abortion, and Jay's older sister, Stacey, wanted a baby but she had something wrong with her ovaries.

Jay had always felt that honesty was called for, but Stacey hadn't felt that it was a good idea at all. She was ten years older than Jay, and she didn't think very highly of him in any case—in terms of his morals, his ideas about life, the drugs, etc.

There's a time and place, she had told Jay, back when Ryan was a baby.

And then later she said: *Why does it matter to you, Jay? Why does it always have to be about you? Can't you think of someone else besides yourself?*

He's happy, Stacey said. *I'm his mom and Owen is his dad and he's happy with that.*

Not long afterward, they had stopped talking to each other. Jay had had some run-ins with the law, and they had argued, and that was that. Jay was hardly mentioned when Ryan was growing up— and then only as a negative example. *Your uncle Jay, the jailbird.* The hobo. Never owned anything he couldn't carry. Got involved in narcotics when he was a teenager and it ruined his life. Let that be a warning. Nobody knows where he is anymore.

And so Ryan hadn't learned the truth—that Stacey was actually his biological aunt, that his little-seen uncle Jay was his "birth father," that his biological mother had committed suicide in her sophomore year in college many years ago, when Ryan was a three-year-old kid living in Council Bluffs, Iowa, with his supposed parents, Stacey and Owen Schuyler, and Jay was backpacking around South America—

Ryan hadn't learned all of this until he was himself in college. One night Jay had called him up and told him all about it.

He was himself a sophomore in college, just like his real mother had been, and maybe that was why it struck such a blow. *My whole life is a lie,* he thought, which he knew was melodramatic, adolescent, but he woke up that morning after Jay had called him and he found himself in his dorm, a corner room on the fourth floor of Willard Hall, and his roommate, Walcott, was asleep under a mounded comforter in the narrow single bed beneath the window, and a gray light was coming in.

It must have been about six-thirty, seven in the morning. The sun wasn't up yet, and he rolled over and faced the wall, chilly old plaster with many thin cracks in the beige painted surface, and he closed his eyes.

He hadn't slept much after his conversation with Uncle Jay. *His father.*

At first it was like a joke, and then he thought, *Why is he doing this, why is he telling me this?* though all he said was, "Oh. Uh-huh. Wow." Monosyllabic, his voice ridiculously polite and noncommittal. "Oh, really?" he said.

"I guess it's just something I thought you ought to know," Jay told him. "I mean it's probably better if you don't say anything to your parents, but you can make your own decision about that. I just thought—it seemed wrong to me. You're a man, you're an adult, I feel like you have a right to know."

"I appreciate that," Ryan said.

But once he'd spent a few hours sleeping on and off, once he'd turned over the facts in his mind a few hundred times, he wasn't sure what he was supposed to do with the information. He sat up in bed and fingered the edges of his blankets. He could imagine his parents—his "parents," Stacey and Owen Schuyler, asleep, back in the house in Council Bluffs, and he could picture his own room down the hall from theirs, the books still on their shelves and his summer clothes still in the closet and his turtle, Veronica, sitting on her rock underneath her heat lamp, all of it like a museum of his childhood. Maybe his parents didn't even think of themselves as fakes, maybe most of the time they didn't even remember that the world they had created was utterly false at its core.

The more he thought about it, the more everything began to feel like a sham. It wasn't just his own faux family, it was the "family structure" in general. It was the social fabric itself, which was like a stage play that everyone was engaged in. Yes, he saw now what his history teacher meant when she talked about "constructs," "tissues of signs," "lacunae." Sitting there in his bed, he was aware of the other rooms, rows and stacks of them, the other students, all of them housed here waiting to be sorted and processed into jobs and sent down their various paths. He was aware of the other teenage boys who had slept in this very room, decades and decades of them, the dormitory like a boxcar being filled and refilled, year after year, and briefly he could have risen up out of his body, out of time, and watched the generic stream of them entering and exiting and being replaced.

He got out of bed and took his towel off the bedpost and figured he might as well go down the hall to the communal bathroom and shower, and he knew he had to get a grip on himself and study for his chemistry test, he was earning a D, C- at best, *Oh God,* he thought—

And maybe it was at that moment that he broke loose from his life. His "life": it felt suddenly so abstract and tenuous.

He had originally just gone out for coffee. It was by that time around seven-thirty in the morning, but the campus was still sleepy. From the sidewalk he could hear the music students in their carrels, the scales and warm-up exercises mingling dissonantly, clarinet, cello, trumpet, bassoon, winding around one another, and it felt like a fitting sound track, like the music you hear in a movie when the character is about to have a mental breakdown and they clutch their forehead in anguish.

He did not clutch his forehead in anguish, but he did think, once again—

My whole life is a lie!

There were many things to be troubled by in this situation, many things to feel angry and betrayed about, but the one that for some reason Ryan felt most keenly was the death of his biological mother. *My God!* he thought. *Suicide. She* killed *herself!* He felt the tragedy of it wash over him, though now it was past. Still, it outraged him that Stacey and Owen hadn't cared whether or not he knew about this. That they found out about it and tsked, and he was probably in the living room in front of the television, three years old, watching some trite and educational program, and they might have shaken their heads and thought what a favor they had done for him, raising him as their own, all the money and effort they'd put into turning him into the kind of kid who could get a scholarship to Northwestern University, into the type of person who could take his place in the top tier, how hard they had worked to mold him. But there was no indication they ever *contemplated* revealing the truth about his parentage, no indication that they realized that this was *important,* no sense that they understood how badly they had wronged him.

Maybe it was melodramatic, but nevertheless he could feel it sink down through the center of his stomach, that fluttery feeling of epinephrine releasing itself. Part of this was also the upcoming chemistry test, which it was likely he was going to fail, and part of it was that it was one of those cold, tinny mornings in October, very windy, and a school of leaves went scampering into Clark Street like lemmings and were run over by a fast-moving car. It made him think of a term he had read in his psychology class. "Fugue state." Maybe it was the combination of the discordant arpeggios from the conservatory and the leaves in the street. "Fugue." A dissociative psychological state marked by sudden, unexpected travel away from home or one's customary place of work, with inability to recall one's past, confusion about personal identity, or the assumption of a new identity, or significant distress or impairment.

Which actually sounded very interesting, very appealing in some ways, although he supposed that if you *decided* to have a fugue state, it wasn't a true fugue state.

He was also failing psychology.

And there were some issues of minor misappropriation of funds, his student loan, and there had been a letter from the registrar: PAST DUE. DEMAND FOR PAYMENT. It would be very difficult to explain to his parents what he had done with that money, how he had managed to forget about paying his tuition, and instead had frittered the borrowed cash away on things like clothes and CDs and dinner at the Mexican place on Foster Ave. How had it happened? He couldn't even say.

And so now here he was in his rented Chevy Aveo driving through the darkened corridor of Interstate 80 in late January and thinking that he would write a song about driving down the interstate alone and no one knows my name and I am so far away from you, or something like that. But not so corny.

Dear Mom and Dad, I realize that the choices I have made recently haven't been exactly sensitive toward you, and I'm sorry for the pain I have caused. I know that I should have contacted you sooner. I realize that at this point the police are involved and that I am probably considered a "missing person," and I want you to know that it wasn't my intention to bring trouble and sorrow into your life. But here I have done it.

Right now I am standing in a motel lobby in _____, and on the wall of the manager's cubicle is this xeroxed sign, one of those kinds of Wise Sayings that people are always taping up on the wall above their computer or whatever, for some reason.

The sign says:

The circumstances of life—
The events of life—
The people around me in life—
*Do not **make** me the way I am.*
*They **reveal** the way I am.*

*And I find myself here thinking about how much you, Mom, would
like that saying, how it might be the thing you would tell me if you
could hear all my excuses. I can imagine that I have **revealed** who I am
to you all of the sudden and that it has turned out to be an unpleasant
surprise. I am not the son you wanted when you took me in as a baby
and raised me as your own and tried to turn me into a good person.
But I guess I am something else. I don't know what yet but—*

But here he was checking into the motel because he was supposed
to have one lodging charge on the Matthew P. Blurton MasterCard
and here was a Holiday Inn with free wireless Internet, and he had to
check Matthew P. Blurton's email and log in to Instant Messenger
and see if Jay might be trying to get in touch.

He had a Matthew P. Blurton cell phone as well, but Jay was cautious about cells and so he was never supposed to call Jay, never supposed to call the house.

He kept worrying that his mother would track him down. She
had claimed for years that she didn't even know Jay's whereabouts,
but if her son was missing, honestly missing, wouldn't she finally
break down and try to locate Jay? Wouldn't she feel that Jay—his
true father—had a right to know? For most of the months, he had
been staying at the cabin in the woods of Michigan with Jay, sleeping on the couch and going on "quests," as Jay called them, whatever they were doing with the credit cards and the social security
numbers and the various lists from the Internet, and it felt like the
right thing to be doing even though he sometimes imagined Stacey
and Owen back in Council Bluffs.

Sitting at the kitchen table, pressing the tines of their forks into one of Stacey's casseroles, lifting a bite. They had always been one of those silent-dinner-table families, even though Stacey insisted all through high school that they *had to* eat together, as if that somehow made them closer, to sit there side by side shoveling food into their mouths until at last Ryan could tilt away from his cleaned plate and say, "Dad, may I be excused?"

Was she sad now? Ryan wondered. Was she worried and terrified and weepy? Or was she enraged?

There had been that one time in high school when he had fucked up, he had been involved with what Stacey thought of as an "inappropriate" girlfriend and he had been skipping school and generally telling lies and sneaking around, and she had acted with such icy swiftness, sending him off to a wilderness program for recalcitrant juveniles, packing him off in the middle of the night with only a duffle bag, the men, the "counselors," standing at the front door waiting to hustle him into the van and carry him off to a two-week-long disciplinary self-help brainwashing session.

He thought about that, too. He could imagine his mother's resolve, her anger, sending out minions to bring him to ground and drag him back to the life that he'd fled.

Ryan sat there at the desk in his room in the Holiday Inn and opened up his laptop. It was probably not useful to dwell on such things, but he nevertheless found himself typing his own name into the search engine and looking again at some of the old articles and such. For example:

No Developments in Case of Missing College Student

CHICAGO—Chicago police have come to a standstill in the case of a Northwestern University college student who disappeared without a trace in the morning hours of October 20. Following one anonymous lead, divers searched the frigid

Lake Michigan waters near the campus but came up empty-handed. Police Sgt. Rizzo said the investigation has come to a standstill, and there have been no new developments.

—which did make him feel guilty, but it was also disappointing. The cops were clearly not particularly good at their jobs. "Without a trace!" Christ! It wasn't as if he were in disguise. It wasn't as if someone had put a burlap bag over his head and spirited him away in a van or whatever. He walked off campus and took the el downtown to the bus station, and there were certainly plenty of people who saw him that day. Were people so inattentive? Was he that nondescript?

And the suicide angle also bothered him—how quick they were to send divers into the lake! That was his mother's doing, he thought. She knew that his biological mother was a suicide, and didn't it figure that was the first thing she thought of.

It had probably been on her mind for a while, he thought. Every time he talked to her on the phone, she was always asking how he felt, why was he so quiet, was there anything wrong, and he saw now the connections that she had been making all along.

There was a ping as someone signed on to Instant Messenger, and he glanced down because it was about time for Jay to contact him—they always had a brief conversation on IM when he was on these trips, just to touch base, but when he opened up the IM window, it was gibberish.

Or actually, someone was typing in what he guessed was Cyrillic. Russian?

490490: Раскрытие способностей к телекинезу с помощью гипноза . . . данном разделе Вашему вниманию предлагается фрагменты видеозаписей демонстраций парапсихологических явлений.

He regarded this string of characters. Was there a problem with Jay's computer? Was it some obscure joke that Jay was playing? Then he typed:

BLURTON: How about trying it in English, dude?

The cursor sat blinking. Breathing. Then:

490490: Господин Ж??? J???

How freaky, he thought.

BLURTON: Jay??

No answer. 490490 had grown silent, though it felt like a kind of watchful silence, a stillness in the motel room, the curtains pulled closed and the television's slate face staring coolly at the bed, and the distant sound of semis passing on the interstate beyond the motel. He thought maybe he should close the IM window.

But then 490490 began to type again.

490490: Mr J. So good to find Mr J. I see were u r.

8

Lucy woke and she was alone in bed. There was the crumpled space where George Orson had been sleeping, the indented pillow, the blankets pulled aside and she sat up as the room loomed over her. The sunlight rimmed the edges of the curtains, and she could see the watchful closet door and the dark stern shape of the bureau dresser and the half-light reflections in the oval vanity mirror, movement, which she realized was herself, alone in the bed.

"George?" she said.

Nearly a week had passed and still they were here at the old house in Nebraska and she was starting to feel a little anxious, though George Orson had tried to be reassuring—"Nothing to be concerned about," he said. "Just a few things that have to be sorted out. . . ."

But he didn't explain further than that. Ever since they'd arrived, he'd made himself scarce. Hours and hours locked in the downstairs room he called "the study." She had actually kneeled in front of the locked door and fit her eye to the keyhole beneath the cut-glass doorknob, and she could see him as if through a pinhole camera, sitting behind the big wooden desk hunched over his laptop, his face hidden behind the screen.

And naturally it had occurred to her that something had gone wrong with their plan.

Whatever the "plan" was.

Which, Lucy realized, she was not that clear about.

She pulled aside the drapes, and the light came in and that felt a bit better. There was a dry, earthy basement smell that was particularly noticeable in the morning, waking up, a taste of underground in her mouth, a taste of rotten fabric, and the windows didn't open, they were painted shut, and it was clear that the house had been sitting in its own dust for a long time. "I've had an exterminator in, don't worry," George Orson had told her, "and a cleaning woman— once every few months. The place has never been *abandoned*," he said, a bit defensively, but all Lucy wanted to know was how long it had been since someone had actually lived in the house, how long since his mother had died?

And he estimated, reluctantly.

"I don't know," he said. "Probably about—eight years?" She didn't know why he acted as if even a simple question were an invasion of his privacy.

But a lot of their conversations had been like that lately, and she lingered at the window in her oversize T-shirt and panties looking down at the gravel road that led from the garage past the house and the tower of the lighthouse and the courtyard of the motel units to the two-lane blacktop that ribboned its way eventually back to the interstate.

"George?" she said, more loudly.

She padded down the hallway, and then she went downstairs to the kitchen and he wasn't there, either, though she saw that his cereal bowl and spoon had been washed and placed neatly into the dish drain.

And so she went out of the kitchen and through the dining room to "the study—"

"Study." Which, to Lucy, sounded British or something, pretentious, like some old murder mystery.

The Study. The Billiard Room. The Conservatory. The Ballroom.

But he wasn't there, either.

The door was open and the room was curtained and carpeted and there was a chandelier made of brass with dangling glass dewdrops.

"That was my mother's idea of elegance," George Orson had told her when he showed her the room for the first time and she'd folded her arms over her chest, taking it in. His mother's "idea" of elegance, she assumed, was not *real* elegance—though to Lucy it was in fact fairly impressive. Beautiful oriental carpet, gold-leaf wallpaper, heavy wooden furniture, shelves full of books—not junky paperbacks, either, but real hardcover books with thread-bound spines and thick pages and a dense, woody smell.

Was there a difference, she wondered, some fine distinction of good taste or breeding that would make it okay to call a room a "study" but not okay to have a light fixture that is called a "chandelier"?

There were a lot of things she had yet to learn about social class, said George Orson, whose college days at Yale had sensitized him to such things.

So what did it say about her that her own experience of chandeliers, studies, and so on was so limited? She herself had come from a long, long line of poor drudgers, Irish and Polish and Italian peasants—nobodies, stretching back for generations.

You could draw her family in two dimensions, like characters in a comic strip. Here was her father, a plumber, a kindly, beer-bellied, muddy little man with hairy hands and a bald head. Her mother: windblown and stern, drinking coffee at the kitchen table before she went off to work at the hospital, a nurse but only a licensed practical nurse, just a vocational degree. Her sister, simple and round like her father, dutifully washing dishes or folding a basket of clothes and not complaining as Lucy sat moodily, lazily, on the couch reading novels by the latest young female authors and trying to emanate an air of sophisticated irritation—

She couldn't help but think of her lost, sadly cartoonish family as she looked around the empty study. Her old loser life, which she had left behind for this new one.

In the study was an old oak desk, six drawers on either side, all of them locked. And a file cabinet, also locked. And George Orson's laptop, password protected. And a wall safe, which was hidden behind a framed picture of George Orson's grandparents.

"Grandpa and Grandma Orson," George Orson had said, referring to the grim pair, their pale faces and dark clothes, the woman with one light-colored eye and one dark—"called heterochromia," said George Orson. "Very rare. One blue eye. One brown eye. Probably hereditary, though my grandmother always said it was because her brother hit her in the eye as a child."

"Hmmm," Lucy had said, and now, alone in the room, she regarded the picture once again, the way the woman fixed her heterochromatic gaze on the photographer. A frankly unhappy and almost pleading look.

And then she unhooked the latch the way that George Orson had shown her, and the old photo swung out like a cabinet door to reveal the nook in the wall with the safe.

"So," Lucy had said when she first saw it. The safe had appeared to be quite old, she thought, with a combination wheel like a dial on an antique radio. "Aren't you going to open it?" she said, and George Orson had chuckled—though a bit uncertainly.

"I can't, actually," he said.

Their eyes met, and she wasn't exactly sure what to make of his expression.

"I haven't been able to figure out the combination," he said. Then he shrugged. "I'm sure it's empty, in any case."

"You're sure it's empty," she said. And she looked at him and he held her gaze, and it was one of those moments in which his eyes said, *Don't you trust me?* And her eyes said, *I'm thinking about it.*

"Well," George Orson said. "I doubt very seriously whether it's full of gold doubloons and gems."

He gave her that dimpled half smile of his.

"I'm sure the combination will turn up somewhere in the files," he said, and touched her leg playfully with the tip of his index finger, as if for good luck.

"Somewhere," he said, "if we can find the key to the filing cabinet."

But now, standing in the study, she couldn't help but take another look at the safe. She couldn't help but reach out and test the brass and ivory handle just to be sure that, yes, it was still locked and sealed and impenetrable.

Not that she would steal from George Orson. Not that she was obsessed with money—

But she had to admit that it was a concern. She had to admit that she was very much looking forward to leaving Pompey, Ohio, and being rich with George Orson, and probably it was true that this was part of the attraction of this whole adventure.

In September of her senior year of high school, two months after her parents' deaths, Lucy was just a depressed student in George Orson's Advanced Placement American history class.

He had been a new teacher, a new person in their town, and it was obvious even on the first day of class that he had a *presence*, with his black clothes and his uncanny way of making eye contact with people, those green eyes, the way he smiled at them as if they were all doing something illicit together.

"American history—the history that you have learned up until now—is full of *lies*," George Orson told them, and he paused over the word "lies" as if he liked the taste of it. She thought he must be from New York City or Chicago or wherever, he wouldn't stay long, she thought, but actually she did pay more attention than she was expecting to.

And then in study hall she heard some boys talking about George Orson's car. The car was a Maserati Spyder, she had noticed it herself, a tiny silver convertible big enough for only two people, almost like a toy.

"Did you get a look at it?" she overheard a boy saying—Todd Zilka, whom Lucy loathed. He was a football player, a big athletic person who was nevertheless the son of a lawyer and did well enough in school that he had been inducted into the National Honor Society, after which Lucy herself had stopped going to meetings. If she had been braver, she would have resigned, denounced her membership. In middle school, it had been Todd Zilka who had started calling her "Lice-y"—which wouldn't have been such a big deal except that she and her sister actually *had* contracted head lice, pediculosis, and were dismissed from school in shame until the infestation could be cleared up, and even years later people still called her "Lice-y," it might be the only thing they remembered about her when their twenty-year reunion rolled around.

"Toddzilla," was Lucy's own private name for Todd Zilka, though she did not have the power to make such a name stick on him.

The fact that a creature like Toddzilla could thrive and become popular was one good reason to leave Pompey, Ohio, forever.

Nevertheless, she listened surreptitiously as he spouted his stupid opinions to his idiotic friends in study hall. "I mean," he was saying, "I'd like to know where a crummy high school teacher gets money for a car like that. It's like, an Italian import, you know? Probably costs seventy grand!"

And, despite herself, that gave her pause. Seventy thousand dollars was an impressive amount of money. She thought again of George Orson standing in front of them in the classroom, George Orson in his tight black shirt talking about how Woodrow Wilson was a white supremacist and quoting Anaïs Nin:

"We see things not as they are, but as we are. Because it is the 'I' behind the 'eye' that does the seeing."

And then one afternoon not long later, Toddzilla raised his hand and George Orson gestured toward him, hopefully. As if they might be about to discuss the Constitution together.

"Yes . . . ? Ah—Todd?" George Orson said, and Toddzilla grinned, showing his large orthodontic teeth.

"So Mr. O," he said. He was one of those teenage jock boys who thought it was cool to call teachers and other adults by trite, jocky nicknames. "So Mr. O," Toddzilla said. "Where'd you get your car? That's an awesome car."

"Oh," George Orson said. "Thank you."

"What make is that? Is that a Maserati?"

"It is." George Orson looked at the rest of them, and Lucy thought that for a fraction of a second she and George Orson had looked directly at each other, that they were in communion, silently agreeing that Toddzilla was a Neanderthal. Then George Orson turned his attention down to his desk, to the syllabus or whatever.

"So, why would you become a high school teacher if you can afford a car like that?" Toddzilla said.

"Well, I guess I just find teaching high school really fulfilling," George Orson said. Straight-faced. He looked again at Lucy, and the corners of his mouth lifted enough so that his dimple peeked out. There was a sharpness, a glint of secret hilarity that perhaps only she could see. Lucy smiled. He was funny, she thought. *Interesting.*

But Todd hadn't liked it. Later, in study hall, in the cafeteria, she heard him repeating the same question, critically. "How can a high school teacher afford a car like that?" Toddzilla wanted to know. "Full-fucking-filling, my ass. I think he's some rich pervert or something. He just likes to be around teenagers."

Which was probably the first time she thought: *Hmmm.* She herself was intrigued by the idea of a wealthy George Orson, his soft but masculine, veiny hands.

They had left Pompey in the Maserati, and maybe that had been the reason she felt so confident. She looked good in that car, she thought, people would look at them as they were cruising down the interstate, a guy in an SUV who watched her as they passed, and he made a display of winking at her, like a silent movie actor or a mime. *Wink.* And she made her own show of not noticing, though in fact she had even bought a tube of bright red lipstick, sort of as a joke, but when she looked at herself in the passenger side mirror, she was privately pleased by the effect.

Who would you be if you weren't Lucy?

Which was a question they found themselves talking about frequently, when George Orson wasn't sequestered in the "study."

Who would you be?

One day, George Orson found an old set of bow and arrows in the garage, and they went down to the beach to try shooting them. He hadn't been able to find an actual target, and so he spent a lot of time setting up various objects for Lucy to shoot arrows at. A pyramid stack of soda cans, for example. An ancient beach ball, which inflated only halfheartedly. A large cardboard box, which he drew circles on with black Magic Marker.

And as Lucy nocked her arrow into the string and drew back the bow, trying to aim, George Orson would ask her questions.

"Would you rather be an unpopular dictator, or a popular president?"

"That's easy," Lucy said.

"Would you rather be poor and live in a beautiful place, or be rich and live in an ugly place?"

"I don't think poor people ever live in beautiful places," she said.

"Would you rather drown, or freeze to death, or die in a fire?"

"George," she said, "why are you always so morbid?" And he smiled tightly.

"Would you want to go to college, even if you had enough money that you'd never have to get a real job?

"Which is to say," George Orson continued. "Do you want to go because you want to be an educated person, or do you only go because you want a career of some sort?"

"Hmm," Lucy said, and tried to draw a bead on the beach ball, which was lolling woozily in the wind. "I think I just want to be an educated person, actually. Though maybe if I had so much money that I never had to work, I'd probably choose a different major. Something impractical."

"I see," George Orson said. He stood behind her; she could feel his chest against her back as he tried to help her take aim. "Like what?" he said.

"Like history," Lucy said, and smiled sidelong at him as she released the arrow, which traveled in a wobbling, uncertain arc before landing in the sand about a foot away from the beach ball.

"You're close!" George Orson whispered—still pressed close up against her, his hand around her waist, his mouth alongside her ear. She could feel the wing-brush of his lips moving. "Very close," he said.

She thought about this again as she went outdoors and stood there in her sleep T-shirt, her hair flattened against the side of her head and nothing attractive about her at all, currently.

"George?" she called—yet again.

And she stepped tenderly barefoot across the gravel driveway toward the garage. It was a wooden barnlike structure with high weeds growing up along the sides of it, and when she drew closer, a flurry of grasshoppers scattered, startled by her approach. Their dry wings made a maraca sound like rattlesnakes; she pulled her hair back into a ponytail and held it with her fist.

They hadn't driven the Maserati since they arrived here. "Too conspicuous," George Orson said. "There's no sense in calling a lot of attention to ourselves," he said, and then the next day she woke and he was already out of bed and he wasn't in the house and she found him at last in the garage.

There were two cars in there. The Maserati was on the left, completely covered by an olive-green tarp. On the right was an old red and white Ford Bronco pickup, possibly from the 1970s or 80s. The hood of the pickup was open and George Orson was leaning into it.

He was wearing an old pair of mechanic's coveralls, and she almost laughed out loud. She couldn't imagine where he had found such an outfit.

"George," she said. "I've been looking all over for you. What are you *doing*?"

"I'm fixing a truck," he said.

"Oh," she said.

And though he was basically still himself, he looked—what?— *costumed* in the dirty coveralls, his hair uncombed and standing up, fingers black with grease, and she felt a twinge.

"I didn't know that you knew how to fix cars," Lucy said, and George Orson gave her a long look. A sad look, she thought, as if he were recalling a mistake he'd made in the distant past.

"There are probably a lot of things you don't know about me," he said.

Which gave her pause, now, as she vacillated at the mouth of the garage.

The truck was gone, and a shiver of unease passed across her as she stared at the bare cement floor, an oil spot in the dust where the old Bronco had been.

He'd gone out—had left her alone—had left her—

The Maserati was still there, still covered in its tarp. She was not completely abandoned.

Though she was aware that she didn't have the key to the Maserati.

And even if she *did* have a key, she didn't know how to drive a stick shift.

She mulled this over, looked at the shelves: oil cans and bottles of nuclear-blue windshield wiper fluid and jars full of screws and bolts and nails and washers.

Nebraska was even worse than Ohio—if such a thing were possible. There was a soundlessness about this place, she thought, though sometimes the wind made the glass in the windowpanes hum, the wind running in a long exhaled stream through the weeds and dust and dry bed of the lake, and sometimes unexpectedly there would be a very startling sonic boom over the house as a military plane broke the sound barrier, and there was the rattle of the grasshoppers leaping from one weed to the next—

But mostly it was silence, a kind of end-of-the-world hush, and you could feel the sky sealing over you like the glass around a snow globe.

She was still in the garage when George Orson returned.

She had pulled back the tarp from the Maserati, and she was sitting in the driver's seat and wishing that she knew how to hot-wire a car. How appropriate, she thought, for George Orson to come back and find his beloved Maserati missing, and it would serve him right, and she liked to imagine the look on his face when she pulled back up the driveway sometime after dark—

She was still fantasizing about this when George Orson drove into the space beside her with the old Bronco. He looked puzzled as he opened the door—why was the tarp off of his Maserati?—but when he saw her sitting there, his expression opened into a gratifying look of alarm.

"Lucy?" he said. He was wearing jeans and a black T-shirt, very nondescript—his version of a native costume—and she had to admit that he didn't look like a wealthy man. He didn't even look like a teacher, with his face unshaved and his hair growing out and his jaw hard with suspicion, he could actually be said to look menacing and middle-aged. Briefly she had a memory of the father of her friend Kayleigh, who was divorced and lived in Youngstown and drank too much, and who had taken them to the Cedar Point amusement park when they were twelve, and she could imagine Kayleigh's father in the parking lot of Cedar Point leaning up against the hood of the car, smoking a cigarette as they came toward him, she remembered being aware of the way his arms were muscled and his eyes were fixed on her, and she thought, *Is he staring at my boobs?*

"Lucy, what are you doing?" George Orson said, and she looked at him hard.

Of course, the real George Orson was still there, underneath, if he cleaned himself up.

"I was just getting ready to drive off in your car and steal it and go to Mexico," Lucy said.

And his face settled back into itself, into the George Orson she knew, the George Orson who loved it when she was sarcastic.

"Sweetie," George Orson said. "I made a quick trip into town, that's all. I had to get some supplies—and I wanted to make you a nice dinner."

"I don't like being ditched," Lucy said sternly.

"You were sleeping," George Orson said. "I didn't want to wake you."

He ran a hand across the back of his hair—yes, he realized it was getting shaggy—and then he reached down and opened the door to the Maserati and climbed into the passenger seat.

"I left a note," he said. "On the kitchen table. I guess you didn't find it."

"No," she said. They were silent, and she couldn't help it, that slow, vacant feeling was opening up inside her chest, that end-of-the-world loneliness, and she put her hands on the steering wheel as if she were driving somewhere.

"I don't appreciate being left alone here," she said.

They looked at each other.

"I'm sorry," George Orson said.

His hand lowered over hers, and she could feel the smooth pressure of his palm against the back of her hand, and he was, after all, possibly the only person left in the world who truly loved her.

9

Back in the days before Hayden began to believe that his phone was being tapped, back when he and Miles were in their early twenties, he used to call fairly frequently. Once a month, sometimes more.

The phone would ring in the middle of the night. Two A.M. Three A.M. "It's me," Hayden would say, though of course who else would it be, at such an hour? "Thank God you finally picked up the phone," he would say. "Miles, you've got to help me, I can't sleep."

Sometimes he would be worked up about an article he had read on psychic phenomena or reincarnation, past lives, spiritualism. The usual.

Sometimes he would start ranting on the subject of their childhood, telling stories about events that Miles had no memory of whatsoever—events he was fairly certain Hayden had invented.

But there was no arguing with him. If Miles expressed any reservation or doubt, Hayden could easily become defensive, belligerent, and then who knew what would happen? The one time they'd gotten into a heated disagreement about his "memories," Hayden had slammed down the phone and hadn't called again for more than two months. Miles was beside himself. Back then, Miles still believed that it was only a matter of time before he tracked Hayden down, only a matter of time before Hayden could be captured or otherwise induced to come home. He had an image of Hayden, calmed and perhaps medicated, the two of them sharing a small apartment, peaceably playing video games after Miles came home from work. Starting a business together. He knew this was ridiculous.

Still, when Hayden resurfaced at last, Miles was very conciliatory. He was so relieved that he told himself he was never going to argue with Hayden again, no matter what Hayden said.

It was four in the morning, and Miles was sitting up in bed, holding the phone tightly, his heart beating fast. "Just tell me where you are, Hayden," he said. "Don't go anywhere."

"Miles, Miles," Hayden said. "I love it that you worry!"

He claimed that he was living in Los Angeles; he had a bungalow, he said, right off Sunset Boulevard in Silver Lake. "You won't find me if you come looking for me," he said, "but if it makes you feel any better, that's where I am."

"I'm relieved," Miles said, and he took out one of the yellow sticky notes he kept on his nightstand and wrote: "Sunset Blvd." and "Silver Lake."

"I'm relieved, too," Hayden said. "You're the only one I can really talk to, you know that, don't you?" Miles listened as Hayden drew an extended breath that he imagined was probably smoke from a joint. "You're the only person in the world who still loves me."

Hayden had been thinking a lot about their childhood—or rather, *his* childhood, since the truth was Miles didn't recall any of the incidents Hayden was obsessing about. But Miles kept his objections to himself. It was the first time Hayden had called him since their argument, and Miles stared down at his little sticky note in silence as Hayden held forth.

"I've been thinking a lot about Mr. Breeze," Hayden was saying. "Do you remember him?"

And Miles wavered. "Well," Miles said, and Hayden made an impatient sound.

"He was that hypnotist, don't you remember?" Hayden said. "He was pretty good friends with Mom and Dad—he was always at those parties back in the day. I think he dated Aunt Helen for a while."

"Uh-huh," Miles said, noncommittally. "And his name was 'Mr. Breeze'?"

"That was probably his stage name," Hayden said. His voice stiffened. "Geez, Miles, you don't remember anything. You never paid attention, you know that?"

"I guess not," Miles said.

Supposedly, according to Hayden, this incident with Mr. Breeze happened at one of the parties their parents used to have. It was late at night, the wee hours, and Hayden came down to the kitchen in his pajamas, couldn't sleep, sweaty from the top bunk, the forced air vent had been blowing from the ceiling onto him, he'd been awake anyway from the sounds of music and laughter and the thick hum of adult talking that came wafting through the floorboards and into his dreams. As for Miles, he would have been peacefully asleep in the bottom bunk. *Insensate,* as always.

The two of them, Miles and Hayden, were eight years old but small for their age, and Hayden was cute and solemn as he drank his glass of water in the kitchen. Mr. Breeze lifted him up and put him on a stool at the counter.

"Tell me, little boy," Mr. Breeze said, in his deep, deep voice. "Do you know what 'cryptomnesia' means?"

Mr. Breeze looked down into Hayden's eyes as if he were admiring his own reflection in a pool, and he took his index finger and let it hover right at the center of Hayden's forehead, though he didn't let it touch.

"Do you ever remember things that didn't really happen to you?" Mr. Breeze said.

"No," Hayden said. He looked, unsmiling, back at Mr. Breeze, in the way he always looked adults in the eye: impertinent. Their aunt Helen had come in and she stayed, watching.

"Portis," she said. "Don't tease that child."

"I'm not," Mr. Breeze said. He was dressed in black jeans and a flowered cowboy shirt, and he had lines around his mouth that looked as if someone had ironed creases there. He peered kindly at Hayden's face.

"You're not afraid, are you, young man?" Mr. Breeze said. Out in the next room, there was the sound of the party, some bluesy rock song, some people slow-dancing; out in the yard, a drunk lady wept bitterly while a drunken friend tried to counsel her.

"We're just going to take a wee peek at his past lives," Mr. Breeze told Aunt Helen. And he beamed at Hayden. "What do you think about that, Hayden? All the people that you used to be, once upon a time!" Mr. Breeze drew in a soft, anticipatory breath, barely audible.

"I so seldom get a chance to work with a child," he said.

This Mr. Breeze was fiercely drunk, Miles imagined. So was Aunt Helen, probably. So were all the other adults in the house.

But even drunk Mr. Breeze held Hayden pinned fast with only the pupils of his eyes. "You want to be hypnotized, don't you, Hayden?" he said.

Hayden's lips parted, and his tongue tingled in his mouth.

"Yes," Hayden heard himself say.

The gaze of Mr. Breeze locked into Hayden like one puzzle piece fits into another.

"I want you to tell me what it was like when you died," Mr. Breeze said. "That moment," he said. "Tell me about that moment."

———

Mr. Breeze had taken Hayden and slit him open the way a fisherman would slit open the belly of a trout. That was what Hayden said. "Not my physical body," Hayden explained. "It was my spirit. Whatever you want to call it. My soul. You know. Inner self."

"What do you mean by 'slit' you open," Miles said uneasily. "I don't get it."

"I'm not saying sexual," Hayden said. "You always assume sexual, Miles, you pervert."

Miles shifted the phone where it was making an uncomfortable, sweaty spot against his ear. It was getting close to five in the morning.

"So—?" Miles said.

"So that was how it started," Hayden said. "Mr. Breeze told me I had more past lives than any other person he'd ever met—"

"*A harvest,*" Mr. Breeze told Hayden. "You produce an unusually large harvest," he said. The lives were clustered inside of Hayden like roe—

"Fish eggs," Hayden said. "That's what 'roe' means."

"Yes, I *know,*" Miles said, and Hayden sighed.

"The thing is, Miles," Hayden said, "no one realizes, once these things have been opened up, you can't close them again. That's what I'm trying to explain to you. If most people had to live with the memories I've had to live with, a lot of them would kill themselves."

"You mean your nightmares," Miles said.

"Yes," he said. "That's how we used to refer to them. I know better now."

"Like the pirate stuff," Miles said.

"*Pirate stuff,*" Hayden said, and then he was witheringly silent. "You make it sound like some little romp through Neverland."

The pirate stuff, so-called, had been one of the recurring nightmares of Hayden's childhood, but they hadn't talked about it in years. It was true that he used to wake up screaming. Horrible, horrible screams. Miles could still hear them vividly.

In the dream Hayden used to talk about, he was a boy on a pirate ship. A cabin boy, Miles supposed. Hayden remembered a coil of heavy rope where he would curl up to sleep. There was the dense flapping of the sails and the creak of the masts as he lay there trying to rest, and the smell of wet wood and barnacles, and when he opened his eyes a crack, he would see the bare dirty feet of the pirates, which always had infected sores on them. He would huddle there, hoping not to be noticed, because sometimes the pirates would give him a kick. Sometimes they would grab him by the back of his shirt or his hair and yank him onto his feet.

"They always want me to kiss them," Hayden would tell Miles. This was back when he was eight, ten years old, and he had woken up screaming. "They always want me to kiss them on the lips." He grimaced: their breath, their nasty teeth, the filth in their beards.

"Gross," Miles said. And he remembered thinking even then that there was an unnatural quality to Hayden's dreams. The pirates would kiss Hayden, and sometimes they would cut off a hank of hair—"as a reminder of yer kisses, me lad"—and one of them even cut off a piece of his earlobe.

This particular pirate was Bill McGregor, and he was the one Hayden feared the most. Bill McGregor was the worst of them— and at night when everyone else was asleep, Bill McGregor would come looking for Hayden, his step slow and hollow on the planks of the deck, his voice a deep whisper.

"Boy," he would murmur. "Where are you, boy?"

After Bill McGregor cut off the piece of Hayden's earlobe, he decided that he wanted more. Every time he caught Hayden, he would cut a small piece off of him. The skin of an elbow, the tip of a finger, a piece of his lip. He would grip the squirming Hayden and cut a piece off of him, and then Bill McGregor would eat the piece of flesh.

"And when I'm finished playing with ye," Bill McGregor whispered, "I'm going to sneak up behind you and—"

Which is exactly what he did, according to Hayden. It was a spring night and Bill McGregor came up from behind him and clapped his hands tightly over Hayden's eyes and slit his throat and tossed him overboard, and Hayden went flailing into the sea with his neck clutched between his hands as if he were trying to throttle himself, blood gurgling out between his fingers. He could see a trickle of blood droplets falling upward as he plunged headfirst into the ocean—he was aware of the moon and the starry sky vanishing beneath his feet, the swallowing sound he made when he hit the water, the fish flitting away as he sank deeper, strands of seaweed, unfurling eddies of jugular blood, his mouth opening and closing, limbs growing limp.

His exact moment of death.

Yes, of course Miles knew about this. Hayden had the dream regularly when they were kids, once or twice a week sometimes. He would jump down into the bottom bunk and under the covers with Miles—and if Miles wasn't awake yet, he would shake him until he was. "Miles," he would say. "Miles! Nightmares! Oh, God! Nightmares!" And he would curl up around Miles as if they were back together in their mother's belly.

Miles had always prided himself on the fact that he was a good brother. He never got angry, no matter how many times he heard the story of Bill McGregor and so on.

But when he mentioned something to that effect, Hayden didn't speak for a long time.

"Oh, *right*," Hayden said. "You were such a good brother to me."

They sat there listening to each other breathing. On Hayden's end, there was the gurgling sound of a bong. Not surprising.

Yes, Miles knew what he was getting at. Hayden thought that he should have stuck by him no matter what. He thought that Miles should have just thrown away his relationship with their mother and the rest of the family and sided with him, no matter how extreme his stories and quarrels and accusations became.

This wasn't a topic that Miles felt comfortable discussing, but with Hayden it was difficult to avoid. Sooner or later, every conversation would circle back to these various obsessions that he had, his nightmares, his memories, his grudges against their family—

"His pathological lies," their mother called them. "He is a deeply, deeply troubled person, Miles," she said, on any number of occasions. She used to warn him that he was too easily deceived, that he was too much Hayden's follower—"his little factotum," she said, acidly.

This was during that period when she was trying to get Hayden institutionalized and she said, "Just you wait, Miles, sweetheart, because someday he will betray you just like he has betrayed everyone else. It's only a matter of time."

And so when Hayden called and said that he needed help, he needed his brother's help—"Just to talk awhile, I can't sleep, Miles, please just talk to me"—well, Miles couldn't keep from thinking of his mother's warning.

It was especially difficult when Hayden would insist so strongly on his version of their lives, his version of events. Events that Miles was pretty certain had never actually happened.

"The thing I'm confused about," Miles told Hayden—they had been talking now for hours about past lives and pirates, and even though Miles was exhausted, he was trying to be good-natured and reasonable. "I'm a little puzzled," Miles said, "about this guy. Mr. Breeze. Because I honestly don't remember you ever telling me anything about him before, and it seems like you would've."

"Oh, I told you about him," Hayden said. "Most definitely."

This was a few weeks after he had begun to obsess about the whole "hypnotist in the kitchen" story. Miles was at a rest area off of the interstate, with his window rolled down, talking on a drive-up pay phone. It was probably about two in the morning. A map of the United States was spread out across the steering wheel.

Hayden was saying, ". . . maybe the problem is that you *repressed* so much about our childhood. Do you ever consider that?"

"Well," Miles said. He took a sip from a bottle of water.

"It's not as if this hasn't been an ongoing ordeal in my life," Hayden said. "Remember Bobby Berman? Remember Amos Murley?"

"Yes," Miles said—and it was true, these were familiar names from their childhood, familiar people from Hayden's nightmares. Bobby Berman was the boy who liked to play with matches, and who had burned to death in a toolshed behind his house; Amos Murley was the teenager who had been drafted into the Union Army during the Civil War, the one who died while dragging himself across a battlefield, his legs blown off below the knee. Their mother used to call them Hayden's "imaginary characters."

"Oh, Hayden," she would say, with exasperation. "Why can't you make up stories about *happy* people? Why does everything have to be so morbid?"

And Hayden would blush, shrugging resentfully. He said nothing. It wasn't until much later that Hayden began to claim these were his own past lives he was dreaming about. That these "characters" were, in fact, people he had actually *been*. That the terrible life he was leading with their family was just one of many terrible lives he had led.

But it wasn't until their father died that Hayden had begun to understand the true nature of his affliction.

At least, that was the version of events he was currently espousing. It wasn't until their father was gone and their mother had remarried and the hateful Marc Spady was living with them in their house. Only then did he begin to grasp the extent of what Mr. Breeze had "opened up" inside him.

"That's the thing I wasn't prepared for, you see," Hayden said. "I came to realize that it wasn't just me—*it was everyone*."

Steadily, he had begun to comprehend, Hayden said. He had become aware that he was not the only person who had these past lives. *Obviously not!* Little by little, in crowds, in restaurants, in faces glimpsed on television, in small gestures of schoolmates and relatives—little by little he had begun to feel vague glimmerings of recognition. An eye, shifting sidelong—the fingers of a cashier, brushing his palm—the discolored front tooth of their geometry teacher—the voice of their stepfather, Marc Spady, which was, Hayden said, the exact gravelly voice of the pirate Bill McGregor.

When their father died, Hayden began to see connections in every face. Where had he come across that one before? In what life? No doubt nearly every soul had encountered the others in one permutation or another, all of them interconnected, entangled, their pathways crisscrossing backward into prehistory, into space and infinity like some terrible mathematical formula.

Clearly it had to do with their father's death, Miles thought. Before that, Hayden was just an overimaginative boy who had nightmares, and Mr. Breeze, if he existed, was just another of their father's unusual acquaintances, drunk at a party.

"Oh, spare me," Hayden said, when Miles tried to suggest this. "How facile!" he said. "Is that what *Mom* told you? That I became a so-called schizophrenic because I couldn't handle Dad's death? I know you don't like me to cast aspersions on your intelligence, but *really*. That's so completely simpleminded."

"Well," Miles said. He didn't want to get into an argument about it, but it had been evident that Hayden had undergone some private transformation in the months following their father's death. That was when they were thirteen, a year after they had started working on the atlas together, and Hayden grew moodier and moodier, angrier, more withdrawn. It had seemed to Miles that Hayden was more susceptible to certain kinds of mementos and reminders of the dead—all the insignificant objects everywhere in the house, now glowing with their father's absence, which Hayden had begun to accumulate. Here: a gum wrapper that their father had distractedly folded into an origami bird and left on his dresser among some loose change. Here: a pencil with his tooth marks, an unmatched sock, an appointment card from the dentist.

His voice on the answering machine, which they'd forgotten to change until one day Hayden called home and their father's voice answered after the phone rang and rang:

"Hello. You've reached the Cheshire residence . . ."

Which was plainly a recording; you could tell after only a second.

But for that second! For that second, a person's heart might leap up, a person might imagine that it had all been a bad dream, that some miracle had happened.

"Dad?" Hayden said, catching his breath.

He and Miles were at the skating rink in the rec center, calling for their mother to come and pick them up, and Miles stood beside Hayden as he spoke into the pay phone.

"Dad?" And Miles could see the brief light of supernatural hopefulness flicker across Hayden's face before it closed down, a light of surprised joy that shrank almost immediately as it dawned on him: he had been fooled. Their father was still dead, more dead than he had been before.

Miles could sense all this, all this passed through Miles's mind as if by telepathy, he experienced Hayden's emotions in the old way that he used to when they were little, when Miles would cry out in pain when Hayden's finger was slammed in a door, when Miles would laugh at a joke before Hayden even told it, when he knew the look on Hayden's face even when they weren't in the same room.

But things weren't like that anymore.

Hayden's expression pinched—he glared abruptly, as if Miles's empathy were a disgusting, groping touch. As if, having witnessed Hayden's display of naked eagerness, Miles ought now to be punished. "Shut up, moron," Hayden said, even though Miles had said nothing, and Hayden turned away, not even willing to look Miles in the eye.

Resolved: never to be happy again.

Was it naïve to think that before their father died they had all been pretty content? Miles had thought about this as he drove down the interstate, as he passed through Illinois, Iowa, Nebraska—Los Angeles still thousands of miles distant.

Things had been nice, Miles thought. *Hadn't they?*

When they were growing up, Cleveland was fairly idyllic, to Miles at least. This was where their parents had settled early in their marriage, on the east side of town, a comfortable old three-story house on a street lined with big silver maples. It was a pleasantly run-down middle-class neighborhood, a little to the north of the mansions on Fairmount Boulevard, a little to the south of the slums on the other side of Mayfield Road, and Miles remembered thinking that this wasn't such a bad position to be in. Growing up, he and Hayden had friends who were both appreciably poorer and appreciably richer than they, and their father told them that they should pay attention to the homes and families of their peers. "Learn what it is like in another life," he said. "Think hard about it, boys. People *choose* their lives; that's what I want you to remember. And what life will you choose for yourselves?"

It was clear that their father himself had thought frequently about this question. He was the proprietor of what he called a "talent agency," though in fact he was all of the employees. Sometimes he worked at children's birthday parties and the grand openings of shopping malls as Periwinkle Clown, making balloon animals and juggling and face-painting and leading sing-alongs and so forth. Sometimes he was the Amazing Cheshire, a magician. ("Amaze Your Clients and Guests with Magical Fun! Trade Shows! Corporate Events! Special Occasions!") Still other times he was known as Dr.

Larry Cheshire, certified hypnotist, smoking-cessation specialist, and motivational speaker; or Lawrence Cheshire, Ph.D., hypnotherapist.

Miles and Hayden had never in their lives seen him perform as any of these characters, though they would occasionally come across photos of him in his various guises laying around the house, even snippets of promotional material he was working on: "Periwinkle Clown and his puppet friends invite you to a magical hour of storytelling . . ." or "Cheshire Hypnotics Workshops will help you discover the powers of your own mind . . ."

Occasionally, they would hear him on the phone, sitting at the kitchen table with his large black appointment book, pausing to bite thoughtfully on his pencil. They found it hilarious that he would take on different voices depending on whom he was talking to. An earnest, boyish dopiness when he was Periwinkle; a sleek managerial smoothness when he was Dr. Larry Cheshire; a baritone stage-trained plumminess when he was speaking for the Amazing Cheshire; a somewhat affectless, calming monotone when he was Lawrence Cheshire, Ph.D.

They would hear such stuff, but it felt disconnected from the man they knew, who was so utterly unlike the various costumed folks in makeup and hats and toupees that he wore over the bald head they were used to at home. Miles didn't remember him doing anything that could have been identified as "theatrical," and in fact he was perhaps even unusually subdued and wistful in his everyday life. Miles supposed it was simply that when he came home from work, he was tired of performing for people.

But he was a good dad, nevertheless. Attentive in his restrained way.

They played cards together, Miles and Hayden and their father, board games, computer games. They went camping a few times, and on nature walks. When they were small, Miles and Hayden were particularly fond of the world of insects, which their father would help them find by turning over large rocks and logs. Identifying the creatures, reciting from his paperback Peterson guide.

He liked to read aloud. *Goodnight Moon* was the first book Miles recalled. *The Return of the King* was the last, finished only a week or so before their father's death.

Even though they were almost thirteen, they liked to sleep next to him when he took his afternoon naps. The three of them, Miles and Hayden and their father, lined up on the king-size bed in their stocking feet, Hayden on one side, Miles on the other, the dog nestled down at the foot of the bed, curled up with her muzzle resting on her tail. Their mother had photographs of them all sleeping this way. Sometimes she would just stand in the doorway, watching. She loved how peaceful they all were, she said. Her boys. She might've been a good mother, Miles thought, if their father had lived.

Their father had been fifty-three years old when he died. It was completely unexpected, of course, though as it turned out his blood pressure had been extremely high and he hadn't been taking care of his body very well. He had been a regular, if secretive, smoker, and he was overweight and hadn't bothered to watch what he ate. "Cholesterol through the roof," their mother had murmured to people at the funeral, and Miles could sense that she was making her way through thickets, mazes of regret and possible preventative measures that might have been taken, and alternate futures, now fruitless but still occupying her thoughts. "I told him I was concerned," she said to people, earnestly, urgently, as if she expected them to blame her. "I spoke to him about it."

In the weeks that followed, Miles spent a lot of time thinking about this. His death. Had they failed his father, had they been inattentive, could they have acted in a way that might have changed the course of events? He would close his eyes and try to imagine what a "massive heart attack" would feel like. Did you just go blank, he wondered, did your mind just empty out, like water spilled out of a cup?

He tried to picture what it might have been like, tried to picture his father standing in front of the audience when the first twinges came upon him. A pain in his left arm, maybe. A tightening in his chest. *Heartburn,* he probably thought. *Exhaustion.* Miles imagined him putting his hands against his toupee, pressing it down tightly with both palms.

Miles thought he knew the basic facts of what had happened. He remembered talking to Hayden about it on the night their father had died.

Their father had been out of town for a weekend event in Indianapolis and he'd died during one of his hypnotism shows.

It would have made a cute news item, Hayden said. One of those jokey, heavily ironic human interest pieces you might read about in *News of the Weird.*

The performance was taking place in a conference room in an office complex on the outskirts of the city; it was a "team-building" exercise for the people in the company, probably some bright idea that a manager in human resources had. *Neat!* they thought. Their father probably convinced them with a pitch about "helping people discover the power of their own mind," and he took volunteers from among the group, people who were bravely willing to be hypnotized, and he brought them up to the front of the room and had them sit down in folding chairs while their coworkers watched, and everyone waited expectantly as one by one their father put each of the volunteers into their own individual trances.

Everyone was delighted. What fun! The coworkers in the audience were tittering to see their colleagues actually hypnotized, deeply relaxed, deeply vulnerable, right there in chairs in front of everyone.

Their father was perspiring a little as he spoke. He pressed the palm of his hand against his forehead, then the back of his neck.

"Ladies and gentlemen," he said, and swallowed a dryness in his throat.

"Ladies and

"Ladies and gen   tlemen."

And then they were all hushed as he raised a finger—*one moment please,* the gesture meant—and then he sat down on a folding chair beside the hypnotized volunteers. The audience chuckled. The last guy in the row was a goofy curly-haired computer dude, slack-jawed, and they were particularly amused by him, he was in such a deep trance.

They waited to see what would happen. Their father put his hand on his chin and appeared to be thinking. He squeezed his eyes shut in a posture of solemn contemplation.

More chuckling.

Probably he died about then.

Sitting in a folding chair—his body balanced, equilibrated, and his audience was still waiting.

A few more chuckles, but mostly expectant silence. A held breath.

Their father's body slumped slightly. Then tilted. Then—at last—fell over, and the metal chair folded shut with a metallic clap onto the echoing tile floor.

A lady cried out in surprise, but still the audience continued to sit there, uncertain, uncertain. Was this part of the act? Was it part of the team-building?

And meanwhile the people who had been hypnotized were not hypnotized any longer. It was, after all, not possible to become stuck in a trance. That is just a myth.

The hypnotized volunteers had begun to stir, to open their eyes and peek out.

Wake up! Wake up! Miles and Hayden's father used to call out in the mornings when they were young. *Wake, my little sleepyheads,* he would whisper, and he would touch their ears lightly with the soft tips of his fingers.

———

In truth, this was not an event any of them—Miles or Hayden or their mother—had actually witnessed, but in Miles's mind's eye it was always as if he'd actually watched it. As if it had been filmed, one of those grainy, boxy educational movies the teachers would dust off on a rainy day at Roxboro Middle School. *Martin Luther King. The Reproductive System. Mummies in Egypt.*

Sometime later, Miles happened to mention this scene, this scene of their father's death, and his mother had studied him.

"Miles, what on earth are you talking about?" she said. She was sitting at the kitchen table, very still, though her cigarette was shaking between her fingers. "Is that what Hayden told you?" she said, and she regarded him worriedly. Her feelings about Hayden were beginning to solidify.

"Your father died in his hotel room, honey," she said. "A maid found him. He was staying at a Holiday Inn. And it was in Minneapolis, not Indianapolis, if you want to know, and he was attending the convention of the National Guild of Hypnotists. He wasn't performing."

She took a sip from her coffee, then lifted her head sharply as Hayden came into the kitchen in his boxer shorts and T-shirt, just waking up though it was two in the afternoon.

"Well, well," she said. "Speak of the devil."

Even then, Miles had begun to realize that many of his "memories" were simply stories that Hayden had told him—suggestions that had been planted, seeds around which his brain had begun to build "setting" and "detail" and "action." Even years later, Miles remembered his father's last moments most vividly in the version that Hayden had described.

Looking back, it was as if there had been two different lives that Miles was leading—one narrated by Hayden, the other the life he was living separately, the life of a more or less normal teenager. While Hayden was delving deeper into the world of the past lives that Mr. Breeze had opened up, while Hayden was becoming more and more isolated, Miles was working on the high school yearbook and playing lacrosse on the junior varsity team at Hawken School, where Marc Spady was director of admissions. While Hayden was going into therapy and staying up all hours of the night, Miles was placidly getting B's and C's in his classes and going out to practice for his driving test with Marc Spady, backing through orange cones in a parking lot while Spady stood a few yards from the car calling: "Careful, Miles! Careful!"

Meanwhile, Hayden's life was moving in a different direction. His nightmares had grown more and more pronounced—pirates and bloody Civil War battles and that burning shed where Bobby Berman had been playing with matches, where the flames sucked the oxygen from his lungs—and this meant that Hayden rarely slept. Their mother made up a new bedroom for him in the attic, and a special bed with cloth straps for his wrists and ankles just to keep him from sleepwalking, or from hurting himself in his sleep. There had been the night that he busted the kitchen windows with the ham of his palms, blood everywhere. There had been the time that their mother and Marc Spady woke to find him standing over them with a hammer, wavering there, mumbling to himself.

And so it was for his own safety, for all their safeties, it wasn't a punishment, but Miles had been surprised at how willingly Hayden had accepted this new arrangement. "Don't worry about me, Miles," Hayden had said, though Miles wasn't sure what, exactly, he was supposed to be worried about. Hayden got video games, cable TV in his new room, and in fact Miles used to be a little jealous of this. He remembered evenings when they would lie there in Hayden's attic room, in bed together, playing Super Mario on that old Nintendo system, side by side holding their game pads and staring at the miniature TV screen on Hayden's dresser. "Don't worry, Miles," Hayden said. "I'm taking care of everything."

"That's good," Miles said.

Hayden had already been through "a battery" of psychologists and therapists, as their mother said. Various prescriptions. Olanzapine, haloperidol. But it didn't matter, Hayden said.

"It's not like I can tell anyone the truth," Hayden said, and the MIDI music of Super Mario was burbling along. "You're the only one I can talk to, Miles," he said.

"Uh-huh," Miles said, mostly focused on the journey of his Mario across the screen. They were sitting there under the covers together, and Hayden slid over and stuck his ice-cold foot against Miles's leg. Hayden's hands and feet were always pale and freezing, bad circulation, and he was always sticking them under Miles's clothes.

"Cut it out!" Miles said, and in the game a mushroom monster killed him. "Oh, man! Look what you made me do!"

But Hayden just gazed at him. "Pay attention, Miles," he said, and Miles watched as the GAME OVER tablet came up onto the TV screen.

"What?" Miles said, and their eyes caught. That significant look, as if, Miles thought, as if he should *know.*

"I told them about Marc Spady," Hayden said, and let out a soft breath. "I told them who Spady *was,* and what he did to us."

"What are you talking about?" Miles said, and then Hayden looked up abruptly. Their mother was standing in the doorway. It was time for them to go to bed, and she had come to strap Hayden in.

Miles had arrived at last in California. This was the first time he had known Hayden's location in quite a while. More than four years had passed. Miles didn't even know what Hayden looked like, though since they were twins, he imagined that they still looked a lot alike, of course.

This was in late June, just after they had turned twenty-two, and their mother and Marc Spady were dead, and Miles had been roaming from job to job ever since he dropped out of college. He came to the end of I-70 in the middle of Utah, then followed I-15 south toward Las Vegas.

When he came at last to the edge of Los Angeles, it was morning.

There was a Super 8 motel near Chinatown, and he slept the whole day on the thin-mattressed bed in his room, curtains closed tightly against the California sunshine, listening to the hum of the miniature refrigerator. It was after dark when he woke, and he groped around on the nightstand and found his car keys and the alarm clock and, at last, the phone.

"Hello?" Hayden said. It was hard to believe that he was only a few miles away. Miles had traced the path he would take to get to the neighborhood where he lived—up past Elysian Park toward the Silver Lake Reservoir.

"Hello?" Hayden said. "Miles?" And Miles deliberated.

"Yes," he said. "It's me."

10

An invader arrives in your computer and begins to glean the little diatoms of your identity.

Your name, your address, and so on; the various websites you visit as you wander through the Internet, your user names and passwords, your birth date, your mother's maiden name, favorite color, the blogs and news sites you read, the items you shop for, the credit card numbers you enter into the databases—

Which isn't necessarily *you*, of course. You are still an individual human being with a soul and a history, friends and relatives and coworkers who care about you, who can vouch for you: they recognize your face and your voice and your personality, and you are aware of your life as a continuous thread, a dependable unfolding story of yourself that you are telling to yourself, you wake up and feel fairly happy—*happy* in that bland, daily way that doesn't even recognize itself as happiness, moving into the empty hours that probably won't be anything more than a series of rote actions: showering and pouring coffee into a cup and dressing and turning a key in the ignition and driving down streets that are so familiar you don't even recall making certain turns and stops—though, yes, you are still *present,* your mind must have consciously carried out the procedure of braking at the corner and rolling the steering wheel beneath your palms and making a left onto the highway even though there is no memory at all of these actions. Perhaps if you were hypnotized such mundane moments could be retrieved, they are written on some file and stored, unused and useless in some neurological clerk's back room. Does it matter? You are still you, after all, through all of these hours and days; you are still whole—

But imagine yourself in pieces.

Imagine all the people who have known you for only a year or a month or a single encounter, imagine those people in a room together trying to assemble a portrait of you, the way an archaeologist puts together the fragments of a ruined façade, or the bones of a caveman. Do you remember the fable of the seven blind men and the elephant?

It's not that easy, after all, to know what you're made up of.

Imagine the parts of yourself disassembled; imagine, for example, that nothing is left of you but a severed hand in an ice cooler. Perhaps there is one of your loved ones who could identify even this small piece. Here: the lines on your palm. The texture of your knuckles and wrinkled skin at the joints in the middle of your fingers. Calluses, scars. The shape of your nails.

Meanwhile, the invaders are busily carrying away small pieces of you, tidbits of information you hardly think about, any more than you think about the flakes of skin that are drifting off of you constantly, any more than you think of the millions of microscopic demodex mites that are crawling over you and feeding off your oil and skin cells.

You don't feel particularly vulnerable, with your firewall and constantly updating virus protection, and most of the predators are almost laughably clumsy. At work you receive an email that is so patently ridiculous that you forward it to a few of your friends. *Miss Emmanuela Kunta, Await Your Reply,* it says in the subject line, and there is something almost adorable about its awkwardness. "Dear One," says Miss Emmanuela Kunta,

Dear One,

I know that this mail will come to you as a surprise since we did not know each other, but I believed that is the will of God for us to know ourselves today and I thank him for making it possible for me to inform you of my great desire of going into long time relationship and financial transaction for our mutual benefits.

Emmanuela Kunta is my name, residing in Abidjan, while I'm 19 years of age, I'm also the only daughter of the late Mr. and Mrs. Godwin Kunta, with my younger brother Emmanuel Kunta who is also 19 years because we are twins.

My father was Gold Agents in Abidjan(Ivory Coast).Before his sudden,death on 20th February in a private hospital here in Abidjan, he called me on his bedside and told me about the sum of (USD $20.000,000,00)Twenty Million United state Dollars, he deposited in a security company here in Abidjan (Ivoiry Coast) for business investment that he used my name his beloved duaghter and only son as the next of kin in depositing the money, because our mother died 13 years ago in a fatal car accident. And that we should seek for a foreign partnerin in any country of our choice where we will transfer this money for investment purpose for our future life.

I humbly seek for your assistance,to help us transfer and secure this money in your country for investment,and to serve as guardian of the fund since we are still students, to make arrangement for us to come over to your country to further our education.Thanks as you made up

your mind to help orphans like us. I am offering you 20% of the total amount for your humble assistnace and 5% is mapped out to refund any expenses incure during the transaction.

Please, I urge you to make this transaction a confidetiallity within your heart for security purposes.and please reply through my private email.

Yours sincerely,
Miss Emmanuela Kunta

And it's pretty funny. Miss Emmanuela Kunta is probably some fat thirty-year-old white guy sitting in his mother's basement surrounded by grimy computer equipment, phishing for a sucker. "Who falls for this?" you would like to know, and your coworkers all have anecdotes about the scams they have heard of, and the conversation meanders along for a while—it is almost five o'clock—

But for some reason, driving home, you find yourself thinking of her. Miss Emmanuela Kunta in Abidjan, Côte d'Ivoire, the orphan daughter of a wealthy gold agent, and she walks along a market street, the crowds of people and beautiful displays of fruit, a large blue bowl stacked with papayas and a man in a pink shirt calls after her—and she turns and her brown eyes are heavy with sorrow. Await your reply.

Here in upstate New York, it is beginning to snow. You pull off the interstate and into the forecourt of a gas station and at the pump you insert your credit card and there is a pause (*One moment please*) while your card is authorized and then you are approved and you may begin to dispense fuel. A thick flurry of snowflakes blows across you as you insert the nozzle into your gas tank, and it is pleasant to think of the glittering lights of the hotels and the cars passing on the highway that runs along the edge of the Ébrié Lagoon, which Abidjan encircles, the palm trees against the indigo sky, etc. *Await your reply.*

———

And meanwhile in another state perhaps a new version of you has already begun to be assembled, someone is using your name and your numbers, a piece of yourself dispersed and dispersing—

And you wipe the snow out of your hair and get back into your car and drive off toward an accumulation of the usual daily stuff—there is dinner to be made and laundry to be done and helping the kids with their homework and watching television on the couch with the dog resting her muzzle in your lap and a phone call you owe to your sister in Wisconsin and getting ready for bed, brushing and flossing and a few different pills that help to regulate your blood pressure and thyroid and a facial scrub that you apply and all the rituals that are—you are increasingly aware—units of measurement by which you are parceling out your life.

PART TWO

—>—<—

Whatever his secret was, I have learnt one secret too, and namely: that the soul is but a manner of being—not a constant state—that any soul may be yours, if you find and follow its undulations. The hereafter may be the full ability of consciously living in any chosen soul, in any number of souls, all of them unconscious of their inter-changeable burden.

—VLADIMIR NABOKOV,
The Real Life of Sebastian Knight

11

Ryan had just gotten back from his trip to Milwaukee when the news came that he was deceased.

Drowned, that was what they were saying.

Friends said Schuyler, a scholarship student, was despondent over poor grades, and police now speculate that

Jay sat on the couch, chopping up a bud of dried marijuana, separating out the seeds, as Ryan read the obituary.

"It's interesting, you know?" Jay said. He was already stoned, in a musing mode as he crouched over the coffee table. He had an old-fashioned Ouija board that he used as a surface for cutting up his marijuana, and Ryan stared down at it—the alphabet laid out in the middle, and the sun and moon at the corners—as if there might be a message waiting for him.

"It's like one of those things that practically everybody fantasizes about, right? *What if you woke up one morning and people thought you were dead?* A classic scenario, right? What would you do if you could totally leave your old self behind? That's one of the great mysteries of adulthood. For most people. "

"Mm," Ryan said, and he lowered the printout that Jay had given him. The obituary. He folded it in half and then, uncertain what to do, slipped it into his pocket.

"It's not that easy to accomplish, you know," Jay was saying. "Actually, it's kind of hard to get yourself officially declared dead."

"Uh-huh," Ryan said, and Jay squinted up at him.

"Believe me, Son," Jay said. "I've looked into it, and it's not simple. Especially these days, with DNA tests and dental records and all that. It's a pretty complicated trick to pull off, truth be told—and here you are, you just slipped into it. Smooth as a feather."

"Huh," Ryan said, but he wasn't sure what to say. Jay sat there, leaned back in his sweats and fleece slip-on shoes, peering up at him expectantly.

It was a lot to take in.

He didn't quite see how they could make such a declaration without an actual body, but apparently, according to the newspaper account, a witness had come forward who claimed to have seen him on the rocks on the shore of the lake, just beyond the student center. The witness claimed they had seen him dive into the lake—a young male of his general description, standing on the big graffiti-covered boulders that lined the shore, and then abruptly jumping—

Which, Ryan thought, sounded highly unlikely, easily contradicted. But apparently the police had decided that this was what had happened, apparently they were eager to wrap things up and move on to more important cases.

And so now, he imagined, his parents were on their way to Evanston for the "memorial service," and he guessed that maybe a couple of his friends from high school might also come. Probably quite a few people from his dorm—Walcott, obviously, and some of the other people on his floor he had hung out with, possibly some acquaintances from freshman year he hadn't seen recently. Some teachers. Some of the various administrative people, deans or assistant deans or whatever, functionaries whose job it was to show up and look regretful.

Jay himself—"Uncle Jay"—would not be in attendance, needless to say.

"Honestly, I'm glad your mother doesn't know how to get ahold of me," Jay said. "She'd probably feel compelled to call me, at this point. After all these years, she'd finally want to make peace. She'd probably even ask me to come to the funeral. Jesus! Can you picture it? I haven't laid eyes on her since you were born, man. I can't even imagine the look on her face if I showed up after all these years. That's definitely not something she needs right now, with all she's dealing with."

"Right," Ryan said.

He himself was trying not to imagine the look on his mother's face.

He was trying not to picture the expressions of his parents as they arrived at last in Chicago and checked into their hotel room and dressed in their somber clothes for the memorial. He compressed that image and tamped it down deep in the back of his mind.

"Dude," Jay said. "Why don't you sit down, man? You're concerning me."

They were on the porch of Jay's cabin, and the cast-iron woodstove was sending out waves of sleepy heat, and Jay gazed up from the old porch couch, pushing his bangs back from his eyes. He gave Ryan a wary, compassionate look—the look you give people when you've told them a difficult or tragic fact—but it was not a gaze Ryan wanted to meet.

"You're upset," Jay said. "You're pretending not to be, but I can tell."

"Hm," Ryan said. And he reflected. *Upset?*

"Not exactly," Ryan said. "It's just—it's a lot to try to wrap your mind around."

"No doubt," said Jay, and when Ryan finally sat down beside him, he lowered his arm over Ryan's shoulder. His grip was surprisingly fierce, and he pulled Ryan close with a hug like a wrestler's grapple, pinning Ryan's arms. It was uncomfortable at first, but there was also a degree of comfort in the weight and strength of that arm. He would have been a good dad to have when you were a kid, Ryan thought, and he experimentally rested his head against Jay's shoulder. Just for a second. He was shuddering a little, and Jay squeezed harder.

"Undoubtedly it's going to take some time to sink in," Jay said gently. "This is a pretty huge thing, isn't it?"

"I guess so," Ryan said.

"I mean," Jay said, "look. You have to realize—at the psychological level, this is a loss. This is a death. And you may not think so, but you probably have to, like, process it in the way you would with a real death. Like those Kübler-Ross stages of grief. Denial, anger, bargaining, depression . . . You have to work through a lot of emotions."

"Yeah," Ryan said.

He wasn't entirely sure of what emotion he was currently experiencing. What stage. He watched as Jay fished a beer out of the Styrofoam cooler at their feet. He took the can when Jay handed it to him. He popped the tab, and Jay observed as he tilted the liquid into his mouth.

"But you're not freaking out or anything," Jay said, after they sat there for a while. "You're okay, right?"

"Yeah," Ryan said.

Ryan sat there staring at the old Ouija board on the coffee table. The letters of the alphabet spread out on it like on some old-fashioned keyboard. Smiling sun in the left corner. Frowning moon in the right. In the bottom corners were clouds, and he hadn't noticed this before but inside the clouds were faces. Featureless, indistinct, but, he guessed, slowly emerging from whatever beyond-place there was. Waiting, off to the side, for someone to call them forth.

"You know I'm here for you," Jay said. "I am your father after all. If you want to talk."

"I know," Ryan said.

They drank a few more beers, and then passed a bong back and forth between them, and after a while Ryan began to feel the concept slowly sinking in. He was dead. He had left his old self behind. He put his mouth against the chimney of the bong as Jay lit the bowl. The realization opened up in slow motion, like one of those time-lapse nature films where seedlings broke through the earth and unwound their spindly stems and unfolded their leaves and lolled their heads in slow circles as the sun crossed the sky.

Meanwhile, Jay went on talking in a placid, soothing, conversational voice. Jay was a man of many stories, and Ryan sat there, listening as Jay held forth.

Apparently, Jay himself had once tried to fake his own death.

This was back in the days when Jay was growing up in Iowa, before he met the girl who would eventually become pregnant with Ryan.

It was the summer after ninth grade, and he had spent a lot of time planning it out. They would find his clothes and shoes in the park along the bank of the river, and he would make sure that someone had heard him screaming for help. He would hide until dark, and then he would hike south, secretly, until he was far out of town, and then he would hitch rides at truck stops until he got to Florida, and then he would stow away on a boat that was going to South America, to some city on the coast near the rain forest or the Andes, where he'd work on the tourists as a confidence man.

"It actually sounds pretty stupid, now that I think back on it," Jay said. "But at the time it seemed like a pretty good plan."

Jay chuckled, his arm still loosely draped over Ryan's shoulder. Jay leaned his face affectionately against him, and he felt the hot, dark, vegetable smell of Jay's smoky breath pass across his neck.

"I don't know," Jay said. " I guess I was feeling a lot of despair at the time—I'd been having some hard times in school. I wasn't much of a student. Not like Stacey. I was just so bored all the time, and I felt like I was disappointing everyone, and I hated my life so much—

"My parents were always putting Stacey up on a pedestal. Like she was the model for how to live, you know. I'm not trying to dis-respect her achievements or anything, but you know, it was hard to take. My mom and dad would hold her up like she was this goddess. Stacey Kozelek! Stacey Kozelek got straight A's! She was so diligent! She had a *plan* for her life! And I was supposed to be, like, 'Oooooh: worship. So impressive.' "

He shrugged, reluctantly. "Not to talk down on your mom. It wasn't her fault, you know—she was a hard worker. Good for her, right? But as for me, that wasn't what I wanted. I never wanted to get to a point in my life where I knew what was going to happen next, and I felt like most people just couldn't wait until they found themselves settled down into a routine and they didn't have to think about the next day or the next year or the next decade, be-cause it was all planned out for them.

"I can't understand how people can settle for having just one life. I remember we were in English class and we were talking about that poem by—that one guy. David Frost. 'Two roads diverged in a yellow wood—' You know this poem, right? 'Two roads diverged in a yellow wood, and sorry I could not travel both and be one traveler, long I stood and looked down one as far as I could, to where it bent in the undergrowth—'

"I loved that poem. But I remember thinking to myself: *Why?* How come you can't travel both? That seemed really unfair to me."

He paused and took a drag of his cigarette, and Ryan, who had been listening dreamily, waited. Outside, it was snowing, and he could feel his heart making a soft shushing sound in his ears.

"I didn't get very far, though," Jay said. "The cops picked me up just after midnight, walking down the highway—after curfew, and my mom and dad were there waiting for me when I got home. Pissed as hell.

"But nobody thought I was dead. They didn't even find my clothes that I'd left on the riverbank. I went back the next day, and there they were, my shoes and shirt and pants, just lying there."

As he listened to Jay talk, Ryan leaned back against the old couch and closed his eyes.

It was a relief. It was actually a relief to be dead, a lot better than committing suicide, which was what he had been considering during those fall months before Jay called him. He had known, all that semester, that he was going to fail out of college. An academic suspension, they would call it, and probably around that time his parents would find out he had wasted the money from his student loans instead of paying the college bills he owed. All that autumn, he could feel the inevitable revelations looming closer and closer, only a few weeks or months in the future, the various humiliations and the sessions in the offices of various administrators, and at last his parents' surprise and disappointment as they learned how badly he had fucked up.

Late one night in his dorm room, he had typed "painless suicide" into a search engine on the Internet and discovered an assisted-suicide society that was recommending asphyxial suicide by inhalation of helium inside a plastic bag.

He was thinking particularly about how difficult it would be to have to face his mom. She had been so happy that he had gotten into a good college. He remembered the way she had obsessed over his college application process. Starting his freshman year in high school, she had kept a chart of his grades, his GPA, how could it be improved? What activities would be most impressive? How did his achievement test scores compare, and were there improvements that could be effected by taking a summer course in How to Take Achievement Tests? What teachers—potential recommenders—

liked him? How could he make them like him more? What would he write about for his college essay? What did a successful college essay look like?

He spent a lot of time dreading the look on her face when she finally found out that he'd screwed up again—her dour watchful silence as he moved back into his old room, as they talked about community college options, or getting a job for a year or so—

It was probably easier on her, in some ways, to be presiding over his funeral.

Easier on a lot of people. He found his obituary posted online, and when he did an Internet search on his name, he saw that a lot of friends had written tributes to him on their blogs, and there was a series of touching farewell messages on his Facebook page. "Rest in peace," people said, "I will not forget you," they said, "I'm sorry that such a terrible event happened to a cool guy like you."

Which, he had to admit, was probably better than the uncomfortable, embarrassed dissipation that would have happened after he'd been sent back home to Council Bluffs in disgrace, the emails and IMs dwindling as he and his friends had less and less in common, knowing that some of them were gossiping about him or flat-out dismissing him, that guy who *flunked out,* or probably after a while he would just not be on their minds at all, their lives would roll forward and after a year or so they would have difficulty calling up his name.

Better for all involved to have this kind of closure.

Better, he thought, to start over entirely.

He had been working on putting together some new identities. Matthew Blurton was one. Kasimir Czernewski was another.

"Clones," Jay called them. Or sometimes: "Avatars." It was like when you were playing a video game, said Jay, who spent a lot of his free time wandering through the endless virtual landscapes of World of Warcraft or Call of Duty or Oblivion. "That's basically what it's like," Jay had said, and he'd fixed his eyes on the large television screen, where he was advancing on an enemy with his sword raised. "It's basically the same idea," he said. "You create your character. You maneuver them through the world. You pay attention, watch what you are doing, and you are rewarded." And then his thumbs began to work rapidly on the buttons of his game controller, as he engaged in battle.

The concept made sense, Ryan thought, though he himself was not as big of a video game person as Jay.

To Ryan, the names were more like shells—that was how he conceptualized them—hollow skins that you stepped into and that began to solidify over time. At first, the identity was as thin as gossamer: a name, a social security number, a false address. But soon there was a photo ID, a driver's license, a work history, a credit history, credit cards, purchases, and so forth. They began to take on a life of their own, developed substance. A *presence* in the world—which, in fact, was probably already more significant than the minor ripples he had created in his twenty years as Ryan Schuyler.

In fact, Ryan had already developed an attachment to Kasimir Czernewski, who had been born in Ukraine, and Ryan parted his hair down the middle and wore a pair of black glasses when he had the driver's license photo taken. Jay showed him how easy it was to establish certain other elements: a fake address—an apartment in Wauwatosa, just outside of Milwaukee; and a job, working from home as a "private investigator" with a specialty in identity theft fraud; and a taxpayer ID; and a dummy website for this fake business; and sometimes people even sent emails to Kasimir's website.

Dear Mr. Czernewski,

I found your website and I seek help regarding the possibility of identity theft. I believe that a person or persons are using my name for the purpose of committing fraud. I have received bills for purchases that I have never made, and money is missing from several of my savings accounts, withdrawals that I never made—

As for Jay, he now had perhaps several hundred "avatars" that he had developed—practically a whole village worth of fake people, discreetly conducting various kinds of commerce from fake addresses in Fresno and Omaha; Lubbock, Texas; and Cape May, New Jersey. Basically all over the map, and layered in such a way, Jay said, interwoven so that even if one were discovered to be false, it would only lead to another counterfeit, another clone, a series of mazes that all led to dead ends.

Who would guess that these dozens of lives were emanating from a cabin in the woods north of Saginaw, Michigan?

It was snowing more heavily now, and Ryan was lucky to have arrived back at the cabin before the storm hit. The place was pretty isolated—a ways off the main highway, through a warren of county two-lane highways and up a narrow asphalt road, nothing but a tangle of trees and shadows until at last the cabin emerged, with Jay's old boxy Econoline van in the driveway.

The cabin was nondescript. A simple one-story, one-bedroom house with log siding and a screened-in porch in front with an old couch and a woodstove; it looked like one of those places weekend fishermen went to back in the 1970s, and it had the smell of damp cedar and mildewed blankets that Ryan associated with almost-forgotten Boy Scout camp buildings.

Out beyond the porch there was a clearing in the woods and the snowflakes fluttered carelessly, curiously, in little wind trails that led at last to accumulations. It hadn't been snowing in Milwaukee when he left, but it might be now. It might be snowing in Chicago, too, in Evanston where his parents would soon be arriving for his memorial service, a drowsy layer tucking itself over the tarmac of the O'Hare airport as their plane circled.

Jay had dozed off on the porch in the heat of the stove, and a cigarette was still pinched between his fingers, which Ryan reached over and gently removed, and a cylinder of cold ash broke off and fell onto the floor. "Mm," Jay said, and pressed his cheek against his own shoulder as if it were a pillow he was nuzzling.

Ryan got up and went into the living room, where a cirrus layer of smoke was still hovering over the clustered tables—dozens of computers and scanners and fax machines and other equipment—and he took a mohair blanket off of the couch and went back and draped it over Jay.

He was slightly drunk himself, slightly stoned, and he drew out another beer from the Styrofoam ice chest. He was trying not to get too anxious, but he was more and more aware that what had happened was truly permanent.

He sat down at one of the computers with his can of beer beside the keyboard and logged on to the Internet and typed his name to see if anyone else had written about his death on their blog or whatever.

But there was nothing new.

Soon, he thought, his name would call forth fewer and fewer results. The tributes would slow to a trickle in a matter of days, and before long any mention of him would be archived and pushed deeper under sedimentary layers of information and gossip and journal entries until he essentially disappeared altogether.

He was thinking about his father.

His father—his adoptive father, Owen—had been going through some mood swings during Ryan's senior year in high school, some gloomy middle-aged forty-five-year-old man thing, and while Ryan's mother obsessed about colleges and so forth, Owen had looked on wordlessly. He had gotten into the habit of the heavy sigh, and Ryan would say:

"What?"

And he would say. "Oh . . . nothing." Sigh.

One night they were standing at the kitchen sink, the two of them washing dishes, his mom in the living room watching her favorite comedy on TV and Owen had let out another one of his melancholic exhalations.

Ryan was drying the plates and putting them away in the cabinet and he said: "What?"

Owen shook his head. "Oh . . . nothing," he said, and then he paused to contemplate the casserole dish he was scrubbing. He shrugged.

"This is stupid," Owen said. "I was just thinking: how many more times in my life will we stand here together washing dishes?"

"Mm," said Ryan—since washing dishes was not something he would miss, actually—but he was aware that Owen was in the midst of some morbid calculation.

Owen shifted. Grimaced over a stubborn bit of noodle that he was trying to scrape off. "I guess," he said, "I don't think I'll see you very much after you go off to college. That's all.

"I can see how restless you are, buddy. And there's nothing wrong with that—I'm not saying there's anything wrong with that!" Owen said. "I wish I'd been so restless, back when I was your age. The way I'm going, I probably won't even manage to see an ocean before I die. But I'll bet you'll see them all. The seven seas—and all the continents—and I just want you to know that I think that's a great thing."

"Maybe," Ryan had said then, and he felt himself stiffening into an uncomfortable formality, embarrassed by Owen's self-depreciation, his maudlin middle-aged self-pity. "I don't know," Ryan said. "I'm sure there are more dishes to be washed together," he said lightly.

But, thinking back, he couldn't help but reflect on such moments—the kitchen in the house in Council Bluffs, the dishes in the sink, specific pieces of silverware he would have been drying that he recalled now with an unexplainable fondness, specific plates—

All the *stuff* he had left behind. The black Takamine acoustic-electric dreadnought guitar Owen and Stacey had bought for his birthday; the notebook full of tabs and lyrics for songs he was trying to write; even mix CDs he'd made, these incredible mixes that now he probably couldn't re-create. It was silly—a childish, morbid nostalgia—that an ache should open up when he thought about that guitar; or when he thought about his pet turtle, Veronica, not even a real pet. What did she care about him, what did she remember?

All these objects, which were themselves like avatars—holding his old self, his old life, inside them.

Okay, he thought. He sat there staring at the computer screen, the photograph and obituary in the Council Bluffs *Daily Nonpareil.* Okay.

The life he had been leading up until now was actually over.

He would never be seen or heard from again. Not as himself, at least.

12

Lucy and George Orson were walking down the dirt road that led to the basin where the lake used to be. Nebraska was still in a drought. It hadn't rained in who knew how long, and puffs of dust rose up from beneath the edges of their foot soles.

Yet another week had passed, and still there was no sign that they would be leaving, despite George Orson's assurances. Something had gone wrong, Lucy assumed. There was some problem with the money, though he wouldn't admit it. "Don't worry," he kept telling her. "Everything is perfectly fine, just a little slower than I thought, a little more—recalcitrant." But then he let out one of his gloomy laughs, which didn't reassure her at all. It sounded so unlike him.

For the past week or so, George Orson had not been himself. This by his own admission: "I'm sorry," he would tell her, when he spaced out, when he strayed off into a distant galaxy, in a trance of private calculations.

"George," she would say, "what are you thinking about? What are you thinking about right now?"

And his eyes would regain their focus. "Nothing," he'd say. "Nothing important. I'm just feeling out of sorts. I'm not myself lately, I guess—"

Which was just a figure of speech, she knew, but it stuck with her. *Not himself,* she thought, and in fact a certain slippage was noticeable— as if, she thought, he were an actor who had begun to lose track of his character's motivation, and even his accent seemed to have changed slightly, she thought. His vowels were looser—was she imagining this?—and his enunciation wasn't as crisp and elegant.

Surely it was natural that his voice would become more casual, as he was no longer a teacher, no longer performing in front of a class. And it was natural that a person would turn out to be a little different when you really got to know them. No one was exactly what you thought they would be.

But still, she had begun to pay closer attention to such things. Perhaps, she thought, it was her own fault that she didn't know what was going on. She had been in a dreamworld for too many days now, almost two weeks' worth of watching movies, reading, fantasizing about travel. So focused on the future places that they were going to go to that she hadn't been paying attention to what was happening in the present.

For example: that morning, she had come into the bathroom and George Orson was leaning over the sink, and when he glanced up she saw that he had shaved off his beard. Actually—briefly—she didn't even recognize him, it was as if there were an unfamiliar man standing there and she'd actually let out a gasp, she'd actually flinched.

And then she saw his eyes, his green eyes, and the face had reconstituted itself: George Orson.

"Oh my God, George," she said, and put her hand to her chest. "You startled me! I hardly recognized you."

"Hmm," George Orson said, moodily. He didn't smile, or even soften his expression. He just gazed down into the sink, where his hair had made a nest in the basin.

"Sorry," he said distractedly, and ran his fingers underneath his eyes, passing his palm slowly down his bare cheeks. "Sorry to startle you."

Lucy peered at him—this new face—uncertainly. Was he—had he been crying?

"George," she said, "is there a problem?"

He shook his head. "No, no," he said. "Just—decided it was time for a change, that's all."

"You seem," she said, "upset or something."

"No, no," he said. "It's just a mood. I'll get over it."

He continued to peer at himself in the mirror, and she continued to hesitate in the doorway of the bathroom, observing warily as he lifted a pair of scissors and cut off a piece of hair, just above his ear.

"You know," she said, "it's not a great idea to cut your own hair. I know that from experience."

"Hmm," he said. "You know what I've always told you. I don't believe in regrets." He lifted his chin, examining his profile in the way a woman might examine her makeup. He made a grimace at himself. Then he smiled brightly. Then he tried to look surprised.

" 'Regrets are idle,' " he said at last. " 'Yet history is one long regret. Everything might have turned out so differently.' "

He gave his reflection a small, wistful smile.

"It's a good quote, isn't it?" he said. "Charles Dudley Warner, a very quotable old buzzard. Friend of Mark Twain. Totally forgotten, these days."

He cut off another piece of hair, this time on the other side of his head, working the scissors in a slow, ruminant line.

"George," she said, "come over here and sit down. Let me do that."

He shrugged. Whatever mood he was in had begun to dissipate— the quote, she guessed, had cheered him up, being able to name a famous person and produce some tidbit of trivia. That made him happy.

"Okay," he said, at last. "Just a trim. A little bit off the sides."

And so now, a few hours later, they were walking silently, and George Orson had taken her hand as they wended their way down the tire track grooves that were still worn into the ground, though it was clear that it had been a long time since a car had come this way.

"Listen," he said, at last, after they had gone on wordlessly for a while. "I just wanted to thank you for being patient with me. Because I know you've been frustrated, and there have been things that I haven't been able to tell you about. As much as I would like to. There are just elements that I haven't quite figured out myself yet, completely."

She waited for him to continue, but he didn't. He just kept walking, and his fingers played along the surface of her palm reassuringly.

"*Elements?*" she said. She had forgotten her sunglasses, and he had remembered his, and she squinted, exasperated, at the dark reflective circles over his eyes. "I still don't know what you're talking about," she said.

"I know," he said. He tilted his head ruefully. "I know, it sounds like bullshit, and I'm truly sorry. I know that you're nervous, and I wouldn't blame you if you're thinking about just—packing up and leaving. I mean, I'm grateful that you haven't left already. And that's why I wanted to tell you that I honestly appreciate the fact that you trust me."

"Hmm," Lucy said. But she didn't respond. She had never been the type who accepted vague assurances. If, for example, her mother had made such a speech to her in that reasonable, gently hopeful voice, Lucy would have been goaded immediately into a fury. There was plenty for her to worry about—obviously! It was ridiculous that they had been here in this place for two weeks and he still hadn't explained what he was up to. She had a right to know! Where was the money coming from? Why was it "recalcitrant"? What was he trying to "figure out," exactly? If her mother had dragged her out to the end of the world without a word of explanation, they would have been arguing constantly.

But she didn't say anything.

George Orson wasn't her mother, nor did she want him to be. She didn't want him to see her in the way her mother had seen her. Bratty. Demanding. Mouthy. A know-it-all. Immature. Impatient. These were among the qualities her mother had accused her of over the years.

And it was her mother's words she would think of when he emerged at last from the study in the late afternoon. She spent her days watching boring old movies, reading books, playing solitaire, wandering around the house and so forth, but when he finally showed his face, she tried very hard not to seem irritable.

"I'm going to make you a wonderful dinner," George Orson said. "*Ceviche de Pescado.* You're going to love it."

And Lucy looked up from watching *My Fair Lady* for the second time, as if she had been completely absorbed. As if she hadn't been in a state of grim panic for the better part of the day. She let him bend down and press his lips to her forehead.

"You're my only one, Lucy," he whispered.

She wanted to believe it.

Even now, uncertain as she was, there was the grip of his fingers along the center of her palm and the occasional brush of his shoulder against her shoulder and the sheer solidity of his body. His focused presence. A simpleminded comfort, perhaps, but nevertheless it was enough to make her calmer.

There was still the possibility that he would take care of her. *Maybe it wasn't a mistake to come here with him.* An idea shooting up a flare into the stark gray expanse of sky. *Maybe they were still going to be rich together.*

She looked down the twin tire ruts that ran through the brush, shielding her eyes from the wind and dust, making a visor out of the flat of her hand.

"Here," George Orson said, and handed her his sunglasses, and she accepted.

It's always the girls who think they are so smart, her mother had told her once. *They're always the biggest fools, in the end.*

Which was one of the reasons she hadn't left yet. The sting of those words still lingered: *Girls who think they're so smart.* And the very idea of returning to Ohio, back to the shack with Patricia. No college, no nothing. How people would laugh at her ego. Her presumption.

It wasn't as if she were being held here against her will. Hadn't George Orson always said she could leave whenever she wanted? "Listen, Lucy," he'd told her—this in the midst of one of the many evasive conversations she'd had with him about their current situation. "Listen," he said, "I understand that you're nervous, and I just want you to know, if you ever feel as if you've lost your confidence in me, even if you ever decide that this just isn't working out, you can always go home. Always. I will regretfully but respectfully buy you a plane ticket and send you back to Ohio. Or wherever you want to go."

So.

So there were alternatives, and over the past days and weeks, she had been evaluating them.

She could almost picture herself getting on a plane; she could imagine herself walking down the aisle and lowering herself at last into a narrow seat next to a smudged window. But where was she going? Back to Pompey? Off to some city? Chicago or New York or

Off to some city where she would

Blank.

It used to be that she was full of ideas about what her future would be like. She was basically a practical person, a person who planned ahead. "Ambitious," her mother had called her, and it hadn't been a compliment.

She remembered one night, not long before her parents died, when their father had been teasing Patricia about her pet rats, joking about how the rats might be keeping her from getting a boyfriend, and their mother, who had been watchfully washing dishes in the background, had stepped in abruptly.

"Larry," Lucy's mother had said sternly, "you had better be nice to Patricia." She turned, and waved a sudsy spatula emphatically. "Because I'll tell you this much: Patricia is going to be the one who will take care of you in your old age. You keep smoking like you do and you'll be wheeling around an oxygen tank by the time you're fifty-five, and it's not going to be Lucy who will be taking you to the doctor and bringing you your groceries, I can tell you that. Once Lucy is out of high school, she's going to be gone, and then you're going to be sorry you teased Patricia so much."

"Geez," Lucy's father said, and Lucy, who was studying at the kitchen table, lifted her head.

"What does this have to do with me?" she said, though her mother was essentially right. There was no way she was going to hang around Pompey, caring for a sick parent. She would pay for a nursing home, she thought. But still—it was weird of her mother to compare her to Patricia in such a way, and she leveled an offended stare in her mother's direction. "I don't know what's so wrong with wanting to go to college and maybe do something different."

At the time, she was thinking that she might go into law, corporate law was where the money was, she had heard. Or investment banking and securities: Merrill Lynch, Goldman Sachs, Lehman Brothers, one of those types of places. She could picture their shining offices, all glass and glistening wood and blue light, the wall-length windows with a Manhattan skyline hanging in the air outside. She had even downloaded information from company websites about internships and so on, though looking back it was clear they didn't give internships to high school students in Ohio.

Her mother had been surprisingly hostile about the idea. "I don't know if I could stand to have a lawyer in the family," her mother had said blithely. "Let alone a banker."

"Don't be ridiculous," Lucy said.

And her mother had sighed humorously. "Oh, Lucy," she said, and adjusted her pink hospital scrub blouse, getting ready to go off to her shift. She was just an LPN, not even a registered nurse; she hadn't even been to a real four-year college. "That stuff is all about 'What's in it for me?' It's all about money, money, money. That's not a way to live."

Lucy was silent for a moment. Then she said, softly: "Mother, you don't know what you're talking about."

Now, as she and George Orson approached the old dock, she was thinking again about leaving, thinking again about the plane lifting off toward some blank space—like a cartoon plane flying off the page into nothingness.

Or, she could stay.

She needed to think over her choices prudently. She was aware that George Orson was engaged in activity that was illegal; she was aware that there was a lot he hadn't told her—a lot of secrets. But so what? It was that secretive quality that drew her to him in the first place, why deny it? And as long as the money itself was real, as long as that part of the situation could be worked out . . .

They'd come to a building at the end of the road. A single-frame storefront, above which a sign said: GENERAL STORE & GAS in old-time letters, and below that a series of offerings were promoted: BAIT . . . ICE . . . SANDWICHES . . . COLD DRINKS . . .

It looked like it had been closed since the days of the pony express. It was the kind of place where a stagecoach would stop in an old Western.

But that was the way things were out here, she'd come to realize. The dry wind, the hard weather, the dust. It turned everything into an antique.

George Orson stood with his head cocked, listening to the faintly creaking hinge of an old sign that advertised cigarettes. His face was expressionless, and so was the face of the storefront. The windows were broken and patched with pieces of cardboard, and there was some trash, a faded candy wrapper and a Styrofoam cup and leaves and such, dancing in a ring on the oil-stained asphalt. The pumps were just standing there, dumbly.

"Hello? Is anyone home?" George Orson called.

He waited, almost expectantly, as if someone might actually respond, some ghostly voice perhaps.

"*Zdravstvuite?*" he called. His old joke. "*Konichiwa?*"

He lifted the arm of a nozzle from its cradle on the side of a gas pump and tried it experimentally. He pulled the trigger that made the gas come out of the hose, but nothing happened, of course.

"This is what the end of civilization will look like," George Orson said. "Don't you think?"

When George Orson was a child, the lake—the reservoir—was the largest body of water in the region. Twenty miles long, four miles wide, 142 feet deep at the dam.

"You have to understand," George Orson told her. "People would come from all over—Omaha, Denver, they'd drive a hundred miles to get here. When I was a kid, it was amazing. That's what's hard to imagine now: it was full of life. I remember when you could look from the top of the dam, and you couldn't even see the end of it. Just huge, especially for a poor Nebraska kid who'd never seen an ocean. Now it looks like pictures you see from Iraq. A geologist friend of mine was talking about the Euphrates drying up and showed me pictures, and it looked exactly like this."

"Hmm," she said.

This was the stuff he liked to talk about. *A geologist friend of mine*—no doubt someone he had gone to school with at Yale, once upon a time. He knew all kinds of people, all kinds of stories and trivia, which occasionally he would trot out to impress her, and which, yes, she did find pretty compelling. She herself would love to know people who would grow up to be geologists and famous authors and politicians such as George Orson's classmates had done.

Lucy had applied to three colleges: Harvard, Princeton, and Yale.

Those were the only places she was interested in, *the most famous places,* she'd thought, *the most important*—

And she could picture herself on their campuses—standing underneath the statue of John Harvard outside University Hall—hurrying through the McCosh Courtyard at Princeton with her books under her arms—or walking along Hillhouse Avenue in New Haven, "The most beautiful street in America," according to the brochures, on her way to a reception at the president's house—

She would have come across as bashful when she first arrived, and though she wouldn't have had any nice clothes, it wouldn't matter. She would've dressed simply, in dark, modest outfits that might even be thought of as mysterious. In any case, it wouldn't have been too much time before people began to recognize her, as George Orson had, for her subtle wit, her sharp sense of the absurd, her incisive comments in class. Her roommate, she thought, would probably be an heiress of some sort, and when Lucy at last shyly revealed that she was an orphan, she might be invited to spend the holidays in the Hamptons or Cape Cod or some such place—

These were not fantasies she could tell to George Orson. He was very critical of his Ivy League education—despite the fact that he mentioned it frequently. He didn't think very highly of the people he'd encountered there. "That grotesque performance of privilege," he said. "All the princes and princesses, primping while they waited to take their rightful place at the front of the line. God, how I hated them!"

He would tell her these things after they became involved, back during the spring semester of her senior year, and she would lie in his bed with her face turned away from him trying to think of how she would probably have to break things off when she went off to Massachusetts or Connecticut or New Jersey. She would have to tell him when the acceptance letters finally came, it would be painful but it would probably be for the best, ultimately.

A few days later, the first rejection had arrived in the mail. She'd discovered it when she came home from school—Patricia was at work—and she sat there at the kitchen table and she could feel her mother's collection of Precious Moments figurines staring down at her. Round-headed porcelain children with large eyes and almost no nose or mouth: reading a book together, or sitting on a giant cupcake, or holding a puppy. All of them arranged on a plastic shelving unit her mother had bought at the drugstore. She smoothed the letter out in front of her: they wished they could be writing with a different decision, they said. They wished it were possible to admit her. They hoped she would accept their best wishes.

In retrospect, she didn't know why she had been so confident. True, she had earned A's in almost all her classes—her grade point average marred by only a couple of B+ semesters in French, the gentle but unforgiving Mme Fournier, who never approved of her accent or embouchure. She had dutifully joined clubs of various sorts—the National Honor Society, Masque and Gavel, Future Business Leaders of America, Model United Nations, and so on. She had scored in the ninety-fourth percentile on the SAT.

Which, she realized now, was not nearly good enough. George Orson was right: a person would have to think in a certain calculated way from early on, from grade school, or before grade school, or, more likely, you would probably need to be groomed for it from the start. By the time you were Lucy's age . . .

The other two rejection letters had come that next week.

She knew what they were even before she looked at them. She could hear the neighbor's dog's dull, aggrieved barking outside, and at last she opened one of the letters and she could guess the contents from the first word.

"After . . ."

She laid the palm of her hand across the page and closed her eyes.

She had been doing so well. Despite her parents' deaths, despite the terrible situation of her home life, the empty refrigerator, the bills she and Patricia could barely pay, the meager income Patricia earned from the Circle K Convenience Store and the remains of their parents' insurance and the two of them eating frozen dinners and canned soups and horrible convenience store hot dogs and nachos that Patricia brought home from work—despite the fact that she didn't have a cell phone or an iPod or even a computer like most normal kids her age—

Despite everything, she had been moving forward, you could even say she'd behaved with a certain degree of dignity and grace, you might even say she was heroic, going off to school every day and doing her homework at night and writing her papers and raising her hand in class and *she had never once cried, she had never complained about what was happening to her. Didn't that count for something?*

Apparently not. Her palm was still resting across the words on the letter, and she peered down at her hand as if it were a discarded glove in a snowbank.

She had been mistaken. She could feel the realization settling over her. The life she had been traveling toward—imagining herself into—the ideas and expectations that had been so solid only a few weeks ago—this life had been erased, and the numb feeling crept up from her hand to her arm to her shoulder and the sound of the barking next door seemed to solidify in the air.

Her future was like a city she had never visited. A city on the other side of the country, and she was driving down the road, with all her possessions packed up in the backseat of the car, and the route was clearly marked on her map, and then she stopped at a rest area and saw that the place she was headed to wasn't there any longer. The town she was driving to had vanished—perhaps had never been there—and if she stopped to ask the way, the gas station attendant would look at her blankly. He wouldn't even know what she was talking about.

"I'm sorry, miss," he'd say gently. "I think you must be mistaken. I never heard of that place."

A sense of sundering.

In one life, there was a city you were on your way to. In another, it was just a place you'd invented.

This was not a period of her life she liked to remember, but she found herself thinking of it nevertheless. This was one of the things George Orson did not understand, one of the things she could never have told him about herself. She couldn't imagine describing the conversation she'd had with a "counselor" at the admissions office at Harvard—the way she'd started crying—

"You don't understand," she said, and it wasn't just that a little sob or whimper had escaped her—it was as if her whole body were draining and becoming hollow, a thick needles-and-pins sensation ran down through her scalp and over her face, and her heart and lungs tightened. "I don't have anything," she said. "I'm an orphan," she said, and the sensation had gone from her lips and for some reason she thought maybe she could possibly go blind. Her fingers were shaking. "My mother and father are dead," she said, and a ragged, heavy space seemed to open up beneath her throat.

This was what real grief felt like—she had never truly felt it before. All the times she had been sad, all the times she had wept in her life, all the glooms and melancholies were merely moods, mere passing whims. Grief was a different thing altogether.

She let the phone slide down and she put her hand to her mouth as an awful and soundless breath came out of it.

And a few weeks later, when George Orson suggested that she leave town with him, it felt like the only reasonable thing to do.

———

They'd reached the edge of the boat ramp, a cement slope that led down into the basin of the former lake, and there was a battered sign that said:

NO SWIMMING OR WADING
WITHIN 20 FEET OF RAMPS OR DOCKS

"I've been meaning to show you this," George Orson said, gesturing out toward some point in the sandy expanse of flatland and scrubby weeds, where the water had once been.

"I don't see anything," Lucy said.

She'd been inside her own head for a while by that time, growing bleaker as their path descended, but of course George Orson couldn't read her thoughts. He didn't know that she was remembering the great humiliation of her life; he didn't know that she was thinking about leaving; he couldn't hear her wondering whether there was any money in the house.

Though naturally he could read her mood; she could see how he was trying to entertain her. Now it was his turn to try to cheer *her* up. "Just wait. You'll like this," he said, clasping her hand, his voice brightening as he guided her along.

Her own private history teacher.

"Down this way is where the town was," he said, and he gestured like a lecturer as they walked. "Lemoyne," he said. "That was what it was called. It was a small village, and when they decided to make the reservoir back in the 1930s, the state bought up all the land and the houses and relocated the people, and then they flooded it. It's not a unique phenomenon, actually. There are, I would guess, hundreds of them all across the United States. 'Drowned towns'— I think that's the term. As the technology for creating these irrigation and hydroelectric reservoirs advanced, the people just had to move aside—"

And he paused, checking to see if he still had her attention.

"Such is progress," he said.

She saw it now. The town. Or rather, what was left of it, which was not particularly townlike after all. The dust was blowing hard in the basin, and the structures ahead were blurred, as if in fog.

"Wow," she said. "This is weird."

"Nebraska's own Atlantis," George Orson said, and glanced at her, gauging her reaction. She could see him planning out what he was going to say, then reconsidering.

"There's a lot of energy here," George Orson said, and he gave her one of his intense, secretive smiles. He was teasing, but he was also serious in a way she didn't quite understand.

"Energy," she said.

His smile broadened—as if she knew exactly what he was getting at. "Energy of the supernatural variety. So they say. They list it in all of those hokey books—*America's Most Haunted, Mysterious Places of the Great Plains,* you know what I mean. Not to say that I discount it wholesale. But I guess if there is energy, it's probably mostly negative, I'd imagine. Not too far from here is where the Battle of Ash Hollow happened. This was back in 1855, and General William Harney led six hundred soldiers onto a Sioux encampment and massacred eighty-six people, many of them women and children. It was part of President Pierce's plan, you see, the westward expansion, the Oregon Trail, the growth of the U.S. Army—"

Lucy frowned. She had been hoping for more about their current situation, but it appeared that this was just another one of his distractions. More chitchat about the things that he found fascinating—cheesy-sounding new age philosophy mixed up with conspiratorial antigovernment historical analysis—though at one time she'd liked it when he would hold forth on such stuff, not least because then she could play the part of the skeptic.

"Oh, right," she said now, and let herself touch once again on their bantering voice, the way they used to talk to each other, the earnest teacher and the wryly challenging student.

"I suppose there are probably secret alien UFO landing bases right around here, too," she said.

"Ha, ha," he said.

And then he pointed, and she felt the back of her neck prickle.

Up ahead, there were perhaps a dozen buildings, rising up among the silt and sand and big tumbleweed-shaped bushes and scrub grass, though "buildings" wasn't exactly the right term.

Remains, she thought. Pieces of structures in various states of collapse and ruin—foundations and scattered slabs of cement—a fat hexagonal block, an oblong column, a triangular corner piece—all with tails of sand pulling behind them. There was a single rocky wall with the rectangle of a door in it. The detritus of an old outhouse or shed had heaved itself over into a pile of rotting boards, covered in silt and algae, and beyond it a crooked, rusted street sign was still posted. At the end of what she guessed had once been the street, there was a larger four-walled frame, some steps leading up the front of the stone block façade.

"Holy shit, George," she said.

Which had always been another part of their relationship. She was the cynic and he was the believer, but she could be persuaded. She could be brought to a state of wonder, if only he was convincing enough.

And he had succeeded this time.

"That was the church," George Orson said. They stood there together, side by side, and she thought that actually he was right about "negative energy," or whatever.

"Doesn't this seem like a good place to perform a ritual?" George Orson said.

And she was aware again of that feeling, that end-of-the-world stillness. She thought of what George Orson had told her back when they were driving through Indiana or Iowa and she was still vaguely talking about going to college: she'd apply again in a year or so, she'd said.

"I wouldn't bother if I were you," George Orson had said, and he'd looked over at her, his lopsided smile pulling up. "By the time you're forty, it's not going to matter whether you graduated from college or not. I doubt if Yale University will even exist."

And Lucy had given him a stern look. "Oh, right," she said. "And apes will rule the earth."

"Honestly," George Orson said. "I'm not so sure there will even be a United States by that point. At least not as we know it."

"George," she said, "I have no idea what you're talking about."

But now, standing in the dried-out basin of the lake, on the steps of the old church where the body of a carp had mummified among a clump of cobwebbed moss—now she could easily imagine the United States was already gone; the cities were burnt and the highways glutted with rusting cars that had never made it out of town.

"It's funny," George Orson was saying. "My mother used to tell us you could see the steeple underneath the water when it was clear—which was a myth, naturally, but my brother and I used to come out here on the pontoon and dive down, looking for it. We're probably about—what would you say?—pretty close to the middle of the lake, and you have to imagine that it was fairly deep at the time. Twelve or thirteen fathoms?"

He was in his own dreamy state, and she watched his finger as he lifted it and pointed upward. "Think about it!" he said. "About seventy or eighty feet above us, there would be the boat, and you could see the two of us dive into the water. You'd be like a shark down here watching the legs splashing and you'd see the surface of the water up there—"

Yes. She could see it. She could imagine being at the bottom of the lake—the membrane of the water hovering above them like the surface of a sky, and the rippled shadow of the pontoon boat, and the figures of the boys in the diffuse blue-green light, their silhouettes like birds skimming the air.

She shuddered, and the fantasy of water and childhood nostalgia drained away.

The pale dust was blowing in horizontal streams close to the ground, snaking in thin, rippling pathways that built tombolos off the scrub plants. All the color around her was washed out by the dust and glare, like a photograph with the brightness and contrast turned up too high.

There was nothing like that in her own childhood, no idyllic vacations at a beach, no pontoon boats or mysterious underwater towns. She could remember summer days at the Pompey swimming pool, or running through the sprinkler in the yard with Patricia, Patricia a plump little girl in a one-piece bathing suit, her mouth open to catch the spray of water.

Poor Patricia, she thought.

Poor Patricia, washing the dishes and doing the laundry and looking sorrowfully at Lucy as she sat there on the couch watching TV. As if she were too good to clean up after herself. Perhaps, Lucy thought, it was better for both of them that she was gone. Maybe Patricia was happier.

"So," Lucy said. "Where is your brother now? Do you ever call him, or talk to him or anything?"

George Orson blinked. He was coming back from some memory himself, she guessed, because at first he was taken aback. As if the question puzzled him. Then he straightened.

"He's—actually he's not around anymore," George Orson said at last. His forehead creased. "He drowned. Somewhere—I guess about five miles north of here. He was eighteen. It was the year he graduated from high school, and I was in college, I was still in New Haven, and apparently—" He paused, as if he were straightening a painting in a room in his mind.

"Apparently, he went out for a swim at night, and—that was it. What happened, it's impossible to know, because he was alone, but they never did figure out *why*. He was an excellent swimmer."

"You're not joking," she said.

"Of course not," he said, and gave her one of his gently reproachful looks. "Why would I joke about something like that?"

"Jesus, George," she said, and they fell mute, both of them looking up to the narrow slate-colored cirrus clouds that were laid across the sky. The former surface of the water, twelve fathoms above them.

She wasn't sure what to think. How long had they been together? Almost five months? All those hours and hours of conversations, all the talk of various kinds of history and movies and his years at Yale and his geologist friend and his magician friend and the crazy computer guys from Atlanta, all this flotsam and jetsam, and yet she couldn't have put together even a basic biography of his life.

"George," she said, "don't you think it's weird that you never told me that you had a brother who died?"

She was trying to maintain their usual bantering tone, but her voice hitched, and she had the awful feeling that she might be overcome by another crying fit such as she had on that day she called the admissions counselor on the phone. She paused; tightened her mouth. "I told you about *my* parents," she said.

"Yes, you did," George Orson said. "And you know, I've always appreciated that you've been so forthright." He shrugged mildly; he didn't want to argue, he didn't want her to be upset. His expression flickered, uncertainly, and she wondered if he had been caught in a truth—the same way some people were caught in a lie.

"Honestly?" he said. "I didn't think you needed to hear any more tragic death stories. With your own loss still weighing so heavily on you? You needed to get away from all that, Lucy. You told me about your parents—you did. But you didn't really want to talk about it."

"Hmm," she said—because perhaps he was right; maybe he did understand her, after all. Was it possible that she was as lost as he seemed to think she was?

"Besides which," he said, "my brother died a long time ago. I don't find myself thinking about it very often. Most of the time, only when I'm out here."

"I see," she said, and they sat down together on the crumbling steps of the old church. "I see," she said again, and here was that pitch in her voice again, that tremor. She thought of that one time when her father took her and Patricia fishing on Lake Erie, the boat with the sonar scanner that would help them find the big fish. She could imagine George Orson sounding his memory, locating the shadow of his brother, sliding through the dark water.

"But—don't you miss him?" she said.

"I don't know," George Orson said at last. "Of course I miss him, in a certain way. I was very upset when he died, naturally; it was a terrible tragedy. But—"

"But what?" Lucy said.

"But fourteen years is a long while," George Orson said. "I'm thirty-two years old, Lucy. You might not realize that yet, but you pass through a lot of different stages in that amount of time. I've been a lot of different people since then."

"A lot of different people," she said.

"Dozens."

"Oh, really?" she said. And she was aware of that wavering shadow passing over her once again, all the different people she herself had wanted to become, all the sadness and anxiety that she had been trying not to think about now shifting above her like an iceberg. Were they merely bantering again? Or were they in the midst of a serious conversation?

"So—" she said. "So—who are you right now?"

"I'm not sure exactly," George Orson said, and he looked at her for a long time, those green eyes moving in minnow darts, scoping her face. "But I think that's okay."

She let him run his palm over the back of her hand. Across her knuckles, her fingers, her nails, her fingertips. He touched her leg, the way he always did when he was particularly focused on her.

He did love her, she thought. For whatever reason, it felt like he was probably the only person left who truly knew her. The real her.

"Listen," George Orson said. "What if I told you that you could leave your old self behind? Right now. What if I told you we could bury George Orson and Lucy Lattimore, right here. Right in this little dead town."

He wasn't dangerous, she thought. He wouldn't hurt her. And yet his face, his eyes had such an odd, unnerving intensity. She wouldn't have been surprised if he was going to tell her that he had done something terrible. Murdered someone, maybe.

Would she still love him, would she still stay with him, if he had committed some awful crime?

"George," she said, and she could hear how hoarse and uncertain her voice sounded, down in this valley. "Are you trying to scare me?"

"Not at all," George Orson said, and he took her palms in his and held them firmly and drew his face close to hers, so that she could see how bright and avid and earnest his eyes were. "No, honey, I swear to God, I would never try to scare you. Never."

And then he smiled at her, hopefully.

"It's just that—oh, sweetheart, I don't think I can be George Orson for much longer. And if we're going to stay together, you can't be Lucy Lattimore much longer, either."

Across the weedy lake bed, the clouds were stacked above the opposite shore, dirty white fading upward into dark gray. A vapor of dust stirred up across the valley where there were once fathoms of water.

13

Miles was sitting in a bar in Inuvik when his phone rang.

He was hovering over his fourth beer, and at first he wasn't sure where the sound was coming from—just a tiny computerized twitter of birdsong that seemed to be emanating from an undisclosed location in the air around him. He glanced at the bartender, and then over his shoulder, and then at the floor below his bar stool, and then at last he discovered the chirping was actually the phone in his jacket pocket.

This was the phone he had purchased at the local wireless place— Ice Wireless, it was called—since he had realized his own phone couldn't get reception. One of the many things he hadn't taken into account when he left Cleveland. One of the many expenditures that had been added to his credit card over the years, in search of Hayden.

But here: this time it turned out to be worth it. The phone was actually ringing.

"Hello?" he said, and there was a blank sound. "Hello? Hello?" he said. He wasn't used to this phone yet, wasn't sure if he was operating it correctly.

Then there was a woman's voice. "I'm calling about the poster?" she said, and at first he was so flustered to encounter a voice at the other end of the phone that synapses in his brain stumbled over one another.

"The poster . . . ?" he said.

"Yes," the woman said. "There was a flyer—a missing person—and this was the number that it said to call. I think I have information about the person on the poster." She had an American accent, the first one he'd heard in a while, and he straightened, patting his pockets for a pen.

"I believe I know the person you're looking for," she said.

He was a terrible detective.

That was one of the things he had been thinking about on the drive to Inuvik. He had spent the entire decade of his twenties looking for Hayden—sleepwalking through various odd jobs and attempts at higher education—and all the while thinking that his "real" vocation was elsewhere. His real vocation was "detective," his real vocation was looking for Hayden, he'd thought, his every attempt at normalcy punctuated—punctured—by periods of intense Hayden-obsession: gathering and sifting through data, spending his money and charging up credit cards so that he could go on these long, fruitless trips.

Though in fact, the truth was, in all these years, he'd done little but accumulate endless notebooks full of unanswered questions:

Is Hayden schizophrenic? Does he have a mental illness, or is that an act?

Unknown.

Does Hayden really believe in his "past lives," and if so, how is that related to his study of "ley lines," "geodesy," and "spirit cities"? Or is this, too, a scam?

Unknown.

Was Hayden responsible for the house fire that killed our mother and Mr. Spady?

Unknown.

Why was Hayden in Los Angeles, and what was the nature of his "residual income stream consultant" business?

Unknown.

What was the nature of his graduate work in mathematics at the University of Missouri, Rolla? How did he get accepted into graduate school when he hadn't even completed an undergraduate degree?

Unknown.

What happened to the young woman he was dating in Missouri?

Unknown.

What, if any, is Hayden's relationship with H&R Block, Morgan Stanley, Lehman Brothers, Merrill Lynch, Citigroup, etc.?

Unknown.

Why did Hayden warn about Mrs. Matalov/Matalov Novelties?

Unknown.

Why is Hayden in Inuvik? Is Hayden in Inuvik?

Unknown.

He sat there at the bar, staring at his spiral reporter's notebook, into which he had printed these and other questions in neat block letters, *his* handwriting, which, ever since childhood, had been a pale imitation of Hayden's more elegant script.

He held the phone to his ear.

"Yes," he said. "You have information about the—the person—the poster?" He was aware that he sounded somewhat incredulous, and he wavered. The woman said nothing.

"We're—as the poster says, we're, ah—prepared to offer a reward," Miles said.

Reward. He supposed he could get another cash advance on his credit card.

He was still addled. Eighty-four hours, with a few sessions of sleeping in the car alongside the road—curled up in the backseat with his knuckles pressed against his mouth, a thin blanket tucked at his neck. Once, he'd awakened and he'd had the notion that he was seeing the aurora borealis in the sky, a wispy, winding smokelike shape, a glowing fluorescent-green, though this was also the color he imagined a UFO would give off as it hovered over you.

By the time he had finally arrived in Inuvik, he was in an out-of-body state. He'd taken a room in a downtown motel—the Eskimo Inn—thinking he would pass out the minute he lay down on the bed.

It was late, but the sun was still shining. The midnight sun, he thought—a dim, dull, yellowy light, as if the world were a basement room lit by a bare forty-watt bulb—and he drew the blackout curtains and sat down on the bed.

His ears were ringing, and his skin felt as if it were lightly shimmering. The buzz of his car's wheels on asphalt had worked its way inside his body, forward movement, forward movement, forward movement, and he wished that he'd had the presence of mind to buy some beer before he checked in—

Instead of sitting there, blinking stupidly, with the old atlas in his lap. A terrible detective, he thought. *Dominion of Canada,* the atlas said, the building block rectangles of Alberta, Saskatchewan, Manitoba, in colors of lilac and tangerine and bubblegum-pink, the Northwest Territories rising above them in mint-green. On this map, Nunavut did not yet exist. On this map, the teenage Hayden had printed a series of runes that ran up the length of the Tuktoyaktuk Peninsula and marched through the Beaufort Sea to Sachs Harbour.

Miles had the image of Hayden wrapped in an Eskimo coat with a fur-lined hood, traveling across the plain of a frozen sea on a dogsled, and behind him the sheet of ice was breaking into jagged jigsaw pieces. The pallid seabirds skated circles overhead, screeching: *Tekeli-li! Tekeli-li!*

It had already occurred to him that this was just another dead end—

Another Kulm, North Dakota—

Another Rolla, Missouri—

Another humiliation like the one at the JPMorgan Chase Tower in Houston—the security guard escorting Miles out of the Sky Lobby and depositing him onto the plaza. *Mister, you've been warned before,* the guard said—

All of those times when he'd been convinced he was on the verge of catching Hayden at last.

He had taken caffeine pills during the last part of his drive on the Dempster Highway, and now his heart didn't want to slow down. He could feel his pulse in the membranes of his eyeballs, in the soles of his feet, in the roots of his hair. And though he was so tired—unbelievably tired—though he stretched out on the thin motel room mattress and pressed his head onto the pillow, he didn't know whether he would be able to go to sleep.

He tried to meditate. He imagined he was back in his apartment in Cleveland, the sheer white curtains were moving in a morning breeze, and his face was pressed against the nice extra-heavy pillow he'd purchased for himself at Bed Bath & Beyond, and he was going to wake up and go to his job at Matalov Novelties, and he had given up on detective work forever.

He was twenty-nine years old when he moved back to Cleveland—this was after his last expedition, his trip to North Dakota—and he had decided that going home, returning to the city of his childhood, would give him a sense of stability and equilibrium. Months had gone by and he hadn't heard from Hayden, and he felt as if his mind were clearing. He was going to enter a new phase of his life.

Cleveland was not in great shape. At first glance, it appeared that Cleveland was in the midst of its final death throes: infrastructure collapsing, stores closed and boarded up, Euclid Avenue—the great central street—dismantled, the asphalt torn off and piled along the sidewalk, the left lane a muddy trench lined with orange construction barrels, the beautiful old buildings—May Company, Higbee's—hollowed out, belts of empty lots and haunted-looking warehouses.

This had been ongoing for as long as he could remember—for years and years the city had been sliding into ruin and despair, people always spoke with nostalgia about the former glory of the city's past, and he had never taken such talk particularly seriously.

But now it looked like a place that had been bombed and then abandoned. Driving downtown for the first time, he had an apocalyptic feeling, a last-man-on-earth feeling, even though other cars were driving a few blocks ahead, even though he saw a dark figure disappearing into the doorway of a ramshackle tavern. It was the feeling you got when you woke up and everyone you loved was dead. Everyone was dead, and yet the world was continuing on, austere and thoughtless, the sky stirred full with gulls and starlings. A blimp floated lethargically in the haze above the baseball field like an old balloon that had been discarded in a muddy lake.

But he needed to try to think more positively! Not everything had to be so morbid, as his mom always said.

He had rented an apartment on Euclid Heights Boulevard, not far from the University Circle area, not far, actually, from the street where he and Hayden had grown up.

But he wasn't going to think about that.

His apartment was in an old brownstone called the Hyde Arms. Third floor, one-bedroom suite, hardwood floors and refurbished kitchen, heat and water inclusive, cats welcome.

He thought about getting a cat, since he was settling down after all. A big, friendly black-and-white tuxedo cat, a mouser, he thought, a companion—and the idea pleased him, not least because Hayden had always had a horror of cats, various superstitions about their "powers."

He had found one of his old friends from high school in the phone book—John Russell—and he had been surprised and actually moved at how happy John Russell was to hear from him. They used to play clarinet together in the marching band and they used to hang out together all the time and John Russell said, "Why don't we go out for a drink? I'd love to catch up!"

Which was exactly what Miles had hoped for when he'd returned to Cleveland. A night out with an old buddy, renewed friendships, familiar places, easy but not unserious conversations. A couple of nights later, the two of them sat in Parnell's Pub, a nice corner bar near the art-house movie theater, and there was a real Irish bartender—"What can I get for you, gents?" he brogued in his pleasant accent—and two televisions mounted unobtrusively in the alcoves above the liquor bottles played a baseball game that people were periodically noticing, as meanwhile the jukebox was emitting rock music that seemed vaguely college-educated, the clientele both reserved and relaxed, not too boisterous, not too aloof.

This could be *my* bar, Miles thought—imagining a scenario in which he and his group of friends met regularly for drinks, and their lives had the fixed rhythms and amusing complications of a well-written ensemble television show. He'd be the funny, slightly neurotic one, the one who might get involved with a smart, edgy younger girl—possibly with tattoos and piercings—who stirs up his life in interesting and comical ways.

"It's fantastic to see you, Miles," John Russell said, as Miles was eking his way through this reverie. "Honestly. I can't believe it's been ten years! Good Lord! More than ten years!" And John Russell put his palms against his cheeks, comically miming surprise. Miles had forgotten about John Russell's odd, nerdy gestures, as if he had learned about emotions from the anime cartoons and video games he used to love.

"So what have you been doing with yourself?" John Russell said, and he raised his eyes as if he were prepared for Miles to reveal a remarkable story. "Homunculus!" as he used to say, back in their teenage years—by which he meant: "Incredible!"

"Miles," he said, "Where have you *been* all these years?"

"A good question," Miles said. "I wonder that myself sometimes."

He was indecisive. He didn't want to get into all of the stuff about Hayden—which would have, he supposed, come across as ridiculous and exaggerated in any case. What would he say? *I've basically been wasting the past decade of my life pursuing my insane twin brother. You remember Hayden, don't you?*

Even mentioning Hayden's name was probably bad luck.

"I don't know," he told John Russell. "I've been somewhat— nomadic, actually. Involved in a lot of different stuff. It took me about six years to finish college, you know. There were . . . some issues. . . ."

"I heard," John Russell said, and he made what Miles assumed was a commiserating expression. "My condolences about your parents."

"Well," Miles said. "Thank you." But what was there to say? How do you respond to expressions of sympathy, so long after the fact? "I'm better now." That was a good answer, he decided. "It was difficult, but—I've gotten myself together, it's been awhile and—and I guess I'm just thinking about settling down for a while. Looking for a job, you know, whatever."

"Most definitely," John Russell said, and nodded as if Miles had been articulate. What a relief! For as long as they'd been friends,

John Russell had always been a blithely, blissfully accepting kid—the perfect friend when you had a crazy brother and a troubled home life and limited social skills—and in personality he was essentially unchanged, though he'd aged radically in other ways: his hairline had receded, and the bare dome of his head now looked more oblong, and his chin had grown weaker, and he'd gotten heavy in the stomach and hips and bottom, so that he was shaped a little like a bowling pin. He was a tax attorney.

"I'm not necessarily looking for anything specific at this point," Miles was saying. He still felt vaguely embarrassed and—he couldn't help it—defensive. "Some job . . . and, I don't know, go back to school? I need to get more focused in my life, I guess. I've wasted a lot of time."

But John Russell only tilted his head sympathetically. "Who knows?" he said. "I actually sometimes wish I'd done more traveling and maybe a little *less* settling." And he patted his round belly wryly.

"I think probably most people waste their lives in one way or another," John Russell said. "You know—one time I tried to figure out how much time I'd spent in my life playing video games and watching TV. My rough estimate is, like, ninety-one thousand hours. Which is actually probably conservative, but that amounts to just over ten years. Which I have to say, I found a little scary—though, it hasn't stopped me from watching TV and playing video games, but—it's sad, I guess."

"Well," Miles said. "It seems like it would be hard to calculate something like that."

"I've actually put together a spreadsheet," John Russell said. "I'll show it to you sometime."

Miles nodded. "That would be cool," he said—and he couldn't help but think how the idea of John Russell's "spreadsheet" would have delighted Hayden.

"That kid is a bigger freak than we are, Miles," Hayden used to say.

And Miles would protest. "We're not freaks," Miles would say. "And he isn't, either."

"Oh, please," Hayden would say.

He remembered how amused Hayden had been by the fact that John Russell went by both his first and last name. "What a ridiculous affectation," Hayden had said. "But I actually kind of like it." And then Hayden had performed a small parody of John Russell's delicate hen-like way of walking. Which, despite himself, Miles had found hilarious, and even now it was hard not to think of John Russell as a humorous character.

But he was not going to think about Hayden.

"Anyway," he said.

He and John Russell had pints of beer, and both of them lifted their glasses to their lips and took a sip. They smiled at each other, and Miles was aware of how urgently he wanted them to be friends, to be normal friends, but instead there was an awkward silence that he didn't know how to fill. John Russell cleared his throat.

"In any case," John Russell said, "people take different paths. Like—for example—did you hear about Clayton Combe? You remember him, don't you?"

"Sure," Miles said, though he hadn't thought of Clayton Combe in years.

He was a boy at Hawken School that both he and John Russell had disliked: a bright, popular student, beloved by nearly everyone, athletic, good-looking, but also, they thought, a condescending ass. He had the most hideously self-satisfied grin Miles had ever seen on a human being.

"You won't believe this," John Russell said, confidentially. "Everybody thought he was going to do so well? As it turns out, he killed himself. He was an investment banker at ING, and there was an embezzlement scandal of some sort. He claimed he wasn't guilty, but he got convicted and he was supposed to get about fifteen years in prison but then he—"

John Russell raised his eyebrows significantly. "*Hung* himself."

"That's awful," Miles said.

And it was, though he didn't necessarily feel that badly about it. He remembered how Hayden had disliked Clayton Combe intensely—how he used to mimic Clayton's way of tilting his head back when he smiled, as if he were being applauded. Hayden would raise his hand and wave to an imaginary, appreciative crowd, like a beauty queen on a float, and Miles and John Russell used to find this parody uproarious.

And then, Miles couldn't help it, the detective part of him woke up and blinked.

Wasn't ING one of those companies, Miles thought, one of the many entities that Hayden bore some grudge against?

Hadn't he mentioned it in one of his emails? One of his various rants?

But he didn't have to let himself go in that direction.

"Poor Clayton," he heard himself murmur. "That's so . . . ," he said. "So strange."

But was it? Was it strange?

He reflected on this, in the week after that conversation with John Russell. Why did it always have to circle back to Hayden? Why couldn't he just sit there and have a pleasant conversation with an old friend? Why couldn't the story of Clayton Combe just be a bit of gossip? And he refused to research it. He was not going to look up news articles about Clayton Combe; he was not going to turn it into some paranoid fantasy.

But then, ultimately, he wrote it down in his notebook anyway:

Did Hayden destroy the life of Clayton Combe and drive him to suicide?

Unknown.

He was feeling very vulnerable at that point. Very vulnerable and unsettled and depressed, and he kept thinking about what John Russell had said. *Most people waste their lives in one way or another.*

I have to change directions, Miles thought. A person can use his life wisely, if he just thinks about it. If he just makes a plan, and sticks to it!

Yet, despite his best intentions, he'd find himself going through his files once again.

He'd find himself staring out the window of his apartment, looking out toward the northeast, out over the suburban treetops. A few blocks away was the street where his family used to live, and he could feel their old house sending out uninterpretable signals, telegraphing its absence, since of course it wasn't there any longer.

He thought about going over to look at the site.

What was left? he wondered. Was it just a grassy lot? Was there a new house where the old one once stood? Was there anything left that he would recognize?

The house had burned down during his sophomore year at Ohio University. Hayden had been missing for more than two years by then, and Miles had never been able to bring himself to come back. What reason was there? His father, his mother, even his stepfather, Mr. Spady, were all dead, nothing to return for except morbid curiosity, which he ultimately resisted. He didn't want to see the remains of the structure, burnt timbers and caved roof, charred pieces of furniture; he didn't want to imagine the windows lit with fire, the neighbors gathering on the lawn as the fire truck and ambulance arrived.

He didn't want to envisage the possibility of Hayden standing there, shadowed in the copse of lilacs at the edge of the yard, perhaps with his arsonist's tools still in a backpack on his shoulder.

There was no real evidence of this—nothing beyond a vivid snapshot in his imagination, a picture so sharp that sometimes he couldn't help but add the house to the tally of Hayden's crimes. The house, and his mother and Mr. Spady.

And now, he thought, there was poor Clayton Combe, hanging himself in a jail cell. He thought of Hayden's Clayton Combe impression: chin up, eyes rolled back, mouth stretched into a rictus of self-regard.

Down below his third-story window, he could see the roof of the building next door; a mummified newspaper, still rolled and rubber-banded but slowly decaying; and a smattering of leaves came running down the alleyway in a formation like birds or football players; and then a helicopter appeared, gliding heavily, passing close to the treetops, its thick propellers chopping the air up. On its way to the hospital, no doubt, though Miles watched it sternly. For years, Hayden had believed that helicopters were spying on him.

A few days later, Miles had found a job. Or rather (he sometimes thought) the job had found him.

He was downtown, had managed to put together a few interviews, low-level programming and IT support, an "associate" position at the public library, nothing spectacular, but who knew? He was settling down, he thought, he had to be persistent and optimistic— though optimism wasn't easy to come by walking down Prospect Avenue. So many empty storefronts with their long-faded SPACE AVAILABLE signs, so many soundless blocks. Probably, he thought again, it was a mistake to come back.

He was thinking this when he saw the old novelty shop, Matalov Novelties, just around the corner on 4th Street, nested among the ancient jewelry stores and pawnshops.

He was amazed it was still there. It was the last place he would have thought of surviving the economic spiral that had overcome most of these downtown establishments. Matalov Novelties hadn't crossed his mind in years—certainly not since his father had died, back when they were thirteen.

When they were children, their father used to take Miles and Hayden with him when he went to the novelty store. A treat—to go with their father to this peculiar run-down establishment. *The magic shop,* he called it

They had never been allowed to see their father perform—not as a clown, not as a magician, certainly not as a hypnotist. At home, he was reserved, untheatrical, which had made their visits to Matalov Novelties all the more impressive in their minds. Their father holding their hands: "Don't touch anything, boys. Just look with your eyes." Which was very difficult, since it was, after all, a magic store—rows and rows of shelves, floor to ceiling, a clutter of antiques and odd devices, wooden figurines like chess pieces in the shapes of gargoyles, Chinese finger traps, feather boas, top hats and capes, an elderly rhesus monkey in a silver cage—

—and then the old woman would emerge. Mrs. Matalov. Aged but not doddering, though her spine was curving into a question mark, a hump raising her bright silky blouse. Her hair was like dandelion fluff, dyed a peach color, and her lips were red with the waxy, glistening lipstick that old silent-movie actresses wore.

"Larry," she said, her voice accented. Russian. "So good to see you!" Their father made a small bow.

When Mrs. Matalov saw Miles and Hayden, she performed a brief dramaturgical double take, drawing a slow gasp through her teeth, her eyes widening.

"Oh, Larry!" she said. "Such lovely boys. They break my heart."

As Miles thought back to this, it felt more like a memory of a children's storybook than an event that had actually happened. Like a lie Hayden would make up. And so he was hardly surprised to find that Matalov Novelties appeared to be closed. A folding metal grate was pulled across the entranceway, and the narrow shop window was covered with paper.

But still—beyond the grate, through the frosted glass of the door, he could see that the place wasn't empty. He could make out shelves, and when he reached through the grate to tap on the glass, he thought he saw movement. He stood there, hesitantly, and soon, enough time had passed that he began to feel foolish he was still waiting.

Then, abruptly, the old woman jerked the door open and peered out at him through the bars.

"No retail!" she shrilled. "No Indians, no Browns, no Cleveland memorabilia. This is not a retail establishment." Her accent was muddy, even thicker than he remembered. He stood gaping as she waved a hand at him: *go, go.*

"Mrs. Matalov?" he said.

Needless to say, she had aged in the seventeen years since he had last seen her. Even when he was a child, she had been an old woman; now she was practically a skeleton. She had grown shorter, smaller. The curve of her spine was so pronounced that her vertebrae stood out in ridges along her stooped back, and her head was tilted toward the ground so that she had to peer up like a turtle to see him. Her hair was very thin, just a few sparse tufts, though still dyed the color of a peach. It was impossible that she was still alive, Miles thought. She must be well into her nineties.

"Mrs. Matalov?" he said again. He tried to speak loudly and clearly, and he put on what he hoped was a winning smile. "I don't know whether you would remember me. I'm Miles Cheshire? Larry Cheshire's son? I'm in Cleveland and . . ."

"One moment," she said crossly. "You're babbling, I can't hear what you're saying. One moment please."

It took more than a moment for her to unlock the metal grate and pull it back, but once it was open, she appeared to be willing to let him inside.

"I'm really sorry to bother you," Miles said, gazing around, the rows of shelves the same as he recalled, the junk-store smell of cigarettes and dust and sandalwood and wet cardboard. "I," he said sheepishly, "—don't mean to intrude. I haven't been in Cleveland in many years and I was just passing by. Nostalgia, I guess. My dad was an old customer of yours."

"Larry Cheshire, yes. I heard you already," Mrs. Matalov said sternly. "I remember. I myself am not a nostalgic person, but come in, come in. Tell me what I can do for you. You, too, are a magician? Like your father?"

"Oh," Miles said. "No, no." As his eyes adjusted to the dimness, he saw that the shop was not, after all, unchanged since his childhood.

It was more like an old garage or attic, and the shelves extended back where the dark aisles were clogged with a disorder of stacks of partially opened boxes. Clustered at the front of the shelves were a number of desks and tables, each one bearing a number of old personal computers of various antiquated generations; and monitors, and tangled birds' nests of electrical cords and connection wires. At one of the desks sat a dark-haired girl—perhaps twenty or twenty-one years old?—wearing black clothes and black lipstick and pointed silver earrings, like the teeth of some prehistoric carnivore. She glanced up at him, expressionless and emanating irony.

"No, no," Miles said. "Definitely not a magician. I never exactly pursued—" And he felt himself blushing, he didn't know why. "I'm not anything, really," he said, and watched as Mrs. Matalov stalked through the maze of desks—a wobbling but unexpectedly swift gait, like someone hurrying over thin ice.

"What a shame," Mrs. Matalov said. She sank into a wheeled office chair, where several ornamental pillows cushioned her back. She motioned for him to come and sit as well. "Your father, I liked him very much. Such a kind and gracious spirit."

"He was," Miles said. She was right: but how much time had passed since he'd remembered his father? An old bit of grief awakened and turned over in his chest.

"Poor man!" she said. "He was a very talented performer; you knew that. If he had lived in a different time, he might have made a lot of money, instead of playing at children's parties." She clucked her tongue at this, a series of soft exclamation points, and Miles felt as if she were going to reproach him, a young man who was squandering his life. But she merely eyed him shrewdly.

"And what of your brother?" she said. "He is not a magician, either, I take it?"

"No," Miles said. "He—"

But what was Hayden? A magician of sorts, perhaps.

"I remember the two of you," Mrs. Matalov said. "Twins. Very pretty. You were the timid one, I think," she said. "Miles. A little mouse name. But your brother—" And here she raised a finger and wagged it, unspecifically. "He was a very naughty one. A thief! I saw him stealing from me, many times, and I would have caught him by his neck! But." She shrugged. "I did not want to embarrass your father."

Miles nodded uncomfortably, glancing over to the dark-haired young woman who was watching him with a look of almost imperceptible amusement.

"Yes," Miles said. "He could be—mischievous."

"Hmm," Mrs. Matalov said. "Mischievous? No. Worse than that, I think." And she regarded Miles for what felt like a long time. "I pitied you," she said. "So shy, and with a brother such as that!"

Miles said nothing. He hadn't expected to find himself in this situation—in this gray fluorescent-lit windowless place, the old woman and the dark-haired girl both observing him closely. He had not expected to find his father—or himself—so closely remembered. What should he say?

Mrs. Matalov took a cigarette from a pocket of her thin cardigan, and Miles watched as she toyed with, but did not light, it. "I had a sister," Mrs. Matalov said. "Not a twin, but very close in age. A terrible show-off. If she had not died, I would never have escaped her shadow." She shrugged, raising her thin eyebrows mildly. "So—I was lucky."

She rummaged again in the pocket of her cardigan, and drew out a clear plastic lighter, which she, trembling, tried to operate. Miles gestured uncertainly. Should he help her?

But before he could decide, the dark-haired girl spoke suddenly. "Grandma!" she said sharply. "Don't smoke!" And Miles sat back.

"Ah," Mrs. Matalov said. She looked at Miles darkly. "This one," she said—referring to the girl, he guessed. "Another naughty one. She doesn't approve of smoking—but drugs! Drugs she likes. She likes them so much that the police come and put an electronic monitor upon her ankle. An electric bracelet. What do you think of that? And now, poor thing, she is my prisoner. I keep her trapped here, and she should be less nosy or I will put a cloth over her cage like a parrot."

Miles was speechless. Too many things, too many odd revelations were revolving in his head, though he did exchange glances with the girl, her curtain of black hair and complicated eyes communicating a series of impenetrable messages.

Mrs. Matalov, meanwhile, had managed to strike the flint of her lighter, and she put her cigarette to her mouth, impressing a tattoo of lipstick onto the filter.

"So—" she said, appraising him. "Miles Cheshire. What brings you here to Cleveland? What is it that you do, if you are not a magician?"

Miles mulled over this question. What was he? He regarded the wall, tiled with framed black-and-white photos, various costumed performers from the thirties and forties, wearing tuxedos and capes, turbans and goatees, expressions of theatrical intensity. There was Mrs. Matalov herself—Mrs. Matalov, age perhaps twenty, not unlike her granddaughter in her dark-eyed beauty, wearing spangled circus-performer's tights and a headdress made of peacock feathers. A magician's assistant, performing at the fabulous Hippodrome Theater, capacity of thirty-five hundred, a beautiful stage, now nothing but a parking lot on East 9th.

And here was a photograph of his father as well. His father, tall and magisterial in a cape, a thin mustache of greasepaint sketched beneath his nose, a wand held aloft in his right hand, bouquets of roses and lilies at his feet. His eyes kind and sad—as if he knew that, years and years later, Miles would look at this picture and miss him once again.

"Do you know about computers?" Mrs. Matalov was saying. "We have very large Web presence. We rarely do business anymore outside of the Internet. I don't open my doors anymore, to tell you the truth. Twenty years now, and I can count on my hands the number of paying customers who have walked into my store off the street. It is nothing out there now but homeless and shoplifters and tourists with their horrible children.

"I have always hated children," Mrs. Matalov said, and her grand-daughter, Aviva, raised her eyebrow and stared at Miles.

"That's true," Aviva said.

And Miles said: "I do know about computers. Actually. I mean, I'm kind of looking for a job."

Later, he found it difficult to explain that this encounter seemed extraordinary without sounding as if he were trying to be melodramatic, without acting as if he believed that something—what?—*supernatural?*—had happened.

"It freaked me out, kind of," he told John Russell later. They were sitting once again in Parnell's, and Miles was thinking of some of the things that Mrs. Matalov had said to him.

I pitied you, Mrs. Matalov had said. And: *If she had not died, I would never have escaped her shadow.* And: *He was a very naughty one! A thief!* And: *He will come to a bad end, your brother. I can assure you of that.*

"I think it's great," John Russell said. "So you're carrying on the family tradition. That's very cool, in a way."

"Yes," Miles said. "I guess so."

And now, sitting in another bar, four thousand miles from Parnell's Pub, these were the things that skated across the surface of his consciousness. These were the images that came to him as he sat at the bar in Inuvik with the cell phone pressed to his ear: The burning house. The helicopter. The knotted sheets around Clayton Combe's neck. John Russell lifting his glass of beer, Mrs. Matalov putting her cigarette to her waxy red lips.

Each image distinct and capsulized, like tarot cards laid down one by one.

"Certainly," he said to the American woman. "Yes, absolutely. I'd like to meet with you. I'd like to speak about this matter in more detail. Could we possibly . . ."

He had spent a good part of the day wandering around Inuvik. It was daylight, still daylight, when he woke up, and when he went outside, the sky was dark blue, fading into white at the lip of the skyline. The clouds were stacked up against the horizon like mountains. Or maybe they were mountains that look like clouds, he wasn't sure. Some concrete slabs had been laid down into a sidewalk that ran between the road and the parking lots of the multiple boxy buildings—all of which had the cheap, hastily constructed look of a strip mall, corrugated siding, satellite dishes bending their heavy heads over the roofs. He had his sheaf of posters, and he paused to staple one to a bare telephone pole, and the paper rippled uncertainly, impermanently, in the wind.

He would blanket the city, Miles thought. He stood there leafing through the glossy *Inuvik Attraction and Service Guide,* which had been available for free at the hotel desk. Where would Hayden have been spotted? Boreal Bookstore? The famed Igloo Church, Our Lady of Victory? The extension campus of Aurora College? He had looked over their list of courses, and he felt a light spark of suspicion. Microsoft Excel: Level 1, with George Doolittle; Foot Reflexology Certification, with Allain St. Cyr; Advanced Wilderness First Aid, with Phoebe Punch. Did those sound like invented names?

Or what about the Inuvik liquor store? The bars—Mad Trapper Pub, perhaps, or Nanook Lounge? Perhaps Hayden would have rented a car at Arctic Chalet, or spent some time in the library, perhaps he'd hired a guide of some kind and headed out toward— what?

God! This was what always happened to him. He would begin in a state of urgent determination, but by the time he reached his destination, his confidence would dissipate.

What did he even know about Hayden anymore? After ten years, Hayden was hardly more than conjecture—a collection of postulations and projections, letters and emails full of paranoia and innuendo, phone calls in the middle of the night in which Hayden ranted about his current fixations. There were a few possessions Hayden had left behind in various apartments across the country, a few strangers who had seen or known some version of Hayden.

In Los Angeles, for example, Miles had found the abandoned apartment of Hayden Nash, whom neighbors described as dark-haired, "possibly Hispanic," a "reclusive guy" that apparently no one ever spoke with, and whose filthy apartment was cluttered with stacks of tabloid newspapers and indecipherable dot matrix printouts, and two dozen computers, all of the hard drives degaussed and irrecoverable. In Rolla, Missouri, professors described Miles Spady as a very bright young mathematician, a thin blond-haired Englishman who claimed to have done his undergraduate work at the Computer Laboratory of the University of Cambridge. There were some fellow students, acquaintances, to whom Hayden had told assorted lies and so forth, which Miles had recorded diligently:

His father was a well-known stage magician back in England, one of these acquaintances told Miles.

His father was an archaeologist who had been studying some Native American ruins in North Dakota, said another.

His parents had been killed in a house fire when he was a small child, said a third.

He was very eccentric, they told Miles. But it was fun to listen to him.

"He had this theory about ley lines. Geodesy, you know? We used to go out to the Stonehenge model on the north campus, and he would take out this old map of the world that he had drawn all over. . . ."

"I think he might have been crazy. He was a good mathematician, but . . ."

"He told me this peculiar story about being hypnotized, and he suddenly remembered all his past lives, a ridiculous story about pirates, or ancient kings or some sort of fantasy world. . . ."

"He said he had a nervous breakdown when he was a teenager, and his mother made him stay in the attic, and she used to tie him to the bed when he went to sleep and he'd lie awake all night thinking that there was a fire downstairs, thinking he smelled smoke. It was hard not to feel sorry for him, he was such a sweet-tempered person. You didn't know what to think when he would tell you these horrible things about his past. . . ."

"He had a twin brother who died in an ice-skating accident when they were twelve. And I gathered that he still blamed himself. I felt bad for the guy, actually. . . . There was a lot of . . . you know . . . deepness . . . under the surface. . . ."

There had also apparently been a girlfriend, an undergraduate student named Rachel, but she had refused to speak to Miles, she wouldn't even open the door when he stood on the porch of her ramshackle student house, she merely peered out at him through the door-chain crack, a single blue eye and sliver of face.

"Please," she said. "Go away. I don't want to have to call the police."

"I'm sorry," Miles said. "I'm just trying to find out some information about. Um. Miles Spady. I was told that you might be able to help me."

"I know who you are," she said. Her eye, framed and disembodied in the slice of door frame, blinked rapidly. "I *will* call the police."

He didn't have the nerve—the aggressiveness, the imposing persuasiveness—of a true detective. He had left as she'd instructed, and walked for a ways, and he could feel his determination lifting up off him, trailing away in the late October drizzle.

There actually was a scale model of Stonehenge on the campus. A half-size replica, the granite stones carved in the university's high-pressure water-jet lab. He stood there looking at it, the four pi-shaped archways facing away from one another, north, south, east, west.

Oh, what was the point, he thought, what was the point in hounding the poor girl? Why was he even doing this? He should just get on with his own life!

It wasn't until a few weeks later, long after he'd left Rolla, that it occurred to him: *Maybe Hayden had been there.*

What if Hayden was there, in Rachel Barrie's house, when Miles came that day? Was that why she wouldn't let him in? Was that why she wouldn't open the door more than a crack? He could picture Hayden, the shape of him, somewhere beyond the foyer, Hayden listening, probably no more than a few feet away from where Miles was standing on the porch.

Too late, he felt the realization settle into him. A shudder. A sickness.

"Hello?" said the voice at the end of the phone. "Hello? Are you still there?"

And Miles straightened. Back in the bar. Back in Inuvik. His memories had been pulling past him in a train of hieroglyphs, and it took him a breath or two to settle back into his physical body.

"Yes," he said. "Yes, absolutely."

He was trying to recover the detective part of himself.

"I . . . ," he said. "We . . . ," he said. "I'm very eager to speak with you. Can we set up a time to talk in person?"

"How about now?" the woman said. "Tell me where to meet you."

14

The message arrived on his computer his first night in Las Vegas, and once again Ryan couldn't help but feel a bit antsy.

This was the third or fourth time a stranger had contacted him out of the blue, writing to him in Russian or some other Eastern European language. In this case, it was someone named "новый друг" and Ryan's Instant Messenger window made its knock-knock sound.

новый друг: добро пожаповать в лас-вегасе

—and Ryan immediately closed the window and shut down the computer and sat there as a creeping feeling dappled its way up his arms and down his back. Why did he let this stuff get to him?

"Shit," he said, and folded his hands over the glass-topped hotel room desk, staring at the blank black screen of his laptop.

He had been doing so well. He had learned the ins and outs of Jay's schemes fairly quickly, had taken to it, Jay said, "like a duck to quack," and it was hardly any time at all before he was juggling nearly a hundred different personas.

"I can tell that you're my son," Jay said. "You've got the talent."

And he had been having fun, for the most part. He loved traveling—driving, flying, riding the Amtrak train—a different city every week, a new name, a new personality that he could try out, a new *role,* as if each new trip were a movie he was starring in. Floating through, that was what he thought sometimes. Floating. There was a great relief of freedom, swashbuckling, becoming a smooth con man criminal thief, the idea of adventure and rule-breaking and shifty, vaguely alluring danger.

And yet, there were times when his calm began to abandon him, brief moments—an unexplained IM, a suspicious clerk at the DMV, a credit card charge abruptly denied—and suddenly he'd feel that old panic crackling across the back of his neck, a shadow had been trailing after him all along, and suddenly he knew that if he turned to look over his shoulder, there it would be.

At times such as this, he wondered if he had the nerve for this lifestyle after all.

Maybe he was just being paranoid.

He had reported this anomaly before, these unexplained messages in Cyrillic letters, and Jay hadn't been concerned at all.

"Oh, don't be such a pussy," Jay told him.

"Doesn't it seem—suspicious?" he'd asked Jay, but Jay wasn't concerned.

"It's just spam," Jay had told him. "Just block it and change your user name, man. There's all kinds of random crap out there."

Jay explained that he had been using Internet servers in Omsk and Nizhniy Novgorod to scramble their IP addresses, and so, he said, it wasn't a surprise that they got occasional Russian junk mail. "It's probably about cheap prescription drugs, or penis enlargement, or hot teenage lesbians."

"Right," Ryan said. "Ha."

"Don't be so uptight, Son," Jay said. And Jay was basically a very cautious person, Ryan thought. If Jay wasn't worried, then why should he be?

Still, he didn't turn the computer back on.

He stood there, holding his cell phone, waiting for Jay to answer, staring from the window on the thirty-third floor of the Mandalay Bay hotel.

Here was Las Vegas spreading out before him: the pyramid of the Luxor, the castle turrets of the Excalibur, the blue glow of the MGM Grand. The Mandalay Bay itself was a big shining gold brick on the edge of the strip. From the outside, at least, the windows were shimmering golden reflective glass, so that no one could see him standing there, peering out. It was a cityscape that looked as if it had been invented, architectural shapes that might appear as the cover illustration for one of those fantasy novels he used to read back in high school, or digital imagery from a big budget SF movie. It would be easy to believe he'd landed on a different planet, or traveled into the future, and he put a hand to the glass, letting these pleasant, calming whimsies settle over him.

The outward wall of his hotel room was a single window, and with the drapes pulled open he could stand there at the very lip of the building like a swimmer on a diving board.

"Hello?" Jay said, and Ryan paused.

"Hey," Ryan said.

"Hey," Jay said. And then there was an expectant pause. Ryan wasn't supposed to call unless it was urgent, but it seemed like Jay was too mellow—probably too stoned—to take Ryan's concerns seriously. Sometimes it was strange to think that Jay was actually his father, strange to think that Jay was only fifteen when he was born, and even now he didn't look like he could be old enough to have a twenty-year-old son. He didn't look much older than thirty. It made more sense, Ryan often thought, to think of him as an uncle.

"So . . . ," Jay said. "What's up?"

"I was just calling to check in," Ryan said. He shifted the phone to his other ear. "Listen," he said, "did you just IM me?"

"Um," Jay said. "I don't think so."

"Oh," Ryan said.

He could hear the gurgling sound of a bong as Jay drew in smoke, and then the arrhythmic clicking percussion of Jay's keyboard as he typed.

"So what do you think of Las Vegas?" Jay said after a pause.

"Good," Ryan said. "Good, so far."

"It's pretty magnificent, isn't it?" said Jay.

"It is," Ryan said, and he looked down into the dusky expanse of the city. Below him a line of taxis was slowly nudging its bovine way up toward the front entrance, the pylon sign that flanked the building with its giant LED screen playing images of singers and comedians flickering above the necklace of headlights along Las Vegas Boulevard—

"It's—" he said.

—and in the other direction, if you faced away from the strip, there was the airport just beyond an old boarded-up courtyard motel across the street; there was a tract of bare desert earth and some strip malls and houses that ran in sheer planes toward the mountains.

"It's great," he said.

"Can you see the Statue of Liberty?" Jay said. "Can you see the Stratosphere tower?"

"Yeah," Ryan said. He was aware of his reflection standing just beyond the edge of the window, hovering in the air.

"I love Vegas," Jay said, and then he paused, reflectively. Perhaps he was thinking of the instructions he and Ryan had gone over together, perhaps wondering if he needed to repeat them—but he just cleared his throat.

"The main thing," Jay said. "I want you to have a good time. Get laid a couple of times, okay?"

"Okay," Ryan said.

Behind him, on the bed, he had laid out his stacks of plastic ATM cards, rubber-banded together in groups of ten.

"I mean it," Jay said. "You could use some—"

"Yeah," he said. "I hear you."

It was April. Months had passed since Ryan's death, and he was doing okay with that. He had basically worked through his Kübler-Ross stages, he guessed. There actually hadn't been much denial or bargaining involved, and the anger he experienced felt kind of good. There was a pleasure in stealing, a warm flush as he moved money from one fake bank account to another, as another credit card arrived in the mail.

In the bathroom, he applied adhesive to his bare scalp and arranged his shaggy blond Kasimir Czernewski wig. He shaved and dried his upper lip and then brushed on some spirit gum so that he could attach his mustache. He had to admit that it was fun to put on a disguise, that instant in the mirror when a new face looked back at him.

He had been traveling away from himself for a long time now, he thought—for years and years, maybe, he had been trying to imagine ways to escape—and now he was actually doing it. It even felt glamorous, in a bathroom such as this: the wall-length mirror and beautiful porcelain sinks, the sunken Jacuzzi tub, the standing shower with its frosted glass door, the commode separate in its own little room, with a telephone on the wall next to the toilet paper dispenser. It was all very sophisticated, he thought, and he adjusted his black Kasimir Czernewski glasses and brushed his teeth.

Get laid a couple of times, Jay had said.

And he thought: *Okay. Maybe I will.*

———

The last time Ryan had sex, he was a junior in high school, and it had turned out to be very problematic.

The girl's name was Pixie—that was what she went by—and she had moved from Chicago to Council Bluffs with her father, and even though she was fifteen, two years younger than he, she was a real city girl—a lot more worldly than Ryan.

She had a lip piercing and an eyebrow piercing and dyed white-blond hair with some strands of pink, and her eyes were traced with black liner. She was just barely five feet tall—thus "Pixie" instead of her real name, Penelope—and she had a body like a cherub or a curvaceous teddy bear, smooth perfect olive skin and large breasts and a full mouth, and even before the end of the first week of school people were referring to her as Goth Hobbit, and Ryan had laughed with everyone else.

So he'd never exactly known what she'd seen in him, except that she sat behind him in period six band. He was a trombonist and she was a drummer, and if he turned his head, he could watch her out of the corner of his eye, and the first thing he noticed about her was this expression, a focused and blissful attention to her page of music, the way her lips parted, the way the sticks moved in her hands as if she weren't even thinking of them, the graceful loose-ness of her wrists and forearms. And, yes, the slight vibration of her breasts when she gave the drumhead a decisive stroke.

And so he couldn't keep from glancing at her from time to time surreptitiously until one day as he was breaking down his trombone after class and lubricating the hand slide, and she stood there star-ing at him with her head cocked to one side. He had arranged the pieces in the velvet indentations of his instrument case, and at last he looked up at her.

"Can I help you?" he said, and she raised one eyebrow—the one with the thin metal ring in it.

"I doubt it," she said. "I was just trying to figure out if there was some reason you keep staring at me, or if you're just autistic or whatever."

He was not that popular; he was used to being made fun of by various people, and so he tightened his lips and inserted his cleaning brush into the mouth of his slide. "I don't know what you're talking about," he said.

And she shrugged. "Okay, then, Archie," she said.

Archie. He didn't know what that was supposed to mean, but he didn't like it. "My name is Ryan," he said.

"Okay, Thurston," she said, and appraised him once more, dubiously. "Can I ask you a question?" she said, and when he continued to pack up his instrument, she smiled, puckering her lips out in a wry, challenging way. "Does your mom buy your clothes for you, or do you honestly intend to dress like that?"

Ryan looked up from his trombone case, fixing her with a look that he thought of as particularly icy. "May I help you?" he said.

And Pixie evaluated this, as if it were a real offer. "Maybe," she said. "I just wanted to tell you that if you did something with yourself, you could probably actually be fuckable." And then she gave him that smile again, lopsided, a gangster smirk.

"I just thought you'd want to know," she said.

He thought about this as he rode down the elevator, and then he pushed it into the back of his mind again, back to the nearly subconscious place where Pixie had been lingering for the past few years.

In the elevator, a miniature LED screen was blaring scenes of some Broadway-style musical entertainment, and the girl standing in front of him shifted her weight from foot to foot as she watched the video. She had a very short skirt and incredibly long bare legs—they seemed to go all the way up to her rib cage, beautiful downy brown legs—and Ryan observed them silently. The skirt ended just slightly below the slope of her buttocks, and he let his eyes run down the back of her thighs to her calves and ankles and sandaled pink-soled feet. He watched as she got off the elevator, and the man beside him made a low sound in his throat.

"Mm, mm," the man said. "Did you see that?" He was a black man, perhaps fifty years old, wearing a pink polo shirt and kelly green pants and carrying a bag of golf clubs. "That was a sight to see."

"Yes," Ryan said, and the man shook his head in exaggerated wonder.

"*Damn,*" the man said. "Are you single?"

"Yeah," Ryan said, "I guess I am." And the man shook his head again.

"I sure do envy you," the man said—and then, before he could say more, the elevator doors opened and three more beautiful teenage girls entered their enclosure.

What if he *did* meet a girl, he thought. That was what people did in Vegas, that was what a lot of people came here for. All over town, he supposed, they were hooking up, seducing their way into one-night stands or stumbling drunkenly into liaisons with strangers. He himself had never picked up someone at a bar, or a casino, though obviously it was possible. You saw it on TV all the time: a man approached an attractive woman; there was some flirtation or suggestive small talk; and shortly thereafter, the couple was having sex. It should be fairly simple to accomplish. If he could get a 2200 on the SAT, he should be able to get laid in Vegas.

But standing there on the main floor of the casino, the very idea of "meeting someone" seemed heartbreakingly complex. How would you even talk to another person in such a place? He peered out at what appeared to be an enormous video arcade, rows upon rows of glowing neon games and slot machines, stretching as far as he could see, hundreds and hundreds of people feeding their individual screens, which showed playing cards or rolling numbers or animated cartoon characters, and he found himself thinking of the photographs he'd seen of sweatshops—cavernous factory lofts, columns of workers sewing seams into blouses or riveting eyelets into shoes, a hive in which each worker was submerged in a constant, lonely activity. Meanwhile, all around him people wandered the aisles and walkways, with that peculiar blankness tourists had as they moved through the paces of being entertained, an aimless shuffle that people took on in shopping malls and national monuments and so forth.

At last, Ryan fell into the flow of foot traffic around the circumference of the main gaming area. In front of him, a pair of blond women in matching capri pants spoke to each other in Dutch or Norwegian or some other language. Up ahead, a mild bottleneck was forming as people paused to watch an elderly man in a cowboy hat and flowered Western shirt performing a card trick. The man held up the ten of spades to show the crowd, and there was a spatter of applause. The magician gave a small, gracious bow, and the blond women stopped and craned to see what was going on.

But Ryan moved past, feeling again in his pockets for his stack of ATM cards, which was almost as thick as a deck of playing cards.

There was a lot of cash that needed to be withdrawn before the night was over.

It was annoying to find himself thinking of Pixie again.

In the past few years, he had been pretty successful at keeping her out of his conscious thoughts, and it was disturbing to find her lingering there now. There was a certain way she would press her nose and lips to his neck, just under the line of his jaw; a way she would slide her hand down on his arm, as if she were trying to make his skin adhere to her palm.

It was not as if he had been in love with her. That was what his mother said later.

"It's just ordinary lust, but at your age you can't tell the difference."

And probably his mother was right. Pixie was not what he had thought of when he'd imagined "falling in love"—and in fact, he couldn't remember if the word "love" had ever been mentioned. It wasn't the type of thing Pixie would have said.

"Fucking"—that was more in line with Pixie's vocabulary, and that was what they were doing within a few weeks of that first conversation in the band room, fucking first in a motel on a band trip to Des Moines, and then fucking after school at Pixie's house while her dad was at work, and then fucking in the school building, in a storage closet in the basement near the boiler room, fucking on top of boxes of industrial paper towels.

"You know what's funny?" Pixie said. "My dad totally thinks I'm this innocent virgin. He's like a zombie since my mom died, poor guy. I don't think he realizes that I'm not twelve anymore."

"Geez," Ryan said. "Your mom died?" He had never known anyone who had experienced that kind of tragedy, and it made him feel even more awkward to be naked in her room, with her girly pink bedspread and her collection of Beanie Babies staring down at them from their shelf.

"She had some deal with her lungs," Pixie said, and she uncovered a pack of Marlboros from a hiding space behind a Harry Potter novel on her bookcase. "Bronchiolitis obliterans, it's called. They don't know how she got it. They thought she could have been exposed to toxic fumes of some sort, or it could have been brought on by a virus. But no one knew what she had. The doctors thought she had asthma or whatever." She looked at him, cryptically, and he watched as she withdrew a cigarette and lit it. She put her face near the open window and exhaled.

"That's awful," Ryan said. Uncertain. What was he supposed to say? "I'm really sorry," he said.

But she only shrugged. "I used to think about killing myself," she said. And she blew a stream of gray-blue smoke through the screen, into the backyard. She peered at him, matter-of-factly. "But then I decided that it wasn't worth it. It's too angsty and whiny, I think. Or maybe . . . ," she said. "Maybe I'm just too beyond caring to bother." She leaned back, kneading the crumple of sheet and blanket with her bare foot, and he watched her toes as they clenched and un-clenched. He was a little stunned by such talk.

"Listen," he said. "You shouldn't think about killing yourself. There are a lot of people who—care about you, and . . ."

"Shut up," she said, but not unkindly. "Don't be a nerd, Ryan."

And so he didn't say anything more.

Instead of going back to school after lunch that day, they stayed at her house and watched movies that Pixie was obsessed with. Fourth period: here was *The Killers,* with Lee Marvin and Angie Dickinson. Fifth period: *Something Wild* with Jeff Daniels and Melanie Griffith. Sixth period: fucking again.

I am actually doing this, he thought. *I am really, really, really doing this—*

The hotels were interconnected. He passed through one casino cavern and boarded an escalator and a series of moving walkways that rivered past mall-like hallways lined with souvenir shops, and then he found himself in a replica of an Egyptian tomb, and then inside another warehouse-size casino floor, and there were a few more ATM machines to attend to, and then there was the Excal-ibur, which was themed to look like a medieval castle, and people were lined up to dine at the Round Table buffet, and he made a couple more withdrawals.

And then, at last, after winding his way through the corridors of the Luxor and the Excalibur, he emerged into the outdoors, into the open air, and he had about ten grand in his backpack. That was the thing about Vegas—you could withdraw five hundred dollars, one thousand, three thousand from an ATM and it was not that unusual, though he knew that he would have to retire Kasimir Czernewski after this trip. Which was sad, in a way. He had spent a lot of time building up Kasimir's life in his mind, trying to conceptualize what it would be like to be a foreigner, a young man starting with nothing and working his way toward the American dream. Kasimir: essentially easygoing, but also crafty in some ways, determined, taking night school classes and struggling to establish his little private investigator business. You could make a television series about Kasimir Czernewski, a kind of comedy-drama, he imagined.

Outside, people were moving down the sidewalk in groups of five or ten or twenty, and the flow had grown more purposeful, more like the movement of big-city people down a street. On one side, car traffic was dragging slowly past, and on the other, hawkers stood and handed out cards to passersby. They were primarily Mexican men, and they would draw attention by slapping their handouts against their forearms—*clap, clap, clap*—and then flicking out a single card and extending it.

"Thank you," Ryan said, and he had gathered about twenty of them before he began to say, "I'm set." "No thanks." "Sorry."

The cards were advertisements for various escort services, pictures of girls, naked, airbrushed, with colorful stars printed over their nipples. Sometimes the letters of their names covered their privates. Fantasie, Roxan, Natasha. *Beautiful Exotic Dancer in the privacy of your own room!* the card said. *Only $39!* And there was the phone number to call.

He was lingering on the street, looking at his collection of escort girls—imagining what it might be like to actually call one of them—when he heard the Russian men approaching.

At least he thought they were Russian. Or they were speaking in some other Eastern European language. Lithuanian? Serbian? Czech? But in any case, they were talking loudly in their native tongue—*Zatruxa* something something. *Baruxa! Ha, ha, ha*—and Ryan looked up, startled, as they approached. There was a bald one, and one with his blond hair moussed into stiff hedgehog-like spikes, and another with a checkered cabbie golf cap. All of them wearing colorful Hawaiian shirts.

They were all three carrying those enormous souvenir drink

glasses that were so popular on the strip, containers that looked like vases, or bongs—round, bulbous bases with long, piped necks that eventually opened into a tuliped rim. He assumed that these glasses had been engineered so that they were hard to spill, and yet held the maximum amount of alcoholic beverage allowed.

They came toward him, noisily joking in whatever Slavic language they were speaking, and he couldn't help it. He froze there, staring at them.

Back when he was a freshman at Northwestern, his roommate, Walcott, used to scold him.

"Why do you always stare at people?" Walcott said, one night, when they were walking down Rush Street in Chicago, looking for bars that might take their cheap fake IDs. "Is that, like, an Iowa thing?" Walcott said critically. "Because you know, in cities, it's not cool to gape at people."

Walcott was actually from Cape Cod, Massachusetts, which wasn't a city, but he had spent a lot of time in Boston and New York, and so believed himself an expert on such things. He also had a lot of opinions about what people from Iowa were like, though he had never been there, either.

"Look," Walcott said, "let me give you some advice. Don't look at people directly in the face. Never—let me reiterate—Never, *never,* *NEVER* make eye contact with a homeless person, or a drunk, or anyone who looks like they are a tourist. It's a super-easy rule to remember: do not look at them."

"Hmm," Ryan said, and Walcott patted him on the back.

"What would you do without me?" Walcott said.

"I don't know," Ryan said. He looked down at his feet, which were weaving along the dirty sidewalk as if by remote control.

He never would have chosen Walcott as a friend, but they had been thrown together by fate, by the administrative offices, and they'd spent an enormous amount of time together that first year, so Walcott's voice was still ingrained in his head.

But now it was too late. He stood, making eye contact, staring, and the bald Russian had noticed him. The bald man's eyes lit up, as if Ryan were holding up a sign with his name on it.

"Hey there, my main man," the bald Russian said, in a thick but surprisingly slangy English—as if he'd learned the language by listening to rap music. "Hey, how you doing?"

And this was the thing Walcott had warned him about. This was the problem with being from Iowa, because he had been trained, for years and years, to be polite and friendly, and he couldn't help himself.

"Hello," Ryan said, as the three men came toward him, grinning as they clustered around him. A bit *too* close, and he stiffened uncomfortably, though he found himself putting on his pleasant, welcoming Midwestern expression.

The man with the spiked hair let out a burst of unrecognizable Russian syllables, and the men all laughed.

"We . . . ," said the spike-haired man, and struggled a moment, trying to think of words. "We—tree—alkonauts! We—" he said. "We come with peace!"

They all found this uproarious, and Ryan smiled uncertainly. He shifted his shoulder, the backpack with his heavy laptop and about ten thousand dollars in cash tucked into one of the pockets. Stay calm. He was at the edge of the curb, and tourists and partygoers and other walkers were moving around them with glazed, bedazzled expressions. Not making eye contact.

He was trying to decide how nervous he should be. They were out in the open, he thought. They couldn't do anything to him right here in the middle of the street—

Though, he remembered a movie he'd seen where an assassin

had expertly severed the saphenous vein in his victim's thigh, and the victim had bled to death right there on a busy street.

The men had formed a circle around him, and he could feel the flow of traffic on Las Vegas Boulevard at his back. He took a step, but the men just gathered closer, as if following his lead.

"You like the cards?" said the bald one. "You like the cards, my main man?"

And Ryan was certain he'd been caught. His hand went automatically to his pocket, where he had his stack of ATM cards. He rested his palm against his thigh, thinking again of the saphenous vein.

"Cards?" Ryan said weakly, and he tried to glance over his shoulder. If he dashed into the four lanes of Las Vegas Boulevard, what were the chances that he would be hit by a car? Fairly high, he guessed. He shook his head at the bald man, as if he didn't understand. "I . . . I don't have any cards," he said. "I don't know what you mean."

"You don't understand?" the man said, and he laughed with good-natured surprise, a bit taken aback. "Cards!" he pronounced, slowly, and he gestured at Ryan's hand. "Cards!"

"Cards!" the spike-haired man repeated, and he grinned, showing his gold-tipped front teeth. He held up a dozen or so of the cards from the escort services, fanned out like a hand of poker, a full house of Fantasie and Britt and Kamchana and Cheyenne and Natasha and Ebony.

And then Ryan realized what they were talking about. He glanced down at the stack of pictures he himself had collected as he walked down the strip. "Oh," he said. "Yeah, anyway, I . . ."

"Yes, yes!" said the bald one, and the men all burst into laughter again. "Cards! Beautiful girls, my main man!"

"Thirty-nine United State dollars! Incredible!" said the man in the golf cap, who had so far been only observing. And then he let out an extended comment in Russian, which was met with more hilarity. The man held out one of his own cards for Ryan to take, offering it.

"You like Natasha. Big titty Russian girl. Very nice."

"Yes," Ryan said, and nodded. "Yes, very nice," he said, and he gazed down the block—Bally's, Flamingo, Imperial Palace, Harrah's, Casino Royale, the Venetian, the Palazzo—all the places he had been planning to visit, all the ATMs he still had to withdraw from before he came at last to the Riviera, where he would check in to the hotel under the name Tom Knott, a young accountant who was attending a convention.

"My name is Shurik," said the bald Russian, and held out his hand to be shook.

"Vasya," said the one with the spiked hair.

"Pavel," said the one in the cap.

"Ryan," Ryan said, and he felt his face growing hot almost immediately as he pressed palms with the three men, one after the other. It was the most basic mistake—his own real name, given thoughtlessly, and he felt more flustered than ever. *Mr. J so good to find,* he thought. Was it significant? Or not?

"Ryan, my main man," said Shurik. "We come with us, yes? Together. Come. We find the best girls. Right?"

"Right," Ryan said. And then, as the three of them parted for him, as they prepared to fall in behind him, following with their giant tulip cups and their cards and their hopeful, friendly expressions, he made an abrupt feint, a zigzag, pushing himself into the flow of tourists on the sidewalk.

And then he took off running.

It was a stupid thing to do, he told himself later.

He stood in the queue at the check-in desk of the Riviera Hotel, his heart still quickened in his chest.

The poor guys. How startled they'd been when he broke off and dashed away. They hadn't made any attempt to pursue. Thinking of their stunned expressions as they watched him flee, he couldn't believe they'd ever been anything more than innocent foreign tourists. A bunch of drunken guys, looking for a native to befriend.

Jay was right: he needed to calm down.

Still, it was hard to shake the adrenaline once it set, that tight, jittery tension, and he sat in his room in the Riviera—Tom Knott, age twenty-two, of Topeka, Kansas—looking again at the escort girls. *Natasha. Ebony.*

This was the thing he hated most about himself, about his old self—that nervousness, worry knitting inside of him. By the time he got to his sophomore year at Northwestern, he spent so much time fretting about all the work he wasn't doing that he didn't have time to actually work.

He guessed that was why he found himself thinking about Pixie again. Despite what had happened, despite the aftermath, the six weeks he had spent with Pixie had probably been the best time of his life. They were skipping classes fairly regularly, and he had been getting home in time to destroy the letters the school was sending about his absences and tardies, and erase the messages on the answering machine from the attendance secretary, and his parents had continued obliviously without noticing anything out of the ordinary. He was, he realized, a pretty good actor. A pretty decent liar. He had not done any homework of significance for a while by that point, and for the first time in his life he had taken a test and he had absolutely no idea what they were asking him. It was his chemistry midterm, and he circled multiple choice questions at random and invented calculations that he had no idea how to perform, and he had a wonderful thought.

I don't care about anything.

It was like the fundamentalist kids when they talked about being born again. "Jesus came into my heart and emptied me of my sin," a girl named Lynette had told him once, and in some ways that was what had happened to him. All his burdens were lifted, and he felt light and transparent, as if the sunlight could shine right through his body.

I don't care about anything, he thought, *I don't care about the future, I don't care what happens to me, I don't care what my family thinks, I don't care, I don't care.* And each time he said it in his mind, it was as if a weight detached and flickered away like a butterfly.

And then one day he came home and his mother was in the kitchen, waiting.

As it turned out, it was not the attendance secretary or one of his teachers who had contacted Stacey; it was Pixie's father. He had apparently intercepted some of the emails they had exchanged, and had found Pixie's journal, and then—this was the aspect that Ryan hadn't expected or understood—Pixie had confessed everything to her father.

Who was enraged. Who wanted to kill Ryan.

"Do you have a daughter, Mrs. Schuyler?" Pixie's father had asked, and Ryan's mother was sitting there at work, at her desk, in the office of Morgan Stanley in Omaha, where she was a CPA, and Mr. Pixie said, "If you had a daughter, you would know how I feel.

"I feel violated. I feel defiled by your pervert son," he told Stacey. "And I want you to know," he said, "I want you to know that if it turns out my daughter is pregnant, I am going to come to your house and I am going to take your son and knock his teeth through the back of his fucking skull."

By the time Ryan came home, Stacey had already called the police, who had charged Pixie's father with aggravated menacing, and she was talking to a lawyer friend who was getting a restraining order, but she didn't tell him this when he came into the kitchen and opened the refrigerator and peered into it. He didn't pay much attention to her. She was often in a bad mood, as far as he could tell. She would situate herself in the kitchen or the TV room or some other area where they could see her being silent, and then she would emanate dense radioactive waves of negativity. He knew better than to look at her when she was in this mode.

And so he got out some milk as she sat there at the kitchen table. He shook some cereal into a bowl and poured milk over it, and he was about to take his snack into the TV room when Stacey looked up at him.

"Who are you?" she said.

Ryan lifted his head, reluctantly. This was also her method, these soft-spoken inscrutable questions. "Um," he said. "Excuse me?"

"I said: who are you?" she murmured in a sadly musing voice. "Because I don't think I know you, Ryan."

He had his first glimmer of nervousness then. He knew that she had found out—what? How much? He felt the expression on his face tightening and growing blanker. "I don't know what you're talking about," he said.

"I thought you were a trustworthy person," Stacey said. "I thought you were responsible, mature, you had a plan for yourself. That's what I used to think. Now I can't fathom what's going on inside of you. I have no idea."

He was still holding his bowl of cereal, which was making almost inaudible whispering noises as the puffed kernels soaked up the milk.

He couldn't think of anything to say.

He didn't want his adventure with Pixie to be over, and he imagined if he just said nothing, it would last for a while longer. He could still be happy, he could still not care about anything, he could still meet up with Pixie in the morning on the north side of school and watch her smoking a cigarette and toying with her lip ring, threading it back and forth through the flesh of her mouth.

"Do you want to ruin your life?" Stacey was saying to him. "Do you want to end up like your uncle Jay? Because that is the way you are headed. He screwed up his life when he was just about your age, and he has never recovered. Never. He turned himself into a loser, and that's where you're headed, Ryan."

It wasn't until years later that he understood what she was talking about.

You are going to end up like your father, that was what she actually meant. His father: Jay, getting a girl pregnant at age fifteen, running away from home, floating from shady job to shady job, never to settle down, never to have a normal life. In retrospect, he could see why she had come down so hard on him, he could even sympathize somewhat. She knew what kind of person he would become, even before he did.

And she was not going to let him end up like Jay. For two weeks, Ryan had been sent to a wilderness camp for rebellious teens, while his mother put the pieces of his life back in order. One of those hiking and team-building and group therapy isolation camps, full of military-esque counselors doling out "tough love" and diagnosing their psychological sicknesses. They had lost their way; they were suffering from unhealthy misperceptions about themselves; they needed to change if they ever wanted to become productive members of society, if they ever wanted to see their friends and family again. . . .

Even when he returned, he was under what basically amounted to house arrest for the rest of the school year. She had taken away his cell phone and Internet privileges, and then she had contacted all his teachers to make arrangements for him to make up all the work that he had missed, and she had him seeing a therapist once a week, and she enrolled him in an SAT prep course, and in a community service program called the Optimist Club, which met three days a week to clean up parks and give toys to poor children and conduct recycling drives and so forth. She switched him out of band, which was the only class he had shared with Pixie, though it actually didn't matter because Pixie herself had been transferred by her father over to St. Albert High. He never saw her again. Her father was found guilty of aggravated menacing and sentenced to probation.

As for Ryan's father, Owen, he was mostly uninvolved during this period, taciturn and glum as he always was in the face of Stacey's stubborn organization. Owen did manage to talk her into letting Ryan take guitar lessons, and that was one nice thing about his last year and a half of high school. He and Pixie had talked about forming a band, in which she would be the drummer and he would be the lead singer, and he used to like to fantasize about that. He liked to sit in his room and make up songs on the Takamine that Owen had bought for him. Ryan wrote a song called "Oh, Pixie." Very sad. He wrote another called "Aggravated Menace," and one called "Soon I'll Be Gone," and "Echopraxia," which, if he ever made an album, might end up being the single.

It was pathetic, he thought, to be thinking about those lame old songs.

It was depressing because he had spent the whole night thinking about Pixie, remembering her, wondering where she was now. What had happened to her? And he was nowhere close to getting laid.

It was even sad that his paranoia about the Russians had turned out to be nothing, after all. Despite his encounter on the street, there hadn't actually been any intrigue, there hadn't been any adventure with gangsters, nothing but the herds of tourists and the workers who went about the job of fleecing them with the grim nonchalance of a clerk at a late-night convenience store.

Maybe he would always be lonely, he thought, and he spread out the escort service cards on the desk and looked at them. Fantasie. Roxan. Natasha.

He sat there at his hotel room desk, contemplating. He typed in his name and room number, and there was a breath as the cyberspace made its connection.

He opened up the Instant Message window, and

No, there wasn't any new greeting in Cyrillic.

And so he just typed a note to Jay. "Mission accomplished," he wrote, and then, he decided, he might as well go to bed.

15

They could be leaving soon. That was one thing. On their way to New York, and then to international destinations.

And they could be rich, too, if everything went according to plan. *If* she was the type of person who would do this sort of thing.

The documents were spread out between them on the kitchen table, and George Orson adjusted and aligned papers in front of him, as if parallel lines could make their conversation easier. She saw him glance up, surreptitiously, and it almost embarrassed her to see his eyes so earnest and guilty—though it was also a relief to have him wordless. Not trying to assure her or convince her or teach her, but just waiting for her decision. It was the first time in a while that a choice of hers had mattered, the first time in months she didn't feel as if she were walking in some dreamscape, amnesia-scape, everything glowing with an aura of déjà vu—

But now it had solidified. His schemes. His evasions. The money.

She lifted a single sheet off of the sheaf that he'd laid in front of her. Here was a copy of the wire transfer. *BICICI,* it said at the top.

Banque Internationale pour le Commerce et l'Industrie de Côte d'Ivoire. And there was a date and a code and stamp and several signatures and a total. *US$4,300,000.00.* Here was the letter confirming the deposit. "Dear Mr. Kozelek, your fund was deposited here in our bank by your partner Mr. Oliver Akubueze. Your partner further instructed us to execute transfer of the fund to your bank account by completing the bank's transfer application form, and he also endorsed other vital documents to that effect. . . ."

"Mr. Kozelek," Lucy said. "That's you."

"Yes," George Orson said. "A pseudonym."

"I see," Lucy said. She looked at him, briefly, then down at the paper: *US$4,300,000.00.*

"I see," she breathed. She was trying to make her voice cool and disinterested and official. She thought of the social worker she and Patricia had to visit after their parents had died, the two of them watching as the woman paged through the papers on her cluttered desk. *I wonder what experience the two of you have with taking care of yourselves?* the social worker said.

Lucy held the paper between her thumbs and forefingers in the way the social worker had. She glanced up to look at George Orson, who was sitting patiently across the table, holding his cup of coffee loosely, as if warming his fingers, even though it must have been eighty degrees outside already.

"Who is Oliver Aku—?" she said, stumbling over the pronunciation, in the way she'd once clumped ungracefully through French sentences in Mme Fournier's class. "Akubueze," she tried again, and George Orson smiled wanly.

"He's nobody," George Orson said, and then after a brief hesitation, he tilted his head regretfully. He had promised to answer any question she asked. "He's—just a middleman. A contact. I had to pay him off, of course. But that wasn't a problem."

Their gazes met, and she remembered what George Orson had once told her about how he used to take classes in hypnosis: those bright green eyes were perfect for it, she thought. He peered at her, and his eyes said: *You must relax.* His eyes said: *Can you trust me?* His eyes said: *Aren't we still in love?*

Perhaps. Perhaps he did love her.

Perhaps he was only trying to take care of her, as he said.

But it was frustrating, because even with all these documents in front of her, he was still vague with the truth. He was a thief, that much he had admitted, but she still didn't understand where the money had come from, or how he had managed to acquire it, or who, exactly, was looking for him.

"I didn't steal from a *person*, Lucy—that's what you have to understand. I didn't take money from a sweet old rich lady, or a gangster, or a small-town credit union in Pompey, Ohio. I've taken money—embezzled, let's say—from an *entity*. A very large, global entity. Which makes things a bit more complicated. I mean," he said, "I remember that you used to be interested in someday working for an international investment firm. Like Goldman Sachs. Right?

"And if, for example, you were able to figure out a way to skim money from the treasury of Goldman Sachs, you would soon come to understand that they would do everything in their power to find you and bring you to justice. They would utilize law enforcement, certainly, but they would probably also resort to other means. Private detectives. Bounty hunters. Would they employ assassins? Torturers? Probably not. But you understand what I'm saying."

"No, I don't, actually," Lucy said. "Are you saying you stole money from Goldman Sachs?"

"No, no," George Orson said. "That was just an example. I was just trying to . . ." And then he sighed, resignedly. A sound unlike George Orson, she thought, almost the opposite of the conspiratorial chuckle she'd first found so attractive and charming. "Look," he said. "I wish things hadn't come to this. I kept thinking I could just sort this out on my own and you wouldn't even have to know about—any of this. I thought I could work everything out so you wouldn't have to be involved."

And he was quiet then, brooding, tapping the edge of his fingernail against his coffee cup. *Tink, tink, tink.* Both of them self-conscious and anxious. It was depressing, Lucy thought—and perhaps it actually had been better when she didn't know anything, back when she was trusting him to take care of things, trusting that they were on their way somewhere wonderful, a shy but witty young woman and her urbane, mysterious older lover, maybe on a cruise ship on their way to Monaco or Playa del Carmen.

She reflected, letting this old fantasy brush briefly over her. Then, at last, she lowered her head to peruse the other documents George Orson had presented to her.

Here was the travel itinerary. From Denver to New York. From New York to Felix Houphouet Boigny airport in Abidjan, Ivory Coast.

Here were the social security cards and birth certificates they would use: David Fremden, age thirty-five, and his daughter, Brooke Fremden, age fifteen.

"I can get the passports expedited; that won't be a big problem," George Orson was telling her. "We can have a rush passport in two to five days. But we would need to act right away. We'd have to go to a courthouse or a post office to put in the application tomorrow—"

But he stopped talking when she looked up at him. She was not going to be rushed. She was going to think about this scrupulously, and he needed to understand that.

"Who are they?" she said. "David and Brooke?"

George Orson gave her another reproachful frown. Still, even now, recalcitrant with his information. But he had promised to answer.

"They aren't anybody in particular," he said wearily. "They're just people." And he passed the palm of his hand across his hair. "They *died*," he said. "A father and daughter, killed in an apartment fire in Chicago about a week ago. Which is why these documents are quite useful to us, *right now*. There's a window of time, before the deaths have been officially processed through the system."

"I see," she said again. It was about all she was able to think of to say, and she shut her eyes briefly. She didn't want to picture them—David and Brooke, in their burning apartment building, gasping in the smoke and heat—and so instead she stared hard down at the birth certificate as if it were a list of test questions she was studying.

Certificate of Live Birth	*112-89-0053*
Brooke Catherine Fremden	*March 15, 1993*
4:22 A. *Female*	*Swedish Covenant Hospital*
Chicago	*Cook County*

Here was the maiden name of the mother: Robin Meredith Crowley, born in the state of Wisconsin, age thirty-one at the time of Brooke's birth.

"So," Lucy said after she had perused this document mutely for a while. "What about the mom? Robin. Won't they ask about her?"

"She actually died some time ago," George Orson said, and made a small, shrugging gesture. "When Brooke was ten, I think. Killed in a, hmmm." And then he grew reticent, as if to spare Lucy's feelings—or Brooke's. "In any case," he said. "The mother's death certificate is there somewhere, too, if you want to . . ."

But Lucy just shook her head.

A car accident. She supposed that was what it was, but maybe she didn't want to know.

"This girl is only fifteen," Lucy said. "I don't look like a fifteen-year-old."

"True," George Orson said. "I hope that I don't look like I'm thirty-five, either, but we can work on that. Believe me, in my experience, people are not good at judging age."

"Hmm," Lucy said, still staring down at the document. Still

thinking about the mom. Robin. About David and Brooke. Had they tried to escape the fire, had they died in their sleep?

The poor Fremdens. The whole family, gone from the face of the earth.

Outside, in the backyard, the late morning sun was burning brightly over the Japanese garden. The weeds were tall and thick, and there was no sign of the little bridge or the Kotoji lantern statue. The top of the weeping cherry rose up out of the weeds as if gasping for breath, the drooping branches like long wet hair.

There were so many, many things that were troubling about this situation, but she found that the one that actually bothered her the most was the idea of pretending to be George Orson's daughter.

Why couldn't they just be traveling companions? Boyfriend and girlfriend? Husband and wife? Even uncle and niece?

"I know, I know," George Orson said.

It was uncomfortable because he was such a subdued George Orson, a diminished version of the George Orson she knew. He shifted in his chair as she turned from staring out at the backyard. "It's regrettable," he said. "To be honest, I'm not particularly happy about it, either. It's more than a little creepy for me, as well. Not to mention that I've never had to think of myself as someone who's old enough to have a teenage child!" He tried out a small laugh, as if she might find this amusing, but she didn't. She wasn't sure exactly how she was feeling, but she wasn't in the mood to appreciate his clever remarks. He reached out to touch her leg, and then thought better of it, drew his hand back, and she watched his proffered smile shrink into a wince.

This wasn't what she wanted, either: the tense discomfort that had developed between them ever since he had begun to tell her the truth. She had loved the way that they used to joke together. *Repartee*, George Orson called it, and it would be terrible if that was gone, if somehow things had changed so much between them, if their old relationship was now lost, irretrievable. She had loved being Lucy and George Orson—"Lucy" and "George Orson"—and maybe it was just an act that they were doing for each other, but it had felt easy and natural and fun. It was her real self she had discovered when she met him.

"Believe me, Lucy," he was saying now, very solemn and not like George Orson at all. "Believe me," he said. "This wasn't my first choice. But I didn't have much recourse. In our current situation, it wasn't particularly easy to acquire the documents we needed. I didn't have a whole variety of choices."

"Okay," Lucy said. "I get it."

"It's just pretending," George Orson said. "A game we're playing."

"I get it," Lucy said again. "I understand what you're saying."

Though that didn't necessarily make it any easier.

George Orson had "some things to take care of" in the afternoon.

Which was almost reassuring, at some level. Ever since they had come here, he had been disappearing for hours at a time—vanishing into the study and locking the door, or driving off without a word in the old pickup, off to town—and today was no different. After their talk, he'd been in a hurry to get back to his computer and she'd stood there in the entrance of his study looking at the big desk and the old painting with the safe behind it, like a prop in a bad murder mystery.

He put his hand on the doorknob. She could tell he wanted to close the door—though not in her face, of course—and he hesitated there, his smile first reassuring, then tightening.

"You probably need some time to yourself, in any case," George Orson said.

"Yes," she said. She watched as his fingertips twitched against the clear cut glass of the doorknob, and he followed her eyes, looked down at his impatient hand, as if it had disappointed him.

"You know that you don't have to do this," he said. "I wouldn't blame you if you wanted to leave. I realize that it's a lot to ask of you."

She wasn't sure how to respond. She thought:

She thought:

Then he shut the door.

For a time, she paced outside of the study, and then she sat at the table in the dining room with a diet soda—it was a hot afternoon—and she pressed the cool damp can against her forehead.

She had been left to her own devices in this way for weeks now, left to watch TV endlessly, adjusting the ancient satellite dish that turned its head with a slow metallic hum, like the sound of an electric wheelchair; laying down hand after hand of solitaire with an old pack of her dad's playing cards that she had brought with her for sentimental reasons; browsing through the bookshelves in the living room, a dreadful collection of old tomes that you might find in a box at an old lady's yard sale. *The Death of the Heart. From Here to Eternity. Marjorie Morningstar.* Nothing anybody had ever heard of.

She was trying to think. Trying to imagine what to do, which was exactly the same thing she'd been doing for almost an entire year, ever since her parents had died. Scoping through the future in her mind, trying to draw a map for herself, looking out into a great expanse like a pilot over an ocean, looking for a place to land. And still no clear plan emerged.

But at least now she had more information.

4.3 million dollars.

Which was a significant and helpful detail, if in fact it could be believed. There were aspects to his story—to this whole thing—that felt exaggerated, or embellished, or distorted. Some aspect of the truth was concealed within what he'd told her, in the manner of those old picture puzzles she used to love as a child, drawings of ordinary landscapes in which simple pictographic figures—five seashells, or eight cowboy hats, or thirteen birds—had been hidden.

She selected an old hardcover from the shelf, and once again she riffled through the pages. Over the past few weeks, she had been through every book on the shelf, thinking that perhaps a note would drop out from between the pages. She had been through every cabinet in the kitchen, every dresser in every bedroom; she had tapped the walls as if there might be a secret door or compartment. She'd even been down to the lighthouse-shaped office of the motel, where she'd looked through the dusty rack of brochures for local amusements that had long ago closed down, where she'd opened boxes to find elderly rolls of toilet paper, still wrapped in plastic, cabinets full of moldering towels; she'd even been into the motel rooms themselves. She'd taken the keys from the hooks behind the counter and opened the rooms one by one—cleared out, all of them, no beds, no furniture, nothing but bare walls and bare floors, nothing but an unremarkable coating of dust.

In all that time, the only clue she'd found was a single golden coin. It was in a cigar box on a high shelf in a closet in one of the empty bedrooms on the second floor of the house, along with some oddly shaped rocks and a tiny horseshoe magnet and some thumbtacks and a plastic dinosaur. The coin was heavy, and appeared to be an old gold doubloon, very worn, though it was most likely just a child's souvenir of some sort.

Still, she had taken it, she had hidden it in her suitcase, and it was this coin that she thought of when she had first seen the deposit slip. *4.3 million dollars,* and childishly she'd had a brief image of chests full of these golden coins.

Of course she was aware that greed was part of her decision. Yes, she knew that. But she did also love him, she thought. She loved the way it felt to be with him, that easy, teasing camaraderie, that sense he gave her that the two of them, only them, had their own country and language, as if, as George Orson used to tell her, they'd known each other in another life—and she guessed that she could even stand to be Brooke Fremden for a while if he were David. . . .

And it could even be fun.

It could be one of those confidential adventures that they shared. One of the stories that made up a private history that only they knew about. They would be at a dinner party in some place like Morocco and someone would ask how they had met and the two of them would exchange private looks.

It was almost three-thirty in the afternoon when he finally emerged from the study. Lucy was sitting in the living room in one of the high wingback chairs that had been draped in a tarp, staring again at Brooke Fremden's birth certificate.

Here were the scrawled signatures at the bottom:

I certify that the personal information provided on this certificate is correct to the best of my knowledge and belief. That was the father.

I certify that the above named child was born alive at the place and time and on the date stated above. That was the doctor—Albert Gerbie, M.D.

And when she looked up, George Orson was standing at the edge of the room. He had been combing his hands through his hair, and now it stood up in tufts, and he had the look of someone who had been reading scientific formulas or columns of numbers for too long, an expression both tense and vacant, as if he were surprised to find her sitting there.

"I have to go out for some supplies," he said. "A few things that we need."

"Okay," she said, and he appeared to relax a little.

"I want to try to buy a few things that make you look younger," he said. "What about something pink? Something a bit girly?"

She looked at him skeptically. "Maybe I should come with you," she said.

But he shook his head emphatically. "Not a good idea," he said. "We shouldn't be seen together in town. Especially not now."

"Okay," she said, and he glanced at her gratefully as he put on the baseball cap he always wore when he was making an excursion. He was thankful, she supposed, that she wasn't arguing with him— and he touched her hand, running his fingers distractedly along her knuckles. She gave him a hesitant smile.

He hadn't locked the door to the study.

She stood at the door of the house watching the old pickup as it turned onto the county highway that led away from the motel. The sky was scalloped with layers of pale gray cumulus clouds, and she folded her arms across her chest as the pickup went up over a hill and vanished.

Even before she turned back to the door, she knew that she would go straight to the study, and in fact she even quickened her pace. That locked study had been a point of contention between them, ever since they'd arrived. His *privacy*—though didn't that contradict all his talk, all the things he'd said about sharing their own secret world, *sub rosa,* he said.

But when she brought this up, he only shrugged. "We all need our personal caves," he'd told her. "Even people as close as we are. Don't you think?"

And Lucy had rolled her eyes. "I don't see what the big deal is," she said. "What, are you looking at porn in there?"

"Don't be ridiculous," George Orson had said. "It's just part of having an adult relationship, Lucy. Giving people their space."

"I just want to check my email," she said—though in fact, there wasn't anyone who would have sent her a message, and naturally he knew that.

"Lucy, please," he said. "Just give me a few more days. I'll get you a computer of your own, and you can email to your heart's content. Just be patient a bit longer."

———

The study was much messier than she expected. Very unlike George Orson—who was a folder of clothes and a maker of lists, a man who hated to see clutter or dirty dishes in the sink.

So this was a side of George Orson she'd never seen, and she stood, uneasily, on the threshold. There was a sense of feverishness, chaos, panic. In any case, there was no doubt that all of those hours and hours he had spent holed up in this room had not been spent idly. He had been working, just as he'd claimed.

There was a jumble of different machines in the room—several laptop computers, a printer, a scanning bed, other things she didn't recognize—all of them connected in a tangle of cords and plugged into a strip of electrical sockets. The lips of his bookshelves were lined with empty soda cans, energy drinks, and there was a smattering of discarded clothes on the floor—a pair of boxer shorts, some T-shirts, a single sock curled up—along with many, many chocolate bar wrappers, though she had never seen George Orson eat candy. Some books were also spread out here and there—their pages tagged and bulging with bookmarks. *The Sacred Pentagram of Sedona. Fibonacci and the Financial Revolution. The Thing on the Doorstep. A Practical Guide to Mentalism.*

And there were papers strewn everywhere—some in piles, some crumpled into balls and discarded, some documents taped to the walls in a haphazard collage. The drawers to the file cabinet—the one he said he couldn't find the key to—had all been taken out, and the overstuffed hanging folders were stacked into various towers around the room.

It could easily be mistaken for the room of a crazy person, she thought, and a nervous feeling settled in her chest, a smooth, vibrating stone forming just below her breastbone as she stepped into the room.

"Oh, George," she breathed, and she couldn't decide if it was scary, or sad, or touching to imagine him emerging day after day from this room as his normal, cheerful self. Coming out of this tsunami with his hair combed and his smile straightened, to make her dinner and reassure her, to watch a movie with his arm draped gently over her shoulder, the day's frenzied activity closed and locked behind the study door.

She knew well enough that she shouldn't move anything. There was no way to tell what organizational principal was at work here, though it might not appear as if there were any. She stepped attentively, as if it were a lake covered with new ice, or a crime scene. It was okay, she told herself. He had promised to tell her everything, and if he hadn't, it was her right to find out. It was only fair, she thought, though she was also uncomfortably aware of those fairy tales that had scared her when she was a child. *Bluebeard. The Robber Bridegroom.* All those horror movies in which girls went into rooms they weren't supposed to.

Which was paranoid, she knew. She didn't believe that George Orson would hurt her. He would lie, yes, but she was sure—she was positive he wasn't dangerous.

Still, she crept forward like a trespasser, and she could feel her pulse ticking in her wrist as she laid one soundless foot in front of the other, picking a slow pathway through the clutter, treading with deliberate steps along the edge of the room.

The papers taped to the walls were mostly maps, she saw—road maps, topography, close-ups of street grids and intricately detailed coastlines—not places recognizable to her. Scattered throughout these maps were some news items George Orson had printed from the Internet: "U.S. Prosecutors Indict 11 in Massive Identity Fraud Case," "No Developments in Case of Missing College Student," "Attempted Theft of Biological Agent Thwarted." She glanced at these headlines, but didn't pause to read the articles. There were so many; every wall of the whole room was papered with 8½ x 11 sheets of paper. Maybe he *had* lost his mind.

And then she noticed the safe. The wall safe he had shown her the first day they had arrived, back when this room was just another one of the dusty curiosities he was touring her through. Back when he blithely told her he didn't have the combination.

But now the safe was open. The painting that had hidden it, the portrait of George Orson's grandparents, was swung back, and the thick metal door of the safe was ajar.

In a horror movie, this would be the moment in which George Orson would appear in the doorway behind her. "What do you think you're doing?" he would purr in a low voice, and she felt her neck prickle even though the doorway was empty behind her, even though George Orson was long gone, on his way to town.

But still she walked toward the safe, because it was full of money.

The bills were in bundles, just like you saw on TV in gangster movies, each stack about half an inch thick, rubber-banded and piled into neat columns, and she reached and took one. One-hundred-dollar bills. She guessed that there must be about fifty bills in each rubber-banded little bale, and she balanced one in the palm of her hand. It was light, no heavier than a pack of cards, and she riffled through the stack, not breathing for a second. There were thirty of these little parcels: about a hundred and fifty thousand dollars, she calculated, and she closed her eyes.

They really were rich, she thought. At least there was that. Despite her doubts, despite the chaos of papers and garbage and the books and maps and news stories, at least there was that. Up until then, she realized, she had almost convinced herself that she was going to have to leave.

Without thinking, she touched the cash to her face, as if it were a bouquet. "Thank you," she whispered. "Thank you, God."

16

They had arranged to meet in the lobby of the Mackenzie Hotel, which was where the woman said she was staying. "My name is Lydia Barrie," she had told him over the phone, and when he gave her his name, there was a moment of hesitance.

"*Miles Cheshire,*" she repeated, a skeptical edge to her voice—as if he had given her some stage name. As if he had told her his name was Mr. Breeze.

"Hello?" he said. "Are you still there?"

"I can meet you in fifteen minutes," she said—a bit stiffly, he thought. "I have red hair, and I'm wearing a black overcoat. We shouldn't have trouble finding each other."

"Oh," he said. "Okay."

Her voice was so curiously clipped, so strange and abrupt, that he felt a pang of uncertainty. When he went around putting up his flyers, he had imagined that—at the very best—he would get a few responses from some local teenagers, perhaps a clerk at the liquor store, or a waitress, or a curious and watchful retiree, or some derelict interested in the reward. That was the type of caller he usually got.

So this woman's eagerness made him uncomfortable.

He probably should have been more cautious, he thought. He probably should have deliberated more before arranging a meeting, he should have prepared a cover story.

All of which came to him too late. Too late he remembered the letter that Hayden had sent him: *someone may be watching you, and I hate to say this but I think you may actually be in danger,* and now he thought perhaps he shouldn't have been so quick to dismiss Hayden's warning.

But the woman had already come into the lobby. She was already peering around, and he was the only person standing there. He glanced over his shoulder, to where the girl at the front desk was talking avidly on the phone, utterly oblivious as the woman came toward him.

"Miles Cheshire?" she said, once again pronouncing his name with a faint touch of skepticism, and what could he do? He nodded, and tried to smile in a way that would seem honest and disarming.

"Yes," he said. He shifted uncertainly. "Thank you for coming," he said.

She was, Miles guessed, a bit older than he was—somewhere between thirty-five and forty, he imagined, a thin, striking woman with high cheekbones and a sharp nose and smooth red hair. Her eyes were large and gray and intense, not bulging, exactly, but prominent in a way that he found unnerving.

He was also aware of how dumpy he looked, in cheap jeans and an untucked, un-ironed button-down shirt, more than a little disheveled, he realized, probably smelling of beer and the cheap barroom fish he'd eaten for dinner. Lydia Barrie, on the other hand, was wearing a light, glossy black trench coat, and emitted a faint scent of some mildly floral businesslike perfume. She fixed her gaze on him, and her eyebrows arched as she looked him up and down.

She removed a thin cloth glove to shake his hand, and her palms were soft and lotioned, very cold. But it was she who shuddered when Miles's fingers touched her palm. She was staring at his face, her big eyes round with suspicious hostility.

"It's striking," she said. "The person in your poster is also named Miles." He watched as her lips pursed: an unpleasant memory. "His name is Miles Spady."

He stood there, blankly. "Well," he said.

Obviously, he should have been prepared for this. He had encountered this particular alias before, back in Missouri—it was an unpleasantly pointed invention on Hayden's part, a secret jab, marrying Miles with the last name of their hated stepfather—and there had even been the time in North Dakota when Hayden had checked into a motel using the name Miles Cheshire.

It was foolish of him to give this woman his real name, a stupid mistake, and he tried to think. Should he show her his driver's license, to prove his own honesty?

"Well," he said again.

Why hadn't he done more preparation? Why hadn't he dressed up a bit, why hadn't he memorized a simple explanation, instead of thinking he could extemporize?

"That's not actually his real name," Miles said at last. It was the only thing that he could think of, and—oh, why not? Why not just tell the truth? Why was he still playing a game that had long ago grown stale? "Miles Spady—" he said. "That's just a pseudonym; he does that all the time. Frequently, he'll use the names of people he knows. Miles is my name, and Spady is the name of our stepfather. It's a joke, I guess."

"A joke," she said. Her eyes rested on his face, and her expression flickered as her thoughts settled into place.

"You're related to him," she said. "I can see the resemblance."

Well.

It took him aback. It was a peculiar feeling, after all this time.

In all the years he had been showing this old photo of Hayden, no one had ever made the connection. For a while, it had dumbfounded him, and then eventually it was just another small, nagging doubt.

They were identical twins—obviously there was a similarity—so why had it been so many years since anyone had remarked on it? Miles guessed that he'd aged differently than Hayden had—he'd gained weight, his face had hardened and grown thicker—but still, he had always felt a little hurt that no one ever seemed to connect his own face with the boy in the poster.

So it was a relief, even a consolation, to hear her say the word "resemblance." It was as if his body solidified for the first time in—he couldn't remember how long.

Miles let out a breath.

"He's my brother," he said at last, and it was such a liberation to say it, such a release. "I've been looking for him for a long time now."

"I see," Lydia Barrie said. She regarded him, and her hostility deflated slightly. She pushed a strand of hair behind her ear, and he watched as she closed her eyes, as if she were meditating.

"Then I guess we have something in common, Miles," she said. "I've also been looking for him for a long time."

He was lonely: that's what he told himself later, when he began to worry that he should have been more cautious, more circumspect. He was lonely and tired and disoriented and sick of playing games, and what did it matter? What did it matter?

They sat at the bar of the Mackenzie Hotel, and he had another few beers, and Lydia Barrie drank gin and tonics, and he told her everything.

Well—almost everything.

It was disconcerting, he found, once he began to put the whole story into words. Their unbelievable childhood—which, even in the blandest summary, sounded like a comic book. Their magician/clown/hypnotist father. The atlas. Hayden's breakdowns, the past lives and spirit cities, the various identities he inhabited, the emails and letters and clues that mapped out a treasure hunt Miles had been pursuing for years now. Perhaps that was the most embarrassing thing to admit, that he had been following this trail for more than a decade now, and hadn't gotten any closer.

How did you explain that? Was it enough to say that they were brothers—that Hayden was the last person alive in the world who shared the same memories, the last person who could remember how happy they were at one point, the last person who knew that things could have been different? Was it enough to say that Hayden was a conduit through which he could pass back in time, the last thread that connected him to what he still thought of as his "real" life?

Was it enough to say that, even now, even after everything, he still loved Hayden more than anyone else? He still longed for the old Hayden every day, the brother he had known as a kid, even though he knew that would sound crazy. Desperate. Pathological.

"I'm honestly not sure what I'm doing at this point," he said, and he folded his hands on the surface of the bar. "Why am I here? I don't actually know."

Over the years, he had imagined himself telling his tale to someone—a wise therapist, perhaps; or a friend he'd become close to—John Russell, maybe, given time and proximity; or a girlfriend, once they'd gotten to know each other and he was sure she wouldn't immediately run away. The girl at Matalov Novelties, Aviva, Mrs. Matalov's granddaughter, with her dyed black hair and skeleton earrings and sharp, sympathetic, knowing eyes—

But he never would have imagined that the person he'd finally reveal himself to would be someone like Lydia Barrie. There were, he thought, few people more unlikely than this owlishly watchful, tightly wound woman, with her gloves and her trench coat and her pale, elegant skin.

But it was, nevertheless, easy to talk to her. She listened intently, but didn't seem to doubt what he was telling her. None of this surprised her, she told him finally.

Lydia Barrie had been looking for Hayden for more than three years—or, to be exact, she had been looking for her younger sister, Rachel.

Hayden was Rachel's fiancé. Or had been.

"This was back in Missouri," Lydia Barrie said. "My sister was attending the University of Missouri at Rolla, and your brother was her teacher. He called himself Miles Spady—he was a graduate student in math. He was supposedly British. He said he'd gone to Cambridge, and his father was a professor of anthropology there, and I think we were a little dazzled by him when he came home with her that December.

"We were five women. It was Rachel and me and our middle sister, Emily, and my aunt Charlotte, and our mother. Our father died when we were young, and so there was that: it was a novelty to have a man in the house.

"And it was also that my mother was so ill. She had ALS, and she was in a wheelchair by that time. We all knew that she was going to die soon, and so—I don't know—everyone wanted it to be a wonderful Christmas, and I'm sure he realized that. He was very charming, and kind to our mother. She wasn't able to talk anymore, but he would sit with her and converse, and tell her about his life back in England, and—

"I believed him. He was convincing enough, at least. In retrospect, I realize that his accent struck me as slightly put-on, but I didn't think too much about it at the time. He seemed very smart, very nice. A little eccentric, I thought, a little *affected,* but nothing that made me feel especially suspicious of him.

"Undeniably, I wasn't paying an enormous amount of attention. I was living in New York, just home for a few days for the holiday, and I was involved in my own life, and I wasn't terribly close to Rachel. We're eight years apart, and she was—always a very quiet girl, secretive, you know? And in any case, I thought it was silly for them to be saying they were *engaged,* since they weren't planning to get married until after she graduated from college, and that was well over a year away. She was a junior at the time.

"And then, in October of the following year—about five months after my mother died—the two of them disappeared."

Lydia Barrie was reticent for a moment. Staring into her drink. Miles wondered whether he ought to tell her about how obsessed Hayden used to be with orphans. How they used to play pretend games when they were children in which they were orphans in danger, runaway orphans, how he used to love this children's book, *The Secret Garden,* about a little orphan girl . . .

But perhaps this wasn't the best time to mention it.

"I was so angry with her," Lydia Barrie said, at last, softly. "We hadn't been talking. I was upset with her, because she hadn't come to our mother's funeral, and so we were out of contact, and it was actually some time before I realized that she was not in school anymore. And there was no way to reach her.

"They left town together, apparently, but no one knew where they were going, and they effectively . . . Well, it probably doesn't sound ridiculous to you if I say that they vanished."

And she looked at Miles with her large, prominent eyes, and he was aware of how pale her skin was, almost transparent, like onion paper through which he could discern her delicate veins. He watched as she reached up and pushed a strand of hair behind her ear.

"My family hasn't seen Rachel since," Lydia Barrie said.

Rachel, he thought. He recalled her name, the name he had been given by Hayden's friends from the math department.

That girl, peering out of the door of the crumbling rental house, the screen door with the torn flap in its mesh, the dusty sofa parked underneath the front bay windows.

It came to him with a shudder. His own appearance in the story that Lydia Barrie had been telling. He had been following it, almost abstractly, picturing that December scene, Hayden in the living room with the mute quivering mother, the two of them staring into the fire, under the shadow of a blinking Christmas tree; Hayden at the breakfast table with these women, buttering toast and talking in his stagy British accent, which, Miles remembered, was one of his favorites; Hayden placing his arm across Rachel Barrie's shoulder as gift-wrapped packages were being distributed, a carol playing from the stereo.

He saw all of this in his mind as he listened, as if he were watching the grainy, sweetly sad home videos of some strangers, and then abruptly Rachel Barrie's eye appeared in a door crack and gazed out at him.

I know who you are, she said. *I'll call the police if you don't leave.*

The two of them, Miles and Lydia, sat there at the bar, both of them quiescent. She lifted her glass, and even though there were other people in the bar, talking and laughing, and there was music playing, he was aware of the faint xylophone rattle of ice in her glass.

"I think I saw your sister, once," he said. And then, seeing her expression brighten, he amended quickly.

"In Rolla," he said. "It was about five years ago. It must have been right before they . . ."

"I see," she said.

He shrugged regretfully—he was familiar with the way those sparks of information could light up and then extinguish. The repeated letdowns, the discouragement.

"I'm sorry," he said.

"No, no," she said. "I didn't mean to seem—disappointed." She looked down at her glass, touched the condensation along the rim.

"It's been ages since I've met anyone who's actually seen her. So: tell me everything you remember. It's important, and useful, even the small things. Did she speak with you at all?"

"Well," he said.

It felt as if there were an intimacy in the way that her eyes had settled on him, waiting, damp and sadly hopeful. What could he tell her? He had talked with some people, other graduate students whom, no doubt, she had also talked to; he had gone to that house, where Rachel was living, and she had come to the door briefly, but she hadn't said much, had she? Just threatened to call the police—which had scared him, he guessed. He was a coward about authority, he had always felt that the cops would side against him, how could you explain a person like Hayden, after all, without sounding crazy? *I know who you are,* Rachel said. *I* will *call the police.*

And why hadn't he been more persistent? Why hadn't he pushed his way inside, sat down with the poor girl and told her exactly who he was, and who Hayden was?

He could have helped her, he thought. He could have *saved* her.

He looked back down at his hand. Even in identical twins, the fingerprints, the creases of the palm, were distinct, and for a moment he imagined telling Lydia this random fact, he didn't know why.

In the beginning, Lydia had tried to contact the authorities. But they hadn't been particularly concerned or helpful.

After that, there had been a series of private detectives.

"But that was very expensive," she said. "I'm not a wealthy person, and in any case, I never managed to hire anyone who was especially bright. They just followed one dead end after the other, charging me hourly plus per diems all the way through, and getting nowhere. Not with your brother.

"These detectives would spend, I don't know—hundreds and thousands of dollars—and then they would come back to me with these ridiculous things. A post office box in Sedona, Arizona. An Internet polling company in Manada Gap, Pennsylvania. An abandoned motel in Nebraska. And then one of them wanted money to pursue some *international leads,* as he called them. Ecuador. Russia. Africa.

"And for a while, I suppose I convinced myself that I was getting somewhere. That I was getting closer, even though—"

She smiled tightly, wearily, and Miles nodded.

"Yes," he said.

He knew the exhaustion that a person began to feel after a few years. Trying to find Hayden required a particular stamina, a patience for small details that might lead nowhere, the perseverance of a cartographer who was mapping a shoreline that wound and raveled into the horizon, that you'd never reach the end of.

He sometimes thought about the autumn after their father died. That was when Hayden had been fascinated with irrational numbers, with the Fibonacci numbers and the golden ratio, making drawings of rectangles and nautilus shells and meticulously filling pages and pages of a notebook with the infinite decimal extension of the ratio.

Miles, meanwhile, found his first semester of algebra almost unbearable. He would look at the equations and he couldn't make them *mean* anything, nothing but a spidery scuttling behind his forehead, as if the numbers had turned into insects inside his brain. He would sit there and glare at the problems—or, worse, he would begin to do them and his own solutions would somehow detour onto an unexplainably wrong track, so that for a time he'd believe that he'd finally figured out a method—only to discover that, in fact, x did not equal 41.7. No, x equaled -1, though he had no idea how that was possible. Sitting before a work sheet of these equations, night after night, was the worst fatigue he'd ever experienced, so eventually his mind felt like it had been eaten away into a lace of thin, almost weightless threads.

"Oh, *please,*" Hayden used to say, and he would gently take the paper from Miles and show him, once again, how easy it was. "You're such a baby, Miles," Hayden said. "Just pay attention. It's simple if you just take it in steps."

But Miles was frequently near tears by that point. "I can't do it," he would say. "I can't think the right way!"

It was that frustration, that sense of futility he would later remember when he began looking for Hayden. He could see the same thing in Lydia Barrie's expression.

Lydia combed her fingers gently through her hair, and looked down critically at her highball glass, which was empty, save for a lime slice that was curled into the fetal position at the bottom. She was, Miles thought, a little drunk, and she looked less refined and dignified. Her hair hadn't fallen back into its previously sculpted form, and a few strands were awry. When the noncommittal pony-tailed bartender came over to see if she wanted another drink, she nodded. Miles was still working on his beer.

The bar was dark and windowless, and replicated the pleasant feeling of night, though outside the sun was still shining.

"It's funny," Lydia said, and she watched gloomily as first a napkin, and then the refilled glass, was placed on the bar in front of her. "Honestly, I suppose I must have spent thirty thousand dollars on these detectives, and after a while I think I just kept pressing forward because I didn't want to believe that the whole thing was a waste.

"I don't know," she said, and drew a breath. "I suppose I can understand why Rachel would leave and never contact me again. I can understand why she wouldn't want to speak with me. I said some very unkind things to her, when she didn't come to our mother's funeral. I said some things that I regret.

"But she hasn't contacted our sister Emily, either. Or Aunt Charlotte. I understand that she was very unhappy, and maybe she was so devastated by our mother's death that she couldn't stand to face it.

"But who just abandons their family in that way? What kind of person decides that they can throw everything away and—*reinvent* themselves. As if you could just discard the parts of your life that you didn't want anymore.

"Sometimes I think, well, that's where we are now, as a society. That's just what people have become, these days. We don't value connection."

She peered at him, and the composure she'd had when they first met had dissipated. There was a precarious aura in the air, an unnerving weight.

"I've done some things," she said. "I've slept with people that I never talked to afterward. I left a job once. I left on a Friday and I didn't call or tell my boss that I quit, or anything. I just never went back. I once told a man I worked with that I went to Wellesley— I guess that I was trying to impress him, and when he asked me about people he knew who had graduated from Wellesley, I pretended I knew them. Because I wanted him to like me.

"But I never *disappeared*," she said. Her hand closed around her drink, her manicured nails, and her fingertips flattened and blanched against the glass. "I never vanished, so that no one could find me. That's a bit extreme, isn't it? That's not normal, is it?"

"No," Miles said. "I don't think it's normal."

"Thank you," she said. She gathered herself, straightened, ran the flat of her palms against the front of her blouse. "Thank you."

Perhaps she was as crazy as he was, Miles thought, though he wasn't sure if that was a comforting thought. Perhaps there were people all over the world whose lives Hayden had ruined, they were a club, a matrix that crisscrossed over the map, who knew how many there were? Hayden's influence expanding outward like the Fibonacci numbers he used to recite—1, 1, 2, 3, 5, 8, 13, 21, 34, 55, 89 . . . and so on.

Meanwhile, Lydia Barrie had pressed the heel of her palm

against her forehead and closed her eyes. Miles thought that perhaps she'd fallen asleep, and he thought about sleep himself. He was so tired—so tired—so many hours of driving, so many hours of daylight and thinking, thinking.

But then Lydia lifted her head.

"Do you think she's still alive?" she whispered.

It took Miles a moment to realize what she was asking.

"Well," he said. "I don't know what you mean."

"I think he might have killed her," Lydia Barrie said. "That's what I mean. I think she might be buried somewhere, anyplace, any one of the places that I've traced them to, or someplace I don't know about. That's why—"

But she didn't finish. She didn't necessarily want to continue with this line of thinking, and so she only sat there, her palm pressed against her face.

"Of course not," Miles said. "I don't think he's—"

Though in fact he *did* think so. He imagined, once again, their old house on fire, he could picture his mother and Mr. Spady in their bed on the second floor, perhaps waking up too late, the room filled with smoke—or perhaps not waking up at all, perhaps only a few seconds of struggle, their eyelids fluttering awake and then closing again as the oxygen vanished and the wallpaper lit up with trickles of flame.

Was it so far-fetched to imagine that Hayden had done something to Rachel Barrie?

"I have some papers upstairs in my room," Lydia Barrie said thickly. "I have some—documents." He observed her as she brought her gin and tonic into the air. As she touched the edge of the glass to her lips.

"I think they are authentic," she said, and took a long sip from her drink. "I think they'll be of interest to you."

17

Sometimes Ryan imagined that he saw people from his past. Ever since his death, this had become a regular occurrence, these minor hallucinations, tricks of perception.

Here, for example, was his mother, standing on a busy street corner on Hennepin Avenue in Minneapolis, her back to him, opening an umbrella as she hurried into a crowd.

Here was Walcott, sitting in the window of a bus full of rowdily singing fraternity brothers. This was in Philadelphia, not far from Penn, and Ryan stood there staring as they were borne past, all of them tunelessly caroling along with Bob Marley.

Their eyes met, his and Walcott's, and for a second Ryan could have sworn that it truly *was* him, though the Walcott on the bus just peered out at him, his mouth moving, "Every little thing gonna be all right," they were singing, and Ryan was aware of motion passing over him, a shadow of a bird or a cloud.

This is what it would be like to see a ghost, he thought, even though he was the one who was dead.

He knew it wasn't really them. He was aware that it was just a trailing cobweb of subconscious, a misfiring synapse of memory, an undigested bit of the past playing games with him. He had been letting his mind wander too much, he thought; that was all it meant. He needed to focus. He needed to meditate, as Jay suggested. "You need to find the silence inside yourself," Jay advised, and one day when he was back from a particularly stressful trip, they listened together to one of Jay's relaxation CDs. "Picture a circle of energy near the base of your spine," the CD told them, while they sat in chairs in the darkened back bedroom, their bare feet on the floor. "Inhale . . . exhale . . . letting your breathing become deep and even . . ."

And it *was* relaxing, actually, though it didn't really help. The next week, in Houston, he thought he saw Pixie—her hair longer and darker but still recognizable—the very image of Pixie, in fact, smoking a cigarette on the curb outside the downtown Marriott, looking bored and wistful as she toyed with the thin ring in her eyebrow.

No.

It wasn't her, he realized, he could see as soon as he stepped out of the taxi that this woman was probably in her thirties or even forties. Why had he even thought there was a resemblance? It was as if she had only been Pixie for a second, appearing just for a few shuttering snapshots out of the corner of his eye. Another little con game his brain had played on him.

Still.

Still, he thought, it was not entirely impossible—even in a country of three hundred million—it was not beyond the realm of possibility that he might eventually encounter someone he once knew.

In fact, he was pretty certain he had actually seen his old psychology professor, Ms. Gill, in an airport bar in Nashville. His connecting flight had been late, and he had been lingering in the terminal of Nashville International, pulling his wheeled carry-on past newsstands and fast-food booths and souvenir shops, looking for some way to distract himself, and there, suddenly, she had been. Sitting in the Gibson Café underneath some guitar memorabilia, she had regarded him casually as he walked by. And then their eyes had connected, and he saw her expression tighten, a startle of attentiveness crossing her face.

It appeared as if she recognized him from somewhere; he saw her puzzling. His head was shaved, and he was wearing aviator sunglasses, and a short-sleeved security guard's uniform, so it was surprising that she would even look twice. But she did. Wasn't he one of her former students? Didn't he look like that boy who had died—who had committed suicide—the one who had been failing her class, who had come to her office to see if there was any way he could do work for extra credit?

No. She wouldn't have made that connection. It was only that he looked vaguely familiar, and she scrutinized him for a second, a sad, single professor lady with a bad haircut and an overbite, she had perhaps contemplated suicide herself, she had thought about that kid, drowning himself in the lake, and she had wondered what that would feel like, she herself had always thought that carbon monoxide would be the way to go, carbon monoxide and sleeping pills, no struggle . . .

And he walked by and she put her vodka and cranberry juice to her lips and he thought about Jay's meditation audios.

"The next energy level is near your forehead," the woman narrator said, in her soothing, dreamy monotone. "Here is the chakra of time, the circle of daylight and nighttime in their eternal passages, which will guide you to awareness of your soul. Let yourself free your mind, and as you accept the power and awe of your own soul, so will you realize the soul within everyone and everything."

He thought of this as he queued himself into the line at the airline check-in desk, and he placed his fingers lightly to his brow.

"That's where the pineal gland is," Jay had told him. "That's where your melatonin comes from, and it regulates your sleep cycle. That's cool, isn't it?"

"Yeah," Ryan had said. "Interesting!"

Though now he wondered what Ms. Gill would have had to say about it all. She had been skeptical, as he remembered, with no patience for New Agey nonsense, and he looked over his shoulder.

Despite his talk of meditation and relaxation and so forth, Jay had been feeling anxious lately, too.

"God damn it, Ryan," he said. "Your jitters are starting to rub off on me. I've got the fucking fantods, man."

Ryan was sitting at one of the laptops, opening a bank account for one of his new acquisitions—Max Wimberley, age twenty-three, of Corvallis, Oregon—and he glanced up, still typing, filling in the blocks of information on the application.

"What's a fantod?" he said.

"I don't know," Jay said. He was at a computer of his own, tapping on the escape key with his index finger, and he shook his head at the screen, irritably. "It's just some old-timey Iowa word that my dad used to use. It's like, when a goose walks over your grave. Do you know that saying?"

"Not exactly," Ryan said, and Jay let out an abrupt, particularly foul set of curses.

"I can't believe this," Jay said, and he smacked the palm of his hand down onto his keyboard, hard enough that two of the letter keys popped out and bounced onto the floor with a small rattle, like a pair of dice. "God damn it!" Jay said. "I've got a bug on this computer! That's the third time this week!"

Jay pushed his hair back from his face, tucked it behind his ears, combing the sides of his head nervously with his fingers.

"Something is going on here," he said. "I've got a bad feeling, Ryan. I don't like it."

Ryan wasn't sure what to think. Jay could get temperamental some-times. He liked to act as if he were the mellow, easygoing philo-sophical type, but he had his own superstitions, his own fears and illogics.

For example, there was that argument they'd had about the dri-ver's licenses. This was back when Ryan had first left college and started working for Jay, back when he was going to the DMVs, trav-eling to various states.

Back then, Ryan didn't truly understand what he was doing. He figured that it was illegal somehow, but then again a lot of things were illegal and they didn't necessarily hurt anybody. He was still trying to get his mind around what was happening to him. His de-cision to leave college. His failure to call his parents, the "search" for him that he had somehow managed to lose control of. He was still trying to adjust to the idea that Jay was his real father, that Stacey and Owen had been lying to him for his whole life.

Participating in a little shady activity fit in with the general murk-iness of his thought process at the time.

Besides which, it wasn't as if he were robbing a bank. It wasn't as if he were mugging old ladies or cheating orphans. Instead, he'd spent a lot of time waiting. Standing in line. Sitting in plastic chairs against the wall across from the Department of Motor Vehicles counter. Reading Wanted posters that had been taped to the wall, various public service things about drunken driving and wearing seat belts and so on.

He watched the other people as they took their tests and made their applications, paying attention to the questions they were asked, the snags they ran into—no social security card, no birth cer-tificate, no proof of residency.

After a while, he had come to be particularly interested in the issue of organ donation. For the clerks, it was a rote question. "Would you like to be an organ donor?" the clerks would ask, monotone, reciting: "Joining the donor registry is a way to legally give consent to the donation of your organs, tissues, and eyes upon your death, for any purposes authorized by law. You could save up to seven lives through organ donation and enhance the quality of life for over fifty others through tissue and eye donation. May I take this opportunity to sign you into the registry?"

Ryan was surprised by how many people were taken aback by this question. In Knoxville, for example, there was one old hippie man, gray ponytail and cutoff jean shorts, who had laughed aloud. He looked over his shoulder at the rest of them, as if a joke were being played on him. Ryan watched as the man's grin wavered, as the man thought briefly about his own death. Being cut up and taken apart. "Heh, heh," the man said, and then he shrugged, making an expansive motion of his hand. "Why . . . sure!" he said. "Sure, by God, why not?" As if this were an act of bravado that the rest of them would be impressed by.

In Indianapolis, there was the old woman in her lemon-yellow jacket and pants, who paused for a long time to think about it. She became very grave, folding her hands over each other. "I'm sorry," she said. "We don't believe in that."

In Baltimore, there was the tough-looking hip-hop guy, muscle T-shirt pulled tight over his chest, jeans sagging down to show his boxer shorts. But he drew back from the clerk in genuine—almost childlike—horror. "No, ma'am," he said. "Uh-uh." As if someone might be waiting in the back room with a saw and a scalpel.

As for Ryan, he didn't have any qualms. It was a basic social good, like giving blood or whatever. Just the right thing to do, he thought, until he had come home that weekend with his cache of fake IDs.

"What the fuck?" Jay said. He had been in a good mood until he had started to look at the licenses that Ryan had given him. "Ryan, dude, you signed up as an organ donor on every goddamn one of these things."

"Uh . . . ," Ryan said. "Yeah?"

"What the hell," Jay said—and his face reddened in a way that Ryan had not yet seen. Jay cultivated a slacker look, his straight black hair down to his shoulders, vintage thrift store clothes. But his expression became impressively hard and threatening. "What the hell were you thinking, man?" Jay said, and gritted his teeth abruptly. "Are you out of your mind? These are ruined!"

"But—" Ryan said. "I'm sorry, I don't get what you're saying."

"Jesus Christ," Jay said. "Ryan, what happens when you add your name to a state organ donor registry?" His voice had grown lower, and he spoke slowly and rhetorically, enunciating Organ. Donor. Registry. Each word a balloon he was poking with a pin.

"I don't know," Ryan said. He was flabbergasted, and he tried to speak lightly, a cautious, apologetic shrug. But Jay didn't stop glaring at him.

"Do you realize that you consented to give the federal and state government access to your private medical and social history? Any confidentiality between you and a doctor is now moot. They are now legally allowed to examine current and past medical records, laboratory tests, blood donations—"

"I didn't know that," Ryan said, and he looked at Jay uncertainly. Was he joking? "Are you sure? That doesn't sound—"

"Doesn't sound what?" said Jay fiercely.

"I don't know," Ryan said again. He thought: *It doesn't sound true.* But he didn't say that.

"You don't know," Jay said. "Did you read the contract you signed?"

"I didn't sign a contract."

"Of course you signed a fucking contract," Jay said, and now his voice was hot with disgust. Controlled contempt. "You just didn't read it, dude. Did you? They told you to sign on the line and you signed, isn't that right? Isn't that what you did?"

"Jay," Ryan said, "it wasn't even my own name."

"Do you think that matters?" Jay said. "The names on these cards are *our* names. We worked hard to harvest these names. They're like

gold to us. And now they are open to government surveillance. Totally useless!" He shook one of the laminated cards between his
thumb and forefinger, repulsed by it, and then flipped it across the
room, where it hit the wall with a tick. "Completely. Ruined. Shit!
Do you get that?"

There were things about Jay that he still hadn't figured out—the
unpredictable bursts of temper, the oddities of philosophy, the supposed facts that sounded made-up, which Ryan guessed were
mostly gleaned from conspiracy theory websites.

Did Jay really believe in the stuff about chakras, for example?
Was he serious when he consulted the Ouija board on the coffee
table, or when he began to hold forth on various "shadow government" organizations such as the Omega Agency and secret societies
such as the Bilderberg Group and the Order of Skull and Bones at
Yale, and the global surveillance network, Echelon—

"We have no idea what our government is up to," Jay said, and
Ryan nodded uncertainly.

"That's why I've never felt like I'm a criminal," Jay said. "The
people who control this country are the real gangsters. You know
that, right? And if you play by their rules, you're nothing but their
slave."

"Uh-huh," Ryan said, and tried to read Jay's expression.

Was he kidding? Was he a bit crazy?

There were times when Ryan was aware that the choices he'd
made would come across as incredibly reckless to an outside ob-
server. Why would he leave behind a pair of stable, loving parents,
and throw his lot in with someone like Jay? Why would he abandon
a good college education to become a petty con man, a professional liar and thief? Why was he so relieved that he would never
have to be part of his nice family again, that he would never have to
take another class, that he would never have to put together a ré-
sumé and go out on a job interview, that he would never have to try

to get married and have a family of his own and participate in the various cyclical joys of middle-class life that Owen had been so attached to?

The truth was, he was actually more like Jay than he was like them; that was what they didn't ever realize.

Stacey and Owen's life, he thought, was no more real than the dozens that he had created in the last year, the virtual lives of Matthew Blurton or Kasimir Czernewski or Max Wimberley. Most people, he thought, had identities that were so shallow that you could easily manage a hundred of them at once. Their existence barely grazed the surface of the world.

Of course, if you wanted to, you could inhabit one or two personas that accumulated more weight. If you wanted, Jay said, you could have wives, families even. He said he knew of a guy who was on a city council in Arizona, and who also ran a real estate business in Illinois, and who was also a traveling salesman with a wife and three children in North Dakota.

And then there were the people who could actually be a single, significant individual. You would have to start work on such a persona from very early on, Ryan thought, maybe from childhood. You'd need a certain precise confidence and focus, and all the abstract elements of luck and circumstance would have to arrange themselves around you. Like, for example, becoming a rock star, building a talent and a name for yourself, working your way into the public eye. He had thought about that a lot, he had liked the idea of turning into a well-known, respected singer-songwriter, but he was also aware that he was never going to be quite good enough. He could sense his own limitations, he could intuit the road blocks that were just a ways down the path of that particular ambition, and truthfully, if you knew you were going to probably fail, then what was the point? Why bother? If you could have dozens of lesser lives, didn't that add up to one big one?

———

He thought of this again as he maneuvered his way through the airport in Portland, Oregon. The rental car safely abandoned, the prepaid wireless phone crushed under the heel of his shoe and dropped into a trash can, the brand new Max Wimberley driver's license and plane ticket produced for the security officer at the front of the passenger security line, his backpack and laptop and shoes and belt and wallet placed in plastic tubs and sent along their way through the X-ray machine on the conveyor belt, and then he himself, Max Wimberley, motioned forward, passing through the doorway-shaped metal detector. All without incident. All simple, no problem, nothing to worry about at all. Max Wimberley could move through the world with much more ease and grace than Ryan Schuyler could have ever managed.

"Okay," he murmured to himself. "Okay."

He sat there in the boarding area, with a chocolate frozen yogurt shake and a copy of *Guitar* magazine, his backpack in the seat beside him. He made a quick, surreptitious scan of the other people in the seats around him. Youngish, tightly wound businesswoman with a palm pilot. Elderly hand-holding couple. Jocky Asian guy in a Red Sox cap. Etc.

No one who looked at all familiar.

There hadn't been any hallucinations on this trip, and he supposed that was a sign. The last vestiges of his old life were finally fading away. The transformation was almost complete, he thought, and he remembered those long-ago days when he drove around trying to compose a letter to his parents in his head.

Dear Mom and Dad, he thought. *I am not the person you thought I was.*

I am not that person, he thought, and he remembered those Kübler-Ross stages Jay had told him about. This was what acceptance felt like. It wasn't just that Ryan Schuyler was dead; Ryan Schuyler had never existed in the first place. Ryan Schuyler was just a shell he had been using, maybe even less real than Max Wimberley was.

He looked down at his boarding pass, and he could almost feel the residue of Ryan Schuyler exhaling out of him, a little ghostly bat with a human face, which dissolved into a shower of tiny gnats and dispersed.

"Okay," he whispered, and closed his eyes briefly. "Okay."

It was late and warm when he arrived in Detroit Metro, 1:44 A.M. after a connection in Phoenix, and he walked purposefully through the hushed terminal toward the long-term parking garage, where Jay's old Econoline van was waiting for him. He stopped at a gas station to buy an energy drink, and then he was on the interstate, feeling very calm, he thought, listening to music. He rolled the windows down and sang for a while.

North of Saginaw, he turned west onto a highway, and then onto a county two-lane, over some railroad tracks, the houses farther and farther apart, his headlights illuminating the tunnels of woods, some trees beginning to bud with spring leaves, some dead bare skeleton branches mummified in a gauze of old tent caterpillar webs, with only occasional squares of human habitation cut out alongside the road. Back in the 1920s, according to Jay, the Purple Gang from Detroit had one of their hideouts up this way.

At last, he turned onto the narrow asphalt lane that would eventually turn into a dirt road that led up to the cabin, deeper into the forest. It was about four in the morning. He saw the lights of the porch shining and as he pulled up he could hear that Jay had his music going, a thump of old-school hip-hop, and he noticed that a couple of Jay's computers had been tossed out into the gravel driveway. They looked like someone had taken a baseball bat to them.

And in fact, just as Ryan turned off the ignition, Jay came out onto the porch carrying a silver aluminum bat in one hand and a Glock revolver in the other.

"Fucking hell, Ryan," Jay said, and he tucked his revolver into the waistband of his pants as Ryan stepped out of the car. "What took you so long?"

In general, Jay didn't tend to carry guns around, although there were a number of them in the cabin, and Ryan wasn't sure how to react. He could see that Jay was fairly drunk, fairly stoned, in a mood, and so he took vigilant steps across the gravel as he approached the house.

"Jay?" he said. "What's wrong?"

He followed Jay onto the screened porch, past the cast-iron woodstove and the cheap lawn furniture, and into the living room of the cabin, where Jay was in the process of dismantling another computer. He was unplugging various wires and USB cords from the back panel of the machine, and when Ryan came in, he paused, running his fingers through his long hair.

"You're not going to believe this," Jay said. "I think some asshole has stolen my identity!"

"You're kidding," Ryan said. He stood there uncertainly in the doorway, and watched as Jay lugged the disconnected computer off the table and let it fall heavily, like a cement block, to the floor.

"What do you mean, 'stolen' your identity?" Ryan said. "Which one?"

Jay looked up, blankly, holding a limp cord as if it were a snake he had just strangled. "Christ," he said. "I'm not sure. I'm starting to feel concerned that they all might be contaminated."

"Contaminated?" Ryan said. Despite the fact that Jay was carrying around a revolver and dismantling computers, he still looked relatively calm. He wasn't as intoxicated as Ryan had thought at first, either, which made things seem more serious. "What do you mean, contaminated?" he said.

"I lost two people today," Jay said, and he bent down and pulled an old laptop out of a cardboard box that had been shoved under one of the tables at the back of the living room. "All of my Dave Deagle credit cards have been canceled, so somebody must have gotten into him a few days ago. And I started to get nervous and I started to go through everybody, and it turned out that someone had cleaned out Warren Dixon's money market account, some fishy electronic transfer—and this happened, like, this morning!"

"You're joking," Ryan said. He observed as Jay began to attach the old laptop to various plugs, watched the machine begin to quiver as it booted up.

"I wish I *was* joking," Jay said, and he stared hard at his screen as it sang out its tiny melody of start-up music. "You better get your ass online and start checking your people. I think we might be under attack."

Under attack. It might have sounded silly and melodramatic, out here in the woods, in this room that looked like a cross between a college dorm room and a computer repair store, the thrift store couch surrounded by tables that were cluttered with dozens of computers, beer cans, candy wrappers, printers, fax machines, dirty plates, ashtrays. But Jay had tucked the revolver into the waistband of his jeans, and his mouth pulled back in a grimace as he typed, and so Ryan didn't say anything.

"You know what?" Jay said. "Why don't you buy us some plane tickets? See if you can get us some reservations for someplace out of the country. Anyplace that's third world is fine. Pakistan. Ecuador. Tonga. See what deals you can get."

"Jay . . . ," Ryan said, but he sat down at the computer as he had been instructed.

"Don't worry," Jay said. "We're going to be fine. We have to pull together, here, but I think we're going to be totally fine."

18

Lucy and George Orson were in the old pickup together, on their way to a post office in Crawford, Nebraska. It was the perfect place to submit their passport applications, according to George Orson, though Lucy wasn't sure why this town was better than another, why they had to drive three hours when there were surely a lot of cruddy post offices closer to home. But she didn't bother to pursue the matter further. She had a lot on her mind at the moment.

The sense of relief she'd felt when she'd discovered the stacks of cash had begun to dissipate, and now she was aware again of a flutter in her stomach. She had a memory of that roller coaster at the Cedar Point amusement park, back in Ohio. Millennium Force, with its three-hundred-ten-foot drop, the way you would wait there, once you were strapped in, the heavy ticking of the chain as you were pulled slowly up the slope to the top of the hill. That terrible anticipation.

But she was trying to appear calm. She sat subdued in the passenger seat of the old pickup, watching as George Orson shifted gears, wearing the hideous pink shirt George Orson had bought for her, with its cloud of smiley-faced butterflies printed down the front. This was his idea of what a fifteen-year-old girl might wear—

"It makes you look younger," he said. "That's the point."

"It makes me look retarded," she said. "Maybe I should act like I'm mentally handicapped?" And she extended her tongue, making a thick cave girl grunt. "Because I can't think of any fifteen-year-old who would wear this shirt, unless she was in some kind of special education group home situation."

"Oh, Lucy," George Orson said. "You look fine. You look the part, that's all that matters. Once we're out of the country, you can wear whatever you want."

And Lucy hadn't argued any further. She just looked balefully at her reflection in the bedroom mirror: a stranger she'd taken an instant dislike to.

She was particularly upset about the hair. She hadn't realized that she'd been attached to her original hair color—which was auburn, with some highlights of red—until she had seen what it looked like when she dyed it.

George Orson had been insistent about this—their hair, he said, should be approximately the same color, since they were supposed to be father and daughter—and he came home from his trip to the store with not only the horrible pink butterfly shirt but also a bag full of hair dye.

"I bought six of them," he said. He put a grocery bag on the kitchen table and drew out a glossy box with a female model on the front of it. "I couldn't decide which one of them was right."

The color they'd eventually chosen was called brown umber, and to Lucy it looked like someone had painted her hair with shoe polish.

"You just have to wash it a few times," George Orson said. "It looks fine now, but it will look completely natural once you've worn it for a couple of days."

"My scalp hurts," Lucy said. "In a couple of days, I'll probably be bald."

And George Orson had put his arm around her shoulder. "Don't be ridiculous," he murmured. "You look terrific."

"Mm," she said, and regarded herself in the mirror.

She did not look *terrific,* that was certain. But perhaps she looked like a fifteen-year-old girl.

Brooke Catherine Fremden. A dull, friendless girl, probably pathologically shy. Probably a little like her sister, Patricia.

Patricia used to have anxiety attacks. That was what Lucy was thinking about as she sat in the pickup on the way to Crawford, her heart vibrating oddly in her chest. Patricia would exhibit all kinds of bizarre symptoms when she was having an "attack": her forehead and arms would feel numb, she would have the sensation of bugs in her hair, she would think her throat was closing up. Very melodramatic, Lucy had thought then, unsympathetically. She remembered standing in the bedroom doorway, impatiently eating a piece of toast, with her book bag over her shoulder as their mother urged Patricia to breathe into a lunch sack. "I'm suffocating!" Patricia gasped, her voice muffled by brown paper. "Please don't make me go to school!"

It all looked very fake to Lucy, though she wouldn't have wanted to go to school, either, if she were Patricia. This was during a period when a group of especially mean seventh-grade boys had singled Patricia out for some reason, they had developed a whole elaborate series of comic routines and sketches that involved Patricia as a character, "Miss Patty Stinkbooty," who they pretended was the host of a children's program with puppets that they also had a series of goofy voices for. All kinds of idiotic gross boy humor that had to do with Patricia farting, or menstruating, or having cockroaches crawling in her pubic hair. Lucy could remember the three of them during lunch, Josh and Aaron and Elliot—she still even remembered their stupid names, three nasty, skinny boys doing their routine at their cafeteria table, laughing and chortling until the milk they were drinking came out of their noses.

And Lucy herself had done nothing. Had merely observed stoically as if she were watching some particularly gruesome TV nature program in which jackals killed a baby hippopotamus.

Poor Patricia! she thought now, and placed her hand to her throat, which felt a bit tight, and her face felt a little numb and tingly.

But she was not going to have an anxiety attack, she told herself.

She was in control of her body, and she refused to let it panic. She placed her hands on her thighs, and let out an even breath, staring fixedly at the glove compartment.

She imagined that all of the money from the safe were there inside that glove compartment. And they weren't in a pickup. They were in the Maserati, and they weren't driving through the sand hills of Nebraska, which, as far as she could see, weren't even sandy, but just an endless lake of rolling hills, covered with thin gray grass and rocks.

They were in the Maserati and they were driving on a road that overlooked the ocean, a Mediterranean blue ocean with some sailboats and yachts floating in it. She closed her eyes and slowly began to fill her lungs with air.

And when she opened her eyes, she felt better, though she was still in a pickup truck, and she was still in Nebraska, where some freaky rock formations were cluttered along the horizon. Were they called mesas? Buttes? They looked like they were from Mars.

"George," she said, after she had gathered herself for a minute or so. "I was just thinking about the Maserati. What are we going to do with the Maserati?"

He didn't say anything. He had been mute for an unusually long time, and she thought that was what had brought on her nervousness, the lack of his conversation, which, despite everything, still might have buoyed her. She wished he would rest his hand on her leg, like he used to do.

"George?" she said. "Are you still alive? Are you receiving transmissions?" And at last he turned to glance at her.

"You need to get out of the habit of calling me George," George Orson said at last, and his voice wasn't as soothing as she'd hoped. It was, in fact, a bit austere, which was disappointing.

"I suppose," she said, "that you want me to call you 'Dad.' "

"That's right," George Orson said. "I guess you could call me 'Father' if you prefer."

"Gross," Lucy said. "That's even weirder than calling you 'Dad.' Why can't I just call you David, or whatever?"

And George Orson had looked at her sternly—as if she really were just an impertinent fifteen-year-old. "*Because,*" he said. "Because you are supposed to be my daughter. It's not respectful. People notice it when a child calls a parent by their first name, especially in a conservative state such as this. And we don't want people to notice us. We don't want them to remember us when we leave. Does that make sense?"

"Yes," she said. She kept her hands in her lap, and when she felt her heart palpitate, she let out a breath. "Yes, Dad," she said. "That makes sense. But I sincerely hope, Dad, that you're not going to talk to me in that condescending tone all the way to Africa."

He glanced at her again, and there was a glint of an edge in his eyes, a hint of fury that made her flinch inwardly. She had not seen him truly angry before, and she realized now that she didn't want to. He would not be a very nice father, she realized. She didn't even know why, but she intuited it suddenly. He would be cold and demanding and impatient with his children, if he ever had them.

She thought this, even though his expression softened almost immediately.

"Listen," he said. "Sweetheart, I'm just a touch nervous about this. This is very serious business, now. You have to remember to answer to 'Brooke,' and you have to be sure that you never, ever call me George. It's very important. I know it's hard to get used to, but it's only temporary."

"I understand," she said, and she nodded, gazing again at the glove box. Out the window, she could see a rock formation that looked like a volcano, or a giant funnel.

"Do you see that up ahead?" George Orson said—David Fremden said. "That's called Chimney Rock. It's a national historic site."

"Yes," said Brooke.

It was weird to be a daughter again. Even a pretend one. A long time had passed since she'd thought about her own real father, for months and months she had been valiantly containing those memories, setting up walls and screens, pushing them back when they threatened to materialize in her daily consciousness.

But when she said the word "Dad," it was more difficult. Her father seemed to genie into her mind's eye as if decanted, his mild, round earnest face, his thick shoulders and bald head. In life, he had never seemed disappointed by her, and though she didn't believe in spirits, in an afterlife, she didn't believe, as Patricia did, that their dead parents hovered over them as angels—

Nevertheless, she felt a twinge when she called George Orson "Dad." A small stab of guilt, as if her father could know that she'd betrayed him, and for the first time since his death, he seemed to lean over her, palpable, not angry but just sort of hurt, and she was sorry.

She had truly loved him, she guessed.

She knew that, but it wasn't something she had allowed herself to think about, and so it came as a surprise.

He'd been a low-key presence in their house, without much of an opinion about the raising of girl children, though Lucy believed he was more temperamentally suited to her than her mother was.

He was a private person, like Lucy, with the same cynical sense of humor, and Lucy remembered how they used to sneak off together to see horror movies, which her mother would have forbidden— Patricia was the type of girl who had nightmares over a Halloween mask, or even a movie poster, let alone the actual film.

But Lucy wasn't scared. She and her father didn't go to such movies for thrills. Watching horror movies was oddly relaxing, for both Lucy and her father, it was like a kind of music that confirmed the way they felt about the world. A shared understanding, and Lucy never got frightened, not exactly. Occasionally when a monster or killer would pop out, she would put her hand on her father's arm, she would lean closer to him, and they would exchange a glance. A smile.

They understood each other.

All of this came to her as she and George Orson drove without a word, and she pressed her cheek against the glass of the passenger seat window, watching as a cloud of birds lifted up from a field, pulling up in a plume as they went past. Her thoughts were not clearly articulated in her mind, but she could feel them moving swiftly, gathering.

"What are you thinking about?" George Orson said, and when he spoke, her thoughts scattered, broke up into fragments of memories, the way that the birds separated out of their formation and back into individual birds. "You look as if you're deep in thought," George Orson said.

Dad said.

And she shrugged. "I don't know," she said. "I guess I'm feeling anxious."

"Ah," he said. He turned his eyes back to the road, touching his index finger lightly to the bridge of his sunglasses. "That's completely natural."

He reached over and patted his hand against her thigh, and she accepted this little gesture, though she wasn't sure if the hand belonged to George Orson or David Fremden.

"It's difficult at first," he said. "Making the switch. There's a bump you have to get past. You get used to one mode and one persona and there can be some cognitive dissonance, when you transfer over. I know exactly what you're talking about." He ran his hand along the circumference of the steering wheel, as if he were shaping it, molding it out of clay.

"Anxiety!" he said. "I've been there, plenty of times! And, you know, it's particularly hard during the first one, especially, because you're so invested in that idea of self. You grew up with that concept—you think there's a *real you*—and you have some long-standing attachments, people you've known, and you start to think about them. People you have to leave behind—"

He sighed, and even grew slightly wistful, maybe thinking about his late mother, or his brother who had drowned, some long-ago family outing on the pontoon when the lake was still full of water.

Or not.

It suddenly seemed so obvious.

What had George Orson said to her? *I've been a lot of people. Dozens.*

She had been in an alternate universe for a long time now, she thought, and she had been floating behind George Orson as if in a trance. And then abruptly, as they drove along toward the distant post office, she felt herself awaken. There was a flutter, a lifting, and then her thoughts began to fall into place.

He didn't have a brother, she thought.

He hadn't really grown up here, in Nebraska. He had never been a student at Yale; nothing he'd told her had been true.

"God," she said, and shook her head. "I'm so stupid."

And he glanced over at her, his eyes attentive and affectionate. "No, no," he said. "You're not stupid, honey. What's the matter?"

"I just realized something," Lucy said, and she glanced down to where his hand was still resting on her leg. His hand, she would recognize it anywhere, a hand that she had held, that she had put to her lips, a palm that she had traced her fingertips across.

"Your name isn't really George Orson, is it?" she said, and—

He was motionless. Still driving. Still wearing those sunglasses, which reflected the road and the rolling horizon, still the same man she had known.

"George Orson," she said. "That's not your real name," she said.

"No," he said.

He spoke gently, as if he were telling her bad news, and she thought of the way the policemen had come to their door on the day their parents were killed, the way they delivered the news in cautious intervals. *There had been a terrible accident. Their parents were severely injured. The paramedics had arrived at the scene. There wasn't anything the paramedics were able to do.*

She nodded, and she and George Orson looked at each other. There was a silent, tender embarrassment. Hadn't this been understood yesterday, when he showed the Ivory Coast bank account, when he'd produced their fake birth certificates? Hadn't it been obvious?

It should have been clear, she guessed, but only now did it begin to sink in.

She looked down at her pink T-shirt, her breasts pressed flat by a sports bra.

"That isn't really the house that you grew up in, is it?" she said, and her voice felt pressed flat as well. "The Lighthouse. All of the stuff you told me. That painting. That wasn't your grandmother."

"Hmm," he said, and he lifted his fingers from her thigh to gesture vaguely, an apologetic fluttering movement. "This is complicated," he said ruefully.

"It always comes to this," he said. "Everyone gets so hung up on what's real and not real."

"Yeah," Lucy said. "People are funny that way."

But George Orson only shook his head, as if she didn't get it.

"This may sound unbelievable to you," he said, "but the truth is, a part of me truly did grow up there. There isn't just *one* version of the past, you know. Maybe that seems crazy, but eventually, after we've done this for a while, I think you'll see. We can be anybody we want. Do you realize that?

"And that's all it comes down to," he said. "I loved being George Orson. I put a lot of thought and energy into it, and it wasn't *fake*. I wasn't trying to fool you. I did it because I liked it. Because it made me happy."

And Lucy let out a small, uncertain breath, thinking: a host of thoughts.

"Why would you want to be a high school teacher?" she said at last. It was the only thing that came to her clearly, the only one of the thoughts that could be articulated. "That doesn't sound fun at all."

"No, no," George Orson said, and he smiled at her hopefully, as if this were the exact right question—as if they were back in the classroom, discussing the difference between existentialism and nihilism—as if she'd raised her hand and she was his beloved student and he was excited to explain.

"It was one of the best things I've ever done," he said. "That year in Pompey. I always wanted to be a teacher, ever since I was a kid. And it was great. It was a fantastic experience."

He shook his head, as if he were still entranced by it. As if high school had been some exotic foreign land.

"And," he said, "I met you. I met you, and we fell in love, didn't we? Don't you understand, honey? You're the only person in the world I've ever been able to talk to. You're the only person in the world who loves me."

———

Had they fallen in love? She guessed they had, though now it felt like a weird idea, since it turned out that "George Orson" wasn't even a real person.

Thinking about it made her feel dizzy and squeamish. If you took away all of the pieces that made up George Orson—his Lighthouse Motel childhood and his Ivy League education, his funny anecdotes and subtly ironic teaching style and the tender, attentive concern he'd had for Lucy as his student—if all of that was just an invention, what was left? There was, presumably, someone inside the George Orson disguise, a personality, a pair of eyes peering out: a soul, she supposed you might call it, though she still didn't know the soul's real name.

Which one did she have feelings for—the character of George Orson, or the person who had created him? Which one had she been having sex with?

It was a bit like one of those word games George Orson had been so fond of offering up to their class—"Strange loops," he called them. *Moderation in all things, including moderation,* he said. *Is the answer to this question no? I never tell the truth.*

She could picture the way he had grinned when he said that. This was before she ever had an idea that she would become his girlfriend, long before she could have imagined that she would be driving to a post office in Nebraska with a fake birth certificate and reservations for a trip to Africa. "I never tell the truth," he told the class, was a version of the famous Epimenides paradox, and then he explained what a paradox was, and Lucy had written it down, thinking that it might be on a test, possibly she could get extra credit.

They had come now almost to the edge of Crawford, and George Orson—David Fremden—pulled over to consult the map he had downloaded from the Internet.

They had parked in front of a historical marker, and after he was finished examining his papers, George Orson sat there for a while, regarding the sign's metal tablet with interest.

Named for Army Captain Emmet Crawford, a Fort Robinson soldier, the city lies in the White River Valley in Pine Ridge country and serves an extensive cattle ranching and farming area. The Fort Laramie–Fort Pierre Fur Trail of 1840 and the Sidney–Black Hills Trail active during the Black Hills gold rush of the 1870s both passed through this site. Crawford has been host or home to such personages as Sioux Chief Red Cloud; former desperado David (Doc) Middleton; poet-scout John Wallace Crawford; frontierswoman Calamity Jane; Army scout Baptiste (Little Bat) Garnier, shot down in a saloon; military surgeon Walter Reed, conqueror of yellow fever; and President Theodore Roosevelt.

It was a sad piece of work, she thought.

Or at least she found it sad, at this juncture in her life. What had George Orson told their class once? "People like to contextualize themselves," he told them. "They like to feel they are connected to the larger forces of the world in some small way." And she recalled how he had tilted his head, as if to say: *Isn't that pathetic?*

"People like to think that what they do actually matters," he'd said, dreamy, bemused, passing his gaze over their faces, and she remembered how his eyes rested in particular upon her, and she'd straightened in her chair, a little flattered, a little flustered. And she'd gazed back at him and nodded.

Thinking of this, Lucy put her hand to her throat, which continued to have that constricted feeling, that anxiety attack feeling.

People like to think that what they do actually matters.

It had occurred to her that, in fact, her own proof of identity— Lucy Lattimore's birth certificate and social security card and so forth—were back in Pompey, Ohio, still in a plastic Ziploc bag in the top drawer of her mother's bureau, along with the ink prints of Lucy's baby feet, and her immunization history, and any other paperwork that her mother had deemed important.

She hadn't bothered to bring any of this stuff with her when she and George Orson had left town, and now, she realized, she probably had more documentation for Brooke Fremden than there was for her real self.

What would happen to Lucy Lattimore now, she wondered. If she no longer entered the public record, if she never held a job or applied for a driver's license or paid taxes or got married or had children, if she never died, would she still exist two hundred years from now, free-floating and unresolved in some record bank in some government dead-letter office computer? At some point, would they decide to expunge her from the official roster?

What if she could call someone? What if she could talk to her parents, for one last time, and tell them that she was alone and broke and about to fly to Africa under an assumed name? What advice would they give her? What would she even ask?

Mom, I'm thinking about not existing anymore, and I was just calling to ask your opinion.

The thought was almost enough to make her laugh, and David Fremden looked over to her as if he had noticed movement. Attentive and dad-like.

"In any case," he said. "I suppose we should get going."

19

Jay Kozelek was standing on the curb outside Denver International when a black Lexus cruised up alongside him and came to a stop. He watched as the tinted window on the driver's side slid down with a faint pneumatic hiss, and a thin, dapper blond dude peered out at him. A young guy, about twenty-four or twenty-five. Preppy: was that the right term?

"Mr. Kozelek, I presume?" this person said, and Jay stood there blinking.

Jay didn't know what he had been expecting, but it certainly wasn't this—this slick-looking character with his designer horn-rim glasses and his natty sports coat and turtleneck and his movie-star teeth. Meanwhile, here was Jay with his old hiker's backpack and army surplus jacket, wearing sweatpants, his hair pulled back and rubber-banded. Not washed in a while.

"Uh," he said, and the guy grinned, pleased with himself, as if he'd pulled off a good practical joke. Which, Jay guessed, he had— and so he tried out a sheepish smile, though he actually felt vaguely nervous. "Hey, Mike," he said, very mellow. "Where we headed? Out to your yacht?"

Mike Hayden regarded him. No reaction.

"Get in," Mike said, and there was a click as the rear door unlocked, and Jay balked just for a second before he climbed into the backseat, pulling his raggedy backpack behind him.

Was this a trap, maybe?

It was a brand-new car, with that leathery sweet chemical smell, spotless, and as Jay adjusted his knees, Mike Hayden turned around and offered his hand. "A pleasure," he said.

"Likewise," Jay said, and when he took Mike Hayden's hand, it was cool and dry. He was apparently not going to be asked to sit in the front seat, which was heaped with papers and a crumpled fast-food bag and a closed laptop and a smattering of cell phones—five of them, clustered in the debris like eggs in a nest.

Their eyes met, and though he didn't know what Mike Hayden's lingering look was meant to convey, there was this expectation in it, and he sat back in his seat as if he had been given a warning.

"It's wonderful to finally meet you in person, Jay," Mike Hayden said. "I'm so pleased that you decided to come."

"Yeah," Jay said, and then sat back as the car accelerated smoothly away from the curb, picking up speed as they slid in and out of the traffic that was nosing its way toward the airport exit, as they pulled onto the interstate and the rain clouds towered above them in the wide sky.

Jay and Mike Hayden had first met in an online chat room, one of those hidden, private spaces where hackers and trolls tended to gather, and they had hit it off right away.

This was back when Jay was living in a house in Atlanta with a bunch of computer nerds who thought of themselves as revolutionaries. The Association, they called themselves, which Jay tried to point out was the name of a horrible band from the 1960s. "You know those stupid songs. Like 'Windy.' Like 'Cherish.' " And he sang a line or two, but they just looked at him skeptically.

And so he was beginning to realize that he was a little too old to be living with them. They had some good ideas about moneymaking schemes, but they were just kids, very juvenile a lot of the time, sitting around watching bad horror movies or arguing about pop-culture crap, pop music and TV and comic books and various websites and memes that the housemates briefly became excited about. They were too stoned and lazy to manage much follow-through, but for Jay it was different. He was thirty years old! He had an actual child out there somewhere, even if the child didn't know that he was its dad. A son, fifteen years of age. Ryan. He figured it was about time to get into more serious business.

"I know what you mean," Mike Hayden had said, as they typed to each other in the chat room. "I'm interested in serious business as well."

At the time, Jay didn't know that the guy's name was Mike Hayden. The guy went by the user name "Breez," and he was well-known among certain circles of the Internet community. All the hackers in Jay's house were in awe of him. It was said that he had been personally involved in a huge national blackout, that he had managed to shut down power grids all across the Northeast and Midwest; it was said that he had stolen millions of dollars from several major banking firms, and that he had engineered the conviction of a Yale University professor on charges of trafficking in pedophilic photos.

"I wouldn't fuck around with that guy if I were you," said Dylan—one of Jay's housemates, a plump, bearded twenty-one-year-old kid from Colorado, with a face the shape of a yam. "That dude is, like, the Destroyer, man," Dylan said earnestly. "He'll trash your life just for the fun of it."

"Hmm," said Jay. It was an odd thing for Dylan to say, he thought, since Dylan and his buddies spent a good portion of their time playing mean, stupid practical jokes on the Internet—posting bestiality porn videos on some lady's bichon frise website, The Wonderful Fluffy World, and uploading graphic accident photos to message boards meant for children; terrorizing some poor girl who maintained a tribute site for a dead pop star they all loathed, sending hundreds of delivery pizzas to her house and getting her power turned off; hacking into the website for the National Epilepsy Foundation with a strobe-like animation they'd decided might send the epileptics into seizures. They sat around doing imitations of convulsions, and chortling wildly as Jay stood by watching with uneasy disapproval. It could get tiresome, he told Breez.

" 'Tiresome,' " said Breez. "That's a polite word for it."

It was about three in the morning, and Jay and Breez had been chatting companionably for a few hours. It was a nice change of pace, Jay thought, to talk to someone his own age, though also intimidating. Breez wrote in complete sentences, in paragraphs rather than long blocks of text, and he never misspelled words or used abbreviations or jargon.

"I do get a bit tired of all of these little trolls," Breez said. "All the antics and the middle school sense of humor. I'm beginning to think there should be a eugenics program for the Internet. Don't you think?"

Jay wasn't sure what the word 'eugenics' meant, and so he waited. Then he typed: "Yeah. Absolutely."

"It's nice to meet someone with some common sense," Breez said. "Most people just can't accept the truth. You know what I mean. Do they think we can just continue on like this, all this babble and bullshit, as if we're not on the edge of ruin? Do they not see it? The Arctic ice cap is melting. We've got dead zones in the oceans that are expanding astronomically. The bees are dying, and the frogs, and the supply of fresh water is drying up. The global food system is headed toward collapse. We're like Fibonacci's rabbits, right? One more generation—ten, fifteen more years, and we'll have reached the tipping point. Basic population-projection matrices. Right?"

"Right," Jay said, and then he watched the small, blinking heart-beat of the cursor.

"I'll tell you a secret, Jay," Breez said. "I believe in the ruin lifestyle. Straight-up anarchy is not that far away. Very soon, we're going to have to start making some difficult choices. There are too many of us, and I'm afraid that before long the question will have to be asked: how quickly can you eliminate three or four of the world's six billion people? Do you get rid of them in the most just and equitable way possible? That's the question humanity should start pondering."

Jay considered. *The ruin lifestyle?*

"There are certainly portions of the herd that deserve to be thinned, that's all I'm saying," Breez said. "Is there still room on earth for people like your loathsome nose-picking roommates? Would the world be better off without the type of people who become investment bankers? Can you think of a lower form of life? These people are supposedly so smart and talented. They go to Princeton, or Harvard, or Yale, and then they become 'investment bankers'? Can you think of a more repulsive waste?"

And Jay didn't say anything. Was the guy kidding? Was he a nut-case?

But still, he was impressed by the things Dylan had told him. "That dude is the Destroyer," Dylan said. "He's stolen probably fucking millions of dollars—" And Jay could feel these thoughts slowly tilting and turning slow Ferris wheels in his head. He was pretty stoned.

And, actually, he had to wonder—a guy like this, did he know things that Jay didn't know? Was he simply paying more attention, while most of the rest of the world was just cruising along, not thinking things through to their logical conclusion?

The ruin lifestyle.

"I'm not sure what to say," Jay responded at last. "There's a lot of things I haven't thought about too deeply, either, to tell the truth." He paused. "It sounds like you're a lot smarter than I am," Jay said.

It was a kiss-ass move, no doubt, but he was curious. What did this guy have besides talk?

"Why don't you call me on my cell?" Breez typed. "I have terrible insomnia. Nightmares. I like the sound of a human voice, every once in a while."

And that was how they had become friends.

That was how he learned that the famed "Breez" was actually a guy named Mike Hayden, an ordinary person who had grown up in the suburbs of Cleveland, and—whatever else he had accomplished, however rich and infamous he was—he still felt lonely. He was looking for someone he could trust, he said. "Which is not so easy to find, in our business," he said.

"No doubt," Jay said, and he chuckled moodily. He and his roommates were living in a bungalow in the Westview neighborhood, southwest Atlanta, and he had to admit, he said, that he was thinking about moving on. They had been involved in mostly amateur crap, he said—sitting in the parking lot outside BJ's Wholesale Club or Macy's or OfficeMax, searching for holes in the wireless networks of the stores, collecting credit and debit card numbers as they were entered into the registers. It didn't seem to be going anywhere.

"It's actually not a bad idea," Mike Hayden said. "I know a guy in Latvia who has a computer where you could store the data—and he knows a guy in China who can imprint blank cards with the numbers. People are doing it. You can get a pretty decent harvest from it, if you're smart and aggressive about it."

"Yeah, well," Jay said, "smart and aggressive is not the name of the game around here. I don't think any of these kids know what they're doing."

And Mike Hayden was thoughtful. "Hmm," he said.

"Yeah," Jay said.

"So what are you going to do about it?" Mike Hayden said. "Are you just going to sit there?"

"I don't know," said Jay.

"If I had access to all of those numbers that you collected," Mike said, "I could really do something with them. That's all I'm saying. We could work together."

"Hmm," Jay said. It was dark in the house, though through one of the doorways Jay could see Dylan, his face lit by computer light, his fingers moving over the keyboard, and Jay lowered his voice, cupping his hand over the mouthpiece of the cell phone he was talking into.

"I have to tell you the truth," Jay said. "I'm in a different situation from these guys. I need to start thinking about the future, if you know what I mean. I'm thirty years old. I've got a kid out there somewhere—a kid, fifteen years old, can you believe it? I'm not in the daydream age of youth anymore, frankly."

This revelation had given Mike Hayden pause.

"Why, Jay," he said at last, "I didn't know you had a child! That's so awesome."

"Yeah," Jay said, and he shifted. "A son. But it's complicated. I gave him up, like, for adoption, in a way. To my sister. He doesn't know that I. That I'm his dad."

"Wow," Mike Hayden said. "That must be intense."

"His name is Ryan," said Jay—and it was nice, actually, to tell someone this, he felt a warm, paternal glow briefly opening up. "He's a teenager. Can you believe that? It seems unbelievable to me."

"That's so cool," Mike Hayden said. "It must be such a great feeling—to have an actual son!"

"I guess," Jay said. "It's not like he knows or anything. It's more like this awful secret thing between me and my sister. Most of the time it doesn't even feel real to me, to be honest. Like it's an alternate universe or something."

"Hmm," said Mike Hayden. "You know what, Jay? I like the way you think. I'd enjoy meeting you. Do you want me to get you a plane ticket?"

Jay didn't say anything. In the living room, he could hear the roommates cackling about some new joke they'd recently come up with, a prank to do with doctored photos of a female celebrity. They hadn't made money in weeks.

Meanwhile, Mike Hayden was still talking about Ryan. "Geez, I wish I had a son!" he was saying. "That would make me so happy. All I've got left is my twin brother, and he's been so disappointing lately."

"That's too bad," Jay said, and he shrugged his shoulders, though he realized that Mike Hayden couldn't see such a gesture through the phone. "I suppose you have to work on these kinds of relationships, right? You can't take anything for granted."

"True," Mike Hayden said. "Very true."

And now here Jay was. A week later, and he and Mike Hayden drove east from Denver, he and Breez, he and the Destroyer, traveling through Colorado, and Jay was basically prepared to betray his former roommates.

He didn't feel that bad about it. They were truly assholes, he thought, though he couldn't help but feel nervous as the sky darkened over Interstate 76, and they passed through the thick plumes of steam that billowed out of the sugar beet factory just beyond Fort Morgan, and a flock of grackles lifted up out of the field, a long, streaming formation. It was as if the world had conspired to seem ominous.

He shifted, picked up his backpack, and moved it a little to the right. It was awkward to be in the backseat, like Mike Hayden was a taxi driver or a chauffeur, though Mike himself acted perfectly at ease with the situation.

"So how's your son doing?" Mike Hayden said, and when Jay looked up, he could see Mike's eyes in the rearview mirror.

He shrugged. "Fine," Jay said. "I guess."

It was awkward. Though at the same time, there wasn't anyone else in the world he'd ever talked to about this stuff.

"I don't know," he said at last. "We— Actually, to be honest, Mike, I've never actually spoken with the kid. You know, after my sister adopted him . . . I had some problems. I was in jail for a short while. And my sister, Stacey. We had a falling out, a lot of it having to do with—her not wanting him to know. She didn't see the point in getting him confused, which I understand, I guess, although— it's a difficult thing to get my mind around."

"So—he's actually never met you?" Mike Hayden said.

"Not exactly," Jay said. "My sister and I haven't spoken since he was about one year old. I doubt if he's even seen a picture of me, except of when I was a kid. My sister has been a real hard-ass about this stuff. When she cuts you off, she cuts you off, and that's it. I did try calling her once. You know, I was curious. I just thought I could say 'hi' to the kid, but she wasn't having any of it. As far as the kid is concerned, I barely exist."

"Wow," Mike Hayden said, and again Jay saw the eye, reflected in the rearview mirror, glancing back at him. A surprisingly sad, compassionate eye, Jay thought, though also unnerving. "Wow," Mike said. "That's an incredible story."

"I guess so," Jay said.

"Tragic."

"I don't know about that," Jay said, and he shrugged. To tell the truth, he didn't know how to feel, exactly—here in the lush, expensive chamber of the Lexus; here with this unexpected Mike Hayden, with his sports coat and trimmed fingernails and formal manner, asking him about all this private stuff.

When they had started talking together on the phone, they'd had some very long, personal conversations—not just about business ideas, but also about their lives. He had learned about Mike's childhood, the father who was a hypnotherapist, who had committed suicide when Mike was thirteen; the abusive stepfather; the twin brother who had been everybody's favorite, who could do no wrong, while Mike was basically invisible.

"I was very close to my dad, and after he was gone, I just felt like a stranger in my own family," Mike told him. "It seemed like they would have been happier without me, and so I left. I never saw them again, and I guess I probably never will."

"I know what you mean," Jay said. "That was what it was like in my family, too. Stacey was ten years older than me, and she was, like, this star student. They were so proud that she became a CPA. A fucking accountant! And I was supposed to be, like, 'Oooooh: worship. So impressive.' "

Mike Hayden found this hilarious. "Ooooh, worship! So impressive!" he repeated, imitating Jay's tone of voice. "Dude, you slay me."

It was Mike Hayden's opinion that Jay should contact his son. That Ryan should be told the truth about his adoption, and all the rest.

"I think he deserves to know the truth," Mike Hayden had said. "That is not a cool situation with that sister of yours. She's controlling, don't you think? And think of poor Ryan! If the people that you think you love are hiding something that important, it's a major betrayal. That's one of those things that screws up the karma of the entire world."

"I don't know," Jay said. "He's probably better off."

But in some ways Jay had taken this advice to heart. Jay was actually thinking a lot about this situation, ever since he turned thirty, and Mike Hayden's friendship and counsel had been important to him.

But at the same time, it felt funny to be talking about it now, with this—stranger. With this young, fussy-looking Mike Hayden. It was always the problem with virtual relationships, Internet friendships, whatever you wanted to call them. There was always a shock, in which you realized that the person you had been building in your mind—the simulacrum, the avatar—didn't resemble the actual flesh and blood in the slightest.

He wondered if it had been such a good idea to leave Atlanta. Perhaps, he thought, he shouldn't have been so forthcoming about the schemes the Association was involved in; perhaps he shouldn't have ever mentioned his son—and he felt a pinprick of unease, imagining the boy, his son, sitting peaceful and unaware back at Stacey's house, "doing so well," Stacey had written, back when Jay was in jail that first time, back when Ryan was just a toddler. "You've done a good thing for him, Jay. Don't you forget that."

And now Mike Hayden—Breez—knew about him. He remembered again what Dylan had said about Breez: *He'll trash your life just for the fun of it.*

He wiped his damp palms on his pant legs, then combed his fingers through his hair as they passed from Colorado into western Nebraska. They were listening to some awful, repetitive classical music, dreadful stuff that sounded like scales being played over and over on a piano.

It was coming on dusk when they pulled into the motel. The Lighthouse Motel, it said, but the neon wasn't lit, and it looked abandoned.

"Home at last!" Mike Hayden said, and he moved the gear stick into park with a flourish. He turned to look over his shoulder, grinning as Jay looked up from his mumbling backseat thoughts.

"This is my place," Mike Hayden said. "I own it."

"Oh," Jay said, and he peered out. It was just an old courtyard motel, with a big replica of a lighthouse at the entrance, a cement cone painted in red and white stripes like a barber pole. "Huh," he said, and tried to nod appreciatively. "Cool."

They walked, Jay and Mike, up the path that led from the motel to the old house on the hill, not saying anything. It was drizzling, late October, and it didn't seem to know whether it planned to rain or snow. The wind pitched the dry high weeds back and forth.

The house that stood above the motel was one of those places you would see in Halloween illustrations, the classic "haunted mansion" sort of deal, Jay thought, though Mike acted as if it were an architectural wonder.

"Doesn't it blow your mind?" he said. "It's called Queen Anne style. Asymmetrical façade. Cantilevered gables. And the turret! Don't you love the turret?"

"Sure," Jay said, and Mike Hayden leaned toward him.

"I managed some extremely interesting things with this estate," Mike said. "The former owner actually died three years ago, but her social security number is still in play. As far as the official record goes, she's still alive."

"Oh, okay," Jay said. "That's cool."

"Wait—it gets better," Mike said. "Because as it turns out, she had two sons. Both of whom died young, but I think they are resurrectable. The best thing is, if they were alive, they would be just about our age! George. And Brandon. They both drowned—when they were teenagers. They were out swimming in the lake, and Brandon was trying to save George. I guess it didn't work out."

Mike Hayden let out a stiff laugh, as if there were something bitterly funny about this fact that Jay didn't quite understand.

"Listen," Mike said. "How do you feel about becoming brothers?"

"Um," Jay said. He glanced at the place that Mike's hand was resting: the ball of his shoulder, and he didn't tighten or flinch. It was one of the advantages that he'd learned from his year in Vegas: a decent poker face.

He was being offered an opportunity. He had dead-ended in Atlanta, and here was a chance to move on.

Did it matter that he himself had been played a little bit? Did it matter that, for a short time, he had actually felt closer to Mike Hayden—Breez—than was probably wise? Did it matter that he'd revealed personal information, did it matter that this guy, whatever his name was, now knew personal details about his life? About his son. His secrets.

Yes, of course it mattered, dumb shit. He had been a fool, and

Mike Hayden—or whoever—was smiling gently. As if Jay were a puppy in a glass case at a pet store.

"One of the things I can show you," Mike Hayden said. "There are some phenomenal things you can do with dead people. Do you have any idea how many unclaimed estates there are in this country? It's like Risk or Monopoly or whatever. You can just land on a property, and basically it's yours, if you know what you're doing."

Mike laughed, and Jay laughed a little, too, though he wasn't exactly sure what was funny. They had come to the porch of the old haunted house, and Jay watched as Mike Hayden withdrew a key ring from his pocket, a thick, jingling wind chime of keys. How many? Twenty? Forty?

But he had no difficulty finding the right one. He inserted a key into the keyhole just below the doorknob and then made another flourish with his hands, like a stage magician: abracadabra.

"Just wait until you see the interior," Mike Hayden said. "There's a library. With an actual wall safe behind a painting! Doesn't that kill you?"

And then Mike Hayden stiffened—as if he were suddenly embarrassed by this burst of goofy enthusiasm, as if he thought Jay might make fun of it.

"I'm so glad that we're going to be working together," he said. "I've always missed having a true brother, you know? When you're born a twin, there's always this part of you that wants that other person in your life. That other—soul mate. Does that make any sense?"

He opened the door and an odd, musty scent poured out. Jay could see, just beyond the foyer, beyond an expanse of faded oriental carpet, some furniture that was covered in sheets, and a large staircase with a coiling banister.

"I've taken care of your associates back in Atlanta for you, by the way," said Mike Hayden. "I suspect that the Feds have already begun to round the little buggers up, so—we're free of that interference, at least."

And with that, he and Jay stepped into the house.

PART THREE

✦

First say to yourself what you would be; and then do what
you have to do.

—EPICTETUS

20

In the photograph, the young man and the girl are sitting on a sofa together. Both of them have gift-wrapped packages in their laps, and they are holding hands. The young man is blond and slender and pleasantly at ease. He is looking at the girl, and you can see in his expression that he is making some gently teasing joke, and the girl is just beginning to laugh. She has auburn hair and mournful eyes, but she is looking at him now with open affection. It's obvious that they are in love.

Miles sat there, staring at the picture, and he wasn't sure what to say.

It was Hayden, all right.

It was his brother, though you wouldn't have ever believed that he and Miles were twins. It was as if this Hayden had been raised from birth in a different life, as if their father had never died, as if their mother had never grown angry and distant and desperate with him, as if Hayden had never lain ranting in an attic room, his hands cuffed to the bed with cloth ties, calling out, his hoarse, hysterical voice through the closed door, muffled but insistent: "Miles! Help me! Miles, cover my neck. Please, please, someone has to cover my neck!"

As if through all that time, some other, normal Hayden were growing up, going to college, falling in love with Rachel Barrie. Slipping into the world of ordinary happiness—the life, Miles thought, they both should have been granted, good suburban middle-class boys that they were.

"Yes," Miles said. He swallowed. "Yes. That's my brother."

They were sitting in Lydia Barrie's room in the Mackenzie Hotel, in Inuvik, but for a moment it didn't feel like they were anywhere. This place, this town, the boxy, flimsy buildings with their corrugated sheet-metal siding, as impermanent as a hastily erected movie set; this room with the rim of steady, implausible sunlight glowing through the edges of the shades on the window—it all felt so much less real than the young people in the picture that it wouldn't have surprised him to learn that, in fact, it was he and Lydia who were nothing but figments.

He let the pad of his fingertip rest lightly on the glossy surface of the photo, as if he could touch his brother's face, and then he watched as Lydia reached down and gently lifted the photograph out of his hands.

"Listen," he said. "Is there a way I can get a copy of that picture? I'd very much like a copy."

There was no way to explain the sense of sadness that he felt, the sense that this photo she was tucking away was almost supernatural: a picture of what might have been. For himself. For Hayden. For their family.

But that wouldn't make sense to Lydia Barrie, he thought. To her, Hayden was merely a fake, a scam artist, an imposter in her family photo. She didn't realize that the person she had known as Miles Spady was a real possibility. An actual existence that might have been.

———

"I imagine that you're hoping to save him," Lydia Barrie said, and she gave Miles a long, searching look he didn't quite understand.

She'd had a lot to drink that night, but she didn't act drunk, exactly. She wasn't stumbling or anything, though her movements seemed more premeditated, as if she had to deliberate before she executed them. Still, there was something very precise about the way she carried herself. She was a lawyer, with a lawyerly sort of grace—a flourish in her wrist when she filed the folder back in its place in her leather portfolio, a sharply choreographed *click* as she opened the matching attaché, an elegant *swiff* of paper as she laid her documents down on the bed between them. You could see that she was drunk only when you looked in her eyes, which had a damp unfocused intensity.

"You think if only you can find him, you can somehow convince him to—what?" She paused, long enough so they could both note how illogical he was.

"What exactly are you thinking, Miles?" she said mildly. "Do you think you can talk him into giving himself up to the authorities? Or perhaps you can talk him into coming back to the U.S. with you, and get some therapy or something? Do you think it's possible that he'll voluntarily allow himself to be committed to an institution?"

"I don't know," Miles said.

It was unnerving to be so transparent. He wasn't sure how she had so accurately articulated his own line of thinking, the doubtful ideas he'd entertained over the years, but hearing them spoken aloud made him aware of how lame and flimsy they sounded.

He didn't exactly have a plan, to tell the truth. He had always thought that when—if—he finally caught up to Hayden, he would have to improvise.

"I don't know," he said again, and Lydia Barrie fixed him with her bright, slurry gaze. Even drunk as she was, he could tell that she had been a terrific prosecutor—deadly, no doubt, during cross-examination.

He looked down with an abashed, rueful smile. He'd had a bit to drink himself, and perhaps that was why it was so easy for her to read him. But, he thought, it was also true that he was not particularly cagey. That had always been his problem—even from the womb, some amniotic chemical must have been washing over him, he had been primed from birth to be the credulous one, the mild twin, easily manipulated.

"He's not who you think he is, Miles," she said. "You know that, don't you?"

She had already told him her various theories concerning Hayden.

Some of them, he basically agreed with.

He knew, without question, that Hayden was a thief, that he had defrauded numerous individuals and corporations, that he had focused particularly on several investment banking firms, from which he had possibly stolen millions of dollars.

Miles doubted that such a large sum was actually involved.

As for Lydia Barrie's other accusations, he wasn't so sure. Was Hayden involved in setting loose various Internet worms—including one that had shut down Diebold Corporation's computers for more than forty-five minutes? Had Hayden hijacked the cell phone of a hotel heiress and for a brief time convinced her father she'd been kidnapped? Had Hayden ruined the career of a Yale University political science professor by planting pedophilic photographs onto his computer? Was he a supporter of and financial contributor to terrorist organizations, including one environmental group that advocated the spread of biological weapons as a means of slowing overpopulation?

Had Hayden orchestrated the suspicions of embezzlement that had forced Lydia Barrie to leave the law firm of Oglesby and Rosenberg under a cloud of unverified accusations, which had marred and perhaps ruined her career?

It was far-fetched, Miles thought, to suggest that Hayden was involved in all of this. So many different things.

"You make him sound like some kind of supervillain," Miles said, and he let out a small chuckle, to show her how silly it sounded. But she merely raised one eyebrow, expectantly.

"My sister has been missing for three years," she said. "That's not a comic book story, for me. I take it very seriously."

And Miles found himself blushing. Flustered. "Well," he said. "I understand. I didn't mean to—belittle—your situation."

He looked down at his hands, down at the meticulous stacks of papers she had arranged for him to examine, staring at the headline of a newspaper article she had photocopied: "U.S. Prosecutors Indict 11 in Massive Identity Fraud Case," he read. What to say?

"I'm not trying to make excuses for him," Miles said. "I'm just saying—it strains credulity, you know? He's only one person. And he's actually— I grew up with him, and he's actually not that much of a genius. I mean, if he's done all the stuff you think he's done, wouldn't someone have caught him already?"

Lydia Barrie tilted her head, and once he met her gaze, she didn't break eye contact. "Miles," she said, "you haven't looked at all the information I've got here yet, have you? We—you and I— might be in a unique position to bring your brother to justice. To try to help him, cure him if you will. To hold him accountable for his actions. He may not be a 'supervillain,' as you put it, but I think we can both agree that he's a danger to himself. And to other people. We can agree on that point, can't we, Miles?"

"I don't think he's evil," Miles said. "He's—troubled, you know? I honestly think a lot of this is just like a game. We used to do all these kinds of games when we were kids, and in a lot of ways it's still the same thing. It's, like, role-playing for him. Do you see what I'm saying?"

"I do," Lydia Barrie said, and she leaned forward, and her expression looked almost sad, almost sympathetic. "You're a very sentimental person," she said, and then she smiled, very briefly and mildly, and rested the cool, smooth palm of her hand against his wrist. "And very loyal. I admire that enormously."

246 | Dan Chaon

He was aware that there was a possibility that she was going to kiss him.

He wasn't sure what he thought about it, but he could sense that odd, heavy feeling in the air, like a barometric drop before a thunderstorm descended. She didn't understand what he was trying to tell her, he thought. She wasn't exactly his ally, he thought, but nevertheless he felt his eyes closing as she leaned toward him. That uncanny sunlight was still glowing around the edges of the window shade as her hand slid up his forearm to his biceps, and okay, yes, their lips were touching.

When Miles woke up in the morning, Lydia Barrie was still asleep, and he lay there for a time with his eyes open, staring at the red numbers on the old digital alarm clock at the bedside. At last, he began to discreetly grope around under the blankets for his underwear, and once he found them, he carefully put his feet into the leg holes and pulled them up over his thighs. Lydia Barrie did not stir as he padded his way toward the bathroom.

Well. This was unexpected.

And he couldn't help but feel a tiny bit pleased with himself. A bit—uplifted. He was not used to this: falling into bed with women, even very drunk women, was not a usual occurrence. He looked at himself critically in the bathroom mirror. He was not double-chinned, but he almost was, unless he kept his jaw lifted. And he was fat enough in the middle that he had man boobs and a round toddler-like gut. How embarrassing! There was a miniature traveler's bottle of mouthwash on the ledge of the sink, and he poured a finger of it into a glass and swished it around in his mouth.

She was deeply crazy, he supposed. Probably that was why she slept with him. He examined his face, and wiped a hand across his unruly hair and combed his fingers through the tight, curly tangles of his beard.

She was as obsessed as he was, if not more so—more conspiracy-minded, more focused in her methods, better organized, more *professional*. It was likely, he thought, that she would find Hayden before he did.

He ran some water into the basin of the sink and patted it onto his cheeks.

And she *was* very attractive. Quite out of his league in a lot of ways, he supposed. He thought again of that photo she had shown him, the picture of Hayden and Rachel Barrie, that hollow sensation in the pit of his stomach as he looked at their happy faces, an old hurt rising up from childhood.

Why couldn't it have been me? he wondered. *Why couldn't a pretty girl fall in love with me? Why does Hayden always get everything?*

When he came out of the bathroom, Lydia Barrie was already up, already partially dressed, and she turned to look at him, wistfully.

"Good morning," she said. She was wearing a bra and a slip, and her formerly coifed hair was tousled into a tangle, like one of the witch wigs they sold back at the magic store in Cleveland. Her makeup was almost completely smudged off, and her eyes were haggard, hungover. You could tell for certain she was getting ready to enter her forties, though he didn't find that fact unappealing. In her rumpled, unpolished state, there was a vulnerability he found himself feeling tenderly toward.

"Hey," he said sheepishly, and he smiled as she put a hand shyly to her hair.

And then he saw the gun.

It was a small revolver of some sort, and she was holding it loosely in her left hand as she smoothed her right hand over her hair, and he watched as she made an attempt to unobtrusively tuck the weapon into her attaché. For a second, she acted as if she hoped he hadn't noticed.

"Holy shit," Miles said.

He took a step back.

Actually, he guessed that he had never seen a gun in real life, though he had probably viewed hundreds of people with guns on television and in movies and video games. He had watched many people get killed; he knew what it was supposed to look like: the small circular hole in the chest or the belly, the blood spreading out in a Rorschach across the shirt.

"Jesus," he said. "Lydia."

Her expression wavered. At first, she seemed to hope that she could play innocent—she widened her eyes, as if she were preparing to say: *What? What are you talking about?* And then she appeared to realize that such a tactic was fruitless, and a cool, defiant look crossed her face before, at last, she shrugged. She smiled at him ruefully.

"What?" she said.

"You have a gun," he said. "Why do you have a gun?"

He was standing there in his underwear, still a bit groggy, still a bit dazzled by the fact that he'd had sex for the first time in two years, still circling through the conversations they'd had the night before, and the picture of Hayden and Rachel, and the sadness he'd felt. Lydia Barrie raised her eyebrows.

"You don't have any idea what it's like to be a woman," she said. "I know you don't think your brother is dangerous, but be realistic. Put yourself in my shoes. I need some security, Miles."

"Oh," Miles said. They stood there, facing each other, and Lydia laid the gun on the bed and held up her hands as if it were Miles who had the weapon.

"It's just a little mousegun," she said. "A little .25-caliber Beretta.

I've carried it for years," she said. "They're not particularly deadly, as guns go—I would call it more of a deterrent than anything else."

"I see," Miles said, though he wasn't quite sure he did. He was standing there in his boxer shorts with their ridiculous hot pepper print, and he crossed his hands uncertainly over his chest. A wobbly shudder ran through his bare legs, and he wondered, briefly, if he ought to make a dash for the door.

"Are you going to kill my brother?" he said at last, and Lydia widened her eyes at him as if astonished.

"Of course not," she said, and he stood there as she pulled her skirt on up over her thighs and zipped up the back, and then she gave him a pinched smile. "Miles," she said. "Dear heart, I asked you last night if you had a plan, and you told me that you more or less expected to improvise, once you located your brother. Well, I'm not going to improvise. When I was fired from Oglesby and Rosenberg, one of the first things I did in my 'free time' was acquire private investigator and bail enforcement agent licenses from the state of New York. Which was an enormous help, as I was looking for— Hayden." She slipped her arms decisively into the sleeves of her blouse. "And the first thing I did when I arrived in Canada was hire Mr. Joe Itigaituk, who is a licensed Canadian private investigator, so that when we take your brother into custody, I won't be interfering with the sovereignty of a foreign power."

Miles watched as Lydia fastened the buttons down the center of her blouse, from the neck to the belly, her fingers moving in a deft sign language as she talked.

He glanced at the door, which led to the hallway, and his leg shuddered again.

"I'm not a murderer, Miles," Lydia said, and they stood there, looking at each other, and her expression softened as she looked him up and down.

"Why don't you put your clothes on," she said. "Mr. Itigaituk and I are flying to Banks Island in a couple of hours, and I thought you'd like to come along with us. That way you can be absolutely sure that no one will hurt him. If you're there, he may come along with us peacefully."

It was Lydia's belief that Hayden was currently occupying an abandoned meteorological station located on the northern tip of Banks Island, not far from the limit of permanent ice.

"Though the limit of permanent ice is not as stable as it used to be," she said as they rode in the taxi. "Global warming and so forth."

Miles was reticent. He leaned his head against the window, peering out at the treeless streets, a row of brightly colored townhouses—turquoise, sunflower-yellow, cardinal-red—linked together like children's building blocks. The dirt along the roads was the color of charcoal, and the sky was cloudless, and he could see the melting tundra just beyond the line of houses and storage facilities. It was green out there, even spotted with wildflowers, though it seemed to him that the landscape wouldn't truly be itself until it was covered again in ice.

Lydia had not given him the full details of how she had traced Hayden to this particular spot, just as Miles had not fully explained his own, less rational methods—the intuition or presentiment or idiocy that sent him driving for days upon days, four thousand miles. But Lydia was fairly confident. "The fact that we're both here in Inuvik seems like a good sign, doesn't it? I feel very encouraged, actually. Don't you?"

"I guess so," Miles said, though now that the prospect of Hayden's capture was looming, he felt a sense of apprehension branching through him, taking root. He was thinking of the way Hayden had screamed when he was put in restraints at the mental hospital. It was one of the most awful things that Miles had ever heard—his brother, eighteen years old, a grown man, bellowing out these dreadful crowlike shrieks, his arms flapping as the orderlies descended on him. It was a few days after the new year, and it was snowing in Cleveland, and Miles and his mother stood there in their winter coats, dandelion fluff snowflakes melting in their hair as Hayden was pressed to the floor, his back arching, legs jerking as he tried to kick free, his eyes wide as he tried to bite. "Miles!" he was crying. "Miles, don't let them take me. They're hurting me, Miles. Save me, save me—"

Which Miles had not.

"You're quiet," Lydia Barrie said, and she reached over and brushed his forearm, as if there were a crumb or a speck of dust. "Worried?"

"A little," he said. "I'm just thinking about how he's going to react. I don't know, it's just—I don't want him to get hurt."

Lydia Barrie sighed. "You're a sweet person," she said. "You have a kind heart, and that's a wonderful quality to have. But you know what, Miles? He's running out of options."

Miles nodded, and looked down to where Lydia had lightly pressed the pads of her fingertips against the back of his hand, just below his wrist.

"He's found himself in a corner," Lydia said. "And I would venture to guess that there are some extremely bad people who are closing in on him. People much more dangerous than I am."

He had suspected as much himself, when he'd gotten that letter from Hayden. *I have been in deep hiding, very deep, but every day I thought about how much I missed you. It was only my fear for your own safety that kept me from contact. . . .*

"Yes," Miles said. "I think you're probably right."

He couldn't help but think again of that photo of Hayden and Rachel, together on the couch at Christmas. He hoped they were still together—that Rachel would be there in the meteorological station with him. He could imagine the moment, when he and Lydia opened the door and Hayden and Rachel stood there in the tiny shacklike room, haggard and startled, and probably thin. What, after all, had they been eating up there in that abandoned place? Fish? Canned goods? Had they been able to shower? Would they be wild-haired like hermits?

Undoubtedly they would panic at first. They would be expecting a looming thug or a swift, efficient assassin—

And then, they would see that it was just Miles. Just Miles and Lydia, a brother and a sister. And wouldn't they, after that first shudder of recognition, be grateful? It would be a reunion of sorts. He and Lydia had come to save them, and they would understand that there was nowhere else to run, that they had reached the end.

And at least it was someone they loved who had found them.

The taxi had arrived at the airfield, where Mr. Itigaituk was waiting for them. The taxi dropped them off, and Lydia paid the driver, and then she turned to wave as Mr. Itigaituk approached. He was a short mustachioed middle-aged Inuit man in a corduroy jacket, jeans, and cowboy boots, and to Miles he looked more like a high school math teacher than a private eye.

The man frowned when he saw Miles, but he didn't say anything. Miles watched as he and Lydia Barrie shook hands, and he stood a short distance away as they spoke together in low voices, as Mr. Itigaituk eyed Miles skeptically and then nodded, his dark eyes resting coolly on Miles's face.

The airfield was about fifteen kilometers outside of town, and he was aware again of the endless sunlight, the green, flat expanse of tundra rolling away from them in all directions, the glint of muddy bogs and melt ponds in the distance.

Just beyond, at rest on the tarmac, was the small six-seater Cessna that was waiting to take them to Banks Island, to Aulavik.

21

Ryan looked up and there was a figure standing in the doorway.

He was almost asleep, bent over his computer, his hands curled into position, his fingertips aligned on *asdf jkl;* and his chin had grown heavy until at last his neck drooped and elbows grew slack and his forehead began a slow descent toward the surface of the table.

It was a particular dream state. After a few beers, a few bong hits; after a long time traveling, crossing time zones—passing from pacific to mountain to central to eastern—after calming his drunk, possibly 'shrooming father who was stumbling around with a gun; after getting him into bed and gently sliding the gun out of his limp hand and putting it away and then sitting in front of the computer screen with his eyes closed.

Dutifully, he had made reservations for them both to fly to Quito, Ecuador, under the names Max Wimberley and Darren Loftus, and the confirmation was still there on the screen, a box floating on the surface of the monitor like a leaf in a pond, and Ryan was thinking, *I should go to bed. I can't believe how exhausted I am.* And he rolled his dry, sticky tongue inside his mouth and peeled open his eyelids.

He'd had dreams like this before.

A man was standing there, silhouetted behind the mesh of the screen door. He stood under the porch light, where moths were circling and bumping groggily against the surface of the ceiling, and there was a revolving shadow-lantern effect above the man's head. Ryan let his eyes close again.

He had been having these small hallucinations for a while now, imagining that he saw people he knew, these flickers that he knew were nothing but the detritus of exhaustion and stress and lingering guilty feelings, too much beer and pot, too much time alone with Jay, no one else to talk with; too much time sitting in front of a computer screen, which sometimes appeared to pulse with a rapid millisecond strobe, like those old subliminal advertising messages he'd read about.

It reminded him of this one time at Northwestern. He and Walcott had been partying all weekend and he was sitting at the window of his fourth-floor dorm room, smoking a joint. His arm was extended out into the open air to keep the smoke from stinking up the room, and he was trying to blow rings out into the foggy spring night, looking down at the empty sidewalk and the streetlamps that were made to look like old-fashioned gaslights, and there was no traffic, and suddenly someone reached up and touched his wrist.

He felt this very distinctly. It was impossible, he knew. His arm was extended four stories above the ground, but nevertheless someone reached up and clutched it for just a second. It was as if he were trailing his arm out of a boat instead of a fourth-floor window, as if his fingers were brushing the surface of a lake when a hand, a drowning person, had reached out of the water to grasp his wrist.

He'd let out a cry, and the joint had fallen out from between his fingers, and he saw the orange light of the lit end tumbling down through dark space as he yanked his hand back quickly into the room. "Holy shit!" he said, and Walcott had looked up from his laptop, regarding Ryan sleepily.

"Huh?" Walcott said, and Ryan just sat there, holding his wrist as if it had been burned. What could he say? *A ghostly hand just swam up four stories and tried to grab me. Someone tried to pull me out of the window.*

"Something bit me," he said at last, calmly. "I just dropped my joint."

All of this came back to him vividly—more like time travel than memory—and he gave his head a shake, the typical gesture of the daydreamer, as if you could rattle your brain back into place.

He squinched his eyes shut, thinking maybe this would wipe the blackboard clean, but when he opened them, the figure in the doorway had actually become more distinct.

The man had come closer. He was in the room now, stepping toward Ryan, a tall man in a black suit, the shiny cloth glinting.

"Is Jay home?" the man said, and Ryan's body jerked as he lifted up into full consciousness. "I'm a friend of Jay's," the man said. Real. Not a dream.

The man was holding a black plastic object, which looked at first like it might be an electric razor. Something that could be plugged into a computer? A communication device, like a cell phone or a receiver, with a pair of metal tongs extending from the end of it?

The man stepped forward quickly with the thing held out, as if offering it to Ryan, and Ryan actually reached out his hand for a second, right before the man pressed it up against his neck.

It was a Taser, Ryan realized.

He felt the electricity pass through him. He and his muscles contracted painfully, and he was aware of the spasms of his arms and legs flailing, his tongue hardening in his mouth, a thick strip of meat as he made a gurgling sound in his throat. His lips shook out spittle.

And then he was becoming unconscious.

It wasn't a hallucination. It wasn't anything except blankness, thick, fuzzy black spots that began to swell over his line of vision. Like mold spreading in a petri dish. Like the film cells of a movie melting.

And then: voices.

Jay—his father—nervous, sidling.

Then a calm reply. A voice from a relaxation tape?

I'm looking for Jay. Can you

help me out with that?

Ouch, Jay said, a little shrilly.

I don't know, I don't

Is the name Jay Kozelek familiar to you?

I . . .

Where is he?

. . . don't know

All I need is an address. We can make this very easy on you.

Honestly

Anything you might be able to tell me will be a big help right now.

Honest to God, I swear

I don't

Ryan's head lifted, but his neck felt like a limp stalk. He was sitting in a chair, and he could feel the pressure of the duct tape that held him—his forearms, his chest, his waist, his calves, his ankles—and when he tried experimentally to flex, he was aware that he was held fast. His eyes slit open and he could see that he and Jay were sitting at the kitchen table across from each other. He could see that a trickle of blood was running from Jay's hair, across his temple and his left eye and along the edge of his nose and into his mouth. Jay made a sound as if he were snuffling, as if he had a cold, and a few droplets of blood spattered out and speckled the tabletop.

"Look," Jay was saying to the man, humbly. "You know what this business is like. People are slippery. I hardly even know the guy," he said, very eager, very helpful, still trying to find a fingerhold on his old charming Jay self. "You probably know more about him than I do."

And the guy standing over him mused on this.

"Oh, really," the guy said, and he stood there looking down at Jay.

It was the guy who had shocked Ryan with the Taser, and for the first time Ryan got a good look at him. He was a big guy, late twenties, narrow shoulders and wide hips, about six foot one or two, and he was wearing a shiny black Italian suit that a mafioso might wear—though he didn't look much like a gangster. He had a boyish, Midwestern, potato-shaped head, a shock of straw-colored blond hair, and he reminded Ryan of no one so much as the graduate student who had been a TA in his computer science class back at Northwestern.

"You know what," the guy said, "I don't believe you."

He lifted his fist and clouted Jay in the face. Hard. Hard enough that Jay tilted back and more blood droplets flew out of his mouth, and Jay let out a high, surprised yelp.

"It's a mistake!" Jay said. "Listen, you've just got the wrong guy, that's all. I don't know what you want me to say. Tell me what you want me to say!"

Ryan was trying to keep himself as small and soundless as possible. He could hear movement—some general thumping and crashing in the next room, and through the doorway he could see men wearing black pants and shirts, two men, he thought, though possibly more, unplugging the hard drives from the rows of computers on the tables and tossing the monitors and keyboards and other extraneous hardware onto the floor, sometimes hitting things with long curved pieces of metal, crowbars, and one of them picked up Jay's Ouija board from the coffee table and looked at it curiously, front and back, as if it were some form of technology he'd never encountered before. Then he paused, maybe sensing that Ryan was looking at him, and Ryan quickly closed his eyes.

"I'm, like, thinking about torturing you," the Taser man said to Jay at last. He had a soft, reasonable, almost monotone voice, reminiscent of a DJ on a college radio station. "Listen to me. It's actually one of the fantasies that kept me going all these years. Thinking about torturing Jay Kozelek is one of the few things that made me happy all the time I was in prison, so don't fuck with me. I tracked him here. I know he's here somewhere. And if you don't tell me where Jay is, I'm going to torture you and your little buddy here until you puke blood. Okay?"

Ryan's lips parted, but nothing came out. No sound, not even a breath.

This was a situation Ryan had never thought too much about. In all the time he and Jay had been engaged in criminal activity, even when he was getting those IMs in Russian, even when he ran from those guys in Las Vegas, he had never pictured himself tied to a chair in a cabin in the deep woods of Michigan with a man who said *I've been thinking about torturing you.*

He was surprised at how useless his mind was. He had always imagined that in some desperate situation, his brain would sharpen—his thoughts would begin to race—his epinephrine would kick in—his instinct to survive would suddenly rise to the surface—but instead he felt a dull, pulsing blankness, a numb heartbeat, like the quick breath of some trapped rodent. He thought of a rabbit, a small animal in the wild, how it will sink into a motionless state as if it is pretending it is invisible. He thought of Jay's meditation tapes: *Picture a circle of energy near the base of your spine. This energy is strong. It connects you to the earth. . . .*

And sitting there, it was as if he was nothing but earth. A sack of dirt.

Meanwhile, the man had his hand in Jay's long hair, and as he was talking, he curled a lock of Jay's hair around each finger, a tangle that he pulled tighter even as his voice grew softer.

"I was in prison for three years," the man was saying. "*Prison.* You may not realize this, dude, but prison has a tendency to make you kind of mean. And you know what? Every single day of every single month, the one thing that made me happy was imagining ways that I could hurt your friend Jay. I thought about that a lot. Sometimes I would just close my eyes and I would ask myself: what should be done with Jay? I would think of his face, and what he would look like when he was tied to a chair, and I would think: What would be the worst thing? What would make him suffer the most?"

The man paused thoughtfully, with a fistful of Jay's hair entwined between his fingers, growing taut.

"And so you see," the man said, "The fact that I don't *have* Jay is really pissing me off."

By this point, Ryan had begun to find their conversation surreal, incomprehensible, but it was hard to focus on anything except the expression on his father's face, Jay's gritted teeth, his blank, trapped eyes.

Ryan guessed that the man had been planning to pull a hank of Jay's hair out by the roots, but this required more force than he initially expected. "Ow!" Jay screamed, but the hair remained stubbornly attached to his scalp, and after a brief struggle the man realized that it would require more leverage, or more muscle, than he wanted—or was able—to expend.

"God damn it," the man said, and instead he gave Jay's head a vigorous shaking, the way a dog might whip a rag with its teeth, and Jay's face jittered rapidly before the man gave up and loosed Jay's hair with a flourish.

He hadn't yanked the hair out, but it had hurt enough that Jay was now whimpering and cringing.

"I haven't seen him in years," Jay said. "I don't have any idea where he is, I swear."

Jay was crying a little, a faint childlike snuffling, a quivering of the shoulders, and this gave the man pause: torturing someone was more work than it had been in his fantasy.

"The last time I saw him, he was planning to go to Latvia. To Rēzekne," Jay said earnestly, and drew in a wet breath through his nose. "He's been out of the picture for a long time, a very long time."

But this wasn't what the man wanted to hear, and Ryan himself had no idea who they were talking about. Was there a different Jay?

"You didn't understand me, did you?" the man said. "You think you can just feed me another line of bullshit, don't you?" And he let out a stiff, theatrical chuckle. "But ve have vays of making you talk," he said, in an imitation of a German or Russian accent.

Ryan watched as the man felt in the pocket of his jacket, the way someone might grope for a lucky coin, and when he touched the object in his pocket, his eyes focused again, his resolve began to return, and his expression settled into a small, private smile.

From his pocket he withdrew a coil of thin silver wire, and he regarded it as if he were recalling some pleasant long-ago memory.

Jay didn't say anything. He just hung his head, and his long hair made a tent around his face, his shoulders rising and falling as he breathed. A droplet fell out of his nose and onto the front of his shirt.

But the man didn't notice. He had turned his attention away from Jay and now looked over at Ryan.

"So," he said. "Who do we have here?"

Ryan could feel the man's eyes fall on him. The brief sense of invisibility lifted away, and he watched as the man unwound the length of wire, a simple rubber handle at either end. The man tilted his head.

"What's your name, man?" the guy said. He gestured casually, stretching the wire out until it was taut, until it quivered like a guitar string.

"Ryan."

And the man nodded. "Good," he said. "You know how to answer a question."

And Ryan wasn't sure what to say to that. He was staring across the table, hoping that Jay would lift his head, that Jay would look at him, would give him a signal, some sense of what to do.

But Jay didn't look up, and the man bent his attention toward Ryan.

"You're Kasimir Czernewski, I guess?" the man said.

Ryan was staring down at the tabletop, on which water stains had spread into a map—a continent, surrounded by tiny islands.

He could feel his skin shuddering—the involuntary physical response he associated with being wet and cold, but this, this was actual fear, this was what being terrified felt like.

"We've been keeping an eye on you, too, you know," the man said. "I think you're going to be surprised to find how many of your bullshit bank accounts are not solvent anymore."

Ryan could hear the words the man was saying, he could process them, he knew what they meant—but at the same time they didn't feel like real sentences. They sunk into his consciousness like a weighted fishing line cast into a pond, and he felt the ripples circle out across his body.

What did he want from Jay right then? What does a son want from a father in such a situation?

To begin with, there is the fantasy of heroic action. The father who might give you a confident, reassuring wink—a little *chk, chk* at the edge of his mouth, and suddenly he breaks free of his bonds and produces a gun that was strapped to his ankle and the bullets enter the back of the torturer's head and he freezes midstep and falls face-forward and your dad gives you a shy grin as he rips the tape from his legs and swings around, gun aloft, aiming for the henchmen—

And then there is the father of steely determination. The father who shows you his gritted teeth: *Stay firm! We'll face this together! We'll be okay!*

Or the father of regret—eyes brimming with tenderness and sorrow, eyes that say: *I am with you. If you suffer, I will suffer tenfold. I send you all my love and my strength . . .*

And then there was Jay. Blood had been running out of his hair into his face, and tears had made pathways through some of the dried blood, and when their eyes met, they barely recognized each other.

For the first time in a long time Ryan thought of Owen. His other father. His former father—the father he had known all his life, who had raised him, the father who thought he was dead. At this very minute, Owen might be waking in Iowa to let the dog out, standing in the yard in his pajamas and watching as the dog sniffed and circled, looking out at the streetlights that were beginning to go dim as the sun came up, bending down to pick up the newspaper from the grass.

For a moment, Ryan was almost there. He might have been sitting like a bird in the old bur oak in front of the house, peering tenderly from above as Owen unwrapped *The Daily Nonpareil* to look at the headlines; as Owen snapped his fingers and whistled and the dog came running, pleased with herself; as Owen glanced up, as if he could sense Ryan somewhere above him, leaning down, a brush of air across the top of Owen's uncombed, sleepy head.

"Dad," Ryan said. "Dad, please, Dad."

And he saw Jay wince. Jay didn't look at him, he didn't lift his head, but a shudder ran through him, and the man in the suit straightened with interest.

"Oh my goodness," he said. "This is an unexpected development."

Ryan lowered his head.

"Ryan," the man said, "is this your father?"

"No," Ryan whispered.

He let his eyes fall back to the cloud-shaped water stain on the table. A continent, he thought again. An island, like Greenland, an imaginary country, and he let his eyes trace along the coastlines, the bays and archipelagos, and he could almost hear the voice of the meditation tape.

Imagine a place, the voice said. *Notice first the light. Is it bright, natural, or dim? Also notice the temperature level. Hot, warm, or cool? Be aware of the colors that surround you. Allow yourself to simply exist. . . .*

A hiding place, he thought, and for a second he could picture the tents that he used to construct when he was a little boy, the kitchen chairs draped with a big quilt, the dark space in the middle where he would pile pillows and stuffed animals, his own underground nest, which he pictured extending outward into soft, dim, winding corridors made of feathers and blankets.

"I'm going to start with the left hand," the man said. "And then the left foot. And then the right hand, and so on."

The man reached down and touched the freckled skin of Ryan's forearm, very lightly.

"We're going to put a tourniquet here," he murmured. "Which is going to be tight. But that way you won't bleed out quite so fast when I cut your hand off."

For some reason, Ryan was almost distracted. He was thinking of Owen. He was thinking of that ghostly hand that had risen up and grasped his wrist, back when he was a student in a dorm room. He was thinking of his cave under the bedspread.

The man said: "Above the wrist? Or below the wrist?"

And Ryan hardly knew what was being asked until he felt the

wire encircling just above his hand, just above the joint of his thumb. He was shaking so badly that the wire quivered, too, as the man tightened it.

"Please don't," Ryan whispered, but he wasn't sure whether any sound had come from his mouth, after all.

"Now, Ryan," the man said, "I want you to tell your father to be reasonable."

Jay had been watching all of this with a stricken, glassy look, and his eyes widened as he watched the man wrap the thin wire around Ryan's wrist.

"I'm Jay," he cried hoarsely, and the sound was like the call of a crow on a branch. "I'm Jay, I'm Jay, I'm the person you're looking for, my name is Jay Kozelek, I'm the one you want. . . ."

But the man only let out a thick, disgusted sound.

"You must think I'm an idiot," the man rasped. "I *know* Jay Kozelek. He was my *roommate.* I know what he looks like. We used to sit around and talk and watch movies together and all that shit, and I thought he was my friend. That's the worst thing. I actually felt personally close to him, so I know exactly what his face looks like. Do you get that? I know what his face looks like. Do you honestly think you can scam me, after all this time? Do you think I'm a moron? Do you think I'm kidding around here . . ."

None of this made sense to Ryan, but he couldn't think properly in any case.

The man had already begun to tighten the grip on the handles of the cutter, and Ryan let out a scream.

It actually took a very short time.

Astonishingly short.

The wire was sharp, and it sank deeply into the flesh until it reached the radiocarpal joint. It hitched just below the radius and ulna, slipping along the edge of bone until it found the softer gristle, and the man tightened his fists around the handles and pulled tighter, pumping his arms in a quick sawing motion, and the hand came off abruptly. Cleanly.

Ukh, the man said.

There was that memory,

       a ghost reaching up out of the air to touch his wrist and

Not really conscious.

Not looking, not looking at his hand, but there was a hard voice—*Jesus fucking Christ, what are you doing?*—and Ryan's eyes opened and he could see the man standing there, looking down at the floor, blinking. The wire still held loosely in his hands, but he had gone pale and there was a wet sheen over his face. A pinched look, as if he'd taken a drink of something he should have spit out.

There was another man there, too, now—one of the ones Ryan had thought of as a "henchman"—saying, *oh my god Dylan are you insane you said you weren't really going to do it,* and Ryan shuddering and woozy as the two figures blurred into silhouettes and then sharpened against a flare of light reflected against the kitchen window, one of them holding a kitchen towel and bending toward Ryan

and Jay's voice—

"He's going to bleed to death, you guys, it's not his fault, please don't let him bleed to death—"

And then the man, Dylan, staring at Ryan with a wide-eyed, horrified revulsion. The rumpled black gangster suit hung on him like a costume someone had dressed him in while he slept, and he stood there, dazed, uncertain, like a sleepwalker who had awakened into a room that he thought he'd only been dreaming about.

"Oh, jeez," Dylan whispered.

Then he bent over to throw up.

22

It was three and a half hours from Denver to New York on JetBlue Airways, time enough to swing from panic to acceptance and back again several times, and Lucy sat upright in her chair in a state of uneasy, pendulous suspension, her hands folded tightly in her lap.

She had never been on an airplane before—though she couldn't bring herself to admit this embarrassing fact to George Orson.

David Fremden. Dad.

She had been trying to wrap her head around the fact that actually there was no such person as George Orson.

It wasn't simply that everything she knew about him had been invented, or borrowed, or exaggerated—it wasn't simply that he had lied. It was larger than that, an uncanny feeling that opened up in her mind whenever she tried to think calmly and logically about the situation.

He didn't exist anymore.

It made her think of the days after her parents died, the laundry basket still full of their unwashed clothes, the refrigerator stocked with food her mother had planned to cook that weekend, her father's cell phone filling up with calls from customers who wanted to know why he had missed his appointments. At first they would leave behind a few empty spaces in the world—customers who relied on her father, patients who were waiting for her mother to nurse them at the hospital, friends and coworkers and acquaintances who would miss them, for a time—but these were very minor rips and tears in the fabric of things, easily repaired, and the thing that shocked her the most was how quickly such absences began to close. Even after a few weeks you could see how soon her parents would be forgotten, how their presence became an absence, and then—what? What did you call an absence that ceased to become an absence, what do you call a hole that has been filled in?

Oh, she kept thinking. *They'll never come back.* As if the idea were supernatural, science-fictional. How could you believe that such a thing was possible?

That was the thought she had, in bed beside him the night he'd told her the truth, as she traced her fingers across the arm, which was not George Orson's arm. *I'll never talk to George Orson again,* she thought, and she drew her hand back.

He was right there, the same physical body she had been with for so long now, but she couldn't help but feel lonely.

Oh, George, she thought. *I miss you.*

And now she thought it again as she sat in her seat next to David Fremden on the airplane and tried to compose her thoughts.

She missed George Orson. She would never talk to him again.

She had never been on a plane before and she was aware of the terrible, unfathomable distance between herself and the ground. She could sense the air quivering beneath her feet, a shudder of empty space, and she tried to avoid looking out the window. It wasn't so bad to look out and see the thick meringue contours of clouds, but it was harder when the earth began to appear through. The topography. You could see the geometric spread of human habitation, the tiny pencil lines of fields and roads and the boxy spatter of towns, and it was hard not to think of how it would be to fall—how long you would have to plunge before you finally landed.

She'd never have told this to George Orson, anyway. She'd have hated to seem so unsophisticated, for George Orson to see her as some silly rube of a girl, atingle with ignorant dread over the idea of air travel, pressing her nails into the upholstery of the seat arms as if somehow that could anchor her.

David Fremden, meanwhile, looked entirely composed. He was watching the miniature television screen that was embedded into the headrest of the seat in front of him, pausing over a program on pyramids on the History Channel, passing quickly by the news and the weather, smiling nostalgically at an episode of an old 1980s sitcom. He didn't look at her, but he let his hand rest on her forearm.

"You still love me, don't you?" he had asked her—and the question pulsed, as if she could feel it through the whorls of his fingertips.

But there were other things she had to bear in mind, as well. Events were moving fairly fast now. The world continued on, and she had to make some decisions, even without reliable information. There was, purportedly, 4.3 million dollars, in a bank in the Ivory Coast, Africa. There was, at least, more than a hundred thousand dollars currently in their possession.

Their carry-on baggage was in the overhead compartment, right there above them, and that was fine so far, though that, too, was a source of unease.

They had spent their last night in the Lighthouse Motel, side by side in the library, each with a cylinder of cellophane tape, each with a stack of hundred-dollar bills.

David Fremden had a big old atlas, 25 x 20, and Lucy had a dictionary and a Dickens novel, and they sat there, affixing bills to the pages.

"Are you sure this will work?" Lucy had said. She was flipping her way through *Bleak House*, fragments of text rising up as she laid a bill on the page and pinned it down. *"The fog is very dense, indeed!" said I.* And she pressed Ben Franklin over the line of words, and then flipped a couple of pages forward. *"It's disgraceful,"* she said. *"You know it is. The whole house is disgraceful."* And she covered it again, though once again some grain of the book rose up: *We found Miss Jellyby trying to warm herself at the fire . . .*

"It's not a problem," David Fremden said. He himself was working more rapidly than she, lining a row of three hundreds down the center of Ireland, pressing a tongue of adhesive tape along the edge of the bills with his thumb. "I've done this before," he said.

"Okay," she said.

"The universe," he observed, *"makes rather an indifferent parent, I am afraid."*

"But isn't there an X-ray machine?" she said. "Won't they be able to see through the covers of the books?"

. . . is the portrait of the present Lady Dedlock. It is considered a perfect likeness, and . . .

"Look," David Fremden said, and he sighed. "You'll just have to trust me on this. I know how these security systems work. I really do know what I'm doing."

And so far, yes, he had been right, though she had been dreadfully nervous. Her body had felt almost mystically visible when they came to the front of the security line, as if her skin were giving off an aura of light. She was shocked that people weren't staring at her, but no one seemed to notice. She put her satchel—which contained a few toiletries and a T-shirt and the books—into a gray plastic tub, and she couldn't help but think of the swollen pages of *Bleak House,* stuffed full of money, even as she bent down to remove her shoes, even as the conveyor belt carried her bag through the tunnel of the X-ray machine.

"Okay," said the security guard, and motioned her forward through the doorway-shaped metal detector, a thick, blank-eyed, weight lifter guy, perhaps not much older than she was, beckoning her through, and there were no alarms, no hesitation as her bag passed through, no second glance at her wretchedly dyed hair, nothing.

David Fremden put his hand on her elbow.

"Good job," he murmured.

And so now the plane was on the tarmac in New York. They were sitting in their seats, waiting for the captain to turn off the FASTEN SEAT BELTS sign, though some of the passengers around them were already impatiently stirring in their seats. Lucy herself was still trying to recover her equilibrium from the experience of landing, the grinding sounds the wheels made as they unfolded, the sudden, quivering bump as the plane touched the landing strip, the way her ears had filled up with a plug of viscous air. She tried to be stern with herself. *You're such an idiot, Lucy. Such a white trash hillbilly, what are you scared of? What are you scared of?*

But the truth was that her leg had developed a tic, she could feel one of the muscles giving a small involuntary twitch and when she put her hand on her thigh she could hear another voice in her head, a small, sad tremor.

I don't want to do this. I think I've made a mistake.

It was like butterflies had begun to alight on her, hundreds of butterflies, and they were each one of them made of lead. It wasn't long before she was covered with them.

There was a soft, deep bell tone, and en masse the rest of the passengers began to sigh and rise, converging into the aisles and opening the overhead compartments and leaning close to the person in front of them, not disorderly, not exactly, but almost like a school of fish or migrating birds, and she looked up as David Fremden stood to join them.

"Brooke," he said. He reached down and took her hand in his and gave it a tight squeeze. "Come on, sweetheart," he whispered. "Don't fail me now."

It was easy enough to get onto her feet. It was easy enough to shuffle down the narrow aisle of the airplane, following behind David— her father—

He handed over her backpack with one of those gently teasing smiles that reminded her so much of George Orson. That grin that had so impressed her back when she was a student in his AP history class, back when he told her he thought she was sui generis. "People like you and me, we invent ourselves," he had said, though there was no way to know back then that he meant it literally.

She missed George Orson.

But she took a breath and fell into the shuffling queue of travelers. It was easy enough. Easy enough to put her head down and trudge through the tight rows of seats. Easy enough to walk past the stewardess, who stood at the front of the plane nodding like a priest, peace be with you, peace be with you, ushering them into the accordion tunnel that led up into the terminal.

"You look peaked," David said. "Are you feeling all right?"

"I'm fine," Lucy said.

"Why don't we get a cup of coffee," he said. "Or a soda? A little something to eat?"

"No, thanks," Lucy said.

They had turned into the rambling avenue that ran past the various gates—counters and podiums surrounded by clusters of anchored chairs, pods full of waiting people, and as far as she could tell, no one was looking at them. No one gave them a second glance, no one wondered if they were father and daughter, or lovers, or teacher and student. Whatever. Back in Pompey, Ohio, the two of them might have caused a stir of curiosity, but here they hardly registered.

Lucy gazed at a trio of women in burkas, blue, faceless, nunlike figures, chatting amiably in their native tongue, and a tall, balding man swept past them, speed-walking, swearing joyfully into his cell phone, and then an old woman in a wheelchair, wearing a full-length fur coat, pushed along by a black man in gray coveralls—

Lucy could feel the weight of her backpack. *Bleak House* and *Webster's Dictionary* and *Marjorie Morningstar,* which between them contained perhaps fifty thousand dollars.

She adjusted the strap on her shoulder, then tugged at the hated butterfly T-shirt as it inched up, exposing her belly. She was aware of how much she would have disliked Brooke Fremden, back in the day. If Brooke Fremden had come traipsing down the halls of Pompey High School, with her cutesy mall-girl clothes and her juvenile, perky backpack, Lucy would have been repulsed.

But when David Fremden looked over his shoulder at her, his look was mild and fatherly and distracted. She was just a girl, just a teenage girl. This was what they looked like; it didn't matter to him as long as she was keeping pace.

He didn't miss Lucy, she thought.

"You've done this before," she said. "I'm not the first."

This was on the night before their trip. They were still in the house above the Lighthouse Motel, and they sat there on the couch in the television room, side by side, their bags packed and the rooms hushed in the way of places that are about to be abandoned.

The books were taped full of money, and they should have just gone to bed, but instead they were sitting there watching the opening monologue of some late-night talk show host, and his face, David's face, was entirely blank, that flat television-watching expression, and at last she repeated herself.

"You've been other people before," she said, and at last he looked away from the TV and glanced at her warily.

"That's a complicated question," he said.

"Don't you think it's fair to be honest with me?" she said. "We're . . ."

Together?

She thought about it.

Maybe it was better to say nothing. It was weird—all this time she'd spent in this musty television room, all the hours she'd spent alone with nothing but old videos for company, *Rebecca* and *Mrs. Miniver* and *Double Indemnity* and *How Green Was My Valley* and *My Fair Lady* and *Mildred Pierce.* Sipping diet soda and glancing out at the raggedy Japanese garden and waiting for the chance to get back into the Maserati and drive away to someplace wonderful.

He had been "a lot of different people." He admitted as much.

So—it was probably logical to think that there had also been other girls, other Lucys, sitting on this same couch and watching the same old movies and listening to the same stillness as the Lighthouse Motel brooded over its dusty swathe of empty lake bed.

"I just want to know—" she said. "I want to know about the others. How many have there been—in your life. In all this."

And he looked up. He pulled his gaze away from the TV and met her eyes and his expression wavered.

"There's never been anyone else," he said. "That's what you don't understand. I've been looking—I've been looking for a long time. But there's never been anyone like you."

So.

No, she didn't believe him, though maybe he had managed to convince himself. Perhaps he truly thought that it didn't matter if she was Lucy or Brooke or whatever other name she would take on. Perhaps he imagined she would remain the same person on the inside, no matter what name or persona she adopted.

But that wasn't true, she thought.

More and more, she was aware that Lucy Lattimore had left the earth. Already there was hardly anything left of her—a few scraps of documents, birth certificate and social security card in her mother's drawer back in the old house, her high school transcript resident on some outdated computer, the memories of her sister, Patricia, the vague recollections of her classmates and teachers, already fading.

The truth was, she had killed herself months ago. Now she was next to nothing: a nameless physical form that could be exchanged and exchanged and exchanged until nothing remained but molecules.

The stuff of stars—that's what George Orson once said when he was holding forth to their history class. *Hydrogen and carbon and all the primordial particles that existed from the very beginning of time, that's what you're made up of,* he told them.

As if that were a comfort.

They would be flying to Brussels, first. Seven hours, twenty-five minutes, on a Boeing 767, and then from there another six hours and forty-five minutes to Abidjan. They had already made it through the most difficult passage, David Fremden said. The customs exercises in Belgium and Ivory Coast were negligible. "We can actually relax now and think about the future."

4.3 million dollars.

"I don't want to stay in Africa for very long," he said. "I just want to get the money situation settled, and then we can go wherever we want.

"I've never been to Rome," he said. "I'd love to spend some time in Italy. Naples, Tuscany, Florence. I think that would be a wonderful, growing experience for you. I think it would be exciting, actually. Like Henry James," he said. "Like E. M. Forster," he said. "Lucy

Honeychurch," he said, and chuckled as if this were a bit of levity she would appreciate—

But she had no idea what he was talking about.

Back in the day, back when he was George Orson and she was his student, she half enjoyed his high-handed trivia, the bits of Ivy League education he would drop into conversation. She used to roll her eyes and pretend to be exasperated by his pretentiousness, the way he raised his eyebrows in that gently reproachful way—as if she'd expressed some lack of knowledge that surprised him. "Who's Spinoza?" Or: "What's sodium pentothal?" And he might have a complicated and even interesting answer.

But that was not who they were anymore, they were not Lucy and George Orson, and so she sat there wordlessly, she looked down at her ticket, New York to Brussels, and

Who's Lucy Honeychurch? Who's E. M. Forster?

It didn't matter. It wasn't important, though she couldn't help but think again of the question she'd asked George Orson the night before: what happened to the other ones, the ones before me?

She could imagine this Lucy Honeychurch—a blond girl, no doubt, a person who wore thrift store sweaters and vintage eyeglasses, a girl who probably thought she was more clever than she actually was. Had he taken her to the Lighthouse Motel? Had they walked together through the ruins of the drowned village? Had he dressed her up in someone else's clothes and hurried her to an airport with a fake passport in her purse, off to another city, another state, some foreign place?

Where was the girl now? Lucy wondered, as people began to stand, as the plane for Brussels announced the beginnings of boarding.

Where was the girl now? Lucy thought. What had happened to her?

23

Here was Banks Island, Aulavik National Park. A polar desert, Mr. Itigaituk told them dryly, in his genial, affectless voice. As they flew, he pointed out landmarks as if they were on a tour: there was a pingo, a conical volcano-shaped hill, filled with ice rather than lava; here was Sachs Harbour, a cluster of houses on a barren, muddy shore; and here were the small interlocking ponds of the dry valleys, and—look!—a herd of musk oxen!

But now, as they walked across the tundra toward the place where the old research station was supposed to be, as the waiting Cessna plane grew smaller and smaller behind them, Mr. Itigaituk was taciturn. Every twenty minutes or so, he stopped to regard his compass, to press his binoculars to his eyes and scan the gray expanse of pebbles and rocks.

Miles had been given a pair of rubber boots, and a jacket, and he took a nervous glance over his shoulder as he trudged along through the damp gravel and puddles and the chill, faintly misty air.

Lydia Barrie, meanwhile, was striding along with remarkable poise, particularly for someone who was surely, Miles thought, colossally hungover. But it didn't show in her face, and when Mr. It-igaituk pointed out a bowl-like depression of gray-white fur—the corpse of a fox, which a goose had made a nest out of—Lydia regarded it with dispassionate interest.

"Gross," Miles said, staring down at the fox's head, the skin tight over the skull, the shriveled eye sockets, the teeth bared and freckled with goose dung. Two eggs lay in the rounded impression of rotten hair.

"Well said," Lydia murmured.

It had been a few miles since they'd said anything to each other. There was, naturally, a certain amount of awkwardness, given what had happened between them the night before, a certain post-intimacy reticence—which wasn't made any easier by the ambient disquiet that had settled over him. A hum in his ear that wouldn't go away.

This was crazy, he thought.

Was it probable that Hayden had come to this place, was it likely that he was actually living here in this tundra flatland, the pinprick of the Cessna still visible, many kilometers behind them?

Perhaps he had been on more futile chases than she had, perhaps he had grown fatalistic. But this didn't look very promising.

"How much farther do you think we have to go?" he said, glancing tactfully toward Mr. Itigaituk, who was by now about ten yards ahead of them. "Are we sure we're going in the right direction?"

Lydia Barrie adjusted the fingers of her glove, her eyes still on the fox, the bones and fur that had made some goose such a comfortable resting place.

"I'm feeling fairly confident," she said, and they looked at each other.

Miles nodded wordlessly.

———

For a while, he had been telling her about Cleveland.

About Hayden, naturally, but also about their childhood, and their father, and even his life today, his job in the old novelty shop, Mrs. Matalov and her granddaughter—

"And yet here you are," Lydia said. "It sounds as if you could have been happy, Miles, and yet here you are, on an island in the Arctic Ocean. It's a shame."

"I guess," Miles said. He shrugged, a little flustered. "I don't know. 'Happy' is a strong word."

" 'Happy' is a strong word?" she repeated mildly, in the way a therapist might. She raised her eyebrows. "What an odd thing to say."

And Miles shrugged again. "I don't know," he said. "I just meant—I wasn't *that* happy in Cleveland."

"I see," she said.

"Just—neutral. I mean, I was working at a catalog company, basically. It wasn't anything special. You know. Spending my nights in an empty apartment most of the time, watching TV."

"Yes," she said, and straightened the collar of her coat as wind blew across them.

It wasn't cold, exactly. Miles estimated that the temperature was somewhere around fifty degrees Fahrenheit, and the endless daylight beamed down upon them. The sky had a glassy, silvery sharpness—more like the reflection of a sky in a pair of mirrored sunglasses. That eerie phosphorescent blue the earth has, when seen from space.

"So," Lydia said at last. "If we find him, do you think you'll be happy then?"

"I don't know," Miles said.

It was a lame answer, no doubt, but honestly he wasn't sure how he would feel. To have things resolved, finally, after all these years? He couldn't quite imagine.

And she seemed to understand that, too. She inclined her head as their feet made soft hushing sounds through the gravel, which was piled in wrinkled ridges like the pebbles in the bed of a stream. Left that way, Miles guessed, by the accumulation and melt of snow.

"And if we don't find him?" Lydia said, after they had trudged in silence for a while. "What then? You'll just get back into your car and drive home to Cleveland?"

"I suppose so."

He shrugged again, and this time she laughed, a surprisingly lighthearted, even affectionate sound.

"Oh, Miles," she said. "I can't believe that you *drove* all the way to Inuvik. That just astounds me." She glanced up ahead at Mr. Itigaituk, who was a dozen or more yards ahead of them, leading determinedly onward.

"You're a very odd person, Miles Cheshire," she said, and regarded him thoughtfully. "I wish—"

But she didn't complete her sentence. She let it drift off, and Miles guessed that she had thought better of what she was going to say.

He was trying to think about the future.

The longer they walked, the more it became clear to Miles that this was yet another one of Hayden's elaborate practical jokes, another maze that he had created, that they were winding their way through.

He *would* go back, he guessed. Back to Cleveland, back to Matalov Novelties, where the old lady was waiting impatiently for him to return to work; and he would return to his corner of the cluttered store, sitting at his computer under the framed black-and-white photos of old vaudevillians, sometimes contemplating the photo of his own father, his dad, dressed in a cape and tuxedo, holding a wand with a flourish.

As for Miles, he was not a magician, nor would he ever be, but he could picture himself becoming a respected figure among them. Their shopkeeper. Already, he had a good eye for the inventory and expenses at Matalov, already he had straightened the disordered shelves and updated the website to make shopping more user-friendly, doing something *useful* at least, making a small pathway through his life that his father might have respected.

Wasn't that enough? Wasn't there the possibility that he could settle in, that he could become happy or at least content? Wasn't there the chance that—after this one last time, the shadow of Hayden would begin to draw away from his thoughts and he could finally, finally escape at last?

Was that so difficult? So improbable?

And then he glanced up as Mr. Itigaituk turned and called back to them.

"I see it," Mr. Itigaituk said. "It's just up ahead!"

Lydia adjusted her sunglasses and craned her neck, and Miles shaded his eyes against the gleaming sky and the wind, squinting toward the horizon.

They all stood there, uncertainly.

"So," Miles said at last. "What do we do now?"

Mr. Itigaituk and Lydia Barrie exchanged a look.

"I mean," Miles said, "do we just walk up to the door and knock? Or what?"

And Lydia regarded him, her sunglasses an unreadable blankness.

"Do you have another suggestion?" she said.

The research station was like a beachfront house. A stilt house, Miles thought, except that there was no water or shoreline in sight, no sense that there would ever be flooding here.

The building itself was little more than three linked mobile homes, propped up on piles, about four or five feet off the ground. It had the white corrugated metal siding he'd seen so much of back in Inuvik, and on the flat roof was a small orchard of metal antennae and satellite dishes and other transmitting instruments. Along the side of the building was a large capsule-shaped tank, such as holds natural gas, and a few metal barrels, also raised on stilts, probably for petroleum. Some wires ran from the main building to a small wooden shack, the size of an outhouse.

"Are you sure this is . . . ," Miles said, and Mr. Itigaituk turned to glare at him with a brisk hunterlike focus.

"Shhhhhhh," Mr. Itigaituk said.

The place was obviously abandoned, Miles thought. The windows—four on each side—were not windows you could look out of. They had a gray opaque film over them, probably a form of insulation. A weathervanc, an aluminum wind spinner, was creaking in the tranquil thicket of metal poles on the roof of the building.

As Mr. Itigaituk crept forward, a raven lifted up from the ramshackle outhouse structure and sailed off.

"He's not here," Miles whispered, more to himself than to Lydia.

He had never believed in any of Hayden's paranormal nonsense, though over the years he had played along with various of Hayden's obsessions: past lives and geodesy, numerology and Ouija boards, telepathy and out-of-body travel.

But he did believe in *something*.

He did believe that when he finally found Hayden, when he finally came within striking distance, he would be able to tell. There would be some extrasensory "twin" radar, he thought. An alarm would be triggered and he would sense it in his body. It would go off in his chest like a cell phone set to vibrate. If Hayden was inside this building, Miles would know it.

"This isn't the place," he murmured.

But Lydia only turned to him, blankly. She put out her gloved hand and rested it on Miles's shoulder.

Hush.

She was watching with an ardent, almost quivering attention. He thought of a gambler, that prayerful second of held breath as the roulette wheel slows and the silver ball settles into its place at last.

She looked so certain and focused that he couldn't help but doubt his own instincts.

Maybe. Maybe it was possible?

She seemed to know things that he did not, after all, she seemed to have done her research.

What if Hayden really was there? What would they do?

Miles and Lydia stood at a distance from the building as Mr. Itigaituk came to the set of wooden stairs that led up to the door.

They watched as Mr. Itigaituk crouched to creep up each step. Together they watched; they caught their breath as he placed his hand on the knob of the door.

Not locked.

Miles closed his eyes. *Okay,* he thought.

Okay. Yes. This is it.

The place was empty.

The door opened unsteadily, and Mr. Itigaituk stood for what seemed like a long while, peering in. Then he turned and looked at them.

"Uninhabited," Mr. Itigaituk said, and finally the spell broke. Miles and Lydia both realized that they'd been standing at a distance, as if waiting for Mr. Itigaituk to defuse a bomb.

"Nothing," Mr. Itigaituk said critically, and gave them both a mild, accusatory look. "Nobody here for a long time."

A *very* long time, Miles realized. Perhaps a year, maybe more. He could tell from the mushroomlike cellar smell of the air as they stepped inside.

The front room, about the size and shape of a semi truck trailer, was gray-carpeted and entirely devoid of furniture. Some pieces of paper were pinned to the corkboard that lined the walls, and they set up a flutter of henhouse anxiety when the wind came in.

"Hello?" Lydia called, but her voice was small and wan. "Rachel?" she said, and stepped hesitantly toward the open doorway that led toward the back rooms. "Hello? Rachel?"

It was darker in the back rooms.

Not pitch-black, but dim, like a hotel room with the shades pulled, and the resourceful Mr. Itigaituk took a small flashlight from his pocket and clicked it on.

"God damn it," Lydia Barrie said, and Miles said nothing.

Here, in this next room, the walls were lined with folding tables, such as you might find in a high school cafeteria. And there was some unplaceable equipment—a large boxy thing, with jagged picket-fence teeth; smaller weathervanes and pinwheel-like wands; a file cabinet with the drawers removed, folders scattered on the floor.

The musky old-clothes smell was stronger now, and Mr. Itigaituk ran the line of his flashlight into a side room that Miles saw was a kitchen and pantry area. Dirty dishes were piled high in the sink, and empty cans and candy bar wrappers lined the counter space, beneath cupboards that were open and mostly empty.

A box of Cap'n Crunch cereal, almost unrecognizably faded, was sitting on the table, next to a bowl and a spoon and a can of condensed milk.

Mr. Itigaituk solemnly turned to look at Lydia, and his expression confirmed what Miles had been thinking. The place had been abandoned for—years, Miles guessed. It wasn't even a close call.

"Fuck," Lydia Barrie said, under her breath, and at last she took a flask from her bag and sipped from it. Her face was drawn, tired, and her hand had a tremor as she offered the flask to Miles.

"I was feeling so confident," she said as Miles took the flask. He considered it, but didn't drink.

"Yes," Miles said. "He's good at this. Fooling people. I guess you could say that it's his life's work."

He held the flask out to her, and she took it, putting it to her lips again.

"I'm sorry," Miles said.

He had been doing this for so long now that this was a familiar feeling—the urgency and anticipation, the swell of emotion. And then disappointment. Anticlimax, which, in its own way, was like sorrow. It was not unlike having your heart broken, he imagined.

And then they both looked up as Mr. Itigaituk cleared his throat. He was standing a few yards away, near the dark entrance to the back rooms.

"Ms. Barrie," he said. "You may want to look at this."

It was a bedroom.

They stood in the doorway, staring in, and it was from here that the smell of old earth and musty cloth emanated most strongly. It was a narrow room, with barely enough space for a bed and some shelves, but it had been decorated extravagantly.

Decorated? Was that the right term?

It reminded him of the stuff they'd talked about in one of the art classes he took at Ohio University. Art Brut, the teacher called it. Outsider Art: and he'd thought then of the dioramas and statues that Hayden used to make when they were kids.

This "decoration" was along those lines, though much more elaborate, filling the entire room. There were mobiles that had been strung from the ceiling, origami fish, origami swans and peacocks, origami nautilus shells and pinwheels; clouds made from cotton batting, wind chimes made of small stones and microscope slides. The shelves were filled with knickknacks that Hayden had made out of rocks and bones, nails, bits of wood and soup cans, plastic wrap, strips of cloth, some feathers, some fur, computer parts, all kinds of unrecognizable junk.

Some of these creations had been arranged into a tableau— and Miles had worked in the magic shop long enough to recognize scenes from the tarot cards. Here was the Four of Swords: a tiny figure made out of clay or mud or flour rested on a cardboard bed, covered in a tiny blanket cut from a piece of corduroy, and above the bed were three nails, pointing downward. Here was the tower—a conical structure made from pebbles, with two miniature paper clip stick people hurling themselves from the turret.

Beneath these objects, clothes had been arranged on the bed. Side by side: a white blouse and a white T-shirt, arms outstretched. Two pairs of jeans. Two pairs of socks. As if they had been sleeping there next to each other and then had simply evaporated, leaving nothing but their empty clothes.

And all around these figures were various flowers: lilies made from goose feathers, roses made out of the pages of books, baby's breath made from wire and bits of insulation. Flecks of mica glinted as Mr. Itigaituk passed his flashlight over the—

Shrine, Miles supposed you would call it.

It was like one of those memorials that one sees along the side of the highway, the jumble of crosses and plastic bouquets and stuffed animals and handmade signs that marked the place where someone had been killed in a car wreck.

Above the empty clothes, some large flat rocks had been arranged in an arch, and on each rock a rune had been etched.

Runes: it was the old game, the old alphabet that they'd invented back when they were twelve, "letters" that were somewhere between Phoenician and Tolkien, which they'd pretended was an ancient language.

He could read the letters well enough. He still remembered.

R-A-C-H-E-L,   it said.   H-A-Y-D-E-N.

And then below that, in smaller letters, it said:

e-a-d-e-m   m-u-t-a-t-a   r-e-s-u-r-g-o

He guessed it was like a grave of some kind.

———

The three of them stood there mutely, and they could all see what this exhibit was meant to convey, they could all tell that they were in the presence of a memorial, or a tomb. There must have been a breeze coming in from the front door, because the mobiles had begun to stir lightly, casting slowly turning shadows on the wall as Mr. Itigaituk's flashlight caught them. The wind chimes made an uncertain, rattling whisper.

"I guess those must be Rachel's clothes," Lydia said at last, hoarsely, and Miles shrugged.

"I'm not sure," he said.

"What is it?" Lydia said. "Is it a message?"

Miles shook his head. He was thinking about the oddly stacked figures of rocks and branches that Hayden used to make in the backyard of their old house, after their father died. He was thinking of the tattered copy of *Frankenstein,* which he'd received in the mail not long after his trip to North Dakota, the passage in the final chapter that had been highlighted:

> Follow me; I seek the everlasting ices of the north, where you will feel the misery of cold and frost to which I am impassive. . . . Come on, my enemy.

"I think it means that they're both dead," Miles said finally, and then he paused.

Did he really think that? Or did he just wish that it were true?

Lydia was shuddering a little, but her face remained still. He didn't know what she was feeling. Rage? Despair? Grief? Or was it merely a version of the numb, blank, wordless hollowness that had settled over him as he remembered the letter that Hayden had sent him: *Do you remember the Great Tower of Kallupilluk? That may be my final resting place, Miles. You may never hear from me again.*

"He left this stuff for me," Miles said quietly. "I guess he thought I would understand what it meant."

Knowing Hayden, Miles assumed that every single object in the room was a message, every sculpture and diorama was supposed to tell a story. Knowing Hayden, each object was built as if it would be given the attention that an archaeologist would give to a set of long-lost scrolls.

And—Miles supposed that he did understand the gist of it. Or at least he could interpret—in the way that fortune-tellers found a story in the random lines of a person's palm or the sticks of the *I Ching;* the way mystics found secret communications everywhere, converting letters to numbers and numbers to letters, magical numerals nestled in the verses of the Bible, incantatory words to be discovered in the endless string of digits that made up pi.

Would it be a lie to say there was a narrative to be found in this jumble of dioramas and statues and mobiles? Would it be dishonest? Would it be any different than a therapist who takes the stuff of dreams, the landscapes and objects and random surreal events, and weaves them into some meaning?

"It's a suicide note," Miles said at last, very gently, and he pointed toward the stack of stones, with the paper clip people throwing themselves from the summit.

"That's the Great Tower of Kallupilluk," he said. "It's . . . a story we made up when we were kids. It's a lighthouse at the very edge of the world, and that's where the immortal ones go, when they are ready to leave this life. They sail off from the shore beyond the lighthouse, and into the sky."

He gazed intently at these objects that Hayden had left for him, as if each one were a hieroglyph, each one a still frame like the fresco cycles of ancient times.

Yes. You could say that there was a story here.

———

In Miles's version of things, he imagined that they had come here in the fall.

Hayden and Rachel. They had been in love, like they were in that photograph that Lydia had shown him. This was a place that they thought they could hide, just for a short time, just until Hayden got things back on track.

They hadn't planned to stay long, but winter came faster than they expected, and they were trapped before they knew it. And Rachel—you could see her in that mobile, there, with the down feathers and bits of colored glass—had gotten sick. She had gone out to look at the aurora borealis. She was a romantic girl, an impractical girl, an amateur photographer—you could see the rolls of film in that diorama, perhaps they could be developed—perhaps they'd contain the pictures she took in her last days—

But she didn't realize. She didn't understand that in this country, even a few minutes of exposure to the elements could be terribly dangerous. You could see her there, delirious in her bed, under those nails—

And by that time, the food had begun to run out, and Hayden didn't know how long the generator would last. And so he'd made a sled for Rachel, and he'd wrapped her in blankets and coats and furs, and he set out. He planned to try to walk to the southern part of the island. It was their only hope.

"No," Mr. Itigaituk said, and shook his head cynically. "That's ridiculous. They would never make it. It would have been impossible."

"He knew that," Miles said. "That's what those stones mean, there. He understood that it was hopeless, but he wanted to try anyway."

Miles looked at Lydia, who had been standing there, listening blankly as he'd talked. As he *interpreted*.

"No," she said. "That doesn't make sense. How could they have been dead for so long? How could—we both have letters from him, recent letters—"

Letters that might have been left with someone, perhaps. Please send these out if I don't come back in a year. Here's a hundred dollars, two hundred dollars for your trouble.

"Maybe you're right," Miles said. "Maybe they're still alive somewhere."

But Lydia had fallen into her own thoughts. Not convinced, but. Even so.

It probably wasn't true, but wouldn't it be nice to believe?

It would be such a relief, Miles thought, such a comfort to think that they'd finally come to the end of the story. Wasn't that the gift that Hayden was giving to them, with this display? Wasn't this Hayden's version of kindness?

A present for you, Miles. A present for you, too, Lydia. You've come at last to the edge of the earth, and now your journey is finished. An ending for you, if you want it.

If only you'll accept it.

24

Ryan had been living in Ecuador for almost a year now, and he had begun to get used to the idea that he would probably never see Jay again.

He was getting used to a lot of things.

He was living in the Old Town part of Quito—Centro Histórico—in a small apartment on Calle Espejo, which was a fairly busy pedestrian boulevard, and he had become inured to the sound of the city, its early waking. There was a magazine stand just below his window, so he didn't need an alarm clock. Before daylight, he would hear the metal clatter as Señor Gamboa Pulido set up his racks and arranged his newspapers, and shortly thereafter voices began to weave their way up into his half consciousness. For a long while, the sound of Spanish sentences was little more than burbling music, but that had begun to change, too. It had not taken as long as he'd expected before the syllables had begun to solidify into words, before he realized that he himself had begun to think in Spanish.

He was still limited, obviously. Still recognizably American, but he could get by in the market or on the street, he could absorb the patter of the disc jockeys on the radio, he could watch television and understand the news, the plots and dialogue of the soap operas, he could exchange friendly conversation at the coffee shops or Internet cafés, he was aware when people were talking about him—watching curiously as he bent over the keyboard, impressed by how quickly he could type with one hand.

He was becoming accustomed to that, as well.

Sometimes in the morning there were occasionally odd twinges. The ghost of his hand would ache, the palm would itch, the fingers would appear to be flexing. But he was no longer surprised to open his eyes and find that it was gone. He had stopped waking up with the certainty that the hand had come back to him, that it had somehow rematerialized in the middle of the night, sprouted and regenerated from the stump of his wrist.

The keen sense of loss had faded, and these days he found that he stumbled less and less over that absence. He could dress and even tie his shoes without much trouble. He could make toast and coffee, crack an egg into a skillet, all one-handed, and some days he wouldn't even bother to wear his prosthesis.

"Eggs" was one of the words that he sometimes stumbled over. *Huevos? Huecos? Huesos?* Eggs, holes, bones.

For the time being, he was using a myoelectric hook, which fit like a gauntlet over his stump. He could open and close the prongs simply by flexing the muscles in his forearm, and he was actually pretty adept at using it. Nevertheless, there were days when it was easier—less conspicuous—to simply button a cuff over the bare empty wrist. He didn't like the interest that the hook aroused in people, the startled glances, the fear from women and children. It was enough to be a gringo, a Yankee, without the added attention.

In the beginning, as he made his way through the Plaza de la Independencia, in the promenade around the winged victory statue, he would find that he attracted notice, despite himself. He remembered Walcott's admonition: *Never look at people directly in the face!* But nevertheless he found that shoe-shining street urchins would dash behind him, making their shrill incomprehensible cries, and the old country women, in their gray braids and anaco caps, would deepen their frowns as he passed. Quito was a city full of a surprising number of clowns and mimes, and these, too, were drawn to him. A ragged, red-nosed skeleton on stilts; a white-faced zombie in a dusty black suit, walking like a mechanical toy through a crosswalk; an elderly man, with lipstick and green eye shadow and a pink turban, holding up a fistful of tarot cards, calling after him, *"Fortuna! Fortuna!"*

Sometimes it would be a college kid, with a backpack and sandals, army surplus clothes. "Hey, dude! Are you American?"

This happened to him less frequently now. He passed through the plaza without much incident. The old fortune-teller merely lifted his head as Ryan passed, the brothel makeup worn down by perspiration, sad eyes following as Ryan made his way toward the Presidential Palace, the white colonnaded façade, the old eighteenth-century jail cells that had once lined the foot of the palace now opened and transformed into barber shops and clothing stores and fast-food joints.

Above the city, on the mountaintops, a Calvary of antennae and satellite dishes gazed down. And through the gaps in buildings he could occasionally see the great statue on Panecillo Hill, the Virgin of the Apocalypse in her dancing pose, hovering over the valley.

Financially, he was doing okay. Despite the setbacks, he still had a few bank accounts that had not been discovered, and he had begun, very cautiously, to transfer monies from one to the next—a little trickle that was keeping him comfortable. He had set up some trusts that were, in fact, producing dividends, and in the meantime he had managed to find a new name that he had settled into. David Angel Verdugo Cubrero, an Ecuadorian national—with a passport and everything—and when people would look at him oddly, he would shrug. "My mother was an American," he told them, and he set up a savings account and got David a couple of credit cards, and it seemed to be fine. He appeared to have escaped.

The men who had attacked them, the men who had cut off his hand, had apparently lost his trail.

He guessed that Jay had not been so lucky.

Whatever had happened that night was still blurry in his mind. He still didn't know what the men had been after, or why they had insisted that Jay wasn't Jay, or why they had left in such a panic, or how Jay had managed to get free from the chair he was taped to. No matter how many times he tried to put it together in his mind, the events remained stubbornly illogical, random, fragmentary.

By the time they reached the hospital, Ryan had lost a lot of blood, and the color had washed out of his vision. He could remember—he thought he remembered—the automatic sliding doors opening as they stumbled into the entrance of the emergency room. He could remember the surprised, quivering nurse in her balloon-patterned smock, puzzled as Jay thrust the beer cooler at her. "It's his hand," Jay said. "You can put it back on, right? You can fix it, right?"

He could remember Jay kissing his hair, whispering thickly, "You're not going to die; I love you, Son; you're the only one who has ever been there for me; I'm not going to let anything bad happen to you; you're going to be fine—"

"Yes," Ryan said. "Okay," he said, and when he closed his eyes, he could hear Jay telling someone, "He fell off a ladder. And his hand—caught on a piece of wire. It happened so quickly."

Why is he lying? Ryan thought dreamily.

And then, the next thing he could recall he was in a hospital bed, the stump of his wrist mummy-wrapped and the ghost of his hand throbbing dully, and the young doctor, Doctor Ali, with his black hair pulled back in a ponytail and his weary brown eyes, telling him that there was some unfortunate news, about his hand, the doctor said they had been unable to reattach the extremity; too much time had passed, and as a small hospital they were not equipped—

"Where is it?" Ryan said. That was his first thought. What had they done with his hand?

And the doctor had glanced at the tiny blond nurse who was standing off to the side. "Unfortunately," the doctor said ruefully, "it's gone."

"Where's my father?" Ryan had asked then. He was comprehending things all right, but nothing was sinking in. His brain felt flat, two-dimensional, and he gazed uncertainly at the door to his hospital room. He could hear the *clip, clip* of someone's hard-soled shoes against the floor of the hallway outside.

"Where's my dad?" he said, and again the doctor and nurse exchanged solemn looks.

"Mr. Wimberley," the doctor said, "do you have a phone number where your father can be reached? Is there someone else that you'd like us to call?"

It wasn't until Ryan had finally looked in his wallet that he had found the note. The wallet—still with his Max Wimberley driver's license—was stuffed with money. Fifteen one-hundred-dollar bills, some twenties, some ones, and there was also a small folded piece of paper, Jay's neat, tiny block-letter handwriting:

R—Leave the country ASAP. I will meet you in Quito, will contact you when I am able. Hurry!

Love always, Jay.

When he'd first arrived in Quito, he kept expecting that Jay would arrive any day. He would scope through the pedestrians on the plaza and the cobblestone sidewalks, he would peer into the narrow cluttered shops, he would sit in various Internet cafés and type Jay's names into search engines, all the names that he could remember Jay ever using. He'd check through every email account he'd ever had, and then he'd double-check.

He didn't want to think that Jay was dead, though maybe it was easier than imagining that Jay just wasn't coming.

That Jay had abandoned him.

That Jay wasn't even Jay, but just some—what?—another avatar?

In those first few months, he would stand at the balcony of his second-floor apartment, listening to the peddler girls who stood outside the Teatro Bolivar, just down the block. Beautiful, sorrowful Otavaleñas, sisters perhaps, twins, with their black braided hair and white peasant blouses and red shawls, holding their baskets of strawberries or lima beans or flowers, chanting "One dollar, one dollar, one dollar, one dollar." At first he'd thought the girls were singing. Their voices were so sweet and musical and yearning, twined together in counterpoint, sometimes harmonizing: "One dollar, one dollar, one dollar." As if their hearts had been broken.

Now almost a year had passed, and he didn't think of Jay quite so much. Not quite so often.

In the afternoon, he'd walk down to Calle Flores to an Internet café that he liked. It was just past the coral-colored stucco walls of the Hotel Viena Internacional, where the American and European students could stay for cheap, and the Ecuadorian businessmen could spend a few hours with a prostitute. Just down the hill, where the narrow side street opened abruptly into a panorama view of the eastern mountains, the stacks and stacks of houses were set in corn-row circles beneath the thin blue sky.

Here. Just an open doorway with a hand-painted sign: INTERNET, and a set of steep, crooked stairs. A cramped back room with rows of ancient, dirty computers.

The proprietor was an old American. Raines Davis, he was called, perhaps seventy years old, who sat behind the counter, slowly filling an ashtray with cigarette butts. His thick white hair had a yellowish tinge, as if stained with smoke.

Often the place was full of students, all hunched over their key-boards, eyes fixed on the box of the monitor, but sometimes in the late afternoon it was more or less empty, and that was Ryan's fa-vorite time, very tranquil, very private, the thin cirrus of cigarette smoke hanging just below the ceiling. Yes, sometimes he would type in "Ryan Schuyler," just to see if anything came up; he would look at satellite photos of Council Bluffs, it was so sophisticated these days that you could see his house, you could see Stacey's car in the driveway, pulling out, on her way to work, he guessed.

He had even wondered what would happen if he contacted them, if he let them know he was alive after all. Would that be kind or cruel, he wondered. Would you really want the dead to come back to life again, after you'd spent so much energy trying to put the world back in order? He wasn't sure—didn't know who to ask—though he could imagine bringing the question up to Mr. Davis someday, when they knew each other better.

Mr. Davis wasn't a talkative person, but they would converse from time to time. He was an old military man, Mr. Davis. A true ex-patriate. He had grown up in Idaho, but had lived in Quito for thirty years now, and he didn't expect to ever return to America again. He didn't even think about it anymore, he said.

And Ryan had nodded.

He imagined there must be a point when you stopped being a

visitor. After the tourists had flown off, after the exchange students had stopped playing native, after the idea of "back home" had started to feel fictional.

How far away, the child he'd been to Stacey and Owen Schuyler. How distant, the gawky, eager boyfriend he'd been to Pixie, the roommate he'd been to Walcott, the son he'd been to Jay.

Was this any less real than the small, transient selves he'd discarded? Kasimir Czernewski, Matthew Blurton, Max Wimberley.

At a certain point, you must be able to slip loose. At a certain point, you found that you had been set free.

You could be anyone, he thought.

You could be anyone.

25

George Orson was losing his cool.

He'd wake up in the middle of the night with a thrashing cry, and then he would sit with his knees pulled up, with the bedside lamp on and the television going. "I'm having bad dreams again," he said, and Lucy sat there uncomfortably beside him as he emanated a long, barren silence.

It was their second day in Africa, holed up in a fifteenth-floor room at the Hotel Ivoire, and George Orson would go out and come back, go out and come back, and each time he returned, he looked more flushed and unnerved.

Meanwhile, Lucy had been sitting there in their room, high in the spire of a skyscraper hotel, bored and pretty freaked out herself, delicately un-taping currency from the pages of books, staring down at the stream of traffic on the highway below. Six lanes of cars, running the circumference of the Ébrié Lagoon—which was not the azure brochure blue she had expected, but just ordinary grayish water, not much different from Lake Erie. At least there were palm trees.

She heard him at the door, rattling the knob, muttering to himself, and when he finally burst in, he threw his key card onto the carpet, his teeth bared.

"Motherfucker," he said, and hurled his briefcase onto the bed. "God-fucking-damn it," he said, and Lucy stood there, holding a hundred-dollar bill, blinking at him, alarmed. She had never heard him swear before.

"What's wrong?" she said, and she watched as he stomped over to the minibar and yanked it open.

Empty.

"Fucking piece-of-shit hotel," he said. "This is supposed to be four stars?"

"What's wrong?" she said again, but he merely shook his head at her, irritably, passing his fingers across his scalp, his hair standing up in dry, grassy tufts.

"We're going to get new passports," he said. "We need to get rid of David and Brooke as quickly as possible."

"Fine with me," she said, and she watched as he went to the phone on the desk and lifted the receiver from its cradle with a flourish of controlled fury.

"*Allô, allô ?*" he said. He took a breath, and it was uncanny, she thought. His face actually seemed to change as he adopted his deep, exaggerated French accent. His eyelids drooped a bit, and his mouth turned down and he lifted his chin.

"*Service des chambres?*" he said. "*S'il vous plaît, je voudrais une bouteille de whiskey. Oui. Jameson, s'il vous plaît.*"

"George," she said—forgetting herself again, forgetting that he was "Dad." "Is there a problem?" she said, but he only held up one finger: *Hush.*

"*Oui,*" he said into the phone. "*Chambre quinze quarante-et-un,*" he said, and then, only after he had set the phone down, did he turn to look at her.

"What's going on?" she said. "Is there a problem?"

"I need a drink; that's the main problem," he said, and he sat down on the bed and took off his shoe. "But if you want to know the truth, I'm feeling just a touch worried, and I'd like to get us some new names. Tomorrow."

"Okay," she said. She set *Bleak House* down on the coffee table and discreetly put the hundred-dollar bill into the front pocket of her jeans. "But that doesn't answer my question. What's going on?"

"Everything's fine," he said, shortly. "I'm just being paranoid," he said, and dropped his other shoe onto the floor. One of those men's slip-on loafers, with leather tassels where the laces should be.

"I want you to go down to the salon downstairs tomorrow morning," he said. "See if they can make you a blonde. And get it cut," he said—and she imagined that there was just a slight edge of distaste in his voice. "Something sophisticated. They should be able to manage that."

Lucy put her hand to her hair. She hadn't yet undone her Brooke Fremden braids, though she hated them. Too childish, she'd said. "Am I supposed to be sixteen? Or eight?" she'd said, though ultimately she had let herself be talked into it, when George Orson insisted.

I never wanted this hair in the first place. That's what she wanted to remind him, but it probably didn't matter. He had taken his palm-size notebook from the pocket of his suit jacket, writing in his fussy, tiny block letters.

"So you'll get your hair done first thing in the morning," he was saying. "We'll get the pictures taken before noon, and we can hopefully have the new passports done for us by Wednesday morning. We'll move to a new hotel by Wednesday afternoon. It would be good if we could get out of the country as soon as possible. I'd like to be in Rome by Saturday, at the latest."

She nodded, staring down at the carpet, which was spotted with the indentations of small black cigarette burns. The remnant of an old piece of gum, worn as flat as a coin. Unremovable, apparently.

"Okay," she said, though now she was feeling nervous as well.

She had not been out of the hotel room without George Orson, and the idea of the hair salon was suddenly daunting. *I'm just being paranoid,* he'd said, but she was sure he was anxious for a good reason, even if he wouldn't admit it.

It would be scary, she thought, going out into the public areas of the hotel, all by herself.

Everyone was black, that was one thing. She would be conscious of being a white girl, she would be visible in a way that she wasn't used to, there would be no crowd to vanish into, and she thought of the times that she and her family had driven through the black parts of Youngstown, how it had felt like the people on the street, the people waiting at the bus stops, had lifted their eyes to stare. As if their old four-door sedan were trailing an aura of Caucasian-ness, as if it were lit with phosphorescence. She remembered how her mother would press the automatic lock buttons on the car door, testing and retesting them.

"This is a bad neighborhood, girls," their mother said, and Lucy had rolled her eyes. *How racist,* she thought, and made a point of lifting the lock on her own door.

This, of course, was different. It was Africa. It was a third world country, a place of coup attempts and armed uprisings and child soldiers, and she had read the State Department advisory: *Americans should avoid crowds and demonstrations, be aware of their surroundings, and use common sense to avoid situations and locations that could be dangerous. Given the strong anti-French sentiment, people of non-African appearance may be specifically targeted for violence.*

But she didn't want to be a coward, either, and so she simply stood, watching as George Orson took off his socks and massaged the ball of his bare foot with his thumb.

"Will they speak English?" she said at last, hesitantly. "At the hair salon? What if they don't speak English?"

And George Orson looked up at her sternly. "I'm sure they'll have someone there who speaks English," he said. "Besides which— Darling, you've had three years of high school French, which should be quite sufficient. Do you need me to write some phrases down for you?"

"No," Lucy said, and she shrugged. "No—I guess I'm . . . I'm fine," she said.

But George Orson exhaled irritably. "Listen," he said. "Lucy," he said, and she could tell that he was using her true name deliberately, to make a point. "You're not a kid. You're an adult. And you're a very smart person, I've always told you that. I saw that about Lucy right away; she was a remarkable young woman.

"And now," he said. "Now you just need to be a little more assertive. Are you going to spend the rest of your life waiting for someone to tell you what to do, every step of the way? I mean, Jesus Christ, Lucy! You go down to the lobby, you speak English, or you patch together some pidgin French, or you communicate through sign language, and I'll bet you can manage to get your hair done without someone holding your hand through the process."

He put up his arms and fell back onto the bed with a private sotto voce huff of frustration, as if there were an audience out there watching them, as if there were someone else he was commiserating with. *Can you believe I have to deal with this?*

She wished she could think of some icy, cutting retort.

But she couldn't think of anything. Speechless: to be talked to in this way, after all of his lies and evasions, after all that time she spent in the Lighthouse Motel, waiting patiently and faithfully, to hear now that she wasn't "assertive"?

"I need a drink," George Orson murmured moodily, and Lucy just stood there, gazing down at him. Then, at last, she turned back to her book, to *Bleak House,* sitting down as with a sweater she was knitting and slowly unfastening the taped bills, observing as the transparent adhesive pulled the letters off of the old pages.

So she would be assertive, she thought.

She was a world traveler, after all. In the past week, she had been to two continents—albeit only a few hours in Europe, in Brussels—but soon she would be living in Rome. She was going to be *cosmopolitan,* wasn't that what George Orson had told her, all those months ago, as they drove away from Pompey, Ohio? Wasn't that what she had dreamed of?

This was not exactly Monaco or the Bahamas or one of the Mexican resorts on the Riviera Maya she used to swoon over on the Internet. But he was right, she thought. It was an opportunity for her to be an adult.

So when he left that morning, promising that he'd be back before noon, she'd steeled herself.

She dressed in a black T-shirt and jeans, an outfit that, while not exactly mature, was at least neutral. She brushed out her hair, and found the tube of lipstick she'd bought back when they were driving cross-country in the Maserati. There it was, barely used, still in a zippered pocket of her purse.

She put five hundred dollars into her purse as well, and the rest of the money she wrapped in a dirty T-shirt at the bottom of the cheap, girly Brooke Fremden backpack George Orson had bought her back in Nebraska.

Okay, she thought. She was doing this.

And she boarded the elevator, coolly and confidently, and when a man entered on the next floor—a soldier, in camouflage and a blue beret, red epaulets on his shoulders—she kept her face entirely expressionless, as if she hadn't even noticed, as if she weren't aware that he was gazing at her with steadfast disapproval and there was a pistol holstered at his waist.

She rode down all the rest of the way, alone with him in silence, and when he held the elevator door and made a gentlemanly gesture—*ladies first*—she murmured *"Merci,"* and stepped into the lobby.

She was really doing this, she thought.

——

It took a long time to get her hair done, but it was actually easier than she'd thought. She was frightened when she first went into the salon, which was empty except for the two employees—a thin, haughty, Mediterranean-looking woman, who looked as if she were examining Lucy's T-shirt and jeans with revulsion; and an African woman who regarded her more mildly.

"Excusez-moi," Lucy said, stiffly. *"Parlez-vous anglais?"*

She was aware of how clumsy she sounded, even though she enunciated as best she could. She remembered how, back in high school French, Mme Fournier would grimace with pity as Lucy tried to bumble her way through a conversational prompt. "Oh!" Mme Fournier would say. *"Ça fait mal aux oreilles!"*

But Lucy could say a simple phrase, couldn't she? It wasn't that hard, was it? She could make herself understood.

And it was okay. The African woman nodded at her politely. "Yes, mademoiselle," she said. "I speak English."

The woman was actually quite friendly. Though she tsked over the dye in Lucy's hair—"terrible," she murmured—she nevertheless believed she could do something with it. "I will do my best for you," she told Lucy.

The woman's name was Stephanie, and she was from Ghana, she said, though she had lived in Côte d'Ivoire for many years now. "Ghana is an English-speaking country. That is my native language," Stephanie said. "So it's pleasant to speak English sometimes. That's one characteristic with the Ivorians I don't understand. They turn to laugh at a foreigner who makes a mistake in French, so even when they know a little English, they refuse to speak. Why? Because they think the Anglophones will laugh at them in turn!" And she lowered her voice as she began to work her rubber-gloved fingers through Lucy's hair. "That is the problem with Zaina. My coworker. She has a good heart, but she is a Lebanese, and they are very proud. All the time, they are worried about their dignity."

"Yes," Lucy said, and she closed her eyes. How long it had been since she had talked to anyone besides George Orson! It had been—what?—months and months, and she almost hadn't realized until just now how lonely she had been. She'd never had many friends, she'd never particularly liked the company of other girls at her high school, but now, as Stephanie's fingernails drew soft lines across her scalp, she saw that this had been a mistake. She had been like Zaina—too proud, too concerned with her own dignity.

"I'm so happy to see that tourists are coming back to Abidjan," Stephanie was telling her. "After the war, after all the French fled, the other countries would all say, 'Do not travel to Côte d'Ivoire, it is too dangerous,' and it made me sad. Once, Abidjan was known as the Paris of West Africa. Did you know that? This hotel, if you could have seen it fifteen years ago, when I first came to this country! There was a casino. An ice-skating rink, the only one in West Africa! The hotel was a jewel, and then it began to fall into disrepair. Did you see that once there was a pool that surrounded the whole building, a beautiful pool, but now there is no water in it. For a while, I would come to work and there were so few guests that I imagined that I was in an old, empty castle, in some cold country.

"But things are getting better again," Stephanie said, and her voice was mild and hopeful. "Since the peace accord, we are returning to our old selves, and it makes me happy. To meet a young woman such as you in this hotel, that's a good sign. I will tell you a secret. I love the art of coiffure. And it is an art, I think. I feel that it is, and if you like what I do with your hair, you should tell your friends: 'Go to Abidjan, go to the Hotel Ivoire, visit Stephanie!' "

Later, when she tried to tell George Orson the story of Stephanie, she found it difficult to explain.

"You look remarkable," George Orson said. "That's a fantastic haircut," he said, and it was. The blond was surprisingly natural-looking, not the fluorescent peroxide color she had feared; it hung straight, cut blunt above her shoulder, with just a little wave to it.

But it was more than that, though she wasn't sure how to articulate it. That dreamy sense of transformation; the intense sisterly intimacy as Stephanie had leaned over her, serenely talking, telling her stories. It was what it must feel like to be hypnotized, she thought. Or like being baptized, maybe.

Not that she could say this to George Orson. It would be too overwrought, too extreme. And so she just shrugged, and showed him the clothes she'd bought at the boutique in the hotel mall.

A simple black dress with thin straps. A dark blue silk blouse, lower cut than she'd usually buy for herself, and white pants, and a colorful African-print scarf.

"I spent a lot of money," she said, but George Orson only smiled—that private, conspiratorial smile he used to give her when they first left Ohio, which she hadn't seen in a long time.

"As long as it's not more than three or four million," he said, and it was such a relief to hear him joke again that she laughed even though it wasn't very funny, and she posed flirtatiously, standing up against the bare off-white wall as he took her picture for the new passport.

He thought he could get them new passports within twenty-four hours.

He was drinking more, and it made her uncomfortable. More than likely he had been a drinker all along, sequestered in his study in the old house above the Lighthouse Motel, slipping heavily into bed beside her in the middle of the night, smelling of mouthwash and soap and cologne.

But this was different. Now that they were sharing a single room, she was more aware of it. She watched him as he sat at the narrow hotel room writing desk, scrutinizing the screen of his laptop, typing and surfing, typing and surfing, taking gulps from his tumbler. The bottle of Jameson whiskey he'd gotten from room service was almost empty, after only two days.

Meanwhile, she lay in bed, watching American movies that had been dubbed into French, or reading through *Marjorie Morningstar*, which had survived the removal of the taped bills better than *Bleak House* had.

They'd had a moment, when he'd seen her new haircut and clothes, a brief return to the couple she'd imagined they were, but it lasted only a few hours. Now he was distant again.

"George?" she said. And then when he didn't answer: "Dad . . . ?"

This made him wince.

Drunk.

"Poor Ryan," he said cryptically, and he lifted his glass to his lips, shaking his head. "I'm not going to screw up this time, Lucy," he said. "Trust me. I know what I'm doing."

Did she trust him?

Even now, after everything, did she believe that he knew what he was doing?

These were still difficult questions to answer, though it helped to know that she was carrying around a backpack that contained almost a hundred and fifty thousand dollars.

It helped that they were no longer in Nebraska, that she was no longer a virtual prisoner in the Lighthouse Motel. When he left the next morning on one of his errands, she was free to wander if she wished, she could ride the elevator down to the lobby of the hotel. She carried the backpack with her, strolling through the corridors and shopping boutiques in her new clothes, trying to think. Trying to imagine herself forward just a few days. Rome. 4.3 million dollars. A new name, a new life, maybe the one that she'd been expecting.

The hotel was a massive complex, but surprisingly quiet. She had expected the lobby to be crowded with people, like the throngs that had rushed along the terminals of the airports in Denver and New York and Brussels, but instead it was more like a museum.

She moved dreamily through a long lobby. Here on the wall was a stylized long-faced African mask—a gazelle, she guessed—with the horns curving down like a woman's hair. She saw two African women, in bright orange and green batik, strolling peaceably; and a hotel employee gently shepherding a bit of litter into his long-handled dustpan; and then she passed outside into an open-air promenade, with tropical gardens along one side, and graceful botanically shaped abstract statues, and a colorful obelisk, decorated with shapes and figures almost like a totem pole; and then the promenade opened up, and there was a cement bridge that led across turquoise pools to a small green island, from which you could look across the lagoon toward the skyscrapers of Abidjan.

Wondrous. She was standing on a path lined with globed street-lamps, under a cloudless sky, and this was probably the most surreal thing that had ever happened to her.

Who, back in Ohio, would have ever believed that Lucy Latti-more would one day be standing on a different continent, at the edge of such a beautiful hotel? In Africa. With an elegant haircut and expensive shoes and a light, fashionable white pleated dress, with the hem lightly moving in the breeze.

If only her mother could see her. Or that horrible, sneering Todd-zilla.

If only someone would come along to take her photograph.

At last, she turned and walked back through the gardens again, back toward the center of the hotel. She found her boutique, and bought another dress—emerald green, this time, batik-printed like the outfits of the women she'd seen in the hallway—and then with her shopping bag she found her way to a restaurant.

Le Pavillion was a long, simple room that opened into a patio, al-most entirely empty. It was past lunchtime, she supposed, though there were still a few patrons lingering, and as the maître d' led her to her place, a trio of white men in flowered Hawaiian shirts looked up as she was led past.

"Beautiful girl," said one of them, bald, arching his eyebrows. "Hey, girl," he said. "I like you. I want to be your friend." And then he spoke to his cohorts in Russian or whatever, and they all laughed.

She ignored them. She wasn't going to let them ruin her afternoon, though they continued to talk raucously even as she held her menu up like a mask.

"I am good lover," called the one with spiked dyed orange hair. "Baby. We should meet us."

Assholes. She gazed at the words on the menu—which were, she realized, entirely in French.

When she came back to the room, George Orson was waiting for her.

"Where the fuck have you been?" he said as she opened the door.

Furious.

She stood there, with the backpack full of their money, and a tote bag from the boutique, and he winged a projectile at her—a little booklet, which she deflected with an upraised hand. It hit her palm, and bounced harmlessly to the floor.

"There's your new passport," he said bitterly, and she stared at him for a long time before she bent to pick it up.

"Where have you been?" he said as she stoically opened the passport and looked inside. Here was the photo he'd taken yesterday—with her brand-new hairdo—and a new name: Kelli Gavin, age twenty-four, of Easthampton, Massachusetts.

She didn't say anything.

"I thought you were . . . kidnapped or something," George Orson said. "I was sitting here, thinking: *What am I going to do now?* Jesus, Lucy, I thought you left me here."

"I was having lunch," Lucy said. "I just went downstairs for a minute. I mean, weren't you just complaining that I wasn't assertive enough? I was just—"

He cleared his throat, and for a second she thought he might be about to cry. His hands were shaking, and he had a bleak look on his face.

"God!" he said. "Why do I always do this to myself? All I ever wanted was to have one person, just one person, and it's never right. It's never right."

Lucy stood there looking at him, her heart quickening, watching uncertainly as he lowered himself into a chair. "What are you talking about?" she said, and she supposed that she should speak to him gently, apologetically, soothingly. She should go over to him and hug him or kiss his forehead or stroke his hair. But instead she just regarded him as he hunched there like a moody thirteen-year-old boy. She tucked her new passport into her purse.

She was the one who should be frightened, after all. She was the one who ought to need comfort and reassurance. She was the one who had been tricked into falling in love with a person who wasn't even real.

"What are you talking about?" she said again. "Did you get the money?"

He peered down at his hands, which were still quivering, making spasms against his knees. He shook his head.

"We're having negotiating problems," George Orson said, and his voice was smaller, the mumbling agitated whisper he'd get when he woke up with his nightmares.

Not like George Orson at all.

"We may have to give up a much larger cut than I expected," he said. "Much larger. That's the problem, it's all corruption, everywhere you go in the world, that's the worst part of it—"

He lifted his head, and there was hardly a trace of the handsome, charming teacher she'd once known.

"I just want one person I can trust," he said, and his eyes rested on her accusingly, as if somehow *she* had betrayed *him*. As if *she* were the liar.

"Pack your bags," he said coldly. "We need to move to a new

hotel right away, and I've been sitting here for a fucking hour wait-ing for you. You're lucky I didn't leave."

As she waited down in the lobby, Lucy didn't know whether to be angry or hurt. Or frightened.

At least she had the backpack with their money. He wasn't likely to leave her without that, but still—the way he had talked to her, the way he had transformed in the last few days. Did she know him at all? Did she have any idea what he was really thinking?

Besides which, she couldn't stop thinking about what he had said about the money. *Negotiating problems,* he'd said. *We may have to give up a much larger cut.* Which upset her. She had been counting on that money, maybe even more than she had been counting on George Orson, and she found herself touching the lumps in her backpack, feeling through the canvas to the stacks of bills that she'd arranged beneath some folded Brooke Fremden T-shirts.

It was late afternoon, and people were arriving at the Hotel Ivoire at a greater pace than they had the day before. There were a num-ber of Africans, some in suits, others in more traditional dress. A few soldiers, a pair of Arab men in embroidered kurtas, a Frenchwoman in sunglasses and a wide-brimmed hat, arguing on a cell phone. Liv-eried hotel agents were trailing along behind various guests.

She should not have come down to the lobby alone, though at the time it had felt like an act of defiant dignity. She had packed her bag angrily as George Orson spoke in rapid, incomprehensible French on the phone, and when she finished with her suitcase, she stood there, trying to piece together what he was saying—until he had glanced up sharply, covering the receiver with his palm.

"Go ahead on down to the lobby," he said. "I have to finish this phone call and I'll be down in five minutes, so don't wander off."

But now it had been more like fifteen minutes, and still he hadn't appeared.

Was it possible that he would ditch her?

She felt her backpack again, as if somehow the money might be spirited away, as if it weren't entirely solid—and she was tempted to unzip the backpack and double-check, just to be positive. Just to look at it.

She scoped again through the expanse of lobby, the cathedral ceilings and the chandelier and the long decorative boxes full of tropical plants. The Frenchwoman had lit a cigarette and stood gently tapping the toe of her high-heeled shoe. Lucy observed as the woman glanced at her watch, and after a hesitation Lucy walked over.

"*Excusez-moi,*" she said, and made an attempt to imitate the accent that once upon a time Mme Fournier had tried to inculcate in her students. "*Quelle,*" Lucy said. "*Quelle . . . heure est-il?*"

The woman looked at her with a surprising benevolence. Their eyes met and the woman took the cell phone away from her ear as she examined Lucy, up and down, with a soft, motherly look. With pity, Lucy thought.

"It is three o'clock, my dear," the woman replied, in English, and she gave Lucy a questioning smile.

"Are you quite all right?" the woman asked, and Lucy nodded.

"*Merci,*" Lucy said, thickly.

She had been waiting for him for almost a half hour now, and she turned and walked toward the elevators, her wheeled suitcase trailing crookedly behind her, the beautiful open-toed sandals she had bought for herself clicking against the glowing marble tile, the people seeming to part for her, the African and Middle Eastern and European faces regarding her with the same wary concern that the Frenchwoman had, the way people look at a young girl who has been a fool, a girl who knows at last that she has been cast aside. *You're lucky I didn't leave without you,* she thought, and when the elevator doors slid open with a deep musical chime, Lucy could feel the swell of panic inside her. The numbness in her fingers, the sense of insects crawling in her hair, a tightness in her throat.

No. He wouldn't abandon her, he wouldn't really abandon her, not after all of this, all the distance they had come together.

She was aware of the elevator beginning to rise, and it was as if the gravity were lifting up out of her body like a spirit, it was as if she could open up like a milkweed pod, a hundred floating seeds spilling out of her, floating off, irretrievable.

She thought of that moment when the policemen stood on their porch, her opening the door to their stony faces; that moment when she called the admissions office of Harvard, that sense of sundering, that sense of her future self, the molecules of her imagined life, unmoored, breaking into smaller and smaller pieces, scattering outward and outward and outward like the universe itself.

For a second, when the elevator came at last to the fifteenth floor, she thought that the doors were not going to open, and she pressed the button with the "open door" symbol on it. She pressed the button again and ran the heel of her hand along the creased line where the elevator doors were sealed together, her fingers shaking, "Oh," she was saying, "Oh," she was saying, until abruptly the doors parted, slid open, and she almost stumbled out into the hallway.

Later, she was glad that she didn't call out his name.

Her voice had left her, and she paused outside the elevator, just breathing, the air filling her lungs in soft, irregular hitches, and her hands scrabbled against the canvas of her backpack, feeling for the solid bundles of currency the way a person in a plunging airplane might clutch for their oxygen mask, and then when she felt the certainty of those stacks of bills, she fumbled in her new purse and found her passport, Kelli Gavin's passport. That was safe, too, and there was the confirmation number for her flight to Rome, and she . . . she . . .

The velocity of her fall seemed to slow.

Yes, this was what it felt like to lose yourself. Again. To let go of your future and let it rise up and up until finally you couldn't see it anymore, and you knew that you had to start over.

Later, she realized that she was lucky.

She was lucky, she supposed, that she was trying to be unobtrusive, trying to get a grip on herself, lucky that she'd stopped outside the elevator door to check her bag once again, lucky because that chill calm had swept down and clutched her in its talons.

Lucky that she didn't call attention to herself, because when she turned the corner, there was a man standing in front of the door to their hotel room.

Posted there, in the doorway of 1541, in the tower of the Hotel Ivoire.

Waiting for her? Or merely blocking George Orson's escape?

It was one of those Russian men she had seen in the restaurant, the one with the spiked orange hair, the one who had called to her: *I am good lover.*

He was standing with his back against the door, his arms folded, and she froze there at the edge of the corridor. She could see the gun, the revolver he was holding loosely, almost sleepily in his left hand.

He didn't look dangerous, exactly, though she knew he was. He would probably kill her if he saw her and made the connection, but he didn't look her way. It was as if she were invisible, and he was smiling to himself as if at a pleasant memory, gazing up at the ceiling, at the light fixture, where a white moth was circling. Mesmerized.

The other two men, she assumed, were in the room already, in the room with George Orson.

26

"We are on our way to the hospital," he told Ryan. "Listen to me, Son. You are not going to bleed to death." He kept repeating it and repeating it, long after Ryan had lapsed into unconsciousness again, just mumbling it to himself the way he used to tell himself stories in that attic room when he was a kid, he could remember that feeling, rocking back and forth and running through the same lines again and again until he'd finally put himself to sleep.

"I promise you are going to be all right," he said, as the headlights illuminated the tangle of branches that overhung the long back roads. "I promise you are going to be all right. We are on our way to the hospital. I promise you are going to be all right."

Of course, he'd said the same thing to Rachel, back when they were in Inuvik, pretending to be scientists, and that hadn't turned out so well.

———

This time, though, he was able to keep his word.

Ryan was in the emergency room, and though there would no doubt be many hours of surgery and blood transfusions and so forth, it would almost certainly turn out okay.

It was nearly six in the morning, a Thursday morning in early May, still before sunrise, and he sat in the fluorescent-lit waiting area in a plastic chair next to the vending machines, still holding Ryan's blood-spattered hoodie, and Ryan's wallet, with the newest driver's license. Max Wimberley. He took the folded stash of currency from his jacket pocket and tucked a few hundreds into the sleeve of Ryan's billfold.

Jesus, he thought, and he put his face down into his palms for a while—not crying, not crying—before at last he found a scrap of paper and began to write a note.

It was probably for the best.

He was sitting in the parking lot, in an old Chrysler he'd found unlocked, and he was weeping a little now, distractedly, as he removed the ignition cover at the bottom of the steering column.

He had been a good father, he told himself. He and Ryan had made a nice life together while things lasted; they had been close in a way that was important, they had made a connection, a deep connection, and even though it had ended sooner—and more tragically—than he'd expected, he had been a better dad than the real Jay ever would have been.

Thinking of Jay, he felt a little twinge of—what?—not exactly regret. All that time they'd spent together, back before he went to Missouri, all that time, he'd done nothing but encourage Jay to contact his son. "It's important," he kept telling Jay. "Family is important; he ought to know who his real father is; he's living a lie otherwise," and Jay giving him that wry stoner stare he had, as if to say: *Are you joking?*

But the fact was, Jay could never bring himself to do it because he was lazy. Because he didn't want to expend the emotional energy, he didn't want to take on the responsibility of truly caring for another person, and that was the reason he wasn't a particularly good con man, either. Hayden had done his best to teach him, but ultimately Jay wasn't all that competent. He made so many errors, so many errors—God! Ryan was so much better suited to the ruin lifestyle than his father ever was—

But with Jay it was just mistake after mistake, even with a perfect avatar like Brandon Orson, even with everything all set up in Latvia and China and Côte d'Ivoire. And so when Jay hadn't returned from that ill-advised trip to Rēzekne, Hayden hadn't been surprised.

Though he had felt sorry that Jay's poor son would never know the truth, he had felt—what?—curious about that son, even during that period when he was living as Miles Spady, back at the University of Missouri, even when he and Rachel were stuck in that godforsaken research station, bickering and getting depressed, even then he'd find himself thinking about Jay Kozelek's long-lost son, and when things went wrong with Rachel and he finally got back to the U.S. and he was sitting in a motel room in North Dakota, he thought—

What if I contacted Jay's son, in his place? What if I did for Jay what he couldn't do for himself? Wouldn't that be a kind of favor, wouldn't that be an honor to his memory?

Well.

Well, as Miles would say.

He sat there in the emergency room parking lot, in the unlocked Chrysler, thinking of this, and then at last he bent down to examine the wires that ran into the steering wheel cylinder, sorting through the tangle of them until he found the red one. It was usually the red one that would provide the power, and the brown one that would handle the starter, and he hunched in the front seat, trying to concentrate. He wiped the back of his hand across his eyes again, and dried the wetness on the front of his shirt.

It would have had to end eventually, anyway. It was amazing he'd been able to convince Ryan in the first place, and certainly over time suspicions would have arisen, questions he wouldn't be able to answer. Probably Ryan would have eventually wanted to move on, maybe even reconnect with his parents, which was fine, which was natural, you couldn't expect these kinds of things to last forever.

Yes. He took out his pocket knife, and carefully stripped away the plastic casing around the wires. A very delicate procedure. You didn't want to get shocked; you didn't want to touch the live current.

He frowned, focusing his attention, and there was a tiny spark as the car shuddered awake. A new life.

"Could anything be more miraculous than an actual authentic ghost?"

He was traveling south down I-75, just past Flint, when this came to him.

A quotation.

He had come across it a long time ago, back in that terrible semester he'd spent at Yale. Thomas Carlyle, the nineteenth-century Scottish essayist, fierce and craggy and bearded, not even someone he'd particularly admired, but he'd memorized the passage anyway because it seemed so beautiful and true and so beyond the rest of the students in the class.

The English Johnson longed, all his life, to see a ghost, Carlyle had written. "But could not, though he went to Cock Lane, and thence to the church-vaults, and tapped on coffins. Foolish Doctor! Did he never, with the mind's eye as well as with the body's, look round him into that full tide of human Life he so loved; did he never so much as look into Himself? The good Doctor was a Ghost, as actual and authentic as heart could wish; well-nigh a million of Ghosts were travelling the streets by his side. Once more I say, sweep away the illusion of Time; compress the threescore years into three minutes; what else was he, what else are we? Are we not Spirits, shaped into a body, into an Appearance; and that fade away again into air and Invisibility?"

He was passing under a bridge, reciting this aloud, and he wasn't really crying though his eyes were leaking a little, the glare of headlights behind him and the glowing reflective circles of markers at the edge of the road and a green interstate sign that said

TO COLUMBUS FOLLOW

"Are we not all of us Spirits?"

He wondered what Miles would have to say about that idea.

He hadn't talked to Miles in a while now, not since the thing with Rachel had gone bad, not since that unfortunate trip to North Dakota, and he wondered. Maybe he could just write Miles a letter, maybe he could send Miles up to the final memorial he had made for himself on Banks Island. *Eadem mutata resurgo:* "Although changed, I shall arise the same." Which maybe Miles would understand. Maybe Miles could move on, Miles could transform himself, too. Live his own life.

Of course, he would have to get Miles up to Canada somehow, but with Miles that wasn't so very difficult. Poor Miles: so obsessive and determined.

He had been reading recently about something called "Vanishing Twin Syndrome," which Miles would surely be interested in. According to an article that he'd read, one in eight people start in life as a twin, but only one in seventy are actually born as twins. Most of the time, the vanishing twin spontaneously aborts, or it is absorbed by the other sibling, or the placenta, or the mother herself.

He was crying again as he passed from Michigan into Ohio, thinking of Ryan, he supposed, though he knew he shouldn't.

He had produced an unusually large harvest of lives, that was what he had been told—and he'd passed from death to death, over centuries, he'd passed from Cleveland to Los Angeles to Houston; from Rolla, Missouri, to Banks Island, NWT; from North Dakota to Michigan, and each time he'd been a different person.

His hands were shaking, and at last he had to pull over to a rest area, he had to curl up in the backseat without a blanket or a pillow, his palms tight against his skull, and outside, the rain had turned into sleet, ticking steadily against the surface of the stolen car.

What if he just settled into a new life and stayed there? Maybe that was the answer. He had failed as a father, and yet he had the soul of a teacher, he thought, and that idea appealed to him, made him calmer, the notion that he could still touch a young life in some way.

What if he became something ordinary, maybe just a simple high school teacher, he thought, and all the students would like him, and he would exert an influence that would extend beyond himself. He would live on through them. Maybe that was corny and stupid, but it didn't seem like such a bad plan for the present, and he pressed himself against the cold upholstery, squeezing his eyes shut hard.

He would never again think of Ryan, he promised himself.

He would never again think of Jay or Rachel.

He would never again think of Miles.

Are we not all of us Spirits? A voice whispered.

But he would never think of that again, either.

Acknowledgments

My wife, the writer Sheila Schwartz, died after a long battle with ovarian cancer shortly after I completed this book. We were married for twenty years. Sheila was my teacher when I was an undergraduate student, and we fell in love, and over the years that we were together, she was my mentor, my best critic, my dearest friend, my soul mate. I spent the last weeks of copyediting looking at the notes that Sheila had written on the manuscript, and it's impossible to express how grateful I am for her wise advice, and how terribly I will miss her.

I have been lucky to inherit a patient, thoughtful, and brilliant editor, Anika Streitfeld, who walked me through this book from conception to completion, and who has been an amazing, supportive, and wise presence throughout. I have also deeply appreciated the help and enthusiasm of the staff at Ballantine during my long tenure there, who have taken such good care of my books. I am grateful to Libby McGuire and Gina Centrello for their long-standing patience and goodwill.

Other people who are dear to me have contributed significantly during the process of writing: my wonderful agent, Noah Lukeman, who has always been a great supporter and friend; my best buddies, Tom Barbash and John Martin; my sons, Philip and Paul Chaon; my sister and brother, Sheri and Jed, who have been reading fragments of this for a long while and offering advice; my writing group, Eric Anderson, Erin Gadd, Steven Hayward, Cynthia Larson, Jason Mullin, and Lisa Srisuco; and all my students at Oberlin College who have, over the years, been an inspiration to me.

This book pays homage, and owes a great deal, to many fantastic and better writers who inspired me, both in childhood and beyond, including Robert Arthur, Robert Bloch, Ray Bradbury, Daphne du Maurier, John Fowles, Patricia Highsmith, Shirley Jackson, Stephen King, Ira Levin, C. S. Lewis, H. P. Lovecraft, Vladimir Nabokov, Joyce Carol Oates, Mary Shelley, Robert Louis Stevenson, Peter Straub, J.R.R. Tolkien, Thomas Tryon, and a number of others. One of the fun things about writing this book was making gestures and winks toward these writers that I've adored, and I hope that they—living and dead—will forgive my incursions.

Support during the writing of this book came in the form of grants from the Ohio Arts Council and the Oberlin College Research Grant Program. I am deeply thankful for their help.

DAN CHAON is the acclaimed author of *You Remind Me of Me*, which was named one of the best books of the year by *The Washington Post, Chicago Tribune, San Francisco Chronicle, The Christian Science Monitor,* and *Entertainment Weekly,* among other publications. Ballantine has also published two collections of his short stories: *Fitting Ends* and *Among the Missing,* which was a finalist for the 2001 National Book Award.

Chaon's work has appeared in many journals and anthologies including Best American Short Stories of 1996 and 2003, the Pushcart Prize 2000, 2002, and 2003, and the O. Henry Prize Stories, 2001. His fiction has been a finalist for the National Magazine Award in Fiction in 2002 and 2007. He was the recipient of the 2006 Academy Award in Literature from the American Academy of Arts and Letters.

Chaon lives in Cleveland Heights, Ohio, and teaches at Oberlin College.

ABOUT THE TYPE

This book was set in Baskerville, a typeface which was designed by John Baskerville, an amateur printer and typefounder, and cut for him by John Handy in 1750. The type became popular again when The Lanston Monotype Corporation of London revived the classic Roman face in 1923. The Mergenthaler Linotype Company in England and the United States cut a version of Baskerville in 1931, making it one of the most widely used typefaces today.